If this book was purchased ̶ ̶ ̶ ̶ ̶ ̶ ̶ ̶ ̶ ̶ ̶ ̶ ̶ ̶ ̶
this may have been stolen or reported to the publisher as "unsold or destroyed." Neither the author nor the publisher has received payment for the sale of this "stripped book."

LIFE, LOVE AND LONELINESS.
Copyright © 2001 by Crystal Lacey Winslow.

All rights reserved. Printed in the United States of America. No part of this book may be used or reproduced, stored in a retrieval system, or transmitted by any means, electronic, mechanical, photocopying, recording, or otherwise, without written permission from the publisher. Although every precaution has been taken in the preparation of this book, the publisher and author assume no responsibility for errors or omissions.

For information address:

Melodrama Publishing
P. O. Box 522
Bellport, New York 11713

Web address: www.melodramapublishing.com
e-mail: melodramapub@aol.com

Cover Photo by Bruce Gomez

ISBN 0-9717021-0-1

This novel is a work of fiction. Any resemblances to actual events, real people, living or dead, organizations, establishments, locales are products of the author's imagination. Other names, characters, places, and incidents are used fictitiously.

INTRODUCTION

Life has no guarantees. So a wise person has to try to be as cautious as possible when making decisions. Every yesterday, we loose a tomorrow of our lives, so to chase pain would be fruitless. Nevertheless, we can all admit we've chased pain. Ran after it until it eventually conquered us. Some of us let pain beat us down until we were so obsessed we started to believe it was a necessity. A normal part of life. And when the pain leaves us, if only for a moment, we tend to want it back. That is when love comes in.

We need to learn to love ourselves first. Now, everyone needs love. And I will let you in on a secret: real love is not so common. In fact, it is as rare as a four–leaf clover. Some people may only experience true love once in a lifetime. Oh, you may have numerous relationships-- I will call them "decoys"-- that come in skillful disguises, and they will make small victories against your resistance to nonsense. However, these decoys are not as strong as they appear to be. You see, it is you who gives them their strength. They eat off your weakness. Any weakness. This is where loneliness plays the biggest part in our lives. Loneliness speaks several different languages and is the principal connection between self–worth and self–hate. Being alone and lonely are two different conditions. When we are alone, that just means there is nobody around at that particular moment to keep us company. When we are feeling lonely, there is something important missing from our lives. When loneliness hits, if we are not careful, it could lead to unproductive things occurring.

I want you to realize from this book that everyday people make mistakes everyday. Whether these mistakes are made because of life, love or loneliness is not what matters. What matters is how we handle the situation. Whether we bow down and take defeat gracefully, or stick out our chest and fight for our integrity. This will define who we really are. Always remember: you deserve

2

better! A very wise person taught me that I have to do what is best for me. That is a difficult lesson to learn without coming off as self–centered. Nevertheless, until you master this, life will always throw you a curve ball when all you ever want is for people to be straight with you.

Lacey.

This book is dedicated to my grandmother,
Callie Bell Winslow,
And her son,
My father,
Tyrone Maurice

THE EIGHTIES

1
LYRIC DEVANEY

"I will never date a married man! Not because of moral issues," I laughed, "I'll never be second to number one." I remember saying those words when I was straight out of high school. Seventeen years ago I was talking to a good friend at the time who was dating our former math teacher. We both graduated with honors from the High School of Performing Arts. I was valedictorian; Stacey, salutatorian. Not bad for two girls from the 'hood. I had applied for Syracuse University and Fiorello H. LaGuardia Community College and I was accepted to both, with full scholarships. I still hadn't decided which to attend.

"Lyric, can I borrow your Gloria Vanderbilt jeans?"

"No," I retorted. That was the end of that subject.

I was half listening to Stacey drone on and on about sleeping with an older man. I studied her for a while. Stacey was extremely jovial. She beamed with enthusiasm. I remember how much I ridiculed her for making such a compromising decision.

"He'll never leave his wife for you," I continued looking at my perfect French manicure. "I mean, she's sophisticated, beautiful *and* the mother of his three children."

Stacey had come to get ready for their date at a secret meeting place. I can still remember how her cheerful mood turned sullen in a matter of moments. She looked aloof and despondent as I hammered her unmercifully. Her cherubic face, despite her age, was distorted and showed visible signs of stress.

I was lying across my bed watching her adjust her outfit in the mirror. She had on a pair of LEE jeans and a fresh pair of black and white Pumas with thick pink shoelaces. What can I say? It was the 80's when

Reaganomics had money rolling in for everyone. It did not matter what side of the law you were on or what color you were painted.

"He's just using you for sex," I volunteered.

"It's more than a sexual relationship. We are soul mates and he loves me," she reasoned.

I looked at my naïve friend and thought about how inexperienced she was. She committed the faux pas of giving herself too much credit. Therefore, I opposed, "How intelligent is your situation? The wife gets the house, car, and pension while you get . . . an occasional bouquet of roses, or candy, or some other gesture of sentimental crap."

"It's not about money either, Lyric. It is about love. I *love* him."

"Whoever said anything about love? Besides, *love* doesn't pay your bills."

"No, *I* pay my bills!"

"As if!"

"As if *what?*"

"As if you're saying something!" I snapped. Then continued, "Independence is overrated. My dream is to marry a millionaire. Someone powerful as Jacqueline Kennedy did."

"Jacqueline Kennedy was the exception. Not the rule."

"Princess Diana," I countered.

"Lyric, come on, you're far from naïve. These white women are from astute, prestigious backgrounds. They are groomed for success. Their lives are pre–planned," she reasoned.

"And so is mine! By next year the whole world will know who Lyric Devaney is."

"Can't you see you're already handicapped by poverty? Look around you . . . you live in the ghetto. There's no getting out of here. No sleeping your way out! No marrying out! No acting, singing, or modeling your way out! So play your position and find somebody nice who can take your mind off your grim reality like I did."

"So I should settle."

"If that's what you want to call it. Yes."

"Settle and love someone who's in love with someone else?"

"He doesn't love her!"

"You're delusional!"

"He loves me!"

"You're stupid!"

"Lyric, not everyone can be non–committal or nonchalant in relationships as you are. When I fall in love, it is the real thing. Not some meaningless escapade," she retorted.

Had she just taken a stab at me?

"Not everyone has the confidence to do what I do," I countered, "if you were smart, you'd use his married ass like a credit card and discard him like yesterday's trash when you were through. But, of course, that would make you one of the smart ones, and you've already established you're a fool in smart clothing!"

"Now you're acting childish! That's what I like about dating an older man. The conversation is mature. If I didn't know how snobbish you were, I'd think you were jealous of my relationship."

"Listen and let your mentor speak. Jealous is an adjective that women use too loosely. To be *jealous* would mean that you are able to obtain something that I cannot. Have you created this misconception all on your own? Or, is that faggot of a man feeding this into your narrow little mind?"

"You heard he's gay?" Stacey exclaimed.

"I don't know. Is he?" I questioned.

"No!"

"Look, Stacey, you're talking apples and oranges. I'm going as far as my looks take me, and my talent will do the rest. I'm street–smart, intelligent, sassy, and classy. I'm beautiful, ambitious, and determined to get in the game. All I have to do is create the opportunity. Love is *not* an option. Nothing is going to hold me back! I just feel sorry I can't take you with me. You've become stagnated. You want to be handicapped by love!"

I refused to feed into the "you're handicapped" nonsense. I believe there is a way out of here and it's not rocket science. It's just good old fashioned magic. You have to create an illusion. Smart people are dumb in a naïve way. They can be gullible. All you have to do is fool people. Leave the ghetto slang in the ghetto and speak eloquently. Leave the street gear to the urban kids and dress classy. But, most importantly . . . lie. Lie a lot. But lie just enough to remember all your lies. I swear on my unborn children, when opportunity knocks . . . Lyric Devaney will be ready!

"Lyric, please!" she whined, throwing up her hands in surrender.

"*Lyric, please!*" I mocked. Her whining was galling. In fact, her entire disposition was irritating the hell out of me.

"Lyric, you must be scorned because you put a damper on all things that are wonderful and fulfilling in love. Your superficial remarks hurt me. Then I say to myself something must have really gone wrong somewhere down your lifeline to make you guard your heart like a fortress. So even though you can be mean, I always end up forgiving you because you have no control over yourself."

"Control? I have enough *control* not to sleep with someone else's husband. You are a hypocritical, selfish bitch. And make a mental note that this is the last time you are invited to my house. I am trying to help you out, and this is what I get? Do not come running to me when he breaks your heart. See if I care!"

"I'm sorry . . . look, Lyric . . . this type of love you can't understand unless you're in a similar situation."

"I will *never* be in a similar situation because I will *never* allow myself to be used by a man in the name of *love*. All you are is an extra piece of pussy. Remember, you heard it here first because my mother taught me love don't love nobody!" I exploded. By this time, she was near tears, but I did not care. Actually, I thrived off weak beings. I really was not as upset as I was projecting myself to be. Her words bounced off me and were stuck somewhere in the atmosphere. I hopped off my canopy bed pushing past her, murmuring, "*Never* will I love a married man."

"Never say never," she warned. I just looked at her disapprovingly and rolled my chestnut brown eyes in despair.

I never did call Stacey after that incident. I just erased her completely out of my life. I was good at removing people, without regret, who were not of use to me. I learned that from my mother.

Thinking back on that day should make me feel like such a hypocrite, but it does not. My mother always said, *"Only those who never sinned should cast the first stone. Everyone is always judging folks. Judge yourself first."* Was that a quote from the Bible? Mother was always taking Bible quotes, revising them, and making them her own philosophy. My philosophy is . . . life . . . it is what it is! That is how I have always looked at it, blocking out any aspirations of ever falling in love. When you are in love, you are vulnerable. When you are vulnerable . . . you are weak! And, anyone who knows Lyric Devaney, knows I am not weak, nor will I ever, ever, be left lonely. I may live alone, die alone, but loneliness is for simple people. I am too charismatic for that!

Unfortunately, seventeen years later, I am in a difficult relationship with a very powerful, very rich, and *very* married man.

1997

2
LYRIC DEVANEY

From tonight on, I will only think positive. I am going to give Richard an ultimatum. He can either start the procedures for a divorce or get the hell out of my life! One day soon, I am going to say those exact words. Leave--no leverage. Whenever we would get into this conversation in the past, it would always come out as a suggestion. Like he had a choice.

"Baby, did you start the divorce procedure yet?"

And, of course, the answer was always an affirmative "no." I would immediately get upset and tell him he had to leave my condominium. At that point, he would always start that crying bullshit, and I would get weaker than a newborn baby trying to lift her head up. I mean, what woman could resist tears? I mean *real* tears. Runny nose, sniffling, slobbering, and all that. Then he would start to beg. I mean it was r-e-e-e-a-l hard for me not to leave him.

Sometimes I would secretly videotape these hysterical sessions as well as our lovemaking. I was into video voyeurism heavily. I often invited my two close friends over to watch, but no one wanted to humor me. They thought Richard looked creepy with his receding hairline, which he usually styled in a comb over, the typical hairstyle bald men usually resort to, trying to save whatever is left. To make it worse, he also spoke with a slight lisp, a speech impediment that he was embarrassed about.

If he knew the library I had on him, he would bust a gut. He was so paranoid. Always talking about his career and his plans for running for President of the United States one day when the time was right. Therefore, his next step was to run for Senator. He said that American people were much too conservative. They would never vote for him if he were involved in a nasty scandal over the divorce of his wife. As a result, once he won State Senate, he would get a divorce, marry me, and then run for President. Everyday I would imagine myself as First Lady with all the perks--the tailored suits, traveling around the world, respected by millions and having my name go down in history books. Now those were dreams of grandeur that were taking too long to realize.

One night when I was marinating in pre–menstrual–syndrome, I decided to give Richard a call.

"Cardinale here."

"When are you leaving her?" I demanded.

"Lyric, your timing is not appropriate. It's late. We'll discuss that at a later date," he soothed.

"Don't try to pacify me, Richard! I am sick and tired of this relationship. You promised you would get a divorce, and you had better make good on that!" I exploded.

"Darling, don't be upset with me. Richard is a bad boy. Forgive me if I seem insensitive to your earnest needs. You know I would divorce Estelle in a second, but first I have to get all my finances together. Estelle will not lie down and play dead. She's made of steel! She will go after my fortune with every ounce of greed her vindictive mind could muster up," he reasoned.

"The Richard Cardinale I know would have made her sign a prenuptial agreement."

"The Lyric Devaney I know would not let something as trivial as a divorce decree throw her off balance. She's too focused."

"I am focused . . . on us! Together. Married. One unit!"

"Soon darling. Soon."

Richard and I hung up the telephone, and he arranged for us to have brunch at my place the next morning. Until then, I had my Absolut on the rocks, a Blockbuster video, and a brand new dildo. What more could a girl want?

3
LYRIC DEVANEY

At 11:00 am sharp, Richard's black Mercedes–Benz arrived. His driver got out and opened the door and Richard stepped out. His right leg extended to the ground, as he simultaneously hoisted himself up, putting on his top hat with his left hand. Goddamn, he was so elegant. With trench coat draped over his forearm he proceeded to reach for a bouquet of long–stemmed red roses. Charming! I leaned out my huge storm window and, in my best Mae West accent, said, "Say sweetie . . . why don't 'cha come up and see me sometime." He looked up and smiled broadly. He was in a good mood. Thank God.

"Richard," I said as I opened the front door. Before he could respond, I pulled him in close by his silk tie and planted a fat, wet kiss on his thin, chapped lips. Then I stepped back, hands on hips, so he could admire my brand new dominatrix outfit. I stood tall, in six–inch black leather heels. I had the black, spiked, leather gloves, bra, G–string, and whip. Smack. I hit the whip to the floor and purred. Then I turned around so he could admire my firm, round ass in my G–string and headed upstairs to my bedroom. Richard tossed the roses on the floor and followed like a good little boy. The house was soundless.

Brunch, as Richard called it, was set–up once a week. We hardly ever ate 'food' during "brunch." It was a lovemaking session. A kinky lovemaking session. Truthfully, I wasn't into sadistic sex. It pleased Richard. Consequently, a good woman knows how to please her man.

"Strip!" I commanded once we were inside my bedroom.

"But, I–"

"Shut up!" Smack. I touched him with my fierce whip. He hurriedly did as he was told. Once naked, I laughed to myself. I looked at his pathetic body. He was grossly out of shape. His shriveled up penis was hardly noticeable because his fat gut hung so low, it covered the shaft. A pair of hairy balls were on display. He kept on his black dress socks which clashed against his pale legs.

"Why do I love this man?" I thought.

"Turn around motherfucker!" I ordered. Richard did as he was told.

"Are you going to hurt me?" he whined. Smack. My whip went across his lower backside and he moaned in pleasure. I grabbed the back of his hair roughly and told him to spread his legs. He did as he was told.

"Bend over bitch!"

Richard bent over and placed his hands firmly on my bedroom walls for stability. I reached in my nightstand and pulled out a strap–on dildo. This one was new. It was huge and painted black, just as Richard liked. The dildo was so fat, I couldn't wrap my hand around it. "Richard will be pleased," I thought. He and I had something in common. We both loved huge, black dick.

I lubricated his anus with my tongue. Richard did not like artificial lubricants. Then I inserted the dildo in him roughly. He shrieked in pain.

"You've been a very bad boy!" I scolded. Then continued, "I have to fucking punish you!" I was ramming his ass and pulling his hair ruthlessly. We were both sweating profusely.

"Ritchie's . . . been . . . a . . . very . . . bad . . . boy!" he panted. Smack. I leaned far back, dildo still inserted in his ass, and let my whip crack across his back. Smack. I hit him again. "Shut the fuck up!" I yelled. Smack. His body then started to jerk involuntarily. He tried to stifle a scream but was unable to. He screamed in pleasure as he came all over my plush, peach carpet.

We both fell to the floor exhausted. Neither one of us speaking for several minutes.

As he lay there marveling over the morning's event, I was proud to see the satisfied expression on his face.

"I'm a bad bitch!" I thought.

"So when are you planning to tell Estelle?" I jumped directly into our situation.

"I have a meeting with my attorney this afternoon. He's helping me hide my assets. See, Estelle and I were married and had lived in California, a commonwealth state, for nineteen years before relocating to New York City. Everything I have made during my career is equally hers. And she knows this," he explained.

"But you will do it, right . . . hide your assets so she can't get her hands on *our* money."

"I most certainly will darling. Don't worry your pretty head. It's the kids I'm worried about. Estelle is witty, but she is no match for me."

That Estelle is not as dumb as I pegged her out to be. However, she was no match for me, either. She was just extra weight waiting to be thrown out like trash.

The real obstacle was his kids. White men had this loyalty for their offspring that I just did not understand. Those little white brats thought divorce was synonymous with Armageddon. Therefore, Richard felt that this was a touchy situation and kept delaying telling his wife the news that he wanted a divorce. He reassured me that the kids were the *only* reason and I believed him. I knew his wife alone was not holding anything up.

I certainly looked better than his wife. Although I have never seen her close up, I had seen her on television, and I am sure television doesn't distort features to the point that you couldn't tell she was ugly.

"Why did you marry her in the first place?" I questioned.

"I was young and wanted children."

"By that ugly thing? You wanted children or Gremlins?"

"Don't be snide with me!" Richard snapped.

"Don't talk down to me!" I snapped back. I got up from the floor and began to take off my outfit. There would be no second session in here today.

"Estelle wears so much make–up it looks as if a box of Crayola markers exploded on top of her face," I joked.

Richard did not seem to find it as funny as I had. I had laughed until I cramped up my stomach, but he did not even crack a smile. He had the stupidest expression on his face, combined with what had just transpired in here, I laughed even harder. Tiny tears streamed down my high cheekbones. I could care less if he did not laugh at my jokes about his wife. I knew the truth hurt.

"You're trying to laugh your insecurities away," he stated with a deadpan gawk. I shut up abruptly. "Negative!" I finally said trying to close the subject, which was now *not* so funny.

"You're insecure when it comes to my marriage. That is why you poke fun at Estelle's appearance."

He began casually putting on the clothes he had only momentarily ripped off in a frenzy. I started to panic. This wasn't going the way I had planned. I felt betrayed. How could he be mad at me for disrespecting his wife. The wife he was supposed to divorce. Whose side was he on? Was he blatantly choosing her over me? Changing the course I was taking, I said, "Are we still going out to dinner tonight?"

"I'll have my secretary call you to confirm." He finished dressing and walked out my front door into a sunny afternoon.

I plopped down on my bed and bit the bottom of my lip. I sulked for hours in that same position until I finally convinced myself that our conversation was strictly a mind game.

"I am not insecure at all!" I reassured myself. I am nothing short of *gorgeous*. I have very fine porcelain features and copper–colored skin. My mother said the sun kissed me when I was a baby in her womb and gave me a permanent glow. I have chestnut–brown eyes and have more sex appeal than Dorothy Dandridge. Everyone has always sung my praises every since I was a toddler. *"You should be a model. You should be an actress. You should be a singer. You should just be able to be seen."*

Yeah, I knew what I was working with. Richard was a big mind–game player. He'll come back. They always do.

4
LYRIC DEVANEY

"Lyric, you're beautiful." That was Richard complimenting my looks over the phone. I have him totally mesmerized. Of course, I demanded he explain what he meant by calling me insecure last week. We were due for our "brunch," and I'm sure he didn't want to jeopardize it.

"You resemble Halle Berry," he crooned. Then continued, "Is that why you style your hair like hers?"

"Excuse me. Halle Berry started styling her hair like *mine*. We had met as adolescents when there was an open call for a Colgate commercial. We hit it off well but never kept in touch. A couple of years later she landed a role in a movie with *my* hairstyle and what happens? Every young black female chops off her locks to capture the look. *My* look, Richard. Most women would have been upset if she had imitated their trademark hairstyle. But I'm flattered because I'm often imitated, but never duplicated. Besides, a million women can try to look like me but the fact remains, they're not." There was a long silence on the other end.

"Interesting," Richard said with skepticism. I could just imagine his right eyebrow arching to express his disbelief. "Are you sure it was *Halle* Berry?" He quizzed me.

"Of course I'm fucking sure. What . . . are you insinuating that I'm lying?" I exploded.

"Well since you mentioned it, are you?"

"Goodbye Richard!" (click) I hung up. I *was* lying. I had picked up the habit as a child and never let it go. I was usually great at convincing people my lies were true, but Richard was the exception. I hated him for that. I also, loved him for it. Richard Cardinale was a challenge.

I'm equally a challenge for the old mayor as well. Woman just don't have my personality. I drive men wild. And once I make love to them, they never stop knocking at my door. I do phenomenal, obscene things in the bedroom. No woman could ever come close to me in bed. Make no mistake about whether it's better having a good pussy or being able to fuck. I've been blessed with both gifts, and I use them wisely. All my men tell me that!

When Richard and I met, he was being deprived of utilizing his manhood. His wife had totally broken him down and their marriage had put a strain on him mentally. She punished him with sex. If they had an argument, no sex. If he was too occupied with work, no sex. If he missed a special occasion, no sex. They hadn't had sexual relations in years. He said he just simply didn't love her anymore. I asked him how he could survive being celibate for so long. Personally, I loved sex and couldn't go without it more than a few days.

When I asked him how they managed to have a three–year–old son if he hadn't been sleeping with his wife, he logically explained she had begged him one night when he was drunk. In a drunken stupor, he said she climbed on top of him and two seconds later he passed out. All he could remember was that six weeks later she said she was pregnant. Richard said he didn't even *want* another baby. But, she had it anyway; she was Catholic and didn't believe in abortion. He said he was furious with her the entire pregnancy, right up to the point when she gave birth to the baby. To his surprise, she gave him a boy. A junior. After having four girls, he had given up on having a son. As Richard Jr. grew, Richard Sr. said he had doubts that the boy was even his child. The boy had a permanent suntan and his hair was naturally curly. He could never request a paternity test. If the press got wind of that . . .

After he told me that, he swore me to secrecy. *Of course, I had my fingers crossed.*

5
LYRIC DEVANEY

Tonight, Richard and I will be going to a dimly lit bar or a romantic, quiet restaurant where everyone minded their own business. We'll grab a secluded table in the back and order the finest red wine. This is going to be my last attempt at getting something concrete regarding the divorce procedures.

I zipped up my black Gucci strapless dress with the middle cut out for seduction. The design Toni Braxton made famous. See, everyone can't wear a dress like this, but they will die trying. Their fat guts oozing out the sides. I can't stand that. But it only makes the *real* women that can handle a dress like this look even better when we slide into it. I decided to wear my brand new $700 dollar Gucci high heels with the black leather sexy straps. My toes were exposed because I had nothing to hide. I had perfect feet. I wore a perfect size six. My motto, if you want to know if someone has money or not, just look at their shoes. The shoes tell it all!

I stood back to see my reflection in the mirror. I looked so alluring in my all-black get up, but I was missing something. I walked over to my dresser and opened my jewelry box. There stood a very expensive selection of the finest jewels women could want. Trinkets of love from former lovers. Oh, how I love diamonds! They're my most favorite gift. I usually kept my jewelry in my safety deposit box along with $200,000 I've managed to hide from the government. But when I'm going on a special date, I take out a couple of pieces and return them the very next day. Everything is insured, but who wants to go through the hassle of reporting to an insurance company when something is stolen. So to avoid that, I keep my jewelry in the safest place I can think of . . . a huge vault in an FDIC bank in the World Trade Center.

I couldn't decide between my 18k white-gold Oyster Perpetual Lady Datejust Pearlmaster Rolex watch.

It was set with diamonds with a white mother–of–pearl dial. This beauty was given to me by a rapper named Jay Kapone. Or my platinum Cartier watch, given to me by a powerful defense attorney named Gabriel. He'd made millions representing members of the Esposito crime family. When one of the under bosses of the family lost in Federal Court and was serving three consecutive life sentences, word got out on the street that there was a contract out on his life. I had unattached myself from that drama. I don't want to get caught in a drive–by shooting and become a victim of a Mafia hit. La Cosa Nostra, my ass! I love making the papers but not in that way.

I decided to go with the Cartier watch, a dainty platinum and diamond tennis chain from BVLGARI with the matching tennis bracelet, and my emerald–cut clear six-karat diamond earrings that Ronald bought me for my twenty–third birthday. Ronald was an investment banker I dated briefly. He had the nerve to ask for them back when I said, "This just isn't going to work out between us." Ronald was too clingy.

He too did that crying routine, but by this time I was already bored. I even yawned to reflect my mood. When he saw that his performance didn't work one bit, he got angry and called me a *"money bitch,"* then demanded the earrings he had purchased for me. That's what I get for going out with someone who had no class.

Now, I know people may find this hard to believe, but where I come from, which I don't tell *anyone*, is the Amsterdam Projects in Harlem, better known as the PJ's. You learn at a very early age that you do not give back shit! This isn't a swap meet. I'll swap you these earrings for your pussy. When I don't get the pussy anymore, we'll just swap back. Please!

So I told him in my most aggressive voice, "Touch my motherfuckin' earrings and I'll buss your ass up 'n here!"

He was shocked but he knew I was serious. He had never heard me use street lingo before. I like to keep that side of me on the low. However, you know what a wise person once said, "You can take the person out of the ghetto, but you can never take the ghetto out of the person." True indeed.

Just as I was examining what I already knew was perfect in the mirror, the doorbell rang. To waste time, I re–touched up my lip–gloss and sprayed a little more of my perfume on. It was Envy, by Gucci, of course. By the third ring, I sashayed towards the door. Mother always said, *"Make a man wait."* I think she was talking about getting me in bed, which I have never mastered. But the door is a start, and you have to start somewhere.

"Say, sweetie, you new 'round town?" I was doing my Mae West impression. Richard seemed impatient. I guess it was the wait. Hell, I am worth it. "Lyric," he said dryly, annoyance written all over his face. He pushed passed me without allowing me to invite him in, which I wasn't going to do because we were supposed to be going out for dinner.

As he started taking off his overcoat and loosening his tie, I knew I was in for a long night.

"Come sit down," he commanded.

"Richard, what is this all about? I don't want to spend another night in my apartment entertaining you." I put emphasis on the *you*. That was an inadvertent threat letting him know that he had better get his act together or he would be replaced. Immediately.

"I take it you haven't read the newspaper?" His words were accusatory.

"Was I supposed to?"

"Do you even read the newspaper *or* listen to the news when it's not headlining your name?" His tone was boisterous and his face was turning fuchsia pink. He flung a copy of The New York Times entertainment section my way. I glanced down and saw his face in a photograph taken at one of the fundraisers he had held early last week for his Senate race. He was right; I didn't read the newspaper unless it was the theater section and occasionally the gossip column. Obviously, we were playing the game of "Clue" and this was my first one. I picked up the article and immediately focused in on my name. I blinked twice to be certain that what I was reading was correct. The reporter had written:

"*Lyric Devaney must be one of Mayor Cardinale's biggest supporters. She's at all of his fundraisers and has been seen having dinner with the Mayor along with other city officials all around town. Who knew actresses cared so much about politics? Or is it the man behind them?*" I could barely contain my excitement, but I knew I had to. "So," I said, and portrayed the best look of bewilderment an actress could project. "So?" he retorted·and let out a demonic laugh. "This could cost me the election!" His eyes were small and beady just like a rat. I never really paid much attention to them until now. He really was an unattractive person. If he weren't a powerful man, he'd be a perfect poster boy for serial killers. He had that next–door–neighbor–on–the–verge–of–pervert look. "We have to cool it for a while. I mean not totally. Just be a little more discrete until after the election. No more accompanying me and my officials, and you certainly cannot attend anymore of my fundraisers." He must have read something in my eyes because his tone softened and he said, "I mean, we're still going to see each other darling, but we're going to have to be more discrete and make arrangements to meet in a hotel and spend a couples of hours there. Your place may become off limits for a while."

He had obviously read the wrong *something* in my eyes.

6
LYRIC DEVANEY

The telephone ringing had startled me in my sleep and for a moment, I didn't know where I was. I must have drunk too much champagne the previous evening with Richard because my head was spinning and I felt awful. I reached for the phone and dropped it in a clumsy attempt to bring it to my ear. Suddenly I felt a rumbling in my stomach, and it was moving north very fast. Without hesitation, I jumped up and did the 100–yard dash to my bathroom and regurgitated every fine delicacy I had devoured for dinner. After rinsing my mouth out in the sink, I looked in the mirror and told myself, "I will never drink again." Suddenly, I smiled. I was thinking that I was saying those same words just last week when I had had 'one too many,' and was in the bathroom throwing up ferociously.

Crawling back to my bedroom, I could hear the operator saying, "If you would like to make a call, please hang up and . . . " "Yeah, yeah," I said to myself because I was alone in my apartment. Richard could never stay the whole night. He had to get back home to his wife and kids at a reasonable hour with a reasonable explanation about his whereabouts. Nevertheless, that arrangement wouldn't last too much longer. Last night I told Richard just what I had planned. The article in The New York Times was an introduction to the conversation. "Look, Richard," I began, "either divorce that husky bitch Estelle or get the hell out of my life!" I said it with so much fury and rage I almost startled myself. I don't know why I had such vengeance in my heart for this woman I had never met. I mean, I'm sleeping with *her* husband. Why am I angry she won't let him go? I should be mad at Richard for using lies and manipulation to get what he wants. Right?

"Lyric, honey, we've discussed this a million times already. Estelle and I are getting a divorce, but now, in the middle of an election campaign, is not the appropriate time to bring the subject up." He looked defeated. He wasn't in the mood for any confrontations. I knew this from the look in his eyes. He had nasty things on his mind and he was ready for me to indulge. However, I wasn't in the mood for play until he told me what I wanted to hear.

"I'm tired of hearing 'now is not the right time,'" I mimicked. "Do you think I'm stupid? Some cheap tramp that you control with your money? I want it all or nothing. I want the prestige, Richard." I was screaming and pointing my index finger in his face. He grabbed my finger and kissed it.

"Sweetheart," he began, "I know you're frustrated. I want to kick myself for putting you through so much pain. I never wanted to hurt you. I only wanted to make you happy. You know how I feel about you." He was looking me directly in my eyes with his small beady rat eyes.

"Do you love me Richard?" I pursued.

"Don't ask me what you already know is true."

"Prove it," I challenged. I was standing with my legs firmly spread apart with my hands folded underneath my breast for strength. He moved in close and touched my chin gently. I didn't stop him. Then he unfolded my arms and pulled me in so close that I could feel his heart beating. Slowly, he brought his lips to mine and began to kiss me softly at first, his tongue greedily exploring the inside of my mouth.

"Make love to me Lyric," he murmured, unaware that I was not responding to his advances. "BITCH!" he screamed, as I bit down hard on his tongue drawing blood. "What the fuck is the matter with you?" he exploded, running into the bathroom to dress his wound with me one step behind him ready for battle.

"I said prove it, not fuck me! Prove you love me Richard and get a divorce from Estelle!" He was ignoring me, too preoccupied with his bleeding tongue.

"I may need stitches," he whined. If there was one thing that annoyed me most, it was a weak man.

"Handle it Richard and quit bitching." My voice was stern and unwavering.

"Why are you acting in such a hateful manner? What happened to my beautiful butterfly? This isn't you Lyric." His eyes were pleading for me to soften up. "Have you been drinking?"

"Drinking? You had better hope I don't get a drink up in me 'cause I will turn this motherfucker out!" I snapped.

"What?" he exclaimed incredulously.

"Listen, I'm everything I pretend to be, Richard!"

"Yes, I'm sure you are. Now what character are you *pretending* to be?"

"Well," I said, ignoring his cockiness.

"Well, what?"

"Are you choosing option number one, which is divorce, or option number two, the front door?" He took a moment to answer searching my eyes to show a sign of weakness.

"If I choose option number one, do I get to see my beautiful butterfly?" His beautiful butterfly was tattooed on my left thigh in between my legs. He said it was very sexy and turned him on. I knew where this conversation was going, but I said nothing. Suddenly, he realized playtime was over.

"Okay, Lyric, tomorrow morning after breakfast, I'll ask Estelle for a divorce. Trust me. I don't want to lose you."

After that, we ordered out, drank champagne and made love for hours in front of my fireplace. I had to show him what he would have been missing if he had chosen option number two. By the time he left, he was drained but still begging for more.

The telephone rang again interrupting my thought. I contemplated not answering it because it was too damn early in the morning. I can't stand nine to five girlfriends. However, that was all I had. None of my friends were performers like me, so as soon as they got to work they were calling me instead of doing what they were supposed to be doing.

"Hello," I said trying to get the right octave on my voice. I hated for people to think I was still in bed sleeping.

"You just waking up?"

25

"Nope," I lied. It was my agent Kenny. He was calling to tell me to get my butt over to the Liberty building on 5th Avenue this Friday. They were casting for a new movie and were looking for black females between the ages of eighteen and twenty–one to audition for the role of a junkie.

"Kenny, didn't I tell you that I'm not auditioning for any ghetto roles."

"Pa–lezze girlfriend! This isn't a ghetto role. They're going to re–make the 1965 classic. It's a m-a-a-a-j-o-r production about the movie Silk."

"Silk *who*?"

"Silk. Don't act like you never heard of the movie. You're old enough to be Janine Holiday's mammy."

"I'm eighteen," I lied.

"Yes dear. I know you are. You've been eighteen for the past twenty years and will be for the next thirty."

"I hardly have to lie about my age."

"Liar, liar. Set your panties on fire," he chimed, then snickered.

"Don't you mean *your* panties?" I challenged.

Kenny was getting on my last nerve. He was always trying to call me out. A hobby of his since the first day we were introduced and I innocently asked him if he were gay. I guess he hasn't gotten over the shock of my forwardness. Unfortunately, I had to deal with him because he was a good agent and the only one who would actually represent my interests. Everyone else thought I'd fuck for a role. Not saying I wouldn't, but they'd want free sex for months before you'd even get a decent audition. With Kenny, I got decent auditions without having to lie on the casting couch. I liked that a lot.

"Tell me more," I entertained, not letting him know his remark had affected me.

"W-e-l-l-l-l," he began, over–exaggerating his words as usual. "They need someone to play the role of the sexy sister who becomes a drug addict."

"Is she a prostitute or something?"

"She's a trifling heifer just like you!"

26

"Look Kenny, I've never seen the movie. I need to know this information, so if I choose to go to the audition, I'm in character. So don't chose today to come out of the closet on me, okay." I added to make him angry.

"Oh, miss thang, I know you didn't just try to come for me!"

"Kenny," I laughed, "what I mean is, is there more to this drug addict? Something exciting like turning tricks to get a hit? Did someone turn her out? I'm not trying to get typecast in low–budget black films. I want to be accepted by Hollywood."

"This is Hollywood."

"I want *white* Hollywood where there's a difference between twenty million a picture or twenty thousand a picture."

"Well, *white* Hollywood isn't paying your bills. This low–budget *black* film can."

He was right. I was low on the cash I'd paid taxes on. On paper, I looked pathetic. Although I had three safety deposit boxes, I really didn't like to dip into them. Moreover, I hadn't had anything major yet, just small roles in low–budget films. That reminds me. Richard was supposed to dig into his fundraising and slide me forty grand. He sure as hell didn't leave the check by the bed on his way out. I'll give him a courtesy call to remind him since I know he's so busy.

"Who's behind it?" I inquired.

"You know that alleged drug–hustler turned rapper named Jay Kapone?"

"Yes."

"Well, Jay Kapone and a silent partner bought the rights and the filming starts in six weeks. Can you carry a note?"

"You know I can carry a note . . . I'm a triple threat, remember. Kenny, I think I recall this film now. Is this the one with Nikki Guy as Sassi and Janine Holiday as Silk?"

"You've just passed your 1st grade entrance examination."

"Who is cast as the lead role, Silk?"

"All the major roles are cast."

"I didn't ask you if all the major roles were cast, I asked who is playing Silk." Kenny had no idea that Jay Kapone was once in love with me. If I had known that a drug–hustler turned rapper would be pursuing bigger dreams in the movie industry, I would have kept him around a little longer. With me back in his life, he won't be using that drug money to re–make old black movies. We'll be doing movies starring John Travolta or Brad Pitt with me co–starring as supporting actress.

"Are you listening to me?" Kenny questioned. I had drifted off into my thoughts for a minute.

"What did you say?"

"I said Terisa Banks is cast as Silk. She's hot right now."

"Yeah, she's hot when I'm not in the room," I said.

I'd die before I'd say something nice about her. Lately, I've been losing a lot of small roles to Terisa. She's the flavor of the month every since she got engaged to Marvin Lee, the famous director Harrington's cousin. She met Marvin on an audition for one of Harrington's latest films. We were both supposed to audition for the role, but I showed up for the audition three days late. She swore that she gave me the correct date, that I must have screwed it up somehow. That audition meant a lot to me. Even agents hadn't known about the casting call. How Terisa was able to get the information was not my business. Anyway, she walked away with the role and my identity. But everything she was, I was.

"She's asking $50,000 for this role, and her agent gets t-w-e-n-t-y percent," he said lavishly. Her acting was hardly worth the fifty grand she was getting paid. I swore one day I'd make her regret the day she crossed Lyric Devaney.

"Nobody crosses me. I cross people!" is what I told her the last time we spoke in public. She just laughed and said, "Lighten up."

"Kenny, this is your lucky day. Not only am I going on this audition, but I'm coming back with the *lead* role and we're asking for *six* figures."

7
LYRIC DEVANEY

It took me two hours to get Jay Kapone's new pager number. I beeped him 911 and entered my old code of 01. When he finally called back, I couldn't adjust to the new attitude he had adopted. Most people say it comes from money. I say it comes from low self–esteem.

"Yo, who dis?"

"Jay Kapone?"

"Who dis?"

"This is Lyric. Do I have the right number? Is this Jay Kapone?" I couldn't make out his voice because he was on a cellular phone and the connection was bad.

"How you git my number, yo?" His voice was very unpleasant.

"Jay Kapone, this is Lyric." Maybe he wasn't sure about who he was speaking to.

"I know who dis is. How you git my number?" he spat. Did I miss something? Last time I saw him he had picked me up in a bear hug and swung me around and declared his everlasting love for me.

"Your mother gave it to me. I told her I wanted to audition for a role in your movie. Plus, I guess I missed you," I added, trying to break the ice.

"You missed me huh?" He was starting to loosen up. I put the charm on real thick and told him that he was my one true love. That ever since I broke it off, I did nothing but regret everyday being without him. So I poured myself into my work and shut everyone out of my life.

"When was the last time dat you fucked?"

"Excuse me?"

"When was the last time dat you fucked?"

"Nothing like getting to the point huh? Well, truthfully it's been about three years," I lied. "I haven't been with anyone since you."

"I know your freaky ass is lying."

"I swear to God. May my mother drop dead," I said continuing my lie.

"So whaddup, yo? What you want 'cause I'm busy. I got meetings 'n shit. Peeps I gotta talk to, paper I gotta git."

"Jay, I want the lead role in your movie," I was always direct in telling people what I wanted. It saved time.

"Ohhhh no. You my peeps 'n shit. But I don't even fuck wit you like dat. What we had was personal, dis business." I felt like I was in the middle of watching Al Pacino in "Scarface" and at any minute he was going to scream, "Say hello to my little friend!"

"I know this is business. That's why I'm calling about *auditioning* for a role. I didn't say give it to me on the strength of our past relationship or remind you that you owe me," I was speaking very softly and seductive just the way he liked me to.

"You sound sexy as shit. You makin' my dick hard." The mere thought of his little slim dick made me remember why I dumped him.

"Jay, stop talking so nasty. You *know* you do things to me when you speak like that."

"Tell daddy what I do to ya." It took about fifteen minutes of phone sex before I could get him to agree to come over to my apartment. I knew that once I got him over to my place and made him give me his word, the role would be mine. All it was going to take was a little persuasion. He said that he would be at my place in an hour. I knew that meant I had the whole afternoon to recover from my hangover before he arrived.

I pushed my hair back with a headband and went into the kitchen and got a can of V–8 tomato juice from my cabinet. I then took two alka–seltzer tablets and diluted them in just a little water. When the tablets were dissolved, I mixed the V–8 and the solution together and forced myself to drink my concoction. I admit that the taste was worse than spinach, but the remedy really worked.

The hot bath was so soothing that it energized me, and I started to make plans to hang out tonight.

Maybe I'd go to that new club called Systems and do a little networking. Before I start planning for club "System," I'd better complete what I started and finish preparing for my afternoon with Jay Kapone. Underneath my bathroom sink, I had my magic weapon. Amongst my tampons, Norforms and pantyliners was my heavyweight. Its called trichotine. Most women don't know about this solvent. All I have to do is put a teaspoon of it into my Summer's Eve douche and I'll have virgin pussy. If I "Ooh, ah, be gentle, you're hurting me" enough, he'll really believe that I haven't been with anyone in the last three years.

8
LYRIC DEVANEY

The sun was shinning so brightly it got inside my soul and gave me the energy I needed to get me through this afternoon. My large storm windows welcomed all the warm rays the sun was sending my way. I decided to clean up my messy apartment because a clean apartment would make the statement that I got my shit together. I took one look around at my huge, dusty duplex and decided to call maid service. Within the hour, I had two Asian women in my house doing justice with a white rag and cleaning liquid. While they were busy, I decided to prepare a carpet picnic on my living room floor for my company. I whipped up a light salad, some strawberries and whipped cream, cheese, crackers and wine. I laid a white picnic blanket on my plush carpet beside the fireplace. Then I propped the red and white–stripped napkins inside the crystal wine glasses and arranged the food on top of pastel–colored Lenox china. I opened the patio door and the warmth of the sun enveloped my body. It was truly a beautiful day. I took this to mean that only good things could happen on such a gorgeous day.

Just when *All My Children* was getting to the good part, my intercom buzzed. I looked at my watch. It was ten minutes before two. Just as I suspected, I had the whole afternoon to get ready. I decided to bite my tongue and swallow my remarks, so I wouldn't curse Jay Kapone out and get him upset. On my way to the door, I could hear him having a very loud conversation, and I was furious that he would bring someone to my apartment. When I flung the door open, he was arguing with someone on his cellular phone. He had three heavy diamond and platinum chains draped around his neck. Two diamond pinky rings dressed each hand. He had on huge, at least five–karat, diamond earrings which should not be on the ears of a man. A black Fubu sweatsuit with a baseball cap turned to the back, and to top it off, he held his beeper in the other hand that had a platinum Rolex watch wrapped around it. This scene was too ghetto. He barely glanced my way as he pushed past me still holding tight onto his cellular phone and intently telling the person on the other end that he'd "better have my dough or else."

"Who the fuck do you think you are coming to my place three hours late?" I screamed, and must have scared him something awful because he dropped his cellular phone and stared at me with his mouth hanging open.

"Lyric," he regrouped. "You still snap like a crocodile."

As he stood there looking like Bozo the clown with his huge nose and thick African lips, I couldn't help but burst out into laughter. Jay Kapone was such a gentle heart trapped in a thug body and lifestyle. It was sad, but there was also an amusing side to this. I sat back and watched him portray being this thug when actually he had grown up in the suburbs, and went to private Catholic schools all his life. His parents were both pediatricians and sent him to NYU to study political science. That's where he hooked up with his thug crowd, laid down some rhymes about growing up in the 'hood, and sold four million records.

Looking back, I think about how somewhere between going to college and getting a record deal, Jay Kapone had met a Columbian girl who used to push about one hundred kilograms of cocaine a week. The money impressed him. She impressed him.

Her connections became his connections. He learned the language and was trusted by her people. When I came into the picture, he was already established in the drug game and making millions. When he met me, he was proposing marriage before I could say, "Hey, I don't even dig you like that." But he didn't hear me. He dumped his Columbian chick and came to my door ring in one hand, roses in the other. The ring was a fabulous ten–karat, platinum creation from Harry Winston. I accepted the ring, of course. But marriage was not in my plans, so I told him let's do a l-o-o-o-n-g engagement. Why not? He tried to convince me otherwise, but once I speak, Lyric has spoken.

He took the token of my accepting his ring as a silent victory and climbed into my bed a proud man. A couple of hours later, someone was banging my front door down. I was reluctant to answer because it might have been one of my other "friends." But then the woman's voice started screaming, "Jay! Jay! I know your black ass is in there with your 'puta' you 'modigon'." She said a lot of other things through the door, but I could hardly make them out in her native language and thick dialect. I looked over at Jay Kapone and he was terrified. This scene hardly moved me. I have been through the same situation, a different player, on numerous occasions. I got up because this was my door she was banging on. She must have been using some of the cocaine she was selling if she thought she could come and disrespect the home where I lay my head every night.

When I opened the door, I'll never forget the look she had in her eyes. They were filled with hate, rage and jealousy as they focused in on my ring. I knew this look well. She was breathing hard and her soft hair was all sweaty and stuck to her forehead. She smelled like a wet dog, but actually was rather cute. A little overweight, but cute in a baby–girl way. Her naturally tanned complexion and dark features were mysterious. But, of course, she had nothing on me. She was a typical Latino. After a quick look over my competition, I was about to say something very offensive to this intruder when she charged me with every bit of strength of a pro wrestler. I was pinned down for about thirty seconds before she started to bang my head on the floor screaming obscenities at me. I was too much in shock to utter a word. I tried to scream for help, but nothing came out. She was pulling at my hair, punching me in my mouth and eyes, yelling, "So you wanna fuck my man, you bitch? I'll kill you! I'll fucking slay your bony ass!"

Now Lyric may be a lot of things, but like Michael Jackson, I'm a lover not a fighter. Jay Kapone finally got the nerve to come and pull her off me.

"Marisol, come on now, stop this shit!" Jay Kapone demanded, grabbing her hands. "I'm not worth it," he reasoned, "you're better than this."

I struggled to pull myself up from the floor to look at her in tears. Crying hysterically, Marisol screamed, "How could you do this to me, poppi? How . . . could . . . you . . . do . . . this?" She collapsed back onto the floor. "I love you . . . I wanna die . . . I can't breathe . . . I'm gonna kill myself!"

I looked at this barbaric creature playing the half–crazed, pathetic, innocent victim. And then I watched this asshole that just asked to marry me getting roped in. It made me want to vomit. I ran in the bathroom to do just that when I looked in the mirror and saw my face. All I saw were colors: black, blue and red.

They were in my kitchen and he was pouring her a glass of water in my crystal glass. He was looking at her with eyes that said, "So, you really love me." Her hands were trembling and she was asking him "why?" I didn't stay to hear his explanation. I ran into my room and got the nickel–plated .25 I kept underneath my mattress and came out as cool as John Wayne in a Western.

"So you feel like dying?" I said. Not waiting for a response, I continued.

"You must, 'cause this is a suicide trip you went on when you decided to fuck with me!" She balled up her fist, and gave me a look like 'Oh, you want some more?' until I had my nickel–plated .25 all up in her face.

Now it's easy to buy a gun, but no one shows you how to aim properly. I just started shooting. I didn't aim my gun at the Columbian sistah; I was aiming at Jay Kapone. When she was on top of me, all I kept thinking was "Why is all her anger directed only at me? Why not fight his fragile ass?" But women are always adversaries when it comes to a man. I should know; I've been there and may go there yet again. You just never know. And even though she fucked with me, I was screwing around with her man, so it was understandable. I knew he had a girl and I just didn't care. And I never will. All I'm saying is, _He_ had a duty of loyalty to her, not me. Although he told me that he had broken it off with her, how many *times do you hear that and they're right back with that same woman? Men don't leave women. They rearrange them. She went from being his main girl to being his chick on the side without even realizing the transition before it was too late.*

I let off about four rounds before I had finally hit him in the ass. I was aiming for his arm but like I said, I don't do this for a living. He had pushed her out of the way while scrambling to get through the door. He would have drop–kicked his Momma if she had been in his way. "Bitch freeze!" I yelled when she tried to make her great escape. I felt like one of Charlie's Angels. Anyway, she had her hands up covering her face, cowering in the corner pleading for her life. Power. Where were the steel balls she had had only moments ago? I guess they left with Jay Kapone?

"You could have died in here tonight for him" I paused. "Ask yourself--is he worth it?" She was looking at me with eyes that were saying, "Please don't kill me." Maybe it was because I still had the gun pointed at her. I had to. I couldn't take the chance that she might charge me again as if she were trying out for the San Diego Chargers football team.

"You knew he was playing you. Most men do, so I do as they do. My advice is . . . play him right back." One lone tear streamed down her face and she said a meek, "I'm sorry."

Just then, I thought about my face and remembered the lumps, cuts and bruises. I finally said, "Get the fuck out!"

Jay Kapone called and cried, cried and called, but to no avail. I did not give into his requests. Who needed the headache? Besides, he was much too weak for me. A lady should be protected at all times. We're very delicate creatures who need to feel that we're safe from harm with our man. But before I bid him farewell, I asked him for money to move out of that apartment. I told him that it held too many emotional memories. He had reluctantly given me enough money to buy the duplex condominium I'm in now. Of course, I had never given him my address until now. In our next to last conversation, he summoned

36

up enough courage to ask for his ring back. In my mind I thought "Why? So he could give it to her." I bet he would be that tacky. Well, I never gave myself a chance to find out how low he'd go because giving back the ring was hardly an option I entertained.

Jay Kapone touched the side of my face and jolted me back into the present. He had a forlorn look on his face as if to ask why we had parted. I had no desire to get nostalgic with him, so I focused on why he was really here.

"Jay, I want the lead role in your movie."

"Lyric, slow down." He was looking around my apartment when his eyes focused on the carpet picnic. His eyes lit up and his grin consumed his face.

"You did all this for me?"

"Jay, I told you on the phone that I missed you. This is just a prelude to our afternoon." I motioned him to come over and sit down on the floor.

"Your place is nice. I can't help but think my money brought you this." There was a sting of resentment in his words.

"Look, Jay, let's let the past be exactly that. The past. I thought you came here because you wanted to. You know very well that you gave me money to get a new place. Are you saying now that you want me to pay you back?"

"No."

"So, what's your real problem?"

"You, baby. It was never about money with you. I would have given you the world, if only you would have given me a chance." I wanted to say I'd given him more than that. I'd given him loving from Lyric, but he had to go and get sloppy. There was no way his girl should have been able to find my place. Anyway, I had to indulge him because at this point he was running the show.

"Jay listen . . . you know how I felt about you. Like I said, I haven't been able to commit to anyone since we broke up. I still think about you, but the ordeal was traumatizing. Think about me for once. You came and proposed to me. Asked me to be your wife, then moments later you're caressing someone else while I lay dying on the floor in *my* home." I was always good at melodrama.

37

A few tears slowly slid down my cheeks. No need to overdo it with hysteria. He would know that I was acting because that wasn't my style. Right now, he was probably thinking that he must have really hurt me because I *never* shed tears.

I tilted my head and looked innocently at Jay Kapone. I wiped my tears away, licked my lips seductively, took a deep breath letting my breast lift up and down, then softly whispered, "Baby, I needed you to love me!"

Jay Kapone's eyes were filled with such pain and guilt I knew I had him. I had never shown vulnerability.

He cupped my face in between his hands and gently leaned over and kissed me. I knew this was going to happen, but I thought he would at least wait until we had lunch. I returned his kisses with soft, playful ones. I was stalling for time. I didn't know if I should play timid, like I was afraid to sleep with him, or attack him passionately, like it had been so long since I had been with him that I actually needed to make love to him. I decided the timid role would be best for this situation. Men like being the aggressor. In their minds it gives them control.

His tongue was exploring the inside of my mouth. He slowly laid me down on the carpet and started to kiss my neck, very gently because he knew I didn't play leaving any 'property marks' on my body. His wet tongue started to kiss, nibble, and lick all areas that are usually overlooked by most. He explored the inner area of my thighs, nibbling gently, and then sucking hard. Jay Kapone flipped me over and focused on the back of my knees. He bit me gently, while inserting his index finger in my vagina. This sent chills through my body. Each layer of clothing was removed and then that area was explored with his tongue. When he started sucking every single toe, one by one, I tried to envision I was with Richard, and he was making love to me this good. Slowly, he glided up in between my legs and gently teased me with his tongue. He was definitely an experienced man when it came to kissing the pussy. He didn't bury his head and start licking like a dog slopping up water. He concentrated on the clit, softly and skillfully applying pressure at just the right moment and keeping each move steady. His tongue fluttered expertly and the feeling was pleasurable. My knees were trembling, and I was grabbing a hold of his head jerking my waist like I was James Brown with the funk in me. When my body started to take on a life of its own, and waves of pleasure overwhelmed me, I started screaming the most common name you could to not get tripped up, "Daddy, Daddy, please don't stop." I have never had an orgasm while having my pussy kissed because most men don't lounge down there long enough. This was definitely star treatment I was getting. When he was so aroused that he was ready to climb up inside of me, I had to start my act.

"Ouch! Do it softer! You're hurting me!"

Then after that performance was over, I flipped him over and climbed on top to do my work. He certainly deserved some appreciation for what he had done in here today. All I kept asking myself was–who had he been sleeping with because his skills had definitely upgraded from a three to a nine and he was pushing a perfect ten. However, his slim penis made him fall short. Why is it all men with little dicks can always fuck better? They actually made love to a woman. They were more sensual. Unfortunately, I had a big dick fetish. There was something about a strong, thick penis that turned me on. The very look of it pointing at me could make me cum in my panties without any penetration.

After we had made love all afternoon, we were both starving. We devoured every morsel of the lunch I had prepared. I was stuffing strawberries in my mouth and washing them down with gulps of wine. I didn't even care about trying to eat like a lady. Anyway, the preliminaries were over and business called.

"Jay, I know auditions are being held for your movie. I don't want a minor role. I want to play the lead."

"The lead role has already been cast. Terisa Banks has–"

"I know Terisa has been cast as the lead. I want to replace her. Give her agent a call and tell her she's been cut from the movie."

"I can't do that."

"What do you mean you *can't* do that? What exactly can you do? We both know that she can't act her way through an 'Annie' movie. She's hot right now from her association with Marvin Lee." My pressure was slowly going up, but I knew I couldn't give up on something I wanted so badly.

"Yeah . . . you right. I told dem not to hire her ass. But we can't cut her. Dis my first movie production; I can't get a name in Hollywood for hiring then cutting loose actresses. That's suicide. Besides, she would sue the shit outta my ass."

He was back to using his Ebonics again. Whenever we would speak about business, he was a thug. Then if we started talking about love, he was a perfect grammar college graduate.

"Look, talk like you got some fucking sense. What the fuck is *dem*?" I corrected. He looked at me for a moment, then said, "What you're suggesting is just not feasible. It's a potential lawsuit. Like I said before, what we got is personal. This is business."

He was relaxing back on my sofa staring contently at me with a satisfied expression. He had a point. She would bring a lawsuit against his company before the movie would even drop. But that was his problem.

"Why do you keep telling me this movie is business as if I don't know what I'm asking you or what I'm into right now? This is my life. I was acting way before I met your ass and way before you tripped up into the movie business because it's a hot fad right now for drug–hustlers."

"I don't deal drugs."

"You murderer!"

"What?"

"You fucking murderer! Do you know how many kids you kill pushing your fucking drugs." Of course, this had nothing to do with the topic. But I was mad as hell and needed to vent. "Why can't I have the part?" I pouted, "I'll audition for whoever I need to. This part is right for me, I can feel it."

I was lying through my perfect teeth. I hadn't even read the script or even knew anything about being drug addicted. I knew that this movie could be a stepping–stone for me. Inwardly, I wondered if the only reason I was passionate about this role was because Terisa had it. I needed this role to put closure on my wound.

"Why do you want this part so bad? I can guarantee you a spot in my film without you auditioning. Pick any of the other characters and it's yours, baby. I know what you're capable of. I'll speak to my partner and get back to you." He was thinking with his cock right now because business just became personal.

"I don't want any other part. I want *her* part and I'm not settling for less. And who is this silent partner of yours? I may need to speak to him because you're thick–headed."

"You don't need to know all of that. Lyric, this part may be bigger, but it's boring. And honestly, if you play the role of the junkie, it's more exciting and if played correctly, could leave a lasting effect on the public as well as Hollywood." Something about the way he said "boring" sent a revelation through my mind.

"Jay, could you go to your office and overnight me the script?"

"I could do better than that. I could have a messenger bring it over tonight. Are you gonna consider taking the role of Sassi?"

"Jay, you said that the role of Sassi is exciting right?"

"Yeah."

"And you said that you didn't want to get sued by Terisa, so I can't get her role right?"

"Yeah."

"Well, what would you say if I had a way to satisfy both you and me?" My brain was racing on adrenaline now. I was in full gear and on overdrive. I was amazed that my Momma hadn't raised any fool.

"What are you getting at?" He pushed forward in his seat to show I had his full attention.

"Well, since Terisa has already signed for the role, let her keep it. But it won't be a major role anymore. I'm rewriting the script and the junkie, who will be me, will be your new leading lady. Anyway, I can certainly carry a film."

I could tell he was actually thinking over my proposal.

"But we're already paying her $50,000 to play the lead role. She'll sue if we give her a pay cut."

"Let her keep the measly fifty grand. The role I'm writing for me is going to cost you $250,000."

"Get the fuck outta here!" He was smiling. I wasn't. After a few more minutes of negotiating, I persuaded him that his money would be wisely invested in me. I told him that we could actually profit off the scandal involving Mayor Cardinale and me. That the publicity alone would generate a whole new audience. The white public would come out to see the woman who was alleged as being involved in a scandal with a top city official. A city official who is currently the mayor of New York, who is running for Senator, and whose next stop is the White House. Of course, I had to assure him that there was no truth in the rumor. By the time he left, he was sold on my idea. All he had to do was convince his silent partner and introduce me to the writer who would have the last say about the changes I would be making in the script.

He left my apartment shortly before five with promises to have a contract drawn up for me to take to my attorney. I was elated! I thought about calling my agent to tell him the good news but changed my mind. Kenny had a way of irking me, and I was on a high that was delightful. I didn't want to spoil it. Just as I was undecided about whom to call, the telephone rang and decided for me. I looked at my caller ID first to see who it was before I picked it up and to my surprise it was Richard. My day was getting better by the second. He was probably calling to tell me what had happened between him and his wife regarding their divorce. Life is so good to me.

9
MADISON MICHAELS

As I approached the steps of Brooklyn Law school, I took a deep breath. This is my last year. Working part–time at the Brooklyn District Attorneys office and going to law school, was a heavy load for anyone to maintain.

Today was the second Friday of September, and the temperature was a warm seventy–nine degrees. The sun was so bright and warm, it complimented the mood I was in. I only had one class on Friday; then I was free to do anything I wanted, which usually meant studying. But since the semester was just starting, I had accepted an invitation from Joshua to join him, his wife Parker, and his close friend Erious in Soho to have dinner. Even though the invitation appeared to be purely innocent, I knew this was the chance for me to indulge in some excitement. Joshua says it's not normal for an attractive woman in her early 20's like me to not go out on dates.

Erious is a professional basketball player drafted from college nine years ago to play for the Los Angeles Lakers. He was recently traded to the Chicago Bulls. Lyle Hoyt and Erious were unstoppable on the court. Since he's been on the team, they've won every championship game. He has three rings to show for it. I am one of his biggest fans and know so many intimate details from Josh. Joshua and Erious have been best friends since grade school, only separating when Erious went to California. But they kept in touch.

I met Joshua four years ago when he interviewed me for a paralegal position at the D.A.'s office. He told me I would be in for a lot of work, but the experience would be gratifying, especially if I was going to apply to law school. Since working at the D.A.'s office, Joshua and I have become very good friends because I don't have any male figures in my life, he's been both father and brother to me.

After class, I immediately went home to take a shower and prepare for dinner that night. I was so nervous. What if he's my soul mate? That question would run through my mind until the night had ended. My palms were sweating and I had lost my appetite. I opened my closet to pull out something to wear and panic struck like a thirty ton Mack truck with no brakes. All I saw were baggy jeans and dark–colored business suits. I needed something elegant but sexy. He's used to dating sophisticated women.

Just while I was contemplating my next move, the phone rang and interrupted my thoughts.

"Hello," I replied, my voice sounding as if someone had just died in the family.

"Hey girl, what's up?" The caller observably could care less about my demeanor, and the voice was only too familiar.

"Hey, Lyric," I replied. Only Lyric could totally disregard someone else's situation. She was self–centered. I also met Lyric through Joshua. They had an 'encounter' a few years back and had been great friends ever since. Neither one of them called the 'encounter' a relationship. They simply called it sex. They had slept together a couple times and realized that nothing could ever become of them as a couple, that being friends was much safer. That was before Joshua had married Parker. I could tell that Joshua was still sweet on Lyric. Most men were. There was something untamable about her that drove men crazy. They would love her so much that they hated her. She was always in very passionate, very conflicting relationships until someone had to say "when" and end it. Even though both Joshua and Lyric both deny ever being intimate, I think Parker suspects that something went on between them. You know women can pick up what the naked eye can't about their man. Parker's very standoffish whenever Lyric's around. So she avoids her, and I think Josh tries not to invite Lyric to functions that his wife is going to be attending to keep the peace.

"I want to know if you want to come to Club Systems with me tonight?"

Lyric was always partying. She went out sometimes seven nights a week. Always saying she had to network. That meant meet people that could help her advance her career in acting.

"Can't," I said, "I'm going out to dinner with Joshua and Parker."

"Come on, Madi. You can go out with Joshua and his lesser half anytime. Tonight, I heard from Kenny, my agent. Lawrence Fishburne is going to be there. He's in town just two nights for his new movie premiere.

"You got tickets for the premiere tonight?" I don't know why I asked because I knew I wasn't going to attend with her. This dinner date was way too important for me.

"No, not yet," she paused. "The premiere is tomorrow night at Ziegfeld's. That's why we have to be at Systems tonight so I can persuade Larry to give me two tickets. Anyway, I thought you said you liked his acting." Lyric said *Larry* like they were old friends.

"I do, but I like Erious Jerome much more." I could hardly contain my schoolgirl excitement. "What does Erious Jerome have to do with having dinner with Joshua? Don't tell me you actually believe all the stories Joshua tells us about Erious being his good friend?"

"Yes, I believe him. I mean, why would Joshua lie?"

"Well, I'm not calling Joshua a liar. Let's just say he embellishes the truth. I've known Joshua longer than you. If Erious was such a good friend of his, why haven't we ever met him?" she argued. "An even simpler question," she added without letting me answer the first one, "where are his complimentary tickets to the season games? He may have known him when they were little or something, but he's just fantasizing because Erious is a celebrity." Her tone was that reprimanding tone my mother used when I did something I should have known not to do.

"Hate to disappoint you, Lyric. It's true I'm having dinner tonight with Joshua and Parker, and *Erious* will also be joining us." There was a vacant silence on the other end of the line. I knew this space well. Lyric's brain was racing.

"What are you wearing?" she casually asked.

"See, that's just it . . . I don't have anything nice to wear. I threw something together, but I really want to go out and buy something and hide the tags, so I could return it tomorrow." I somehow suspect Lyric knew the answer to her question before I replied.

"You don't have to be a pigeon," she laughed. I also joined her in her laughter. A pigeon is someone who does unscrupulous things such as go into a department store and make a purchase, wear the item, then return it with the excuse "it didn't fit."

"I'm a sporadic pigeon. In life or death dilemmas only. I'm not full–fledged yet."

"Why don't I come over and bring you something to wear?"

"Would you really do that for me? Do you think you have something that could fit me in your closet?"

"Of course I do. And Madison, don't sound so grateful. It's scary. Anyway, it's only a dress. I'll bring it over in a hour. Sit tight. Later."

I sat fidgeting around my apartment, which was a very large loft that a Jewish girlfriend of mine let me sub–lease while she was attending law school at Berkeley. Her parents were wealthy, so she could afford not to make a profit off her loft. The only stipulation was that when she came for holidays, she came to stay in the apartment with me. Which was cool; she's a very entertaining person and I like her company. Her only detriment is that she gets lonely and finds herself in loveless relationships and, out of pure desperation, accepts anything. It's sad, but Beth has a big heart, and she'll always be a friend of mine.

10
MADISON MICHAELS

When I opened the door for Lyric an hour later, she took my breath away. I was admiring her like a bridegroom does his bride on his wedding day.

"You look gorgeous, Lyric," the words rolled from my tongue directly into her ego.

"And you look like bad wallpaper," she retorted. "I'm glad I decided to go to this dinner engagement or you would have embarrassed not only yourself but Joshua as well." She was walking towards my bedroom with a garment bag draped over her arm.

"Lyric, you've decided to join us," I said hoping she didn't hear the disappointment in my voice.

"Yeah, why not? Besides there's nothing else for me to do."

"What happened to Club Systems and Lawrence Fishburne?"

"Damn, Madison! If I didn't know any better, I would think you didn't want me to go." Her voice was firm now, and she was looking me directly in the eyes trying to rattle me.

"Yes, I want you to go," I nervously explained. "But I was just thinking that this dinner wasn't your speed. We're really not doing anything exciting afterwards. I know how short your attention span is. Plus, Josh might trip."

"What do you mean '*Josh* might trip?' Listen Madison," she countered, "I don't need your permission to meet up with my friend. Joshua is *my* friend. And for you to try and come between that is very selfish." Her eyes were getting very small like they usually did when she was upset. "Do I see a hint of green in your hazel eyes?" she challenged.

"Lyric, please don't be mad at me. I'm so sorry if I hurt you." By this time I was so confused and feeling so guilty I would have done anything for her to forgive me.

"It's only a misunderstanding," I continued, praying with every syllable that she might accept my apology.

"You're my friend till the end," I said hoping she would respond to my sincerity.

"You're my friend till the end," she said, her face softening up. I don't know why I felt so threatened that Lyric would be joining us. But I knew she had the power to make all men fall in love with her seductive ways. It wasn't her fault that she was so flirtatious. Underneath all her sex appeal was a very insecure woman. She needed men to adore her to validate her ego.

The dress Lyric brought me wasn't exactly what I had in mind. Lyric had beautiful things in her closet and she brought me a dress that I had never seen before. It looked a little worn and faded, with a pasta stain on the front.

"Lyric . . . maybe I'll just wear what I have on." I said as I examined the dress more carefully. It was a spaghetti strap spandex dress. It looked like one of the cheap cotton dresses you saw in every ten–dollar store on Pitkin Avenue.

"Don't be silly. You can't wear a business suit on a dinner date. This dress is sexy. Trust me . . . he'll be pleased," she said, ignoring the plea in my eyes.

"I never saw this dress in your closet," I casually replied.

"Maybe you just overlooked it. Besides, why are you rummaging through my closet taking inventory anyway?"

"No, I wasn't. I just . . . forget it. I'll go get dressed."

"You do that," she retorted.

I went to change my clothes alone in the bathroom. I was very shy and self–conscious about my body.

I took a rag and wet it with cold water and scrubbed the stain out. Then I took the blow dryer and put the warm air on the wet spot until it was dry. Next, I put the dress on and it clung to every curve I had. My breasts were oozing out the front of the dress and my buttocks were protruding out the back. I took one look in the mirror and knew that I could never wear this dress. I walked back in the room to show Lyric how awful I looked and she exclaimed I looked fabulous.

"Girl, don't you dare take off that dress! You look hot."

"I don't like it."

"Because you're not used to wearing sexy clothes, Madison. I've never seen you show off your assets. I wish I had your boob size. Mother Nature was definitely cheap in *my* department."

"Lyric, I feel very uncomfortable because this isn't me. It's trashy. I thought you were going to bring me something elegant like what you have on." Lyric's face was distorted with rage. It didn't take much for her to explode, and lately I was pushing her buttons.

"Well, maybe it's not the dress. Maybe, it's the person wearing it. Elegance isn't something you buy in a department store; it's something you're born with. Some of us have it, some don't." She was on me, lifting up the dress and trying to pull it off me. "If you don't appreciate the dress," she continued, pulling and tugging at it, "I'll just bring it back home." I gently moved her hands away and adjusted the dress as much as I could. My guilt was so thick it formed a lump in my throat. I had to swallow hard to speak.

"Lyric, the dress is fine. I'm just a little self–conscious . . . you know that. I know that I could never look as good as you do in your clothes. And I'm sorry if I sound ungrateful. I'm just a little nervous about tonight." Once again she accepted my apology and we gathered our things to head towards the restaurant.

11
MADISON MICHAELS

For the whole ride to the restaurant, I sat fidgeting in Lyric's Mercedes–Benz. We drove over the Manhattan Bridge and got caught in traffic at Canal Street. I was so uncomfortable in this dress I wanted to scream. I was angry inside for not standing up for myself. I didn't want to hurt Lyric's feelings after she had gone through so much trouble to make sure I looked good for the evening and all I did was insult her. I'm sure I must look okay if she said so. Lyric wouldn't deliberately lie to me about my appearance.

I sat looking out the window at the New Yorkers walking through the traffic as if they had built–in bumpers, all rushing to get to the same places, to do the same things they had done the night before. Lyric's silver Mercedes–Benz E–class 320 with midnight blue leather interior dipped in and out of traffic with such grace, I started to fall asleep just before we arrived at the parking lot.

"How much longer?" I asked, trying to create some conversation to see if there was any tension still left in the air from the discussion at my apartment.

"About five more minutes. Damn girl . . . you're really serious about hooking up with Erious." She was smiling, which relieved some of my anxiety. I would hate to start off a perfect evening with my best friend mad at me.

Lyric's cell phone was vibrating. She asked me to reach into her pocketbook and hand it to her. Before she answered the telephone, she looked at her caller ID to see who was calling. The number came up "unavailable." She swore softly underneath her breath, then answered it anyway.

"Girl, I almost let your ass get my machine," she exclaimed. "What have I told you about calling me from private numbers?" It was Portia calling to see if Lyric had any action going on for the night. Portia was Lyric's friend. She never became mine. I became very annoyed when she invited Portia to come meet us at the restaurant without asking me first. When she hung up the phone, I voiced my disapproval.

"Lyric, how are you going to invite Portia to have dinner with us when you know she doesn't like me?"

"She doesn't dislike you, so I did nothing wrong."

"The only reason she's coming to an event she knows I'm at is because you told her that Erious Jerome was going to be there."

"Listen Madison, it is what it is. Your insecurity is really irking me. We're women. He's a man. Everything is fair game."

"What do you mean by that?" I hoped I wasn't taking her words in the wrong context.

"What I mean is what I said!" she said through clenched teeth. "It's only dinner with friends. Don't personalize everything. You. You. You." We were inside the parking garage on Spring Street, and Lyric was getting out of the car without letting me conclude. I decided to keep quiet and let the night play out as it was meant to. Lyric ducked out of the parking lot before paying the $25 for the space. I wasn't surprised. That was classic Lyric and 'thrifty' was her middle name.

12
MADISON MICHAELS

The restaurant was cozy and eclectic. It had huge tropical plants in every corner with brick stucco on the walls. There were large lounge chairs with different color velvet cushions decorating the place. Candles created a luminous atmosphere while a jazz band played old 20's melodies from center stage. Towards the back of the restaurant was a bar with patrons ordering drinks. There was a heavy burgundy curtain used as a divider between the bar and dining area, and a bed in the corner where patrons would climb on top and order from a menu. Many of them were tourists and were taking pictures, laughing and enjoying the mystique of Soho. Four huge television sets were placed on mute with various sporting events broadcast on each channel for entertainment.

Immediately after walking in, I spotted Erious at a table having a conversation with a woman. It looked as if she had asked him to sign something for her, and then he leaned in real close while a girl snapped a picture. Joshua and Parker were sitting there with big grins on their faces as if they were the proud parents of Erious Jerome. My heartbeat accelerated and my palms began to sweat again. This always happened when I was nervous. I glanced over at Lyric. Her cool demeanor was unnerving me. Why was she never intimidated?

Lyric led the way through the crowd, one leg extending after the other, with the grace of a panther. Her hips would sway one way, her head the other and vice versa. I walked behind her trying to emulate her walk. In a clumsy attempt, I tripped over my feet and bumped into a waiter.

"Oh no!" I screamed as he spilled a cold glass of white wine down the front of my dress. I stood there stunned. Too humiliated to even move. He began to immediately wipe between my breast with a towel.

"Are you alright?" he asked.

"Yes, I'm fine," I replied.

"I could get a glass of seltzer water to make sure the dress doesn't stain."

"I'm sure this dress could withstand a glass of white wine. You have a good night." Lyric tugged on my arm and pulled me in the direction of the table. By this time Joshua and Parker had wiped their silly grins off their faces and replaced them with looks of resentment. I know they were both mad at me for bringing Lyric, but I'd explain to them later that I had no choice.

"Peace Madison. Are you okay? You're all wet." Parker had to remind me of the obvious. I was almost hoping that they didn't see; they all did.

"Madison . . . you look . . . *different*." Joshua was looking me up and down, and his eyes said everything I feared about the dress was true. I immediately sat down trying to conceal what I could of this awful dress. I wrapped my arms around my breast and didn't dare move them for long. Lyric continued to stand and extended her hand towards Erious.

"Lyric Devaney," she said, and her eyes spoke in a language I hadn't learned yet.

"Pleased to make your acquaintance, Erious Jerome." He had stood up and taken her hand into his. When he slowly bent down to kiss her hand, I nearly fainted. He then pulled her chair out for her and she sat down like a lady. He then remarked on how lovely she looked in her dress and commented on how "fly" her shoes were. He said he loved a woman who wore expensive shoes. They had all but disregarded the rest of us sitting at the table before Joshua said, "Erious, I'd like you to meet Madison. She's the one I've been telling you about."

"Nice to meet ya," he said, hardly glancing my way. I didn't even respond because he wouldn't have heard me anyway. Lyric had his full attention. Joshua was making small talk with me trying to divert my attention from the obvious. At one point, he gave me a look that said, "What did you expect?" But I wasn't going to regret bringing Lyric along. I don't know what made me think that he would have been attracted to me anyway?

13
MADISON MICHAELS

By the time the waiter came over with the third round of drinks, Parker had started flirting with Erious as well. She leaned in real close and said, "Let me see your watch," gently grabbing a hold of his wrist. "Not every man can wear a watch like this. They may look too effeminate. But not on you." Erious had on a Chopard, flooded with dangling diamonds in the dial. Parker was smiling and batting her eyes in his direction.

"You're right," he said, turning his attention towards Parker. What ever happened to modesty?

"Parker, I didn't know someone who brought their husband a Timex was interested in anything of value. Is this a new hobby of yours? Or is the interest just for tonight?" Lyric said coyly. Lyric was right. Parker had no interest in material things. She was pro–natural, pro–black and had a "Free Mumia" T–shirt on to prove it. Mumia is a black man who was convicted of killing a white police officer. He has always maintained his innocence.

"Well, I may not be as experienced as you are with watches. I mean you get to experience a different watch every night, while I only get to fiddle with my old Timex. Don't hate me because your eyes are getting old and worn out from time."

If they were going to bicker all night, I could have stayed home. I was having a miserable time anyway. And why wasn't Joshua interrupting or telling his wife to tone it down with her disrespectful behavior. I guess because he was too busy nursing his gin and making eye contact with the young Hispanic girl sitting across the table with her girlfriends.

"LYRIC!" the voice shouted above the music and was approaching fast by the second. I knew it was Portia by the look in Parker's eyes. Portia made her way through the crowd huffing and puffing as if she had run in the New York Marathon.

"Lyric, girl, I thought you tried to play me and give me the wrong fuckin' restaurant. I went to two other motherfuckers 'fore I found dis one." She was speaking to Lyric but looking at Erious. "Don't be silly, I said *Tutti Fressi*, on Broadway darling," Lyric replied.

"I dunno all dat I–talian names 'n shit. I went into another joint and I'm like 'is the BALLPLAYER up in here?' They looked at me crazy, yo." She was removing her shawl and her face was beaming with joy.

"Show me some luv nigga . . . " Portia said, lightly tapping Erious on his shoulder.

"Erious Jerome." His eyes were on the breast that she had thrust in his face. He didn't get up though. She grabbed an empty chair from the next table and squeezed in between Erious and Parker. She wouldn't have dared to come in between him and Lyric. Finally she said "whaddup" to everyone. Then her eyes fixed on me intently.

"*I know you ain't got on my dress!*" she screamed looking me directly in the eyes with rage.

"Who me?" was all I could say.

"Yeah, you!" she countered. All eyes were staring at me, but I could not meet them back. I was too ashamed. Everyone was silent waiting for me to say whether or not it was Portia's dress I had on.

"Well if it is your dress . . . she looks lovely in it." Joshua had finally broken the ice. I know my cheeks had taken on a rose petal tone from the embarrassment. Portia sucked her teeth and rolled her eyes while everyone started to look at me to see just what 'lovely' he saw. I was on display and I didn't like it one bit.

"Why do girls borrow each other's clothes? That is so nasty to me. I could never have my homeboy running 'round in my sweats. His balls brushing up against the crotch area, then after banging some chick all night, give them back all funky. Hell no, man! Keep that," Erious said.

"That's the nature of women. They bond like that." Joshua replied.

"Word up, man. I know chicks who do it all the time, but not my lady," Erious said, then corrected, "If I had one, my girl would have enough clothes for every occasion not to have to borrow someone else's shit."

"So you take care of your lady?" Lyric was smiling as she asked the question because he was saying what she wanted to hear.

"I always take care of my woman. I was raised the old–fashioned way. I believe the woman should be pampered by her man. Shit, if I had the perfect woman I'd never let her ass go."

"And what's the perfect woman in your eyes?" Parker pursued.

"That's simple. All men want a good girl that's bad in bed," Erious smiled slyly. Then continued, "I'm curious, what do women want?"

"A big dick and a large bank account!" Lyric said flatly and everyone erupted in laughter.

"What about independent women?" The words rather fell out of my mouth before I could stop them.

"By independent, do you mean have her own career?" Erious responded.

"Yes. I was just curious and wanted you to clarify that when you said 'pampered,' you simply meant 'treated like a woman'. The part about buying her clothes is vague, and I don't want to misinterpret your intention," I said.

"Yeah, I want to treat my lady like a lady. Buy her clothes, whatever she needs, she can take the charge card and go get it. Wherever she wants to go, take the jet and make it happen. I mean I just signed a contract for $130 million for three years. I'm the highest paid ball player around, not to mention my endorsements. So, no doubt, my lady has to look good to represent me."

He looked at his perfectly manicured fingers, then continued, "As far as her having her own career, that's an obstacle that causes complications to arise. And then I'm not the focus of her life and my needs aren't getting met."

"So you like to pay the cost to be the boss," I said.

"Exactly."

"Most men with careers, whether it's athletes, businessmen, actors, just men with money, I guess, are always attracted to beautiful woman who *need* a man to support them. Why is that?" I had asked a question I already had an answer to, but I wanted to know if he could give an earnest answer considering he was a man with money.

"We don't go out looking for broke–down bum bitches who are on welfare with a sign around their neck, 'I will fuck for food.' They have to have certain qualities to gain the title of a millionaire's wife. For one thing, they have to be gorgeous. Therefore, when you're photographed in the press, other men and women will admire what you have. You can show her off. My preference is fine features, thin nose, lips and nice teeth. I like women who are lighter than myself. So when we have kids they'll have a nice complexion. In addition, they have to have a top of the line body. When she puts on a dress, she wears it, not the other way around. Last, she has to have that good hair. I like long hair, but it doesn't have to be long . . . but it *has* to be naturally soft. Not the shit that needs a perm and a weave. When I run my fingers through it, it's soft and when she gets it wet it just curls up. That's the shit I'm talkin 'bout!" Erious slapped his hands together and got excited in his seat.

I guess everyone at the table felt he was describing them, so no one was offended but me. Portia tossed her long, soft hair in his direction a few times. I knew at this point I didn't have a chance with Erious. He was looking for someone who was either white, or half–white, because no all–black girl has fine features and that curly 'good hair' as he described it. Moreover, I've never needed a weave, but every six weeks I invest in "Revlon."

So I said, "These women never intend to have a career because they're banking on their looks to get them the house, the car, and the seven–figure safety net. That's why you'll read in the society section in the papers 'John Doe, top record executive has just married Jane Doe, she's a supermodel.' And you know you've never seen her in any magazines."

"Word." Portia said, and then continued, "Yup, dat's true, yo. Like Martin's wife. I read in some magazine that she some beauty queen and a model. I ain't never seen her tired ass in no Vogue. Shit I'mma model too. You feelin' me."

"Portia, you don't even subscribe to Vogue. And if you knew anything, you'd know that some models get printed in catalogs, do runways, or advertise different products you may not be familiar with. So for you to criticize something because you're not in their field would be to step on their craft," Lyric said.

I knew Lyric interjected because she always wanted to shut someone down. If you say "tomato", she'll say "tomahto."

"But you'll have to admit, Lyric, all these women are not models. They just look good enough to be one," Parker retorted.

"It is what it is," Lyric responded.

"Erious, don't you feel these men are afraid of a woman who can do for herself. They need a subservient woman who will stroke their ego everyday of their lives."

I was back drilling Erious for a deliberate answer. Everyone was listening very intently for his response. This conversation had struck a nerve with me because I was hoping he was different. He's just another shallow celebrity.

"Damn Madison, why you wildin'? Why a nigga can't hook up his chick? If he got enough cheddar, he should be hittin' her off wit da paper. They both should be bling blingin'. There ain't nothin' wrong with a girl bein' loyal to all her man needs. He washes my back, I'll wash his. I'll scrub dat ma'fucker!" Portia said, trying to score some points. She flung her long, thick, black wavy hair back then batted her slanted Chinese eyes at Erious, her light skin glowing underneath the florescent lights.

"Well, Portia, if you even have to ask, then you're already lost and living in the land of the obtuse."

"Lost? Ob– what? Wait a minute bitch 'cause you playin' me right now. Tryin' to sound all smart 'cause you in law school? I'm not even feelin' you right now. I should slap your smart ass silly."

Portia wasn't screaming, but her tone was just as intimidating. I had overstepped my boundaries and I needed to back down. However, I didn't. I pushed on and said, "What does my current educational status have to do with how I feel about women being submissive for a man?"

"So what made a pretty, timid, young feminist lady like yourself decide to prosecute big, bad criminals?" Erious interjected. I wasn't sure if he was mocking me or not. However, his tone was soft, almost flirty. He had picked up his drink, took a big gulp, then stared in my eyes intently.

My heart started to beat irregularly from the compliment he had given me. I knew I was blushing when I said, "Well you need to be corrected. I don't want to prosecute big, bad criminals. I want to defend them!" My voice was equally soft. Was I flirting as well? I know I was definitely trying to shock him by saying "defend." You can't be timid when you're defending big, bad alleged criminals.

"You work for Joshua right?"

"Absolutely. But that's preliminary . . . I mean I have to support myself, right?"

"Madison, I'm appalled. Where's the devotion? So you're only working for me to put food on the table?" Joshua joked. He put a sad expression on his face and pretended to be offended. Joshua knew I had planned to go into private practice and be a defense attorney as soon as I graduated from law school. The D.A.'s office was a good background because I will have a head start on how my opponent will maneuver.

"What made you choose defense, Madi?" Erious paused. "Can I call you Madi?" Erious was twirling the olive from his dry martini around his tongue. Then he bit down into it as if it was the best thing since sex in the sixties. I started to get butterflies in my stomach and forgot all about the previous conversation and my not respecting him. All those feelings took a quick nap and I was fantasizing about him kissing me with that long tongue he had just displayed. "All my friends call me Madi. It's cool."

"Am I your friend?" he was flirting again.

"Yeah . . . I guess so. I mean your Joshua's friend. But we could build our own friendship." I was flirting again, too. Moreover, it wasn't subtle. As soon as I said the word "build," I felt as if I was a basketball groupie. I don't think I've ever been this aggressive before. He didn't respond to my last remark. Everyone just sat looking around at each other and the moment became awkward. I decided to break the silence, "Umm . . . I decided to get into defense because I'm intrigued by people who use illegal means to get material things." That response went on deaf ears and that was the best I had to offer. Usually it impressed people. This was a tough crowd to please.

"What about you Lyric?"

"What about me?"

"Do you want to build a friendship with me?"

"This conversation is boring me. Pardon, I think the ladies room is more exciting than this train wreck."

Lyric excused herself and headed towards the fine black person posted up in front of the ladies room nursing a drink. Erious looked a little annoyed at being dismissed but immediately recovered by starting idle conversation with Portia. He was leaning all over her like they were attached at the waist. She loved every minute of it. I peered to my left and saw Joshua slide his hand in between Parker's legs. She blushed then leaned over and they started to playfully kiss, tuning out everyone around them. The handsome black guy, who I had just recognized as the CEO of his own record label, was conversing with Lyric. I should have known she wasn't having a conversation with an ordinary Joe. He and his Bad Boy Imagine were worth millions. I saw him reach into his pocket and give Lyric a business card. Then Lyric reached into her oversized Louis Vuitton bag and extended him the same courtesy. I'm sure his actress/ girlfriend wouldn't have been too pleased by this exchange.

"Portia, are you still working at The Gap?" I was trying to have small talk to break up their intimate conversation.

"Nah!" Portia said in a less than friendly tone. I ignored her rudeness and tried to continue.

"So, where do you work at now?"

"Damn yo, can a bitch breathe wit out you ridin' me? Your whiney voice is fuckin' up my high. You sound like revenge of the nerds 'n shit!" Portia retorted.

"Well, that wasn't a very nice thing to say. How would you like it if I called you a nasty name."

"Like what? Virgin!" Portia sneered.

"I wish I could call you such a name, Portia. How could a jezebel be anything as pure as a virgin?"

Portia took a moment before she screamed, "Jezibel? Jezibel! Dat's some hoe name right? I know you ain't just call me a hoe. Name a nigga I fucked dat you know!"

"I could name plenty but it would take the rest of the evening."

I was on a roll. I had to admit there was fire in me because I was jealous that Portia, of all people, took Erious' attention away. I glanced over at Lyric, who had now walked back over, and she had the strangest expression on her face. I think she was actually proud that I was finally standing up to Portia.

"Well I fuck who I wanna fuck. Holla back, ya heard!" She put her hand up to give Lyric a high–five. Lyric just ignored the gesture. Embarrassed by Lyric's blatant disrespect, she continued. "Your fat–ass is just jealous of me, bitch! I'd be wrong if I japped the shit outta you. Matta fact . . . " And she did slap me. In fact she slapped me so hard my left hoop earring flung out of my ear and landed across the room. My head snapped back so fast I knew I had whiplash. My hand immediately went up to cover my face just in case she was going to return for seconds. Joshua jumped up and restrained her before she could land another blow. Meanwhile, Erious was laughing his butt off.

"What's wrong with you!" Joshua yelled. "Don't you know how to defend yourself with words instead of resorting to violence?" His eyes were black with rage. Portia yanked away from him then diverted her anger towards Lyric.

"Madison can only know my shit, Lyric, if you tellin' it to her! Playin' both sides against the middle." Her voice was aggressive, but leaned more on the verge of embarrassment.

"Portia, you are a paranoid one, aren't you? The whole borough of Brooklyn knows your business because you are less than discrete. Let's face it, you kiss and tell. Now you're saying they're all *tales*. You're a very confused little girl. I have no time for this, let's order." Lyric dismissed Portia, then waved for the waiter to return. Joshua and I were on the same page.

"Madison, are you okay? Do you want to file charges?" He was the only one genuinely concerned about the assault that just took place. When Joshua mentioned pressing charges, he shot Portia a nasty glance.

"No, I'm fine." I lied. I wanted to cry hysterically from the pain on the side of my face.

"Lyric, I don't know how you can think someone wants to sit through dinner after what just happened. Your best friend was just assaulted, and you want to eat dinner?" Joshua was disgusted. He had a right to be. He was assistant district attorney for Brooklyn, and he was sitting at a table where people were being attacked.

"Look, Joshua, don't start in on me, too. I've been through enough with Portia trying to put me on a guilt trip here. Madison is a big girl. She has to learn to defend herself. You're not always going to be there to fight off the bad people and kiss her wounds. How is she supposed to be an attorney defending people if she can't defend herself?" Lyric reasoned.

"Jesus, Mary, and Joseph, she's 24-years-old, Lyric. That's still a kid in my eyes. She's not as worldly or as old and experienced as you." Joshua's voice was leveled and filled with genuine concern for me. Since I didn't have any brothers and I never really knew my father, Joshua was like a surrogate parent. Lyric's eyes grew very small and we all knew he should have never said the "o" word.

"Old! Oh, *I'm* old. And 24–year–old women are babies to you? What a hypocrite you are Mr. Assistant *District* Attorney. What about the little minor you've been fucking for the past year. Last I heard fucking minors was against the law." She stood up then said, "The evening's over!"

She had controlled the whole engagement. Before Joshua could defend himself, Lyric was out the front door. He turned to Parker to say something, but she put up her hand to dismiss his rebuttal. I saw the hurt in Joshua's eyes as he lowered them to the floor. Everyone knew that he had trouble being faithful in his marriage. Joshua was a philanderer of the old school. He's always had a weakness for women. My mother would have called him a womanizer. However, that's a little extreme for me. Lyric would once again be the reason for a Joshua and Parker argument. Everyone started to get up and gather his or her things. Erious called for the check then turned to Portia and asked her if she played Chess.

"No," she responded.

"Backgammon?"

"Nope."

"What about checkers?"

"Yeah, sure . . . why?"

"I wanted to know if you wanted to go play checkers with me in my hotel suite?"

"Hell, yeah!" Portia said, and her smile said for me to go eat my heart out. Everyone froze like we were in a time projection movie and someone had pushed the freeze button. I could hardly believe he wanted to date Portia and not Lyric. And what about me? I'm the one who he was supposed to be dating. Erious confused me; I thought he and Lyric had chemistry. Joshua gave Erious a look that said Portia was trouble. Then Erious gave Joshua a gesture that he seemed to understand and the tension from Joshua's eyes went away. He smiled at Erious and told him to have a goodnight. I said goodnight to everyone, and then left the restaurant.

Lyric had gone to the garage and now was double–parked in front of the restaurant waiting for me. A long, sleek, black stretch Lexus limousine was out front waiting for Erious.

I hopped in the front seat of Lyric's Mercedes and watched her eyes focus on Erious and Portia leaving together. Portia was draped around Erious arm.

"I . . . don't . . . believe . . . it." Lyric said slowly.

"Me either, Lyric. I told you not to invite her. I knew I didn't have a chance, but I thought he would find you more attractive than Portia, with her raunchy ways."

"You know, Madison, you have a lot to learn. Of course, he finds me more attractive than Portia. Why wouldn't he? All her men find me attractive. I can take any man she wants. She has a pale face and a big head, but that's beside the point. He's going to get something tonight from Portia that I wasn't offering."

"Like what?"

"You know your naïve act for the past four years is starting to be redundant."

That was the last thing Lyric said to me the whole ride to my house.

14
JOSHUA TUNE

The consequences of my actions were merely superficial wounds. Papercuts. Never cutting deep enough to hit a major artery like my heart for instance. My heart has never been snubbed in all my years of dating women. Again, I had gotten away with the insinuation that I was cheating. The routine was maniacal. All I had to do was listen to Parker pontificating about how a married man should conduct himself, and then tell her I was done with my infidelities.

This morning started off superbly. After perusing The New York Times financial section, confirming that my stock was doing well, I dropped down and did 100 push-ups. Feeling elated, I decided to prepare for my morning in court. I had to be in to work early because we were doing voir dire jury selection.

I was prosecuting a guy who married a pretty, young bride. It was a blissful romance that would eventually end up in murder. Five months would go by before she was supposedly thrown from her car. Her husband would rush her to the hospital's emergency room where the doctors would pronounce her D.O.A. Her parents remembered asking him at the hospital whether he had taken out a life insurance policy on their daughter because they remembered her mentioning she had one. He replied that he hadn't. Her parents paid to bury her, and the next day he takes off for California to "get away." When the family is tipped off that he did in fact have a $1 million life insurance policy on their daughter, which doubled for accidental death, they alerted authorities, who promised to look into the matter. During the investigation the police found out that he'd asked two other women to marry him the same week he had asked his deceased wife. Unfortunately, their daughter was the only one who had accepted. Then, they found out that he was not in California at all, but in the Cayman Islands, getting a Caribbean suntan with a beautiful young woman he was having an affair with. That was enough for the State to get her body exhumed after four months and have another autopsy performed. The medical examiner could not discover any natural cause of death upon autopsy. The toxicological investigation revealed no possible cause of death. Further probing turned up two tiny needle marks, one on the side of her neck, the other between her thighs on her right leg, suggesting that she had been killed by something injected into her body tissue. She was apparently so "roughed up" from the alleged car throwing that her needle marks were previously undetected.

Body tissue samples were taken and sent to the lab. A forensic scientist found traces of succinylcholine chloride, a muscle relaxant used in general anesthesia surgery along with an artificial respirator. The respirator is needed because the drug causes a cessation of breathing. This meant when he injected her with the first needle it left her immobile. All her muscles relaxed, and she wasn't able to move; but she was still able to see who was killing her. Imagine being murdered and not being able to fight back or scream for help no matter how hard you tried? Think about her frustration as she watched her loving husband inject her with the second lethal dosage.

Thinking of this schmuck gave me a hard on. I wanted to go and awaken Parker to help me relieve some of my tension. Unfortunately, Parker was soundly asleep. We didn't have the old–fashioned marriage where the wife got up and had breakfast prepared for her husband so he could have enough energy to make it through the day. But I knew she wasn't very domestic before I asked for her hand in marriage. She'll probably wake up shortly after twelve noon just in time to make it to her three o'clock afternoon classes. She's studying interior decorating. A girlie major. She wants to have her own television show, giving people tips on how to decorate lavishly on a moderate budget. I took a quick glance around our apartment and wondered when she was going to start using some of the skills she was learning. I sure know that her damn tuition costs a fortune! I could just as well be sending her to medical school. Everyday I wonder where my money is going.

Parker has no concept of budgeting. She squanders away money on incense, toe rings, Malcolm X tapes and pomade/wax. She wastes her weekends shopping at all the vintage and thrift stores she can find. How a person could actually invest money in used clothing is mind–boggling. Now she keeps complaining we need a bigger place. How am I supposed to afford one with her relinquishing the money before my direct deposit clears at the bank?

I looked at my beautiful wife sleeping peacefully on her stomach, the covers lying loosely across her buttocks with her bareback and long legs exposed. Her natural fiery red dredlocks, hanging just below her ass, were exceptionally sexy this morning. I leaned over and gently kissed her freckled chocolate–brown face. I loved the way my skin contrasted with hers. It turned me on.

I walked to the hallway closet to pick the suit I would be wearing. I decided to go with a navy blue suit with a light blue tie to bring out the color in my blue eyes. I'm jumping to a conclusion when I assume there'll be many attractive women waiting to be selected for the jury. Still, I try to look my best so I have their full attention. Not that my technique isn't up to par because it is. My looks are just extra. Sort of like ice cream with chocolate fudge on top. Just extra.

The defense attorney is an old eccentric guy named D. Lee Scialla. He had quite a reputation in his early days. He had gotten an alleged child molester off. The press had already determined the man's guilt before the trial had begun and had no qualms about putting it in print. Nevertheless, he walked. Unfortunately, two weeks later someone had to pay with their life. They found a ten–year–old girl strangled to death in the trunk of his car. Scialla took the blow hard and some say he lost his edge. He was forced into early retirement at thirty–eight. He had started drinking heavily and showed up to court too many times intoxicated. But before he could have his license revoked, he just never renewed it. He spent years as a recluse. Some say he was fighting the demons of all the murdered victims whose killers he allowed to get off.

Two years ago he came back after twenty years in retirement. They say he's had a protégé in training--a young woman from Harvard Law School. He had made a promise to her father that he would guide her since she had chosen the same profession. That was on her father's deathbed. Now he's sober, and apparently, the young woman is out of law school sitting co-counsel to him. I have yet to meet her. I'm not worried about Scialla, a formerly retired drunk. I don't care if his reputation precedes him.

"What time is it?" Parker said, smiling up at me as I walked back into the bedroom. I looked in the full-length mirror at my reflection then turned back around to face my wife.

"Seven thirty." I was smiling back.

"Come here, Blondie," she joked.

I turned around and started to walk towards her when my pager started to vibrate on the night table, making an awful noise as it moved its way to the end just before falling off. I tried to dash toward it, but she was quicker than I was. She picked it up and pressed it to reveal the number. I had that "Gomer Pyle" look on my face.

"Whose code 300?" She asked.

"Huh?" I responded. Some prosecutor I was.

"If you can huh, you can hear. Who is code 300? And why are they not leaving a telephone number for you to call them back at. That's what pagers are for right?"

"That's Dominick at the office. His code is 300. That's to say he's already in his office, why am I not in mine? You know he's second chair on the case I'm trying today."

"Call him!"

"What? Why are you acting childish?"

"I said call him! I'm going to get the other phone and I want to hear you ask him why he paged you."

"Parker, this is ridiculous. You know I love only you. Why I'd walk through hell with gasoline briefs on if you were waiting for me on the other side, pumpkin."

"I said fucking call him!"

"You're acting crazy again, Parker. Cut it out before I have you admitted," I said, refusing to become indignant.

"You think I'm stupid? That's your young bitch! She's putting in a code now because you two are tired of getting busted!" She had jumped out of bed and was standing with her hands on her naked hips.

I was drawn to her immediately. I grabbed her roughly and began to kiss her lips passionately. "Pumpkin . . . I'm not seeing anyone," I murmured through each kiss. She started to respond and I grew more excited. She started pulling at my clothes aggressively, and I was ripping them off just as quickly as I had put them on.

We fell onto the bed groping each other like two young college kids. Our foreplay was rushed and intense. I wrapped my hands around her soft dredlocks and pulled myself inside her tunnel with force. She was moist and warm as I eagerly mounted myself on top. Parker moaned in pleasure. She wrapped her legs tightly around my waist and we moved in unison. My tongue explored the inside of her ear, the nape of her neck, then sucked each finger savoring the taste like expensive delicacies.

As our passion increased, so did my stamina. I stroked harder and faster, sweat dripping down the small of my back. "I want you to cum all over me," Parker whispered. Not wanting to break my stride, I ignored her request. Parker tightened her vagina muscle, then pushed my shoulders back. I hoisted myself back on my hind legs and watched Parker massage her ripe breast. My penis was brick–hard as I grabbed it and jerked off all over my wife's chest. Cum squirted everywhere! Parker squealed from enjoyment. As she rubbed the hot liquid all over her nipple–erect breast and stomach with her fingers, she was staring at me intently enjoying the moment. When she spread her legs open even wider, I knew she wanted more . . .

15
JOSHUA TUNE

We engaged in lovemaking twice before I fell back out of bed quarter after eight. I had to move my ass to make it into the office before nine. Parker had forgotten about the beeper and channeled all her attention into pleasuring me. I couldn't take another minute of arguing. Friday night after we got home from our dinner engagement, Parker intensified the evening by verbally berating me. She was furious at the remark Lyric had made at the restaurant. She said that she would no longer tolerate my humiliating her by chasing after young girls. I denied everything. I told her that Lyric was just being bitchy. After I gave her a full body massage and ran her a hot tub, she started to give me small talk, asking me to pass her things like her brush or a magazine. We knew perfectly well that she could have reached for the brush herself *and* the magazine. She was letting me know she wasn't going to be mad all night.

I have to make a mental note to call Kaisha and remind her that I said never to call me again. I thought I had been clear that under no circumstances was she to contact me. Our relationship had been exposed and I was sure that Parker would threaten to leave if she felt that the relationship was ongoing. I never divulged to Parker that I was having an affair, but she knew. Women have a way of knowing when their man is being unfaithful. They just know. They don't have to catch you being disloyal to accuse you of disloyalty. Talk about circumstantial evidence. She always says her sixth sense told her. Intuition. Women live by that feeling! Like it has it's own passage in the Holy Bible. Anyway, I disengaged myself from that arrangement. Parker meant way too much to me to lose her to a sexual fulfillment. Kaisha was a stripper in club "Heat" up in the Bronx. She had a body that was shaped like a Coke bottle. She did things to me in bed that made me the most envied individual around when having discussions about our love life with the guys at Tabbie's Pub, our favorite bar in Manhattan.

Again, a good day was about to be ruined. But luckily, she is being a little less temperamental. Maybe she's up to something. I know my wife; she wants something. We've been married for two years now; our third anniversary is three months away.

It's distressing because my parents won't have anything to do with her. When I first introduced them to her, they thought I was going through a phase. That I was experimenting with life. That whole slavery bit–that every white man wants to sleep with a black woman to feel superior like a slave master. My father had this conversation with me. My father has a Ph.D. in psychology; he's the best–selling author of numerous books dealing with this subject matter. However, this was the conversation he was having with his only son concerning the woman he was in love with. My mother was worse. She announced, "Black women are only good for one thing. Keeping a man satisfied in the bedroom. They do them kinky things that we respectable white women won't do. However, you don't marry them, son. If they were marriage material, then why don't their black men marry them instead of propagating all these babies and making us good white folks foot the bills?"

This from a woman who has her Masters degree in criminology. Many important officials have used my mother in high–profile cases. And when it came to common sense, she was out to lunch.

So I call them on their birthdays and send presents on Christmas every year. They ignore me just as much as I adjusted to ignoring them. They say I've disgraced their name but somehow I beg to differ. My father did many unscrupulous things when he and my mom were young. I remember catching him and my babysitter in an uncompromising position on my bed when I was about five. I don't think my father fathoms that I remember that incident because I was so young. But, I do.

My mother knew of his infidelity. Nevertheless, she would never divorce him. She said it was against her

Catholic religion. Instead, she would get lost in a gin bottle, then go out drunk on the corner of our block and disturb the peace by calling to the young women who passed, "Whore! You can't stay away from my husband." Yes, my childhood was definitely not customary. And our family name, Jesus, everyone knew the loony Tune family. How much damage can a person do to a name like that?

So why was I attracted to black women? I think I've always been fascinated with black women. It's sort of like how a gay man who just came out of the closet admits that he's had fantasies about men growing up, but never acted them out. I used to have fantasies about a young black girl in my ninth-grade, but wouldn't dare ask her out because I was afraid that she wouldn't be attracted to me because I was white. I didn't care what my friends thought. I told a couple friends that I was interested in her. They all agreed that they would sleep with a black girl but would *never* be seen in public dating one. I still remember her name: Monique. Pretty Monique with the thick black hair worn in two ponytails and double-deep dimples. She had a small button nose and a rear end that could give shade to ten men on a sunny day.

Sometimes when I get nostalgic, I wonder where my life would be if I had gone with my feelings back then. I wonder if she would have been my wife. I wonder what she's doing with her life, what career she chose. After high school, I never saw her again. I went to John Jay College for Criminal Justice and she went away to Spelman in Atlanta, Georgia.

I walked into my office five minutes before nine. I felt euphoric. I had an inkling that this was going to be a good day. I told my secretary to get Kaisha on the line for me, to have my paralegal get the case files for the Denver case, and to get ready to head over to the court. Dominick came into my office with a top hat and overcoat. It was an exceptional eighty-four degrees outside. New York One weather reported that the last time the temperature hit eighty-four on this day was 1969.

"Jesus, Mary, and Joseph! Dominick, is there supposed to be a hurricane that only you know about? You're making me sweat just looking at you."

Dominick was a little overweight and was rapidly balding by the day. He had been with us for the past six months, and it seems every morning he comes into work he's missing a little more of his hair. He's very personable and has a great personality; his wife could be a top supermodel. She is exceptionally beautiful. She could make Cindy Crawford feel like the ugly duckling. They make a unique pair. When I inquired how he managed to get such a dynamite–looking wife on his salary he joked that he had gone to a Third World country, found a woman who couldn't speak any English, brought her back to America, married her, kept her away from any American women and taught her very little English. Sometimes I wondered how much of the story was true.

"Joshua, come on man! We have to be in court in twenty minutes," he protested.

"The court is a couple of blocks away. Relax. Judge Madden will be late as usual," I replied.

"I think you feel like you can take advantage of her because she's a woman. For some reason, you feel like you have this magic over women and you just bat your baby blues and they're all over you," he countered.

"My reputation speaks for itself," I joked. "I just have to make a quick telephone call. I'll meet you in the lobby in five minutes. We'll walk over together."

Dominick stayed in my doorway for about fifty seconds after my secretary buzzed me to say she had Kaisha on the line. I had to give him a "will–you–excuse–me" look before he had gotten the hint.

"Kaisha?"

"Hello . . . Joshua."

"Why did you page me this morning? I thought we discussed that we had to keep our distance. My wife won't keep tolerating my lustful endeavors."

"Oh, Joshua . . . I *miss* you." She was sobbing in the telephone uncontrollably. I glanced at my watch and knew I had no time for this conversation. Missing me was of no relevance. "Kaisha, where are you? At home?" That was a redundant question. Where did I have my secretary call her?

"Yes, I'm home. Why? Are you trying to hang up on me? I need to talk to you about something important."

"I have to be in court in ten minutes. I'll call you as soon as I get through."

"Promise?"

"Without my fingers crossed," I said.

This situation had to be resolved. I was always up front with Kaisha. I explained I had a wife. That I loved my wife. That I was not going to leave my wife for her or any other woman under any circumstance. She said she understood. She said she had her own things going on, and never got caught up in one man. That she was a big girl and could handle adult relationships. Kaisha was just seventeen years old, and the feeling in my stomach was telling me that I had made a grave mistake involving myself with a teenager. I was thirty–five years old. I should have known better. Shouldn't I?

16
JOSHUA TUNE

Dominick was in the lobby sucking up to our boss Michael Hoffman, a gray-haired conservative. Hoffman didn't know my face from the latest serial killer, but he knew my name well. I had received countless e-mails on the magnificent work I had done on cases every now and then. As I approached, I overheard Dominick inviting him to have dinner with him and his wife. He respectfully declined, then excused himself and scurried into the elevator.

"Why are you always exploiting yourself, man?"

"What?"

"You know *what*."

"I was just killing time."

"Where do you plan to go in this agency? Where do you see yourself in five years, because sucking up to the boss will get you nowhere fast. And soliciting your wife! You should be ashamed," I joked. "You have to get your name recognized by prosecuting and winning high-profile cases as I do. My next step is to run for New York State District Attorney."

"He doesn't know you either Mr. Big Shot."

"He doesn't know my face. But my name is synonymous with success in his mind. And you know what . . . " I was thinking about the future. "Mark my words . . . there's going to be a time when my face is the only face he'll know, and I'm going to pretend like I don't know who he is. Give him a taste of his own medicine. I'm going to get ahead on merit, not bullshit."

We had reached Supreme Court on Adams Street, which was only a couple of blocks away, and Dominick was breathing uncontrollably and sweating profusely.

"Are you all right man?" I was worried.

"I'm fine . . . fine. I just need to catch my breath."

We stood there for about five minutes. I was going over my opening statement in my head when I glanced behind me to see my paralegal pushing a cart filled with my case files. How inconsiderate were we. I forgot all about him. My mind had been so distracted since the first thing this morning.

"David, I'm sorry we didn't help you. I sometimes get absent–minded before a case."

"It's okay Mr. Tune. I can manage," he said with a smile on his face.

David was a paralegal that I had hired with a two–year degree. I usually went for the four–year degree, but something in this kid's eye told me he needed a break. His interview clothes were very worn and on his resume the last job he had down was manager in McDonald's. I gathered he paid his way through school trying to better himself. He told me during the interview that he'd been out of school for six months. He had an Associates degree and everywhere he interviewed he was told he had to have at least two years of work experience in a law firm. But how was he supposed to get the experience if no one wanted to hire him because he didn't have two years of work experience? It was a catch–22. That was a relevant point that no one seemed to acknowledge. So I did and gave him the job.

We all entered the courtroom with egos intact. You have to be confident when you're an attorney. This is an egotistical profession. You lose in court, you hardly think about the defendant getting off. All that matters is that you lost. And everyone will know about it. Well, at least I do. The defendant getting off is secondary, the afterthought.

I took a look around the courtroom and D. Lee Scialla was sitting, talking with his client. He began to whisper when we entered. His client was a middle–aged man who looked like the time he was sitting behind bars at Rikers Island awaiting trial was taking a toll on him. He looked worn and tattered like a well–used history book. I counted on the defense playing the card that he adored his wife and had no reason to kill her, yadda, yadda, yadda. I'd counter that he had two million reasons to kill his wife. The ultimate motive is greed. In this case I was seeking the death penalty; and if I could get a jury to believe that this murder was premeditated and that all the defendant needed was a victim, anyone would do, they should all want to flip the switch.

I can imagine the press will be all over this place around noon to get the story for the five o'clock news. I recognized his parents. His father was in his late 60's with a full head of silvery–white hair. His thick–framed glasses took up most of his face. He held an unlit pipe, which he twirled around in his hand out of habit. His mother was dressed conservatively in a dark blue two–piece suit. Her lips were pursed together tightly. She had a prominent jawbone and a full head of dyed black hair. She was in her early 50's. Their smug faces were trying to rattle me. The courtroom started to fill up pretty fast. The victim's parents and family sat behind the prosecution, while relatives of the defendant filled in all the empty wooden church seats on his side. A lot of spectators were there, and the judge had allowed an artist to sketch the trial instead of letting the media record live. That pissed me off. New York trials are hardly ever recorded to go on "Court TV." I wanted my three minutes of fame.

I was so engrossed in going over witness statements that I didn't notice that second chair counsel had come into the courtroom. She was sitting on the far left of the defense table. I couldn't see her face, but I saw her complexion. She was a deep cherry–colored chocolate, with her hair pulled back tight in a French bun. I took a moment to overlook the superficial aspects of the case and concentrated on reality, which was, Oliver Denver was as guilty of murder as I was of adultery. And that was one hundred percent. I got my strength back and my adrenaline pumped up. Then it happened. The court officer led the potential jurors in and asked everyone to quiet down and please rise for the judge. I felt strangeness, like someone was watching me. I turned to my left and there she was: Monique. Sweet Monique was staring at me. Our eyes locked and gathered memories of the time that had passed over the years. She was even more beautiful than I had remembered. But it was Monique. The judge was saying something, but all I heard was Monique wishing me well in my new college on high school graduation day.

Dominick nudged me back into reality, and before I knew it, I was asking potential juror one if he was capable of just evaluating the facts of the case and not letting the media play a part in any decision he would make. I turned around to look at the defendant to make a dramatic statement. I liked to look at defendants with a look of disapproval. It's an underhanded technique of mine that I find most effective. However, as I looked into his eyes, someone else's eyes were penetrating my glare, breaking my concentration. My eyes were drawn to Monique's. I returned her stare and she smiled. Was she smiling at me?

17
LYRIC DEVANEY

My doorbell was ringing, and I climbed off the sofa and went to the door feeling exceptionally good. I had on a Gucci sweatsuit and my hair was short, soft and silky between my fingers as I ran them through it. I opened the door and Denzel Washington was standing there holding a dozen long–stemmed red roses. As I stood there, he smiled at me and motioned for two delivery guys to bring in thirty–dozen more in every pastel color you could think of. Within minutes my living room was filled with the aroma of fresh flowers. Just as I was going to give Denzel a luscious "thank you" kiss, I heard a loud banging . . .

"Lyric! Open up if you're there!"

The banging had bolted me back into consciousness. I realized I was dreaming.

"Who is it?" I yelled, and felt a sharp pain in my head. Where was I? As my eyes struggled to open and I started to gain some consciousness, I realized I was home in my bed. I had gone out to Club Systems with Kenny last night and didn't return until seven o'clock this morning. What time was it anyway? And who the hell was banging my door down? I turned over to look at the digital clock. It was just barely eleven o'clock in the morning. My eyes were puffy, and my mouth had a thick filmy paste lining my teeth. I tried to remember last night, but just couldn't. The last thing I remembered was getting into Club 'Systems,' and going over to Larry's table where he had ordered Cristal champagne, then dancing, grinding and grooving my body to almost every record the D.J. played. The way my head was spinning, I must have had a good time. Fortunately, Kenny will tell me all about it I'm sure. The banging started up again and so did the banging in my head.

"Wait a minute!" I yelled. "Hold your goddamn horses!" I dragged myself out of my mahogany wood bed and walked my bare feet downstairs to the door and flung it open without seeing who my visitor was. I stood there looking at Erious Jerome in the face. He was smiling at first, and then upon closer inspection of me, his smile disappeared.

"You look like shit!" he said.

"What are you doing here?" I managed to get out.

"And you smell the same," he replied ignoring my question, but this time he smiled. I was furious that I had gotten caught looking less than my best from a potential fling. Careful not to open my mouth again, I motioned with my hands for him to come in, and he did.

I went upstairs and locked myself in my bathroom. I looked in the mirror and hoped I had had as much fun as I should have had. I grabbed the Listerine mouthwash and went to work. After I scrubbed my teeth and face, I contemplated hopping in a quick shower to freshen up. Why not? Who knows what the morning could have in store? Instantly, I remembered he went home with Portia last night, and I was not playing second to that tramp. I popped a Valium in my mouth, then went in my bedroom to throw on that Gucci sweatsuit I had just dreamed about.

When I opened my bedroom door, Erious was spread eagle, butt–naked across my bed with only his white Nike cotton socks on. I jumped because he had startled me. I had left him downstairs in the living room.

"No need to jump baby, I don't bite." He looked down at his penis, then grabbed it and ran his hand up and down the shaft. And it was a l-o-n-n-n-g and equally thick shaft. His dick was absolutely huge. It matched his long fingers and toes. I started to feel all tingly inside as I often do when confronted with a huge penis. But I had to control my urge. This jerk had ignored me last night, and the nerve of him to come and expect me to give him some after he had just slept with my friend. Besides, big dick or not, I don't sell myself for cheap. That's what separates me from Portia. Portia will sleep with a guy for the thrill. That's enough for her. And even though I think we both have the same insatiable appetite, I need incentives. The big moron expected to get a piece and then bounce.

"Neither do I," I retorted after a long pause. "I don't bite, I don't lick, I don't kiss, and I don't fuck basketball players. So get the crack of your tired ass off of my silk sheets before I make you very sorry!" I moved towards my bed and started to pull my sheets from underneath him. He pulled them back and we were in a tug of war before I could decipher how we had gotten this far. He would yank the covers toward him, and I would go flying into the bed. Then, I would gather up my strength and yank the cover into me and he would hardly flinch.

"You're not a lesbian, are you?"

"Do I look like I need to lick pussy?"

"You look like you've indulged a time or two."

"You wish, you undercover fag!"

"Oh, BLOW me!"

"With your momma's mouth!" This was child's play. I had a naked basketball player in my bed, and I was kicking his butt to the curb. He was a psychopath stripping down to his birthday suit. No one is going to believe me when I tell this story. But just in case, I'll take out a little insurance.

"Wassup with you girl? I know you want it. I could see that in your eyes last night. You just mad that I chose your friend over you." He put his arms behind his head and laid back and relaxed on my bed. He stopped struggling with me from pulling the covers, so I pulled the top sheet completely off the bed. He remained in place, penis as straight as six o'clock. My head was throbbing, and I was weak from lack of sleep. Struggling with him over the covers had exhausted all of my energy. I wanted to crawl back into bed and not come out until tomorrow. I walked towards the phone and tried to pick it up. He stopped me by grabbing the phone from out my hands.

"What are you doing?" he said.

"I'm calling the police!" I yelled back at him. I was tired of his shit. I paid the mortgage on this condominium.

"Cut the fucking act before you turn me off. Look what I got to offer you!" Once again his penis was on display.

"Give me back the phone, Erious."

"Give me back the phone, Erious," he mimicked. Did he know who he was dealing with? I would hate to have to get my nickel–plated .25 and cap a bullet in his ass.

"Lyric, stop being a player–hater. Listen carefully. You might learn something. There are three types of women and rarely do you come across all three at the same time. There's the one you know you could fuck on the first night. The one you could fuck, but she wants something monetary before. And last, the one you could fuck, but not before mentioning you would like to get married and settle down one day soon." He was talking like a scholar. I had no idea where this conversation was going. He continued, "So? I fucked Portia last night. I came here early so I could fuck you. 'Cause I know your gold–digging ass will probably want to go shopping of some sort, which is fine with me. Then I'll go and court innocent Madison over the weekend, and fuck her brains out before I take the red–eye back to Los Angeles Sunday night."

He was irrepressible with his cockiness. Now I knew why I didn't date athletes. They're used to those college–groupie chicks being at their disposal. Most of them couldn't spell C–A–T and probably had had twice over every venereal disease known to mankind. I looked in his eyes and saw the seriousness.

"First of all, if I slept with you, and I assure you I wouldn't, there wouldn't be any other stops. You'd be sitting here stuck–on–stupid trying to figure out how many karats my engagement ring will be!"

I had had enough of his smug ass. I really didn't care for him anyway. Madison had made her interest my interest. If I wanted to pursue a basketball player, it would most likely be Penny Hardaway. He has megabucks, plus he looks better.

I walked around to the side of my bed where I kept my nickel–plated .25 underneath the mattress.

When I leaned over to slide my hand underneath my mattress to get it, he grabbed me roughly by my shoulders and flung me onto the bed. I lay on my back and he positioned himself on top of me with his penis pointing directly in my face. I tried to squirm out of the position, but he had me pinned down. He started to aggressively kiss my lips, face and neck. I tried to reach up and slap his face, but he grabbed both my hands and pinned them by my sides with his thighs holding them in place. I wanted to kick the shit out of him, but my legs were also immovable. I managed to scream, "Help" once, and he slapped me silent. I then knew that he was going to screw me one way or another. I refused to become a victim though. I went to scream again but his hand covered my mouth so I couldn't make a sound. I wiggled my head until I was able to bite down hard on the side of his hand. He screamed in agony and released me.

Without skipping a beat I tried to lunge forward, but he was too swift. He pulled me from behind, grabbing the back of my head. I tried to grab my night table for support, but it tipped over and my lamp fell crashing to the floor. He wrapped both his hands around my neck and squeezed until I had stopped fidgeting. I lay still with my eyes closed and pretended to have passed out hoping he would leave. All I kept thinking was, "My God, is he serious?" He slowly let his grip on my neck loose and sat on top of me for a minute. I could feel his eyes staring at me; I knew his mind was contemplating what he should do next. Then I heard this mechanical laughter. It startled me. It mimicked that of a demonic creature in a horror film.

"You ain't dead, bitch! You're a silly ma'fucker, ain't you?" I opened my eyes and he was looking down at me in amusement. "Oh, I forgot . . . you're some sort of actress." Once again came the laughter. Adrenaline from deep inside the depths of my body mixed with hatred. My body felt hot with rage. I reached up and dug my nails deep into his face and left Freddy Kruger scratches on him. I then screamed a bone–chilling, blood–curdling call for help. He immediately put his hand over my mouth to stop the screaming. He wanted to silence me so badly, that his huge hand covered my nose. He was using his feet and one free hand to pull my pajama pants off me. He then ripped my shirt and my breasts were exposed. Tiny tears of frustration slowly slid down my cheeks, and my eyes spoke what my mouth couldn't. I was so angry that this was happening to ME! Lyric Devaney. In my home! In my bed.

He was still applying so much pressure to my mouth and nose that I started to wiggle and fight even harder because I couldn't breathe. This must have turned him on because he said, "Yeah, baby . . . I like it rough. Keep fighting me you sexy bitch!" He then entered me with such force, I think something ripped inside of me. If I could have screamed, I would have. But my heart was screaming from the pain and humiliation. He kept thrusting his hips with such force and moaning and groaning in my ear, telling me "I know you like it," slobbering all over my face with his wet kisses. All of a sudden he started to thrust extremely fast; he then put both hands over my face and just before I passed out from lack of oxygen, I heard him scream, "Damn . . . you got some good pussy!" Then he exploded inside of me.

18
LYRIC DEVANEY

I don't know how long I was passed out because the clock said eleven o'clock. My bed was completely made up, and I was in it fully dressed in a nightgown. This must have all been a dream. "But it seemed so real," I thought to myself. Then, I tried to move and my body told me that I hadn't been dreaming. I had been raped. Vivid images of Erious came flooding back. He must have thought he had killed me because any signs of a struggle had been cleaned up. He had probably dusted his fingerprints before making a discrete, speedy exist. But how did he do all that in fifteen minutes? Was I going crazy? I have to get up and get some answers. I walked back into my bathroom and when I looked in the mirror, I saw my eye was slightly bruised. But I could have gotten that from the club last night.

I pulled up my gown and sat on the toilet to pee. The liquid stung when it left my body. I screamed in pain. When I reached for the toilet tissue to wipe myself, I looked and there was blood mixed with a slimy white substance. I was old enough to know the white substance was sperm. That confirmed that I couldn't have dreamed it. Erious did rape me!

I ran into my bedroom to look for my pajamas I was wearing. I rummaged through every drawer but couldn't find my things. I looked underneath my bed, my closets, pulling out everything, throwing it around in a hysterical frenzy. I was a mad woman. I ran downstairs to my kitchen to inspect my garbage, and buried underneath The New York Times, Michelini's Italian entrees, and a milk carton were my pajamas. The shirt buttons were all popped off and my bottom sheet was there, too. Bloody. I was so angry I wanted to murder that bastard. But I'm no murderer. The events came flooding back all at once. I fell back on the floor because my knees went weak. I just sat there staring into space unable to arrange my thoughts into any order. I thought,

"Denzel . . . it's not Denzel . . . Erious? . . .Erious! . . . rapist . . . you're hurting me . . . Club Systems . . . I'm Lyric Devaney . . . Stop it!"

Someone was screaming with pain. Deep moans, sounding like a wounded hound. I lifted my hands up to cover my ears from the sound and realized that it was me screaming in agony. My telephone ringing interrupted my hysteria. "Pull yourself together Lyric!" I told myself. I let my answering machine pick up. It was Madison; she was at work and was wondering why I hadn't returned any of her phone calls all weekend. I realized it was Monday morning. I had been passed out for two days. I pulled myself to my feet, went to the kitchen cupboard, reached in and found a bottle of Absolut Vodka. I looked in the refrigerator for some pineapple juice to mix with it, then decided against it and closed the door. I put my Absolut on the rocks and went upstairs and ran me a warm bath, grabbed two Valiums and thought about what I was going to do next. It is what it is . . . but I wanted to make it more!

19
MADISON MICHAELS

The reddish–yellow sunrise came bursting through my Venetian blinds, while the rays playfully kissed my face; I pulled my body up from my bed and over to the window. I think I stood there looking at it for nearly ten minutes. The morning air was brisk, and the apartment had that fall chill in the air. I sat back on my bed, just staring at the sun and loving the tranquility it brought me. It's amazing how a little thing like watching the sunrise can make you appreciate life.

I clicked on the television and turned to "New York One News." I had to keep abreast of my current events. It was early Sunday morning, and I had no reason to be up so early. I got up and went into the kitchen and started to brew some coffee and warm me up a blueberry bran muffin. The apartment was silent and empty. "Just like my life," I thought. I wondered what I would do for the day. Every weekend I did the same thing. Sat around my apartment either cleaning or reading some romance novel, getting caught up in the characters of someone else's imagination.

I opened my door to get my Sunday New York Times, and after flipping through each section, drinking two cups of hazelnut coffee and three more bran muffins, I realized I was lonely. I felt like something was missing from my life, and I could not put my finger on it. I contemplated calling Lyric to ask her if she wanted to have brunch, but she hadn't returned any of my phone calls. I can only assume she's busy rewriting her new script, so I'll leave her alone. I could bother Joshua, but I know he and Parker are probably doing some husband and wife thing and three's a crowd . . . sometimes. I thought about all the things I've been meaning to do, and decided maybe I'll hop on the uptown train and go to the Metropolitan Museum of Art. "What a wonderful idea!" I thought. I haven't been there in years. So it's planned. I'll have brunch . . . alone, then go to the

Museum and see some exhibits. I suddenly felt important. Like I had a life, with priorities and was going to do something meaningful, not just mope around the apartment and lose another day of my life. I'd hate feeling that I wasted another weekend.

    I went into my bathroom and prepared a hot bubble bath. I put Johnson baby oil, Dead Sea salt, and aromatherapy bath beads in it to help relax me. I lay in the tub until my fingers and toes began to wrinkle and my skin felt silky smooth. Next, I decided to give myself a French manicure and pedicure. I took off my old dark brown polish that was chipped and applied a neutral beige and delicate white. The end results were fabulous. I have never had a French manicure before; that's Lyric's trademark. But just once, I decided to copy her style and do something different. I smiled. I liked the idea that I could try and emulate Lyric. Just a little bit, for fun. Maybe, after the museum, I'll go catch a movie. Maybe?

20
MADISON MICHAELS

The Renaissance exhibition was simply fabulous. The deep rich colors, deep burgundy, wine and earth tones were beautiful. I loved that era. I loved all eras. I went from room to room studying each painting and trying to remember what I had learned in Art History many years ago in high school. I went from Greek mythology to Egyptian hieroglyphics and was in complete awe. Each room had a different era; I saw ancient, medieval and non–European art and was still looking for more when a gentleman came up beside me as I was studying a painting. At 6 feet 3, he stood tall and intimidating. He had a presence with his broad shoulders and sleepy eyes. He was as black as the night is dark, with perfect white teeth. His teeth looked like elephant ivory.

"Hello," he said with a smile.

"Hello," I replied. He was staring intently at the painting I was looking at. The inscription said, "Krishna and Radha in Pavilion." It was beautiful. It was two lovers on a canopy bed embracing each other. They were painted in blue.

"I love Indian art, don't you?" he said.

"I guess so. Actually, I just love beautiful things and art is one of them. I don't have one particular era or category."

"How old are you, if you don't mind my asking?"

"Um . . . why do you ask? I mean it's impolite to ask a lady's age."

"It's only impolite if that lady's in her 30's. I can see clearly that's not the case."

"I'm twenty–four."

"I'm Maurice. Maurice Mungin. Nice to meet you." He extended his hand. I aggressively took his hand and gave him a firm handshake.

"Madison Michaels. Nice to meet you too." I looked in his dark eyes and was immediately attracted to this stranger.

"Why did you ask my age?" I still wanted to know.

"Because, your attitude about life is still untainted. The comment about you loving beautiful things was almost childlike. You have an innocence that surrounds you." My face lit up like some Fourth of July fireworks. He turned back towards the painting and began to explain it to me.

I was in awe of how eloquently he spoke. He talked about his favorite painter being Jacob Lawrence, and his favorite Lawrence work being "the Migration of the Negro." And how he's been to Japan's Miho Museum and the Robson Gallery in California. He was amazing! He's traveled the world and has seen many interesting things but took the time to have a conversation with a plain Jane like me.

After the museum, Maurice asked me if I wanted to get something to eat. I said "yes," although I had just eaten less than two hours ago. We took a cab to midtown, and when I reached in my wallet to give him half of the fare, he refused.

"A lady should never be expected to pay her way when she's in the presence of a real man." His eyes were smiling at me. I was trying to figure out how old he was. He was dressed neatly, and I could tell he worked out because his body was muscular. I wondered if he was a male model.

We stopped at a café and the waitress sat us in a cozy corner. We ordered frozen drinks with turkey club sandwiches, and then he leaned in real close and said, "Tell me all about yourself." The alcohol from my two frozen strawberry daiquiris had calmed me, and I was by now comfortable around him. He was soft-spoken and so polite. He was absolutely charming. I could have talked to him all night. It's rare that men want to hear about you. They're always more interested in talking about themselves and what they like. He was different. He was a gentleman. I told him all about Joshua, Lyric, and myself, my mother, my job, and law school. Everything!

And he listened, following up with questions, showing he was paying attention to me. An hour had passed and we were still there laughing and enjoying each other's company.

"What do you do?" I finally decided to quiz him on his life. "Well, I do . . . um . . . I'm really uncomfortable talking about what I do on my first date with a woman. I'm afraid I might scare you away."

"What occupation can be scary? I mean you're not a hit man are you?"

"A hit man huh? Don't be silly Madison!" he smiled, then responded, "Well, if you really must know I guess I'll have to tell you. You're sure this discussion can't wait until our second date?" He took both my hands and wrapped his warm, soft hands around mine. I felt warm and tingly inside. He was indirectly asking me to go out on a second date with him. I guess this was officially a first date. I realized he was waiting for me to answer.

"Are you asking me out on a date Mr. Mungin?"

"Why yes, Miss Michaels."

"Yes . . . I will go out on a second date with you, but only because you asked me to. And no, it cannot wait until then. Let me know what you do for a living. And don't tell me construction because your hands are too soft." He smiled, maybe even blushed and said, "You smell nice. Like a baby. What are you wearing?" He leaned over the table and brought his face close to my face. I could feel his breath on my neck, and I was turned on by the single thought of his bringing his lips to mine.

"You're being evasive." I playfully pushed him back down in his seat.

"Well?" I said.

"You're very persistent Miss Law Student. Okay, but whatever I tell you doesn't leave the room. It's very confidential." He looked directly in my eyes to be assured he had my complete understanding that this was serious.

"I promise." I said, intrigued by this whole afternoon.

"I'm a federal agent working with the Atlanta bureau. I've been working on a case undercover for the past three years. They put me inside the operation to gather enough evidence to convict a major drug distributor. We're going to indict him on RICO. I'll be here for about two more weeks, then I'm gone back home where I belong for good." His face was intent and he had kept his voice very low.

"That must be a very dangerous job. How can you manage to keep your sanity? How do you separate the two lifestyles?" I whispered.

"It's difficult. But I manage. I do things like what I did today. Go to the museum, take long walks, roller–blade. Anything to keep my sanity. I'll tell you Madison, the things I've seen, the people I've come into contact with, it's so sad. They have no value for human life. It's all about the almighty American dollar. The green. Paper or cheddar is what they call it in their world."

"Are you required to wear a wire?"

"I've worn a wire in my boots . . . sometimes. Only on certain occasions when I knew something big had gone down and I needed to get it on tape. If you could see me in my street clothes, you would trip. I wear my baggy jeans, my Timberland boots; I have my pager and my cellular phone. I have about six imaginary girlfriends that I have to sporadically call "bitches" so they can hear me. There's also a woman; she's with the Manhattan bureau that was brought in to be my main girl. They feel comfortable around her, so she's been a big help in this investigation. Anyway with technology, we're so advanced at the bureau, we have equipment the underworld isn't ready for."

"What about your family back home in Atlanta, don't they miss you?"

"I have no family back home in Atlanta. My mother passed away five years ago. I was an only child and the usual story . . . I never knew my dad. So there you have it. The evolution of Maurice Mungin."

"I'm sorry to hear about your mother."

"Me too . . . me too." He looked down at his empty plate. I could tell he was hurting. There's no telling what I would do if I had lost my mother.

"Where do you live while you're working?"

"The bureau pays for me to live in a rental at an undisclosed location. It's a two–family house and I'm supposed to be renting out the top floor. The first floor is our safe house; a lot of surveillance is done from that apartment. My apartment is lavishly decorated, meeting the satisfaction of my drug–dealing cohorts. Big screen television, leather sofa, thick carpet, things like that. It's grand . . . very grand. But I could never take you to that apartment because it is too dangerous."

"Oh, I understand."

"But, when I need to get away and find piece of mind, I stay at the Plaza Hotel on 57th street."

"That can be a very expensive retreat. But I'm sure it's worth it."

"Madison, what are you missing in your life?" He diverted the conversation because I guess today was one of the days he had to escape. I took a moment to think about the question. I thought it was a little forward of him to assume that I was missing anything.

"I can't really answer that question. I guess when it finds me . . . I'll know that I must have been missing it all along."

"Is *it* love?"

"You tell me. You're the one who asked the question," I said. I suddenly felt very vulnerable. Like tattooed to my forehead was "*needy.*"

"You sound a little upset. Just a little bit. I'm very observant. I have to be in my line of work. I just see a longing in your eyes. Like you haven't been totally fulfilled yet. I may be wrong . . . but you seem to be in search of . . . something." When he said the word "*fulfilled,*" my stomach felt squeamish.

"Don't tell me you think I'm so naïve that I believe in fairytales, like Cinderella. Maybe I'm in search of a white knight?"

"Are you pessimistic? Do you think white or black knights exists only in fairytales?"

"Absolutely!"

"Well, my little princess . . . you're wrong."

"Am I?"

"I won't tell you. I can do better than that, I'll show you!" he exclaimed. Then asked, "Do you have anything that you like to do that's private?"

"Private?"

"Yeah . . . something you do that you don't share with anyone else?" he explained. I thought about what he asked, and then said, "I write poetry. I write poetry that I don't share with anyone. No one knows this is my hobby. Sometimes I go into New Jersey to a small café named "Bogies" and listen to poets such as Flowmentalz, Kirk Nugent, Tammy Carr, and many more. These poets or spoken word artists are phenomenal. They take me to a whole new universe where I find myself. I don't share that I write poetry because it's common to get up during open mic and express yourself. I'm too shy for that."

As I spoke the words, I wondered why I had disclosed this intimate side of myself. I hadn't even told Joshua about the collection of poems that has stacked up in my journal. He listened intently, but before he could respond his pager started to vibrate and it ended our wonderful afternoon.

"It's business. I got to go. Can I have your telephone number so I can see you again before I go home?"

"Sure . . . only if I can have yours."

"Madison, it's too dangerous. What if something goes down and you somehow get involved. I can't take a chance like that."

"What about your cellular?"

"That's only for business too. It's too risky. But I'll tell you what, you give me your telephone number and I promise you won't regret it. How does that sound?"

"That sounds just perfect."

He paid the bill and we rushed out of the little café. He offered to put me in a cab, but I insisted I take the train. He had to go to the Plaza Hotel first to get something he had left in his room before he went to meet one of his drug–dealing, soon–to–be indicted criminals.

The whole concept was dangerously exciting. I watched him hail a cab, and I walked very slowly towards the train station trying to savor every word, every moment of this afternoon.

21
MADISON MICHAELS

I sat flicking through all 79 channels my cable company had to offer waiting for Maurice to call. By 10:30 p.m. I was exhausted from waiting for the telephone to ring. I picked up the phone and called Joshua to see if he was still up.

"Hey, Josh, it's me, Madison."

"Is everything alright? It's *way* past your bedtime," he joked.

"Everything's cool. Listen, I wanted to talk if you had a moment."

"Shoot."

"I met a guy today and I really want to speak to him, but he hasn't called me yet. What does that mean?"

"This is girlie talk. Shouldn't you be talking to Lyric about these things?"

"Well, I've been calling her and she hasn't returned any of my phone calls."

"Now that you mention it, she hasn't returned any of mine either. I thought that was because she was still sour about our altercation at the restaurant. I hope everything's alright."

"I'm sure everything's fine." I tried to cut that conversation short; I knew Joshua would love to spend an evening discussing Lyric. "Anyway," I continued, "do you think that means he's not going to call or is that what guys do normally? Like waiting a couple of days before they call you."

"No. That's what women do. Playing all hard to get. That's what my baby did, isn't that right honey?" I heard Parker agree in the background. I could tell she had no idea what he was talking about. "Listen, Madison, if he's interested he'll call. He just probably got caught up in something. Be patient."

"I'm trying."

"Well, you know you could always call him. Did you think about that?"

"If I could, I would. But I don't have his telephone number."

"You didn't *exchange* numbers? I wish I could have gotten away with that when I was younger. If I asked for a telephone number, the woman asked for my telephone number in return. Then when I didn't want to be bothered anymore, I would receive a slew of hang-ups until I broke down and changed my number. I'm glad I don't have to go through that anymore, right honey?" He was talking to Parker again, trying to convince her that he was faithful. He must be out cheating again. I'm sure she saw through his whole routine.

"Joshua, are you talking to me or Parker?" I think I sounded a little possessive.

"I'm talking to the both of you. Now, how does that sound?" Before I could answer, my two-way line beeped.

"Hold on a moment, Josh, it's my other line." I reached for the receiver and clicked for the second line to come through.

"Hello."

"Hello, gorgeous." It was him! I could recognize his voice. My heart started to pitter-patter.

"How are you? I didn't think you would call."

"I apologize for calling so late but I had to. I don't think I could have let the night end without hearing your sexy voice tell me goodnight."

"You're so sweet."

"When am I going to see you again?"

"Whenever you want to see me again." I replied sweetly.

"Did you have someone on your other line?"

"Um . . . yes . . . I forgot to click back over." I admitted, embarrassed at the concept.

"He's going to be very upset with you."

"How do you know it was a *he?*" I was flattered that he was showing a jealous side. But I didn't want him to think I was up late talking to males all night. What would he think of me?

"You're a very beautiful woman, Madison. I won't try to pretend that men aren't interested in you. I can see you have a lot to offer."

"Offer. Like what?" If I had so much to offer, why weren't men banging down my door like they did Lyric's or Portia's? I'm the one who always goes unnoticed.

"For one, like I just said, you're gorgeous. You're intelligent, wholesome. You don't have any children; and if you did, I don't think you'd have a handful of baby daddies. You're independent. You have your own place, and you have a job, not on the welfare line. So I must reiterate, you have a lot to offer."

"Well, no one has ever outlined my life in a positive way. My friends are always telling me what I don't do and what I don't have. That I never have enough energy to concentrate on what I can do and what I do have." He had genuinely made me feel special. How could he know more about me in one day than anyone in my circumference ever had?

"Not to overstep my boundaries, but your friends are shallow. Everything you've told me about them sums up their interpretation and evaluation of you." He sounded livid. I should be livid as well. He was right! My friends were shallow. Lyric with her clothes and diamonds and Joshua with his string of mistresses and BMW. How could they recognize someone of quality when they were imitating life? There was a long silence on the phone while I was trying to digest everything Maurice was telling me.

"Madison?"

"Yes?"

"Goodnight, princess."

"Goodnight."

And just like that he was gone, leaving me wanting more. I could have stayed on the phone all night. Until dawn if he would have allowed it. But I think I made my first mistake. Lyric said never to let a guy end the conversation first. She says to always hang up first; it annoys them and messes with their ego. Leaving them wanting more instead of vice–versa. I let that inhibition go, and decided I'd be more skeptical of the advice Lyric offered. I closed my eyes and had sweet dreams of my prince.

22
JOSHUA TUNE

After court this morning, I left the office early. I went to the deli to order a couple of smoked salmon steaks, picked up a bottle of Merlot red wine, then stopped at Macy's and bought a dozen of their scented candles. I was planning a romantic dinner for Parker and wanted to have it prepared before she came in from school. I loved to cook. Actually, I was an excellent cook. I cooked with ease, whereas some people, such as my wife, found it hard to make scrambled eggs. After dinner was prepared, I still had about thirty minutes before she came home, so I hopped in a warm shower and put on my Giorgio Armani cologne. I wanted to smell sexy for my wife. Since I was doing this whole seduction thing, I put on my crème color silk T-shirt and tan slacks. I then lit all twelve candles and put the wine on chill. I flipped through our enormous CD collection and put on Pavaratti to set the mood right. Then I remembered Parker hated opera music. So I had to decide between her love of R&B or Rap. Jesus, Mary, and Joseph! I deplored them both but I could tolerate Teddy Pendergrass. I decided Teddy would best represent the sexual mood I was in.

Time was moving quickly, and I realized she was twenty minutes late. When the doorbell rang an hour later with the five dozen long-stemmed roses I had ordered for her, I was livid. Where was she? I wanted her to be the one to open the door for the delivery. She was always ruining something! Then I realized she had no idea that I was planning this, so how could she be held responsible for anything not going according to plan? I had the delivery guy help me arrange the roses around the living room. When he left, I took a couple of roses and plucked the petals off and dropped them on the floor leading to the bedroom. Maybe I'll just wait for her in bed in my birthday suit. I was feeling very romantic and the apartment aroma was an aphrodisiac. I wanted to make love to Parker without more ado.

Three hours later I woke up naked on our bed alone. I began to panic because I checked my pager and she hadn't called me all evening. I called her name to see if she was in front. That was a silly thought, but I had just woken up, so my senses were still numb. As I was walking to the front of the apartment, the door opened and slammed.

"Is that you pumpkin?" I said. I was waiting for her to rush me and shower me with a million kisses, but instead I got, "Who the fuck is Cynthia?" She was rushing towards me with her fist in a ball.

"What are you talking about? I don't know any *Cynthia*?"

"You are a liar, Joshua."

"Baby, please not tonight. I said I do not know any Cynthia. Who is she supposed to be?"

"Some fucking whore you're cheating on me with, that's who!"

"Pumpkin . . . don't you know I'd walk through hell with gasoline briefs on if you were waiting for me on the other side."

"If you're so in love with me, why do you keep cheating?"

"Look, I'm tired of this shit, Parker. Okay!" I exploded.

"You're tired of this shit? No, I'm tired of *your* shit!"

"Well, leave then." I had enough of her paranoia. Here I was going out my way to make her day special and all she could do was bicker about another woman the way she usually did. And this time I really didn't know any Cynthia. I take phone numbers just like any other regular Joe. It doesn't mean I call all of them back. I walked my stark naked–ass back into the bedroom and started to get dressed. She stormed in the room with tears streaking her face.

"You want me to leave?" Her voice was barely a whisper. This hardly fazed me.

"You can do what you want. If you're so tired of my shit, as you put it, leave!" My voice was stern and unwavering.

"But who's Cynthia. Are you seeing her?"

"You tell me who she is. I don't know."

"Don't lie to me, Joshua."

"Jesus, Mary, and Joseph! All you do is nag and fucking nag me all damn day. I said I don't know who she is!" I bellowed.

"You're lying. I got her number from off of your pager yesterday. I called her. She admitted that something is going on between you two."

"Stop playing fucking Columbo all the time! And stop trying to pretend like you're the one with the law degree. You can't coerce me, Parker."

"You think you're so intelligent, then why are you always getting busted!"

"I'm only going to say this one time. Get a life Parker and stop living vicariously through the lies of women who have nothing better to do than to string a neurotic wife along. And you let them. Then when it becomes too much to take, you break down. Why do you put yourself through this?"

I was fully dressed by now and was heading out the front door before she could respond. When she realized I was leaving her alone, she had the stupidest expression on her face. And that's how I left her standing. . . dumbfounded.

23
JOSHUA TUNE

I strolled to the corner where I had parked my black 328 BMW, jumped in, hit the CD selection and let Mozart filter out of my speakers. The music was soothing as I drove around Cobble Hill awhile, flirting with the females who were flirting with my car. I then aimlessly ended up crossing the Brooklyn Bridge and found myself in lower Manhattan. My cellular phone kept ringing every five minutes, but I didn't answer it. It was Parker. I knew she wanted to apologize and ask me to come back home. After she dialed three more consecutive times, I was curious enough to pick up.

"What!"

"Hello?"

"What is it? I mean, who is this?" The voice on the other line was not Parker.

"This is Monique. Is this Joshua?" Her voice was smooth as silk, almost purring in the phone. I perked up immediately. I had given her my number after court last week, but she hadn't used it. I knew she'd call. Women like to play hard to get. I knew it was only a matter of time before her patience grew thin. After court we had gone for drinks and caught up on old times. I told her how I felt about her when we were in school, but I was afraid she might reject me. She confided that she always had a crush on me as well, but she couldn't tell any of her girlfriends because they would have looked at her with disapproval, so she said she admired me from afar. That race card playing both ends against the middle. "Did I catch you at a bad time?" she purred.

"No, I was just out cruising. Say, what are you doing? Would you like to accompany me for a drink?"

"Right now?"

"Certainly right now! I'll come pick you up. Where do you live?" She gave me her address, and I told her I'd be there in half an hour. I could really have been there in ten minutes, but I know women like to take time to beautify themselves before a date.

I went to Amoco to get a quick car wash. I wanted the beamer to look good when she saw it for the first time. I got out and let my car ride through the assembly line. I rarely took it to brushless car washes because they tended to leave tiny scratches, but Seville's Hand Wash in Brooklyn, where I usually go, was closed at this hour. When the attendant finished wiping down my car, I had to rush over to it because my phone was ringing. It had to be Monique.

"Hello." I had that eagerness in my voice that most men have when they're first getting acquainted with a woman. The pre–sexual voice.

"Joshua," the woman on the other end said. My mood had dropped ten stories when I heard Parker, her voice cracking from crying all evening.

"What!" I screamed.

"Joshua, where are you?" There she goes again playing Columbo.

"Why?"

"Because I wanted you to come home so we could talk."

"I don't want to talk Parker." I was already driving towards Monique's apartment.

"Fine . . . we don't have to talk. You prepared a fabulous evening for us. Let's not ruin it, let's make up." I really didn't hear most of what she had to say; I was trying to see the fastest way to get to Monique's.

"Josh . . . are you coming?" she continued.

"Not now Parker. I'm still upset. You're always ruining something with your petty antics."

"I'm sorry, baby."

"Parker, I work hard all day trying to be a good husband and provider, I don't have time to be involved with another woman. You're enough to deal with."

"I know. I don't know why I get so jealous . . . it's just that I love you so much that I don't want to share you with anyone. You're *my* husband. I want you to want only me."

"And you have that, but you keep pushing me away. I married you, didn't I?"

"Yes."

"That says a lot."

"I love you so much Joshua and I'm so, so, so sorry. It will never happen again. Now come home, I have a surprise for you." Her voice elevated with hope.

"Okay, honey."

"You're on your way home now?"

"Yes!" She gave me a kiss through the phone and we hung up right as I pulled in front of Monique's apartment. I shut my cellular phone and pager off. I knew in less than an hour Parker was going to blow the both of them up.

24
JOSHUA TUNE

Monique's apartment was very plush. She had Parquet floors sanded to pale beige. A huge Sony sixty–inch flat projection color television with surround sound was blasting the Giants football game. A very expensive brown leather sofa with huge pillows completed the decor. Her dining room set was a dainty peach marble with a beautifully decorated table. Her bedroom door was closed and her apartment smelled of jasmine incense.

She had huge candleholders everywhere lamps should be. She had done very well for herself. I was impressed. Her Midtown address and doorman facilitated my admiration. I managed to keep my composure. She looked so adorable when she opened the door. She was wearing a ponytail with a baseball cap turned to the back. A gray sweatsuit and a pair of Nike air trainers. I expected a backless dress and some slip on shoes. She unknowingly took me off guard. If I didn't know any better, I would have thought I was taking an adolescent out on a date. She didn't look any older than fifteen. She greeted me with a kiss on the cheek and an "I'm–happy–you–came" smile. "You ready?" she said. I thought we would get comfortable in her apartment first, but I guess that could be later on when I dropped her off.

"Yeah, sure . . . are you wearing that?"

"Yes. Is something wrong?"

"No. I just wasn't sure if you wanted to change or not." I felt awkward now. I had on my silk shirt and slacks and she had on a sweatsuit. I had given her enough time to throw on something sexy to seduce me. She looked me up and down and began to laugh hysterically. I got on the defensive side.

"What's so funny?" I gritted my teeth and clenched my fist together. I was looking at her directly in the eyes and I wasn't smiling.

"Your gear. Who taught you how to dress . . . big bird?" Once again, her uncontrollable laughter came. She unrepentantly took me off guard.

"Big Bird? Is that some sort of joke? I am sorry, but I beg your pardon. I consider myself decked out in Todd Oldham silk and slacks. Am I not up to par?"

"First of all, your silk is too tight. You look like an advertisement for a gay bar. And those slacks are cut all wrong for your shape. You look like a pencil. Designer wear or not . . . you need some lessons!" I felt disrespected. Her flippant remarks had insulted me. If this were anyone else, the night would have just ended. But this was Monique. I had to just swallow my ego and proceed. Anyway, when she sees my ride she will be singing a different tune.

We walked towards the elevator a little tense. I started with small talk to ease the tension. "How long have you been living here?"

"Not long."

"How long have you been in New York?"

"Not long," she responded. She was inspecting her fingernails. Was I just imagining it or was she purposely being evasive? That's what us men do. I'll ask one more question to be sure.

"Where were you before you came here?"

"Around." That confirmed it! She was making me feel like I was fucking Columbo.

"Where did you park?" she said.

"Up the block on Second Avenue."

"Good, your car will be safe there. We're taking my car. I feel like driving." There was a knot in my stomach the size of a football and it was all aggravation. "Are you sure you want to drive because I have a really nice car. The ride is smooth and with these New York streets a good car is a necessity."

"Oh, I have a good car. The ride will be fine."

We rode her elevator down to the lower level, which was the parking garage. We walked past some Fords and Buicks and then she started to slow down when we got near a Mitsubishi but then walked on past it. To my amazement she stopped in front of a midnight blue 850i BMW. She clicked the alarm and hopped in like a superstar, just as I do with my car. I was unable to move for a moment. She rolled down her window, smiled, and said, "Are you coming or not?" I walked around to the passenger seat and got in. Just then I thought to myself, should I let her pay the bill at the end of the night?

25
JOSHUA TUNE

The night was terrific despite any anxieties I had. She was charming, gentle and tough all wrapped up in one. She was intelligent and savvy. We started the night by ordering a Cosmopolitan for her and a Long Island Iced Tea for me. After the second round, she let her guard down a little. She was very flirtatious with me as well as the waiters. She justified this behavior by saying all Gemini women were flirts. "It's in the Zodiac" she said.

I wasn't big on Zodiac signs. It was a lot of superstition to me. I sat laughing and giggling at all her jokes. She had a great sense of humor. Then she got serious and said, "Tell me about your wife." I swallowed hard and then put my drink down on the table. She was looking me directly in the eye, challenging my credibility. No one ever asks about Parker. Once I tell them that I'm married, they pretend from that day on that Parker doesn't exist. She put me on the spot and now I had to explain my situation. "Well, she's a great lady," I started slowly. I felt very uncomfortable.

"Wives always are," she took another sip from her drink.

"Yes, I guess you're right. But she really is a great person. But lately we've been going through marital problems and she keeps pushing me away."

"Another woman is involved?"

"God no! We've been married for two years and I've been faithful," I lied. "It's just that she's not very supportive, and now I'm starting to feel a void in my life. She never has any time for me, always too busy with her friends and affairs. Like tonight for example, I cooked this lavish dinner for her and she brushed me off. I waited six hours for her to come home and she never did. I finally got in my car and just started to cruise."

"I'm sure she has a good excuse for blowing you off."

"Does she?" I questioned.

"Do you think another man is involved?"

"Regrettably I'm starting to suspect my wife's having an affair!"

"Why would you think that? What inclinations do you have?"

"It's nearly two–o'clock in the morning and she hasn't paged or called my cellular phone yet! Where is she?" I ran my fingers through my hair and took a deep breath. When I let out my frustration, I could tell I had her going.

"Are you keeping me company because you're going through problems with your wife? Because if that's what you're looking for, it isn't fair to me."

"No. It's not like that at all. When I saw you again, Monique, my knees went weak and I couldn't breathe. I think about you day and night now. No . . . I've thought about you day and night since the first time I laid eyes on you. I can open up and talk to you with ease. I'm not able to do that with most women. I've never cheated on my wife, but I can't help thinking how your lips taste." I avoided eye contact purposely; I wanted her to think that I could be bashful.

"What are you looking for?"

"What I've always been looking for . . . you."

"Joshua, I can't do this. I can't have an affair with a married man. I feel guilty just being out having drinks with you. What if somebody saw us?"

"Monique . . . can we just take one day at a time? I promise I will never hurt you or make a promise I can't keep. Can you do me a favor and trust me?"

"You're taking me out of character."

"And you've taken me totally out of mine."

We sat there until the owner kicked us out at 3 a.m. When we got back to her place, she wouldn't let me come upstairs to her apartment. She dropped me off in front of my car.

"I didn't figure you for a three–series man. I had a three–series my second year in college. But then I graduated." She joked on my car. This time I wasn't offended. I loved it, but before she could make another wisecrack, I silenced her with a kiss. Her lips were soft and plump. Her mouth was wet and experienced. She soon pulled back as I got more aggressive and ushered me out of the car.

"It's not going to happen," she said. "Well, at least not tonight," she continued. I got the hint and reluctantly got out of her car remembering that I would be seeing her in court in a few hours. I sped over the bridge doing over ninety mph; switching gears with the taste of Monique's kiss fresh on my lips. To my amazement, her lips tasted like peach nectar Snapple.

26
LYRIC DEVANEY

The long hours with my writing partner were really paying off. We had an excellent script. Much to my chagrin, tonight should have been our last night together. The writer's name was Ed. I was surprised with Ed. He was the only straight man that didn't try to make a pass at me. I knew he was straight because I could sense such things. I don't know if it was the late hours or my ego feeling slightly bruised that he wasn't hitting on me. So I made a pass at him. Why not? Luckily, he turned me down, stating his devotion for his girlfriend. That was a first, and I was glad because the last thing I needed was him putting the moves back on me. I immediately grew to respect him; and when his girlfriend came to pick him up, I was nice to her. They even made a cute couple. He was short, dark and plump, and she was short, light and plump. She was a little too sweet, though. I couldn't help but be skeptical and wonder if it was genuine or an act.

I felt a little solemn when we wrapped up. He had taken so much of my time the last few weeks, I hardly had time to feel depressed about my life. Writing fiction had taken my mind off reality. I closed the door behind my guests and wondered what I would do now. My non–stop ringing telephone was at it again. Between Jay Kapone and the mayor, I couldn't get a moment's rest. Fooling around with the both of them was really starting to become complicated. I picked up the phone on the third ring, "Yes . . . who is it?" A long silence greeted me. Here we go again with the crank telephone calls. It was probably a distraught girl wanting to know if her man was seeing me.

"Who is it?" I said with a little baseness in my voice. I had cleared my throat twice before I heard, "What the fuck is this shit, Lyric!" The caller's voice was icy but recognizable. "Hello, darling," I said with a false sense of cheer.

"You scandalous bitch!" He yelled into the telephone. I felt myself get hot, but maintained my composure.

"Why Erious . . . you shouldn't talk so nasty."

"This video . . . and the money . . . it's blackmail. You're fucking blackmailing me!"

"Erious, I suggest you shut the fuck up and listen carefully." I had waited two days for this telephone conversation, so I was more than up for the battle. I continued, "Either you have fifteen million wired into my Swiss bank account by *next* Friday, or that video will be given to every news station from New York to LA. Your pretty ass face will be splattered all over the evening news for rape and attempted murder. Now you can gamble if you want to . . . but you know the odds when you gamble, don't you!" I knew I had his full attention.

"I can't get– "

"I don't want to hear what you *can't* do. You better start believing in what you can do or you can kiss your celebrity lifestyle goodbye . . . you sorry ass, pussy stealing rapist!" I really hated him for the shit he pulled.

"And Erious, just to let you know, I have the doctor's report to back up my accusations. I could fax it to you if you want me to," I lied.

"That won't be necessary," his voice was barely a whisper.

"Good. Then our business is concluded?"

"How do I know that once I give you the fifteen, you won't keep coming back for more?" He sounded like a little whiney brat. I was in control of this trip. The tables had turned!

"Listen, don't think that I'm going to sit here and hold your hand through this. Life has no guarantee. You fucked up! Now you have to make amends and face it. The only thing I will guarantee you is that the money is the easy part. If you don't believe in karma, you'd better start. Because somehow . . . someday . . . you're going to regret what you did to Lyric Devaney!"

I slammed the phone down and felt a little better . . . just a little though.

27
MADISON MICHAELS

I ran around my apartment feeling frantic. I couldn't find my matching blue shoe, and Maurice would be here any minute. I looked everywhere! Under the bed, in the closet! Just everywhere! I started to perspire underneath my arms and it created a big wet spot on my silk blue blouse. My heartbeat accelerated as my palms began to simultaneously sweat. In frustration I just plopped down on the bed and cried. This was my fourth date going out on the town with Maurice, and I wanted to look my best. He's treated me so nicely, better than any other guy has ever treated me. And it appears everything that could go wrong, has gone wrong.

I have a major problem with acne. I have a big pimple right smack in the middle of my forehead, but he pretended he didn't notice it. So I mentioned it because I was embarrassed myself, and he leaned over and kissed it, then said, "I don't see anything." I just laughed and got caught up in a special moment.

Tonight, he was taking me to the South Street Seaport for seafood dinner. I think I'm going to order steamed lobster. Normally I wouldn't dare order such an expensive dish, but he can afford it. He has already given me a beautiful sterling silver charm bracelet, and he always brings me roses. I was very hesitant about accepting a gift from someone I had just met. I wasn't sure what his expectations were. But I feel like I've known him all my life. I haven't told him but I think he's my soul mate. We've been together everyday or evening since I first met him a week ago. Sometimes, he just comes over, and we'll watch a Blockbuster movie and I'll cook dinner.

Yesterday we were in here nibbling on the shrimp cocktail I had prepared, and then he started to nibble on my neck. I didn't want to stop him too soon, nor did I want him to stop too late. I was confused and nervous as to what I should do. When he started to slide his hands down my pants, I panicked and screamed "No!" He just pulled back and looked at me very strangely. Then he smiled, jumped up and put on a Mary J. Blige CD and pulled me in real close and started to dance with me. The stiffness in his penis was pressing aggressively against my pelvis. I felt vulnerable. But soon that pressure subsided and the words to Mary's "Not Gonna Cry" played over and over in my head. That song would ultimately be our song, but at that time, I thought the lyrics were so sad that I'd have to find another one.

The doorbell rang and I stood up and looked in my mirror. I looked horrible. My eyes were puffy and swollen. My blouse was soaked with perspiration, and I had one shoe on. I hobbled to the front door hitting my big toe on the side of my nightstand. I screamed in agony hopping to the door at the same time. I opened the door and rushed immediately in his arms blurting out my dilemma. "Shhhsh . . . slow down baby. Tell me what happened." He was walking me into the living room, wiping my eyes with his handkerchief. He sat me down and told me to explain why I was crying. I slowly rehashed my terrible trauma. He bent down on one knee and started to slowly give me a foot massage. It was so pleasurable I just relented and let the feeling take over me. Then he took off my other shoe, told me not to move and came back with a black pair that would look just as nice with my outfit. When he realized that I had perspired underneath my arms and stained my silk shirt, he brought me into my room and told me to relax. Then he opened my closet and started to search for a replacement. He picked a blue knitted pullover. "Cotton. It'll absorb perspiration better." He then moved in real close and told me not to be afraid. He started at the top of my shirt and unbuttoned each hook, his eyes glancing occasionally from my shirt to my eyes. Then he slowly removed my blouse and dressed me in the cotton one. I shivered slightly, blushing involuntarily. But then I calmed myself because he had a gentle, unobtrusive presence that didn't intimidate me.

We took a cab to the Seaport, talking the whole ride there. He was very knowledgeable. He spoke about the stock market, his portfolio, 401K, IRA, online investing. He'd made thousands investing, sometimes getting a twelve percent return on his money. He then reluctantly told me that his case was over; those indictments were passed down. He said that he could go back to Atlanta whenever he wanted to, so he had purchased a one–way ticket back to Atlanta the first thing the next morning.

28
MADISON MICHAELS

We entered the restaurant and I was solemn. The news of his departure had shattered all positive vibes. What was I going to do now?

Once we were seated in the restaurant and drinks were ordered, I looked him in the eye and said, "Don't go." Our eyes met and locked momentarily. He smiled a sheepish grin and said, "If I don't go . . . where will I stay?"

"You can stay with me . . . I mean I hope I'm not sounding too forward, but stay with me until you can get settled here in New York. What's in Atlanta for you anyway?"

My hands were trembling because even though I really wanted him to stay in New York, I didn't really want him to stay with *me*. I mean that's not really my apartment, I'm sub–leasing. What if Beth freaks out? And speaking of freaking out, I have never lived with anyone except my mother. I'm certainly not ready to live with a man. Where would he sleep?

"Madi, my feelings for you are increasing. Every night before I leave you, I hold your hand a little tighter, afraid to let go. But I must because I'm afraid of what you might do to me. Staying here with you could be putting myself in an uncompromising situation, and to sound a little bit like a sissy, I don't want to get hurt. I've been there and I don't like it."

His eyes were so vulnerable, I felt myself inside his soul. How could I let this go? Everything inside me said that I wanted to be with him. I had to swallow my fears and pursue this relationship if it was special to me.

"I've been there too and I would never treat someone the way I didn't want to be treated. I have these strong feelings for you Maurice, and I would never hurt you. I care about you too much. So stay . . . here . . . with me . . . until you get yourself settled."

"Well, what do you mean? Like just move in tonight?" He put up a cantankerous front. I offered a wide grin at the thought.

"Why not? What do you have in New York that's really yours . . . Maurice the person . . . not Maurice the federal agent. All the furniture and props are the bureau's, right?"

"You are actually right. But soon I will have to go to Atlanta to clear up some things. My finances. And I would also have to put in for a transfer with the bureau to work in a New York office. Gosh, Madi, I really would be rearranging my life. Do you think you're strong enough to stay with me through this long haul, or will you give up if things get too complicated?" He exhaled and made a lemon–sucking face.

"I'm not a quitter . . . check my resume," I smiled and suddenly felt very mature. Like I was a responsible adult making grown–up decisions.

Briefly I wondered what Lyric or Joshua would say. I know they're going to be in shell shock. Neither one of them has met him yet. But they soon will. At first I was excited about introducing him to Lyric, so she could see that I was dating someone attractive and with the status as Maurice. Then I felt a twinge of jealously and decided that their encounter could wait. I should feel ashamed for feeling this way but Lyric is hard to understand. I know she doesn't mean to be so flirtatious, but she just is and there is no excuses for her behavior. But on further consideration, when I take that fictitious layer off, I realize that I have just as much low self–esteem as Lyric does when it comes to men. We both just exhibited our behavior in different ways. I decided that if she stole Maurice's attention from me, then he wasn't worth keeping around anyway. So, I made up my mind and realized that he should definitely meet my best girlfriend.

"Remember that . . . your words . . . you're not a quitter. I'm the first to admit that I'm no Prince Charming." He was sipping on his Long Island Ice Tea. The only drink he seemed to enjoy.

"No. You remember, Mr. FBI person." I winked my left eye at him and smiled shyly, devouring his humility, the type of person he was.

"Madison, maybe I should wait this out a couple of months in Atlanta until I get my finances together so I could take care of you right. These credit cards and cellular phones are the bureau's account; it would be illegal to continue to use them. Besides, they should be in the process of shutting down as we speak." His voice was serious, and I started to wonder whether he really didn't want to stay but just didn't know how to tell me. I decided to give it one more try before I let him do what he wanted to do anyway. I couldn't look in his eyes afraid he might see my desperation, so I found a spot on the table and concentrated on it. Then said, "I'm cheap as a pair of jellies and tend to hold on just as tight. I make enough to handle all my bills, and I would prefer to cook dinner than eat out! You can't catch a cold for less."

Before dinner was over, Maurice had decided to temporarily move in with me. I was so excited. A live–in boyfriend was very chic. All my college friends had done it years ago. I was graduating from law school this spring. What did I have to worry about? I was a big girl, if not in weight alone. Which reminds me . . . I think I'd better start that new diet I've been thinking about. I could stand to lose ten or fifteen pounds.

29
MADISON MICHAELS

When we arrived at my apartment together, I rushed around trying to make Maurice feel comfortable in the living room. I didn't know how to ask him if it would be okay if he slept out there. He sat down on the sofa for a hot two minutes then said he was beat and wanted to take a shower and go to bed. He mentioned he had a lot to do in the morning if he was going to stay in New York with me. Moments after he had gotten into the shower, he called for me to come join him. I respectfully declined, saying that I was too tired and that I was just going to go to bed. Now that upset me because I would have to wait until morning to take a shower and I really wanted to take one that night. But if I got in after him, there's no telling what he may think. He may think that I was childish or that I was ashamed of my body. Or he may get bored with me because I'm not fun in a sexy way. I don't know what guys think, but all those possibilities made me anxious. Then I wondered if he was going to think that I had bad hygiene going to bed without bathing first. Living with a man was going to be tough to pull off, and once again, I realized that I might have just gotten myself into something that I could not handle.

When I heard the shower water cut off, I panicked and started to rip off my clothes. I ran to my armoire for my nightgown and tore the side pulling it over my head. I shut off the lights and dashed into my bed, shut my bedroom door, closed my eyes tight and pretended to be asleep. He slowly opened the door, and the light from the living room came shining in. I didn't move or acknowledge his presence. I heard wet feet hitting the parquet floor coming towards me. I still didn't open my eyes. "Madi . . . are you asleep already?" I pretended that I was fighting to open my eyes back up from fatigue, and when I did open my eyes, Maurice was standing in front of me stark naked. I gasped, then bit down hard on my tongue to keep from yelling out.

"Madi . . . where do you keep the linen? I need a towel to dry off." I quickly diverted my eyes away from him and jumped up to get him a towel to cover his naked body. He came walking behind me to the linen closet so he would know where to get the linen himself when I wasn't home. On my way back to the bedroom, he walked right behind me and clicked on the light. He finished drying off in the mirror admiring the reflection of his naked body. I tried not to look but I couldn't help myself. I had this strange feeling he wanted me to look and admire his body. I could see him taking quick sneak peaks from the corner of his eye. He reached for the Johnson's Baby Oil and started to methodically apply the moisturizer into his baby–soft skin.

The more I watched his body, the more my body felt hot. It felt like a forest fire was going on inside my panties. The feeling was foreign, pleasing, and was also driving me crazy. I clasped my hands together and slid them in between my thighs. The presence of heavy weight so close to my vagina made my body react and it jerked involuntarily. I looked up immediately to make sure he hadn't just seen what had happened. He was still making love to his body. Making every section glow from pleasure. Finally, he turned around and we made eye contact. I tried to close my eyes, but I just couldn't. He clicked the light off and then closed the heavy oak wood door. It was pitch black in the bedroom, and I couldn't see him. But I felt him climb into bed next to me. My mind kept telling me that I should say . . . something. Tell him to sleep on the sofa, but my body was curious and wanted him to stay exactly where he was. I lay there very still for what seemed like days and to my dismay I was upset that he had not tried to touch me.

My body was tense and I was barely breathing. Then slowly, I felt his hand go underneath the covers and glide up and down my body. Then his hand slid underneath my nightgown and went straight to my breast. He gently massaged that area until my nipples were hard. Next, he rolled on top of me and started to suck and lick my nipples. All the while I said nothing. I just lay there wondering what he was going to do next. His lips kissed mine softly at first, then the kissing became more aggressive and passionate. I closed my eyes tightly and didn't realize that my hips were rocking back and forth and my vagina was pulsating with such ferocity it felt like my body was going to explode. He was getting excited too, a little too excited because he tried to lift my gown up around my hips. I took my one free hand, because the other one was behind his head, and pulled my gown back down. "No . . . Maurice . . . don't." I was whispering a meek plea. He silenced me with another long, wet kiss. Then he started to slide underneath the covers and was headed to my 'private sanctuary.' That's what I called it. I put both hands on his head and told him to stop now. But that was a weak plea too. I've heard so many stories about how it feels to have a guy "go down on you" that I was curious to know if it was an exaggeration. I was also conflicted as to how I would feel later about letting him do that to me. What would he think of me? Would he think I was a slut? With all these questions running around in my head, he was getting closer to his destination. Before I knew it, he had my panties off, nightgown pulled way up, and was heading inside face first.

"Maurice . . . no . . . p-l-e-e-e-a-s-e!" His warm wet tongue was massaging my clitoris and the feeling was inexplicable. It was simply heaven. He expertly moved his tongue, darting it in and out. My hips were moving to his rhythm, and I was loving every moment. I no longer thought about what anyone would think of me; the feeling was too good. My hands had grasped his head, and we were both in perfect unison. After a while my knees began to tremble uncontrollably, and he stopped and started to kiss my belly moving north towards my mouth. I no longer sang the word "no;" I wanted more. My new words were, "Oh, yes! Maurice . . . don't stop." Just like the women do in the movies. His wet, long tongue licked and sucked every inch of my body. He sat me up and pulled my gown completely off, then laid me back down. By this time our eyes had adjusted to the light and we could see each other.

He looked at my body for a long while then said, "Do you have any condoms in here?"

"Condoms?" I hadn't thought that we were going to go all the way. I thought we'd just explore each other. What was I doing? "No." I finally managed to say when he reached over into my nightstand. His penis was erect and intimidating.

"Maurice, maybe we should wait." I continued, "Since we don't have any condoms or anything . . . and I'm not on the pill." I added for good measure.

"Wait? No, baby, I cannot *wait*. I'll pull out I promise."

"Pull out of where? What are you talking about?" This was getting out of hand. He was now threatening me that if we didn't make love he was going to pull out of this relationship.

"I'll pull out of you. I won't cum inside of you, I promise." He then started to move his body up against mine and it felt s-o-o-o-o good. I gently pushed him back and said a firm "No!"

"Goddamn it, Madison. I'm not a fucking kid! *Stop . . . no . . . don't.* I need some loving; I'm a man Madison. A man!" He got up and went to sleep in the living room. I was almost relieved. Almost. I could tell he was very upset. He had slammed my bedroom door behind him. I had also noticed he called me Madison, not the friendly 'Madi' that he preferred.

30
MADISON MICHAELS

I don't know what made me do it, and until I die, I may never understand my actions, but I slowly got up and went into the living room where he was tossing around on the sofa. He looked so frustrated. I gently touched his face and sat down next to him. He stopped fidgeting and brought his hands up and cupped my face and slowly pulled me into him and kissed me softly. I stood up and let my bathrobe fall around my feet and he stood up to meet me. We walked slowly back into the bedroom. This time when he climbed on top of me I didn't utter a word. I remained silent as he pushed my legs open and positioned himself in between my vulnerability. My body was trembling because I knew what was about to happen. When I felt his penis against my vagina walls, I held my breath, then exhaled regret. After tense strokes of pressure, his angry penis finally broke through. I let out a moan of agony then swallowed my screams. Tiny tears streaked the side of my face as he pumped in and out. My body stung with pain and my right leg couldn't stop shaking. My left leg began to cramp up, but I didn't say a word. I just lay there lifeless. Perhaps five minutes of his synchronized rhythm had passed when he broke the monotony and sped up.

"I'm gonna cum . . . I'm gonna cum . . . oh God . . . this shit is s-o-o-o-o good!" he crooned. He made one final thrust, then collapsed on top of me. His body weight was solid, and he was sweaty and breathing rapidly. After about thirty seconds, he eased his penis from inside of me.

My body still couldn't move and my mind was trying to assess everything that had just happened. In between my thighs stung and felt wet and sticky. I put my index finger gently in between my thighs, then lifted my finger up so that the light shining through the Venetian blinds could reflect on the sticky substance. My finger picked up a dark burgundy gel that I knew was blood. "So this is it," I thought to myself. I had liked the pre–sexual feelings I was getting more than I liked intercourse. "Madi," he said. I didn't answer. He continued anyway. "Why didn't you tell me you were a virgin?" The words stung me like a bee, and my morality took a dive out the window. What had I done here? I was saving myself for my husband. I wanted to be a virgin on my wedding night. I was so disappointed with myself. When I thought about all the relationships I had lost from holding on to my virginity. And Aaron. He was a stockbroker I dated for about nine months. He was extremely patient for a while. Then he became irritable and said he'd rather let me go, than cheat on me. He said the same words to me that Maurice had said. He said that he was *a man!* I didn't even realize that I was sobbing uncontrollably but I was. He turned to comfort me, but I turned my back to him.

"Madi . . . there's nothing wrong with being a virgin. You don't have to be ashamed. I'm not mad at you. In fact . . . I'm glad. I'm glad you wanted to give me something special."

He had no idea why I was crying. I wasn't ashamed of being a *virgin!* I was disappointed that I no longer was one. For all I knew he could leave me and be gone tomorrow. I looked over at my digital clock. The hand had just turned a minute past midnight. The beginning of a new day. How would I face tomorrow?

31
LYRIC DEVANEY

It was shortly after five in the morning when the make–up crew knocked on my trailer for make–up. Yesterday, I sat in that make–up chair for two hours and then the stylist set my hair, which subsequently took another two hours thirty minutes. She had to add hair extensions and dye my sandy brown hair jet–black, which I despised but the overall look was very becoming. The dark features made me a little more sinister. The false eyelashes and fake mole complemented my high cheekbones. I looked exactly like my mother did when she was my age. These perks would take place for the next eight weeks of filming. It was nice being pampered. One long look in the mirror, and I was in full character.

It was the second day of the shoot, and tension was high on the set. Yesterday Terisa came on the set with her entourage and exploded on Jacob the director and Jay Kapone the producer. She demanded to know who the executive producer of the movie was and who "O.k.'d" the script change. She had said my name a few times, but she had never even glanced in my direction. She accused Jay Kapone *and* the director of screwing me.

To be realistic about myself, I am thirty–five years old and I'm losing my youth by the second. Although I don't look a day older than nineteen because black skin ages so well, time was still running out. If I don't get a break through soon, my film career will be over before it gets started. I *need* this to work. God knows this is a fantastic script, and I intend to be the most savvy, intelligent, conniving, the-one-your-momma-warned-you-about, drug–addicted, sex symbol! If people thought Nikki Guy was sexy, and she was, they just haven't seen Lyric Devaney steam up the screen. I had my vocals and movements coordinated. Thank God my mother screwed Big Benny to get me singing lessons. I was doing all lead vocals on the soundtrack. Terisa couldn't sing a note, so no royalty checks for her.

Terisa was too smart to give me any *extra* satisfaction from a confrontation. I made a mental note to get up in her face as soon as the opportunity arose. Inside I beamed. I think it showed on my face because my complexion radiated. Everyone said I had a glow. She slung a few nasty words in the atmosphere about me, but I pretended not to hear her. I acted as if she didn't exist and continued to get fitted for costume along with everyone else. I was careful to act as quiet as a church mouse and as innocent as a virgin. I didn't want to generate bad press. If people start spreading the word that I was difficult to work with, no one will want to hire me. I knew I hadn't made it yet to show how vain I really was, so I decided to act as simple as Madison does. In fact, I had Madison's character down to the last 's' in her last name. Thinking about my best friend, I decided to give her a call. It's been a few weeks since I had a long conversation with her. I was so wrapped up in myself and still am, but maybe I'll fly her down to Los Angeles and have her spend a weekend with me. I know she'd like that. California was simply gorgeous with the palm trees, Rolls Royces, and the money. I hadn't had free time to go shopping, but I intended to hit Gucci, Prada, Fendi, Tiffany's, Fred Segal and every other boutique Rodeo Drive had. I hope Madison is up to it. I think she mentioned that she was seeing someone . . . named Martin . . . or something like that. Madison with a guy? He's probably as clumsy and goofy as she is. Anyway, whoever he is, he will have to part with my best friend for a weekend because I miss her very much.

32
LYRIC DEVANEY

Terisa was livid. And she had a right to be. I cut her part down so much she couldn't be considered a supporting actress. But I was careful not to cut it down too much because then she would pass it off as if she were signed on to do a fifty–thousand–dollar cameo. Her lines were meaningless but not stupid. That would hurt the film. The clever thing I did was write it so at the end of the movie, when she's supposed to have a big break at Doveland Hall and she starts to sing, the camera flashes to me when I was alive singing the same songs. So the camera will reflect her mind as if she's thinking about me, as she's singing trying to emulate my movements. Brilliant! This film would certainly help bury her career. I thought she would leave the fifty thousand and turn the role down. But she didn't. So I came to the conclusion that she must really need the part *and* the money. Things must have slowed down for her a bit. And I saw late last night on "Inquiring Gossip Show" Terisa and Martin Lee were through. He dumped her for the "Babe Watch" actress with the bigger boobs. I would attribute her behavior to this, but she was always intolerable.

Much to my amazement, I had the biggest trailer, then came Winston Love, a hot theatre actor playing Leroy Slade. He was more sexy than cute, and he was known for causing havoc on any set, not him exactly, but the groupies that went crazy for him. All the women practically threw their panties at him the first day on the set. However, he was too busy rehearsing or engrossed in thought. They say he's a method actor and takes his roles seriously. I revere his talent and want to learn all I can from him.

We'll have our first scene together this morning. In the script, we're supposed to be introduced by my sister, Silk. The scene closes with me watching him escort Silk out of the club. In this scene I'm supposed to convey curiosity in my eyes. Not hard to do . . . not hard to do at all considering the players. I was curious as to what he had to offer. I could see a dick print through the torn Levis he had on when we were first introduced.

The director came in to tell me how important that look was. He expressed that even though there were limited lines between Leroy and Sassi for this scene, that look carried the whole film because everyone will know my motive is to get with this rich player even though my sister is dating him. This scene shows Sassi has no integrity. A quality that is overvalued.

A hard knock on my trailer door, and I was told that I was needed on the set. I took a deep breath and reminded myself that I was supposed to treat the staff with respect. Terisa was going to get the bad reputation, and everyone will say how genuinely sweet I am. I laughed out loud because doing the movie and playing a drug addict was the easy part. Playing sweet was really going to be acting.

33
LYRIC DEVANEY

It was a short walk to the set where we were on location, a small nightclub in Compton, California. We would be filming about two scenes there. The club was dark and the area was desolate. Graffiti filled the concrete walls and many bystanders were forming a crowd outside, trying to catch a glimpse of someone famous. I was moving fast and purposefully to the set. A young guy cat–called me a couple of times, and when I didn't answer, he called me a "bitch." I smiled graciously, said "thank you" and kept it moving.

A few things inside the club were taken down and replaced temporarily with fixtures that were more reminiscent of the 60's. Aretha Franklin's music was playing on the jukebox. Winston was bellowing out the tunes word for word. His deep, baritone voice overshadowed the low jukebox and sent chills through my body. In costume and character he was the exact image of Leroy Slade–a pimp–looking brother with a perm. He had all the gestures down perfectly. Jay Kapone stood off to the side with Jacob. They were engrossed in a conversation, but Jay Kapone managed to give me a sweet smile. I reciprocated. Jay Kapone was dressed in green army fatigues and Jacob had on an all–black T–shirt, jeans and a black baseball cap with the word 'director' stitched into it. Someone walked up to Jay, and handed him a cup of coffee. "It must be one of the crew on the set," I thought. But there was something familiar about her.

I decided to come in and join Winston on vocals. "Ain't no way . . . for me to love you. . . if you won't . . . let me . . . " I belted out. "It ain't no way . . . I know that a woman's duty . . . "

I took a couple of more steps into the set when I heard loud noises coming from behind me. The commotion was so loud it jerked Winston out of character, and everyone just swung around to watch the door. Terisa flew in like thunder and lightening on her broom and landed right in front of me. She spoke breathlessly for everyone to hear. "Look at me! Look at what that *bitch* has done to my hair! I can't work like this." She was in full diva character now. "Kapone! Jay Kapone get over here now!" Her voice was high–pitched and irritating the hell out of everyone. You could see it written on everyone's face. She purposely bumped me when she passed by to meet Jay Kapone mid–way. I lost my balance momentarily, but then recovered. If I wasn't in Madison Mode, I would have grabbed her by the back of her Shirley Temple hairdo and pulled out her hair weave. She was "live on stage" and "doing shows" as Kenny would say.

"Kapone, what the fuck is going on? You're actually paying that *bitch* of a stylist to fuck up my hair?" She had her hands on her bony hips and her lips were pursed tightly together. Jay Kapone put his two index fingers to each temple and rubbed. He exhaled and then looked over at the stylist who was less than pleased to be called so many bitches. She had come running in after Terisa, comb and hair sheen in each hand.

"Terisa, what's the problem?" Jay Kapone was talking low in an unobtrusive way.

"My hair is the fucking problem! This isn't sexy. I look like an adolescent. I want my layered flip or I will flip this bitch all around this set!"

"That's it. I quit!" The stylist dropped her comb and hair sheen right on the spot and walked out.

"No, you're fired bitch!" Terisa yelled after her. While Jay Kapone tried to calm Terisa down and everyone thought that that was the last of that confrontation, the hair stylist came back with fire in her eyes.

"What did you say to me?" She startled Terisa who was still in the middle of bitching to Jay Kapone.

"Excuse me?" Terisa was buying her time.

"You heard me twice the first time." Her icy blue eyes said she was not the one to be disrespected.

Jay Kapone stepped in between the two before blows were thrown. He asked the stylist if she could remain on the set and that he'd give her a bonus. He needed her for all the extras and he had only hired two–hair stylists. She reluctantly agreed. I guess she needed the gig, too. Once she left the set, Terisa was at it again.

"Kapone, I am not using her again. I want the hair stylist that does Lyric's hair. Or do I have to fuck you, too?" I looked at Terisa's supercilious expression. Jay Kapone turned red in his dark–brown complexion. Then I heard a familiar voice say, "Listen Terisa. I do the hiring and firing. If you don't respect this set, I will fire your unemployable ass right here on the spot. This is my shit, and a bratty, snobby, replaceable actress is not going to throw the two million dollars I've invested down the drain. We both know you need this movie! So you better not fuck with me. Comprende?" It was Marisol. Jay Kapone's girlfriend who had kicked my ass years ago.

"And Terisa, if I hear–"

"Listen . . . you got this all–"

"I'm on a roll baby . . . please don't interrupt my flow. If I hear that you are disrespecting any of my staff, you're out! And take that airbrush mango and banana color off your nails. Did you even read your character? You're supposed to be innocent. Have them put on a pale beige nail polish."

So . . . she and Jay Kapone were still together. Men were such liars. She looked a little different. She had lost that baby weight which did her a lot of good. She looked wonderful. She also exerted confidence. Marisol glanced at me and smiled slightly. I nodded, then smiled obsequiously at her. "So she's running the show," I thought to myself. Jay Kapone's silent partner.

She dismissed Terisa back to her trailer where my stylist would style her hair in a mushroom. Marisol said that a layered flip was not a 60's hairdo. If Terisa was upset, she didn't say word to Marisol. She bit her tongue and then turned towards me and rolled her eyes. I casually flipped her the finger, making sure no one saw me. She then mouthed the words, "I'll get you." I retorted with, "I can't wait."

Marisol went over to talk with Jacob, and I went over to talk with Winston. I needed to get to know him a little before we started shooting. I was actually hoping he'd say or do something that would make me want to fuck him. I wouldn't though. I just wanted that curious look to be perfect. It's just so important for the film. We were already twenty minutes behind schedule due to Terisa's fiasco. He was visibly irritated. He said he couldn't stand when people let their fame go to their heads. Winston said he'd seen a lot of people rise to fame fast and just as fast fall flat on their faces, with no one there to help them back up. For a man with his praise and status, who was well–respected in the industry, he was very humble, a quality that was attractive. But I reminded myself he was off limits. The last thing I wanted to do was be like Julia Roberts, dating every leading man she can get her cute, big, pink lips on.

Jacob finally announced on his bullhorn that we'd "start in five." He said that he had contemplated shooting around Terisa, who would be at least another two hours, but that Marisol decided that she wasn't important for the scene and we'd shoot without her. This particular scene was after the two sisters performed and were back stage in the dressing room, and everyone comes in the back to congratulate them on their great performance. I guess it'll be minus Terisa. The audience will either assume she left after the performance, or she's out front in the bar mingling with the patrons. "It'll work!" she said when everyone looked around in shock. And it did.

34
JOSHUA TUNE

The rain hammered on my car roof without mercy. My beige London Fog trench coat did a great job of shielding me from the rain. Judge Madden had ended early to review our motions to ascertain whether she was going to allow evidence obtained by my office. I was on my way over to Monique's house where she'd be waiting for me. We had a rule to *never* discuss our case. And we both honored that; we were both professionals. We had been secretly seeing each other for the last two weeks. Jesus, Mary, and Joseph! If anyone ever found out we were seeing each other during the trial . . .

Parker was beginning to become a pain in my ass! Everyday and night she was screaming about something or another, "You're not spending enough time at home," "You don't do anything with me." Well, how am I supposed to when she's complaining all the time? Her nagging is running me out of the house. Some nights I plan on going home, then I think about her constant bickering and detour right to Monique's house. I don't understand her tiff; I pay all the bills and give her whatever money she wants, and still she's not satisfied. She's not approachable anymore, so I stay my distance.

This is the first time I've been involved with someone and took the chance of staying the *whole* night out. I admit, when I woke up the next morning at Monique's, I was scared shitless. But then I remembered who wore the pants in our marriage. And when I went home, she was furious. I tried explaining that I had gotten drunk after work and crashed at a friend's house. She wasn't hearing it, so I turned right around and went back to Monique's. I realized that she could assume I was out screwing around all day. But could she prove it? All she had was circumstantial evidence. The next day when I came home she was silent and solemn. I guess that was supposed to make me feel guilty or something.

You know how women are. And to tell the truth, it felt *good* to sleep all night next to Monique.

When I left Monique's and came right back, the look on Monique's face was pure shock. "What are you doing back here?" she said.

"I went home and she started yelling." I was taking off my jacket again and untying my shoes.

"Well, what did you think she'd do?" Actually, I hadn't thought ahead that far. I was so consumed in my own pleasure; I never stopped to think about Parker's pain. I sat there with my ""Gomer Pyle"" look on again. Monique saw this and started to laugh hysterically.

"What are you laughing at?" I yelled.

"You! Just tell me what was going through your mind when you said, "I'm just going to fuck up completely tonight?" She was completely amused by this whole episode.

"Monique, do I make you laugh? Do I amuse you? Am I here to fucking amuse you?" I was imitating Joe Pesci, in Goodfellas. She laughed. I laughed. However, the jokes were not penetrating enough for me to take my butt back home and mend my quarrels with Parker. That situation wasn't funny. I was very comfortable at Monique's, and I enjoyed her company. She made me feel young and virile. She tapped into my sensitive side; the funny side I never knew existed in me. I enjoyed her. We enjoyed each other.

Monique had chilled a bottle of Dom Perignon champagne, and we sat in front of her huge television set eating homemade pizza. Monique was an excellent cook. Her mini–movie theatre was just what a man needed after a hard day of work. We were watching the New York Knicks getting wasted by the Detroit Pistons. We were both yelling at the television as if the coach, referee, and the players could hear. I don't know if it was the flames from the fire she had set, bonding with her during the game, or the champagne, but she looked so alluring, I wanted to become one with her. I leaned over and grabbed the remote. I put it on mute, then turned my attention towards her. I wanted to get to know her better. With a mouth full of pizza she was already voicing her objections. I smiled, then said, "Monique, let's talk." She swallowed her pizza hard, then said, "Talk is overrated. Let's fuck."

At that moment I knew I had fallen in love with Monique. I wondered if that were possible because I was still in love with Parker. People ask the question all the time, so I won't get any medals for originality, but how can you be in love with two people at the same time?

35
JOSHUA TUNE

The night air was brisk as I walked up the walkway to my apartment. It was almost eleven o'clock. I hadn't spoken with Parker since I had left the apartment this morning to go to work. I meant to give her a call during my lunch break, but it slipped my mind. Monique and I had made love six times that night. She was a real stallion matching my stamina mile for mile. I thought a lot about loving two women, though. It was a conflicting thought. And I guess my love for Parker pulled me out of Monique's bed to return home. I missed her.

Monique gave me a long, succulent kiss goodbye, careful not to kiss me with her lipstick on. Actually, she was careful about everything. She was even more cautious than I was. She'd practically kick me out of bed, so I could make it home at a decent time. Whenever I'd call Parker from her apartment she'd sit in silence, blowing kisses at me careful not to make a sound. She never squirmed when I reciprocated Parker's "I love you." In fact, she taught me a thing or two or three about cheating cautiously.

My mind quickly went back to our first encounter when she said she could never date a married man. She led me to believe that she was a reluctant participant in the cheating arena, and this would be her first relationship of that kind. Had she lied to me? I shrugged off my skepticism and decided to attribute her words to her love for me. Did she love me? Neither one of us had said the word yet. But then I thought that she clearly must love me because women fall in love way before men do. And I'm in love with her, so it's only natural that the feeling would be reciprocated. I made a mental note to tell Monique how I felt very soon. I knew she would be hesitant to say it first considering I have a wife. She probably thinks I'm just in it for a free ride. Then I thought, "What am I in this relationship for? What am I seeking with Monique? What is it that I want out of life?"

The ride home was slow. I deliberately drove the speed limit. I needed the time alone to clear my head. I said a silent prayer before I put my key in the lock asking God to please let Parker be asleep, so I could just crawl into bed and hold her all night.

God had answered my prayer after all. When I went inside Parker was in the bed and all the lights were out. I quickly slid my clothes off and climbed into bed. When I wrapped my arms around Parker's back, she turned around to face me. She didn't say a word. She just stared in my eyes. Her eyes were consumed with hurt and pain. I thought that she was going to start with her investigating questions again as if she was Columbo. But she didn't. She touched my face gently, then brought her lips to mine. We started to kiss and it was the "I want to make love kiss" she was giving me. I backed off slowly, but she reached for my penis and I gently pushed her away. I hadn't taken a shower before I left Monique's because Parker would smell the soap on me and that'd be another argument. I had learned my lesson with taking showers at the Marriott after leaving Kaisha. Parker had exploded when she smelled how fresh I smelled. So now, I just wipe it off and throw on more cologne to kill any scent of perfume.

Usually, when I pushed her away, she'd turn over angrily, but she'd leave me alone. But tonight, she came back a little more aggressively. How long had it been since I made love to her? I was becoming careless. What was I going to do? I couldn't sleep with my wife right now with Monique's juices still on me. I mean I have morals. What to do?

Parker slid underneath the covers to try and persuade me with a blowjob. I gently pulled her head back up. She looked in my eyes and when I saw her pain, I sighed heavily with guilt. There was only one choice and that was I had no choice.

After Parker and I made love, I felt like a prick. First of all, I was already completely drained from Monique, so I couldn't completely please my wife. In fact, I made her do all the work. I had her on top the whole ride. I was surprised I could even get it up. But being the man that I am, my penis responded accordingly. When we were, well, when she was through, she started to cry hysterically. I was too tired to even talk to her, so I grabbed her close and caressed her the best way I could. I told her over and over that it was the trial that was draining me, and when the case was over, we'd go on a vacation. She slowed her sobs down to a sniffle then said, "Joshua, I want a baby." My tired, lazy eyes shot open. "I want us to have a family. I want to be the mother of your children," she continued. She was rubbing my chest, as she lay cuddled in my arms. "Parker, let's talk about this at another time please . . . I'm exhausted." I closed my eyes tight and prayed for the last time for this to all be a dream.

36
MADISON MICHAELS

I stood waiting for Joshua in his office, looking out the window at the season that had just changed. I love fall. The orange, red, and brown leaves falling from the trees were beautiful. And I felt beautiful. Maurice had been living with me, and I hadn't told a soul. It was my little secret.

Joshua came into his office looking terrific. He had on a dark–green cashmere sweater, black trousers, and black suede Salvatore Ferragammo shoes. He had styled his hair differently, with it combed towards the front, with some hair gel on the ends making a wild effect. It was also highlighted, and I could tell he had been to one of those tanning spas. He looked like a movie star; his piercing blue eyes sparkling with contentment. We embraced and it felt good. We sat down, and he had his secretary bring us croissants and coffee.

I told him everything about Maurice, even the part I wasn't supposed to. I let him know that Maurice was with the federal government. An FBI agent. I had to. He was looking too skeptical when I told him that he had moved in with me after only a week. I didn't tell him that I had given my virginity to Maurice, but I can assume Joshua knew. I could tell he was forcing himself to sound optimistic about my situation because I was so happy. Joshua was a little over–protective of me. So I knew that he'd accept my dinner invitation, if only to put his mind at ease. I left his office with plans to have drinks with Joshua around seven at Tabbie's Pub. When I asked whether he was going to invite Parker, he squirmed, then said he doubt it. I left it at that. I hoped everything was all right in his household. But I didn't pry.

I went to my work area to call Maurice at home. When the answering machine picked up, I didn't leave a message. I then tried him on his cellular phone. His cellular phone service came on, too. I wondered where he was this early in the morning, but left a detailed message as to where I wanted him to meet Joshua and me later.

37
MADISON MICHAELS

Joshua and I took a cab over to Tabbie's Bar together. We laughed and caught up on each other's events. Joshua invited me to the "Pirates of Penzance" opera and I accepted. I missed him so much.

Joshua really looked fabulous, like a man who owned the world. He confided in me about Monique. He spoke of this Monique with a great deal of respect. How could he respect a home wrecker? His blue eyes twinkled and made me feel a little uneasy. Joshua fell fast for a lot of pretty women; that was his Achilles heel, but he said Monique was different from anyone else he dated.

"She's everything I've always looked for. She does not like drama. She has a nonchalant attitude that I admire. She's funny, strong, and whenever she hears some of the quandaries Parker puts me through, she says she'd never behave like that."

"That's easy for her to say because she's not your wife. She is the woman trying to take you away from your wife, so she will say *anything* she thinks you want to hear. Do not let her inconspicuous demeanor fool you; you're too smart for that."

"She doesn't want to take me from my wife. She knows I love my wife. She just wants to have a good time, that's all."

"Everyone thinks the grass is greener on the other side."

I had to remind him that he was married and that although he was my friend, I loved and adored Parker and that I did not approve of what he was doing. He shrugged it off, said he was just being a man. I called him a little doggie. He laughed. I sympathized. How many times could a man fall in love and remain unsatisfied?

When the cab pulled up to Murray Street, Maurice was on time outside awaiting our arrival. I had a big Kool–Aid smile on my face when I saw him. My face lit up like a light bulb. Joshua looked around to see why I was smiling and then he saw Maurice smiling back at me.

"So this must be him," Joshua said as he extended his hand for Maurice to shake.

"Whaddup? Nice to meet you finally, man. Madi has told me so much about you."

"Really?"

"Madi said you're like her big brother."

"Big, bad ass brother who won't tolerate my sister getting hurt. But I'm sure I won't have to take out a can of whip ass on ya, would I?" Joshua's voice turned stern but he tried to disguise it as cynical humor. My eyes dashed towards Maurice to see if he was going to fall for the bait. He did not. Instead, he said charismatically, "I hear where you're coming from my man. If I had a baby sis, I would protect her from some of these cats out here myself. They give us decent guys a bad name, you know?" He smiled, then leaned over and kissed my cheek. From behind his back, he pulled out a single red rose.

"How was your day baby?" I greedily accepted my rose. I wrapped my arm around his waist and moved in close so I could smell the Nautica cologne I brought for him.

"It was great. How about we go inside and get a table." We all walked inside and grabbed the first available table. Before we could order our first round of drinks, Joshua started in on Maurice again. "So Maurice, what brings you to New York? Madison says you lived in Atlanta."

"Yes. Well actually, I really didn't care for New York until I met Madison. In a few moments, my life turned around. Wherever she is . . . that's where I want to be."

"I used to do things on impulse myself back in high school. However, as an adult, you have to prioritize your life. Just because something may feel right today . . . it can be the worst situation tomorrow. It's best to thoroughly think a situation through."

"Yeah . . . well . . . I'm wise enough to know a good thing when I set my eyes on it." I smiled at

Maurice's compliment. He always made me feel adored. Joshua was not letting go of his fear about my relationship. He continued, "So I hear you're not working?" I nearly choked on my drink, and then looked at Maurice with eyes that said I am sorry. He shrugged off my insecurities and held my hand tight underneath the table. He said, "As a matter of fact, I start back working on Monday. I was waiting for my transfer paperwork to go through. I wanted to tell Madi alone tonight because she has been so supportive, but among her friends is just as good." He leaned over and gave me a soft, sensual kiss. Joshua squirmed in his seat at our affection. He looked uneasy. This seemed to make Maurice happy. "Since we're celebrating, we might as well do it in style," Maurice exclaimed. He called the waiter and ordered a bottle of Moet champagne.

"Expensive taste," Joshua remarked dryly.

"Anything for my baby," Maurice retorted.

"So what exactly do you do? Madison never did tell me." Joshua lied. Before Maurice could answer, I interjected and answered for him. I lied right back at Joshua for putting Maurice on the spot. This was supposed to be a light evening full of fun and laughs. "He's in sales with an advertisement firm," I said. Joshua smirked, then said, "Is that right?" Maurice backed me up and said, "Exactly." The waiter came and poured our glasses to the rim, and then Maurice held up his glass to toast. "To the most beautiful woman inside and out that I have ever met. Madison, to say you are beautiful is much too common. You are enchanting." Our glasses clicked together and my life flashed before my eyes. My future. I wanted to marry Maurice and have his children. I wanted to wash his dirty clothes and make Sunday dinners, inhale his cologne on our sheets while waiting for him to come home from work and make love to me. I loved him! I was in love, and no one was going to take that away from me.

Before the evening ended, I noticed that Maurice had started to win Joshua over. They started to bond as men do talking about sports, cars, and things that I had no interest. Maurice mentioned that he wanted to join a gym to keep in shape. He had a gorgeous body. He was so sculptured he looked like a Greek sculpture. Triceps and biceps toned to a perfect "t." Joshua invited him to come to his gym on his buddy pass and Maurice accepted. I turned to Josh, leaned in close, and planted a fat–wet kiss on his cheek. He blushed and said, "What was that for?"

"That was just because. Just because I love you so much."

When the evening was ending and we were getting our things together, Maurice reached inside his blazer jacket and pulled out a long, rectangle, black velvet box. "I almost forgot. I bought this for you today Madi. I hope you like it." I reached for the box, my hands shaking as I opened it. Inside was a diamond and ruby heart–shaped necklace that astounded me. I gasped at the sight of it. The diamonds sparkled so much that they nearly blinded me. Before I could say anything, Maurice spoke, "The diamonds represent how pure you are to me. Your innocence. The rubies represent my love for you. Each time you wear it I want you to think about my love for you." As he spoke the words, my heart opened up and enveloped this sweet, sensitive man. Tears streamed down my face and said everything I wanted to say. All I could think about was what Lyric would say when she saw it. If Joshua was skeptical about Maurice, this certainly sealed it for him.

We said our good–byes, and then Maurice and I went home to make love.

38
MADISON MICHAELS

Maurice liked to sleep late on Saturday mornings, so when I got out of bed to make breakfast, I didn't wake him up. As the sunny–side–up eggs were frying, Maurice decided to sneak up on me and scared my black hair white. I screamed as if I was in a horror movie. He laughed and picked me up and swung me around. "What are you doing up so early this morning?" I scolded him, and then continued, "I was making you breakfast in bed."

"Let's eat very quick because I have an appointment with a used–car dealer today," he playfully slapped me on my ass.

"You're getting a car?"

"Well, I need one. Hell, *we* need one. I could drop you off at work in the mornings en route to my office. These cabs in New York are very expensive. " He was nibbling on the bacon that I had already cooked on top of the stove. His lips were greasy and he was smiling. I loved the fact that he included me in everything that he did. "*We*" he had said.

"What type of car are you thinking about buying?"

"A Lexus. What do you think about that car?"

"They're beautiful, but they're very expensive."

"That's why we're going to a used car dealer. I could probably get one for $20,000."

"$20,000 is still too much to pay for a car. That's a down payment for a house, Maurice. Why don't you get a used car for maybe $2,000 and keep the rest in the bank."

"Practical Madi. Do you ever buy yourself something that you really want and not feel guilty about it the next day?"

I thought about it then said, "Honestly, I try not to spend over my means."

"Madi, get dressed."

"For what?"

"You're going with me to the dealer."

"Why? I wanted to do my house–cleaning today."

"Because I want you to help me pick out the car. You know I can be a little indecisive."

Actually, I never picked that trait up in him. He was always decisive.

"And put on something sexy and wear the necklace I brought you."

"Don't you think that necklace is too expensive to wear to a used–car lot?" He didn't answer. He just motioned me to the room to get dressed.

The dealership on Hillside Avenue in Queens had a selection of beautiful cars. A heavy-set woman in her early 30's came walking towards us. Her thighs were rubbing together in her too–tight black pantsuit. There was an area inside her upper thighs that had busted out the seams, but she had re–stitched the area in white thread. That was very tacky.

The salesmen were like sharks, and we were the bait. Everyone was scrambling to get the next meal. As she approached, sweat was running down the side of her face and along her faint mustache. She extended her hand and said, "Mr. Mungin, we have all your paperwork ready. The deal is set up." It was then I realized that Maurice had been there already.

"Do you want Madison to see the car you picked out?" she knew my name as well.

"Yes. Thank you." Maurice said and she led us to a crème color 1997 Lexus GS300.

After we all got inside the car and said our "ooh's and ahh's," it was time to go back to the fat lady's cubicle for Maurice to discuss payment possibilities. I also noticed that the car was a whopping $35,000. How dare they charge so much for a second–hand vehicle? I didn't want to know the sticker price of a brand new one. Maurice seemed excited, and I was a little too. Then the fat lady said, "What's your social security number dear?"

"Excuse me?" I said. Then Maurice interjected and said. "She needs your social security number."

"For what?"

"So we can get approved for the car." Suddenly that *we* didn't sound so attractive.

"Why does she need my number? I thought you wanted a car because I don't need one." Something about what was going down didn't seem right to me. My stomach was doing somersaults and back flips.

"Madi, baby, I need to get the car in your name because of my situation that I told you about." What did he tell me about?

"What situation?"

"I told you I couldn't be traced. It's too dangerous. I'm in New York where I just locked up a dozen bad guys. It was all over the papers . . . didn't you see it?" He was whispering in my ear so the fat lady wouldn't hear. I hadn't seen any big drug busts on the news lately.

"You never said you needed me to do this . . . this is a big step for me. You're asking me to do a lot here. I need time to think." I was irritated. What if he missed car notes or has a history of late payments? I don't know that much about Maurice Mungin.

"What about what you asked of me? I rearranged my whole goddamn life for you!" He was no longer discrete and whispering. The words came bellowing out and everyone turned around to see what the commotion was. I pushed far back in my chair because it looked like he was about to strike me in my face. His eyes held all the rage they say you see in bulls. I was trembling and at a lost for words, but I knew that I had better say something fast.

"You're right," I started out by saying, then continued, "In relationships you're supposed to make sacrifices for each other. I'll do it. It just took me by surprise that's all."

My hand involuntarily went up and fingered my necklace. Then I realized how selfish I was being. Maurice was going to be my future husband and father of my children. He's given me everything he possibly could, and I was only thinking about myself.

After I filled out the paperwork, it only got worse. "How much of a deposit will you be putting down?" She looked directly at me and not Maurice. So I looked at Maurice.

"How much money do you have Maurice?" I said, hoping he had at least half of the now $38,000 car loan. The fat lady sat looking at us with a tickled expression on her face. She knew exactly what was going down, but all she cared about was the commission she would make off of this sale. Maurice leaned in again and said, "Madi, how much money do you have in the bank right now?" Before I could answer he said, "I tied up all my loose cash yesterday when I purchased that necklace for you. I wrote out a check for $60,000, and it hasn't cleared with my bank yet. Once that clears, I'll give you your money right back and everything else I owe you."

The price of the necklace stuck in my throat. I had no idea that it was so expensive. Maurice hasn't said it yet, but he must love me. He has to. Lyric always said, "Men and money don't part . . . unless you've done something special to their heart!" I must have done something special to Maurice's heart. I looked adoringly at my handsome boyfriend and said, "Do you really want this car that bad?"

"Madison, I'm a big boy; this isn't the latest candy bar. I need this vehicle." Momentarily, I wondered what had happened to the "*we.*"

"Well, how long will it be before I get my money back?"

"Just a couple of business days for the bank to clear my check." His eyes and movements were growing impatient with me. I thought about where I would get the money for a down payment. I had $500 that I would be sending out in a couple of days for this month's rent. I guess I could give that as a down payment and when Maurice's check cleared he could reimburse me, and I could pay the rent at that time. We still had two weeks in the month anyway so I felt safe. "I can give $500," I offered proudly. Maurice looked as if he had eaten a piece of chicken that I had just told him was rat meat. "That's not enough!" Maurice and the fat lady sang in unison. "Madi," Maurice continued, "I need at least fifteen grand to close the deal."

"$15,000!" It was my turn to start screaming and act the fool. Where did he think I would get $15,000? Then I answered my own question. My big mouth had told him about the money I had in the bank. The CD had just cleared last week. My mother saved $2 a day from the first day I was born. She gave it to me on my 21st birthday.

I searched in my wallet and pulled out my checkbook and wrote out $15,000 regrets. I signed my name on the dotted line and felt like I had just sold my soul to the devil. Only Maurice wasn't a devil; he was my man and I needed to be supportive. What did Maurice have over me that I would put him on a higher pedestal than I did myself?

39
LYRIC DEVANEY

"What do you see in him Lyric?"

"What business is it of yours?"

"Lyric, a lot of things are going down in New York that I think you should know about. The mayor is out of fucking control. Did you know that an unarmed black female was shot twelve times by three white police officer's for mistaken identity, and the mayor holds a press conference commending their actions! He's a racist Lyric. The fucking anti–Christ himself. You'd better stay far away from him," Joshua was in an uproar.

"Why are your panties so tight today, Joshua?"

"Pardon me?"

"There has to be more to this than a dead black girl. You're calling across the world to say the mayor is being naughty. What do you want me to do? Spank him?"

"I'm sure you'd do that anyway for pleasure. I'm talking politics right now."

"Oh fuck you. And fuck the dead girl, too. Don't go dumping no heavy shit in my lap right now because I am not in the mood."

"Lyric, you're a cold–hearted bitch! Where's your remorse for the woman who has lost her life because the cops wanted to play Cowboys and Indians?"

"Josh, I'm not going to be too many of your bitches. What the fuck do I care about someone who was in the wrong place at the wrong time? I mean, I feel for her . . . a little . . . I guess. But what can I do?"

"You can get a clue!" That was the last thing he said before he slammed the phone down hard in my ear. I didn't even bother to call him back.

I had heard the news on CSNN. The mayor was taking a lot of criticism for his choice of words and his handling of the situation. He had never given his condolences to the victim's family, and to make the situation worse, he had the police commissioner release her sealed juvenile record to negate the press, headlines like--"Innocent Black Female Shot Dead by the Police Department." Apparently, when she was fifteen years old, she was caught shoplifting from Harry's Hardware, but that was ten years ago. The mayor had used bad judgment or he had been badly advised. Since the Harry's Hardware incident, she had been a model citizen. She had never even received a traffic ticket. She had just joined the Navy and was going out to celebrate her departure with friends when the terrible incident occurred. The cops said that she was one of the suspects in a recent bank robbery on Astoria Boulevard in Queens. They had received a tip from an informant that the suspect was hiding out in Kew Gardens. Police were given the wrong address. Witnesses said that she was startled and dropped her pocketbook. When she bent down to pick it back up, thirty-three shots rang out. She picked up twelve.

The three white police officers released a statement indicating they thought that she had been reaching for a gun and that they had felt that their lives were in immediate danger. Reverend Clifford Dale had previously received the news. He had already been on the evening news at the podium telling the world that the incident was racially motivated. "When a innocent black woman can't come out of her home without getting shot by the same people who were supposed to protect and serve the community, we have not progressed at all . . . " He stated that racial profiling needed to stop. Then, the mayor made a statement. Richard said, "She isn't as innocent as her parents and press are making her out to be. She has been arrested before and has a criminal history." He never did add that she was a minor when that incident occurred.

40
LYRIC DEVANEY

My disagreement with Joshua had irked my nerves. What did he mean, "get a clue?" And the way he said it. Joshua was a pompous asshole. I shook off those negative vibes and picked up the phone to call Richard on his cellular. He picked up on the third ring.

"Cardinale, here."

"Richard, darling I miss you," I said flatly.

"Lyric, my butterfly, how is the West Coast treating you?"

"The sun is terrible for my skin. Other than spending a fortune on Clinique sun–blocking lotion, everything else is fine."

"Are you meeting any handsome celebrities that want to steal you from me?"

"Baby, no one can *steal* me. I'm not a commodity. But if you're asking if my heart still belongs to you, the answer is yes."

"Good. Good. I'm glad to know I still have you in my corner."

"Richard, I miss you. Why don't you come out here and spend some time with me?"

"I'm sorry darling but that is not feasible. I have several engagements I'm involved with at this moment. In fact, I can't stay on the phone. I have a late meeting, I'll speak to you soon, love." Before I could object, he hung up. That was twice in the same day someone dismissed me. I was furious. And although I didn't call Joshua back, I definitely dialed Richard back. I must have called his phone twenty times, and each time his voice mail came on. I didn't leave a message.

I was supposed to be studying my lines for tomorrow's shoot, but Richard had taken away my concentration. How dare he treat me like that? Then I realized–he's going through a lot in New York with the shooting incident. But didn't he realize he could talk to me about anything? Maybe he's seeing someone else?

Richard cheating on me? No! I'm just being paranoid. Richard loves me. He wouldn't dare jeopardize what we have by seeing someone else. My mind raced to review his recent behavior.

Since I've been in Los Angeles, he hasn't called me once. I've initiated each call.

Cheating.

But when I do call, he's usually sweet and his voice sounds happy to hear from me.

Not cheating.

I've invited him down here three times and he's turned me down.

Cheating.

Every time I speak to him he's makes a comment about the men and sounds really jealous.

NOT CHEATING!

I slowly inflated the air back into my self–esteem and fixed myself a drink. Absolut on the rocks. Now where in the hell did I put my Valium?

41
LYRIC DEVANEY

"Five, four, three, two, . . . "

"Mr. Slade I've heard a lot about you."

"Well, a sexy lil' thing like yourself shouldn't believe everything you hear."

"I believe nothing I hear and only half of what I see."

"And what do you see when you look at me?"

"I see that a man like yourself should be careful of girls like me."

"And why is that?"

"I'll make you fall in love."

"Would you want me to fall in love with you?"

"Why wouldn't I? You're handsome, rich and have the right connections."

"You sure know how to pay a fella a compliment."

"I know how to show a fella a good time too."

"Well is that right?"

"Only if you say so."

"I do. I do indeed."

"Cut! That's a wrap." The director ran over to me.

"Lyric, if you could see in the tele–prompter, you would want to screw your own self. Goddamn, you're hot! You're going to do for the 90's what Marilyn Monroe did for the 60's. You're a sex kitten."

Jacob, the director, was all excited about the scene we had just shot. Terisa was on the set, and her eyes were burning holes into the back of my neck. I thought this was the right opportunity to have a little fun. I was in a bad mood, and I'm sure a confrontation with her would have balanced my emotions. I sauntered over towards Terisa who was standing around with some extras. She had been on the set since sun–up waiting to shoot her few lines. By this time, word around the set was that she was a nobody and her career was fading fast. Her cocky attitude had changed to meek with everyone except me. She couldn't wait for a confrontation. Every time I took a step towards her, I decided that I would bypass her and keep walking. Why not? I'm the star on this set.

I walked directly to my trailer to relax before my next scene. I had been in the trailer for a hot two minutes before my door flung open. Terisa was standing there with her arms folded over each other and her lips poked out. She'd had a nose job and a boob job. Her fake silicones were at attention in her extra small cashmere sweater.

"You think you're so clever, don't you Lyric?"

"I am."

"Really?" She said that with such skepticism as if I hadn't just masterminded the best deal of the century. As if I didn't rip her role out from under her and maneuver myself into the lead role with just one fuck.

"Are you doubting my talent T-e-r-e-s-s-a?"

"It's Terisa!"

"Whatever."

"You're not going to get away with this, Lyric. I've already been booked for The Evening Show and I'm going to tell $20 million viewers how you screwed me out of my role. Literally."

"Go ahead, and you'll be blacklisted from every social event. You know as well as I do that Hollywood hates a snitch–bitch."

"You're a bitch, Lyric."

"Likewise," I said flatly. I had stripped down to my panties and bra to show off my hourglass figure. Let her see what a real woman looked like. She was more artificial than my dildo. She stared me up and down then came all the way into my trailer and shut my door. I stared her down hard to see if she was about to make a move, but instead she broke down crying. She collapsed on my sofa and let out a loud wail.

"I . . . I . . . can't take anymore," she wailed. Her nose was blowing snot bubbles and tears streaked her face. She continued, "I needed this role. I'm washed up at twenty–two . . . "

Twenty–two? She had to be joking. "T-e-r-e-s-s-a, I don't have time for your hysterics. I'm back on set in two hours. I need my rest."

"Lyric, please don't ruin my career. It was a misunderstanding. I really thought I gave you the correct date. Ask yourself why I would lie to you? What would I gain?"

"How about a starring role in a Harrington Lee movie?" The logic stung her. She choked back a quick rebuttal, then composed herself and said, "I earned that role."

"I'm sure you did," I said dryly.

"Not like that!" she screamed, then lowered her voice and said, "Can you help me get my lines increased? I know you can do it, Lyric, if you really want to. You can do anything you want once you put your mind to it. We were once friends. That must mean something to you."

She went to my vanity and took a napkin to blow her nose. Her eyes were red around the brim and puffy.

"Are you asking me to choose friendship over Hollywood?"

"Why do you have to make a choice? You can still be the star, just make me supporting actress."

"If I had them rewrite the script and make you supporting actress, how do you know it would help your failing career?"

"Lyric, we both know this movie is going to be a blockbuster. It's going to put your career in orbit. Every script being written will be Federal Expressed to your front door before the ink is dry. All I'm asking is that I get to eat off the same plate. I know I fucked up and I'm sorry. I'm begging for my life here. We're two young black females trying to make it in a white man's world. We need to stick together with black unity."

Black unity? I laughed in her face. She ignored my blatant sarcasm. Her voice was soft and her tears seemed genuine. I thought briefly about the lunches we'd had and how we would go shopping together and spend an obscene amount of money at Bergdorf's.

"T-e-r-e-s-s-a, let me explain something to you. I've made plenty shed tears. Men and women. It doesn't move me. I've demoted friends to acquaintances, immediate family members to distant relatives, but *only* after they drew first blood. This scenario you're going through is just an internship. Preparation for what I have planned for you. I told you I'd get you back and you challenged me to validate my threat. So I say to you 'check.' The next move is yours."

I was completely naked at this point. Terisa's eyes were poking out her head. She was in complete shock. I enjoyed vibing off of her fear. So I continued, "I'm not going to stop until you're some crackhead begging for a hit up in Harlem or committed to some insane asylum for overdosing on your misery."

I walked over to her and grabbed her by her arm and ushered her to the door. She yanked away and swallowed hard. She wiped her tears away and adjusted her outfit. Her scene was over. Now if she could only act half as good on screen, her career wouldn't be in shambles.

"One day you're going to mess with the wrong person, Lyric Devaney, and it'll be your turn to beg and plead for *your* life back!"

"Oh . . . lighten up!" I challenged.

"You fuckin' lighten up!"

"T-e-r-e-s-s-a," she turned around to face me once again. Her eyes said she hoped I had changed my mind. I smiled my Lyric Devaney trademark, winked and said, "Checkmate!" She stormed out of my trailer leaving my front door ajar. I fell back on my temporary bed laughing my ass off. She will hate herself in the morning for groveling in front of me. Where was her self–respect?

42
LYRIC DEVANEY

I went to my portable CD player and put on the hottest rap single of all time–"Hot Boys" by Missy "Misdemeanor" Elliot. I was in my birthday suit and a pair of silver stilettos. As I was dancing around my trailer, high off hate and gyrating my body like a professional stripper, I felt someone watching me, that strange feeling you get at the back of your neck when your senses tell you you're not alone. I swung my sexy naked body around, still gyrating, to see Marisol in my doorway watching me.

"Nice moves," she complimented.

"What do you want?"

"I saw Terisa come in here, I was just coming to make sure she didn't start anything."

"I can take care of myself . . . you should know that."

"That you can." She invited herself all the way in and closed the door behind her. She had this authoritative manner. Something new. I needed to find out what was up with her. I programmed myself out of "bitch mode" and started my investigation.

"So, Marisol, you walk around here like you own the world. What's up with that?"

"Do you want to go get a drink?" she said not responding to my question. Curiosity was definitely my weak spot. I knew she had something she wanted to say, and I wanted to indulge her. I threw on a tank top that had "Pervert" across it, a pair of 'Frankie B' jeans, Manolo Blahnik sling back shoes and was ready.

We hopped in her convertible rental. It was a classic low–rider with hydraulics. "Nice ride. Very LA." Instantly my nasty mood had disappeared and I felt at ease in her company. Her skills behind the wheel were almost as good as mine. She dashed in and out of traffic with ease. The wind was blowing through our hair and she put on "The Chronic" by Dr. Dre and Snoop Dogg.

She passed me an "el" and I lit it up quickly. I was feeling nice. We were both singing the lyrics and shaking our heads to the music.

We drove to a quaint restaurant in Oakland because I had to be back on the set in a little over an hour. When we hopped out, we were greeted by a lot of men trying to get the digits. We bypassed them and went straight to the bar. I ordered an Absolut on the rocks and she had a frozen Margarita. Once inside, I got straight to the point.

"So tell me, what's up with you, Jay Kapone, and this damn film? Who's frontin' who?"

"Very perceptive Lyric. Let me be honest. That night in your apartment you taught me something and I felt indebted to you. When you said, "Play them right back" I took heed. So when Jay Kapone called and said you wanted a role in the movie, I said 'hire her.' When we thought that there'd be trouble with Terisa, I knew you'd think of something to correct it. Some people make things happen, others watch things happen."

"So this is your movie?"

"Absolutely."

"So Jay Kapone is the frontman?"

"Lyric, I was truly in love with Jay Kapone. When I found out he was cheating, it crushed me. When I first saw you, I freaked out. You were gorgeous. I felt you were the bad guy not him. And that instant, when my life flashed before my eyes, I grew up. I grew wise. This world is about having your own. Make your own money, have your own mind, be your own boss."

"So you hired a ghost writer and produced a movie?"

"I did more than that. Jay Kapone's first album sold one million copies. That was all him. But when it came time to go into the studio to push out another album, he didn't have any material. All his money had gone to his record label, and his first deal took most of his publishing rights. Jay Kapone really is a one–hit wonder. He's not a rapper; he's just someone who made a rap album. Nor is he a drug dealer, just someone who sold some drugs. Lyric you know what I do and what my family does. I needed to legitimize my money. I brought all his publishing points for his second album and got my record company, Sky's the Limit, incorporated. First I sat back to see how his sales would do. They were mediocre. So I brought up his entire unit. He went seven times platinum. He gets to keep his platinum status, and I get all my money laundered into my legitimate business. I pay taxes on drug money! I have credit and respectability."

"Very smart indeed." I had to give credit when it was due. This cute, Colombian sister was a fast–thinking businesswoman. During our female bonding, she admitted that she didn't need Jay Kapone anymore but she still cared about him.

"Are you and Jay Kapone screwing?" She looked me eye to eye and waited for me to answer. I evaluated the situation.

If everything she told me was true, which I think it was, she didn't have any use for Jay Kapone unless she was still in love with him. And if she's the one pulling all the strings, then I don't need Jay Kapone either and I certainly don't love him. I need to get on her side and I can't mess that up. Besides, she feels like she owes me something for opening up her eyes.

I told her what she wanted to hear and we left the restaurant. On the ride back, I felt like I had made a smart business decision. I would no longer make love to Jay Kapone! He was a nobody. Despite our differences, I decided that I liked Marisol. She's still a little soft, but I can help her work on that. Truthfully speaking, she's much too good for Jay Kapone. And I don't doubt that he doesn't love her, I think he does. However, I know that he's not *in* love with her. And although she's financially stable, mentally she still needs him. In five years, she could be one of the most powerful women in the industry. And if I know anything about success, power, and money, is that it creates the illusion that we as human beings don't need anyone. She'll drop him. And when she does, he'll realize that if he didn't love her, he should have. That'll be his lesson in life. At least one of them.

43
LYRIC DEVANEY

"This is no ordinary love." I was listening to Sade. My tank was full on Absolut and I was feeling miserable. I was homesick and dick–sick. I hadn't had a dose of either one in a long time. Lying in my hotel suite crying, which I only did when I was intoxicated, I was singing the words out of tune and feeling sorry for myself. I picked up the phone and dialed Richard. I wanted to fuck his brains out. Since cutting Jay Kapone off, my sex life was dry. I needed to feel a human body next to me. I was tired of my plastic dildo. I wanted to be held.

"Cardinale here."

"Yeah, Cardinale. Why aren't you h-e-e-re?" I slurred.

"Lyric, are you drunk?"

"You've just asked the million–dollar question."

"Why are you drinking? I thought I told you to lay off the booze."

"Richard, I n-e-e-ed you. I want you to take a flight out here to see me right now." I was screaming and crying into phone. My voice was wavering with every syllable.

"Lyric, are you alright?"

"No, I'm not alright!" I felt like I was losing him. I felt like I was losing all my friends. Joshua wasn't speaking to me and Madison wasn't returning any of my phone calls. Richard exhaled, and then said, "Lyric, I can't come see you right now. I'll have to check my schedule and get back with you to confirm."

"Either you get your political ass out here A.S.A.P, or I'm taking the next flight out of here and heading straight over to Gracie Mansion!"

"Are you out of your mind? The press will go crazy."

"You . . . " I hiccupped. "Excuse me. You heard what I said. I mean it Richard. Either surprise me with a visit tomorrow night, or I'll surprise you!"

A long pause followed from the other line.

"Make the arrangements, Lyric. I'll be there. Someplace discrete, I can't take any chances." He hung up the phone and I drifted off to sleep. Satisfied.

Today, I wasn't shooting and had the whole day to myself. After I made the reservations for Richard, I called downstairs to have them send someone up to my room for a full body massage. I also needed a facial, manicure, pedicure, and full body wax. I was so excited and I didn't know why. Richard was definitely "the one." I mean, I can get any man. But how often do you come across "the one?" My mother told me that you come across true love once in a lifetime, and when you do, you hold on tight and didn't let go. I intended to not let Richard go, no matter how much I threatened him that I would leave him. My heart wouldn't let me. He's the only one I have a soft spot for. The *only* one. We had a lot of things to sort out. I needed to talk to him about our future. He never did get back to me regarding whether he had told Estelle about the divorce. That subject was as foreign as Japan to me. But I knew I needed to be persistent. That's the only way to get what you want in life.

44
LYRIC DEVANEY

The morning had me feeling a little nauseous, so I opened up seltzer water. It must have been the Absolut I drank last night. I reached for my Valium when the phone rang.

"Talk to me," I whispered.

"I just wired that last payment into your account."

"Why, Erious, darling, where's your manners? What happened to good morning?" I had perked up.

"Don't be coy with me you blood–sucking bitch!"

"Tsk, tsk, you are such a naughty lil' boy. Somebody should wash your mouth out with soap."

"Somebody should shove dynamite in yours." I loved infuriating Erious. It was so easy to push his buttons. Especially since I was digging into his pockets. I didn't have any qualms about him calling the police or recording these conversations because if he had me arrested by the FBI for blackmail, he would throw his career down the drain. I know he'd never cut off his nose to spite his face, so I indulged in these conversations.

"Erious, what's the lesson for today?"

"Excuse me?"

"Negative! The lesson for the day is NEVER screw Lyric Devaney because it'll cost you." I felt him holding in his rage. But instead of exploding, he remained calm and continued with his question, "When are you going to send me the tape?"

"I'll Fed–Ex it today."

"And there aren't any copies . . . you're going to send the original?"

"Would I lie to you? The deal stated I get the money, you get the original."

"Lyric?"

"Yes, dear."

"If you screw me on this deal, they'll find your body in pieces in the trunk of MY car!"

"I'll look forward to our next encounter, player." We didn't say our good–byes. We both just hung up the phone. What the hell was eating him? Threatening my life like that. He needs counseling. A hug. Something.

I was a millionaire! The word was so grand. I was back on top of the world. I was going to send Erious a *copy* of the rape–tape. There was no way he was getting the original. Maybe, I'll make copies and send them to Joshua and Madison and tell them not to watch it unless something tragic happens. Just for good measure. What if he hired a hit man to take me out? But then he would have done that before he wired $15 million into my account.

45
LYRIC DEVANEY

Richard arrived on a 9 p.m. flight. My driver brought him to the hotel on schedule. When I opened the door, he looked wonderful. Balding, fat gut, beady eyes, lisp and all looked wonderful. He felt like home. We embraced and I held on for dear life. He ended the embrace and walked inside. Was I being paranoid, or did he look annoyed? He barely glanced at me and I had on Victoria Secret's best. I had ordered steak, his favorite, but he said he wasn't hungry. The scented candles, champagne on ice and soft music did nothing for him. He was ruining a special moment by being grouchy. Again, I put it off as being caused by his problems in New York. I knew how to make him relax and forget about his troubles. I started to kiss his neck and he practically ripped my face off of him.

"Ouch!" I yelled. "What the fuck is the matter with you?"

"Lyric have a seat."

"Fuck you!"

"Not tonight, baby!" Why was he being so hostile? This was supposed to be a romantic evening and he was bringing his bad vibes into our special evening.

"Richard, whatever you're going through in New York can stay there. This is my time and I don't want to spend it working out your hostilities."

"Lyric, my obligations in New York are handled. I'm here about us. It's over. I don't want to see you anymore. I have changed all my numbers so you won't be able to contact me after tonight. Please don't make this difficult; here's some money. A parting gift. I want you to accept it." He reached inside his breast pocket and pulled out a check.

Someone let all the air out of my lungs because I couldn't breathe. I was gasping for air and felt faint. He ran over to me and sat me down on the sofa. Still, I was unable to talk. So he continued, "I know you can be a fire starter, and up until now you haven't seen my bad side. Don't make this ugly. You'll regret it." These words from the man I was in love with. He was so cold. What did I do? Something must have happened.

"Richard . . . what's going on . . . I thought we were getting married?"

"You're not very bright are you?"

"Excuse me?"

"Lyric, it was fun while it lasted. It's just that simple. I enjoyed the ride." He was talking to me as if I was a whore and meant nothing to him! There had to be another woman. That's where men get their strength. But I sure wasn't going to make this easy for him and his new mistress. I looked at the check he had in his hand and took it. I was curious to see what he thought I was worth. It was for one hundred thousand dollars. I laughed in his face then ripped the check up. How dare he insult me like that? We were at war! I regained my strength and countered, "Richard, I invited you out here to celebrate."

"Celebrate what?"

"To celebrate the arrival of our baby. I'm pregnant. Where going to have a baby."

"You're a whore Lyric. Your insides are probably so polluted you couldn't even get pregnant. And if you are, the baby's not mine."

"We'll Mr. Mayor, I am pregnant. You could certify that. And the baby *is* yours. You could send that certified mail to your wife because that's a fact."

"We used condoms."

"Sometimes. Sometimes not. You remember these words, 'Baby, let me just feel your juices.' Does that sound familiar?" I could tell he was going back to those nights where the sex was so hot that nobody wanted to stop to get a condom.

"Take the money and get an abortion!" His voice had gotten louder and his face was beet red. I loved to see him furious. He'd lost his composure in a matter of seconds.

"That money was an insult. Now this is plan 'B'. You're either going to get a divorce from Estelle and marry me and then I'll have an abortion. Or, we can get

167

ghetto, and have your black baby's face on every tabloid from here to London. You will be laughed out of office, your marriage will be ruined anyway, and, this is the most important part, I'll still collect child support from you every month. And in the long run, it'll be more than that measly hundred–grand. Do I make myself clear senator? Excuse me . . . mayor."

"Crystal."

"Now get the fuck out of my hotel suite and take a moment to make up your mind. But please, don't take too long because every day this baby grows inside me."

"You're nothing but a savage in–house nigger! Wanting to have a baby from the mas'ser to pretend that you're better than the rest of the niggers out here. A half–white baby so you can compete in this all–white world is not going to buy you a seat at the front of the bus."

His words slapped the shit out of me. Knocked me right on my ass! Joshua was right; the mayor was a racist. He just used me to fulfill some fantasy. To fuck a black girl. A *nigger* as he put it. I was deeply hurting but I kept my cool. Nothing Absolut and two Valiums couldn't fix.

"My race is not savage. Savages are the people who came to a country and stole my ancestors then auctioned them off. Made them slaves, raped our women, and killed our men. Savages are the people who became millionaires off slave labor. Stole our history. Wouldn't allow them to vote or learn how to read. Treated them as cattle. Can I identify with these people or you? Savages are the people who hunt people like animals. Cut them up into tiny pieces and bury the parts in their backyard. These serial killers are savages. And when you see them on television, what skin color are they? Can I identify with these people or you? Savages are the people who are cannibals. The people who *eat* people for no psychological rhyme or reasoning. Can I identify with Jeffrey Damher? Or can you? Savages are the white yuppies who slaughter their parents in their sleep. Can I identify with these people or you? I think you need to redefine savage, sweetheart, because my people are survivors. I'm a survivor," I said.

He looked bored at my analogy. He lifted his buffed manicured hand and said flatly, "Lyric, are you blackmailing me?"

"Richard, get a clue!" I said. And I knew exactly what Joshua meant.

"If I were you, I'd be very careful."

"Likewise!"

After Richard left, I thought about what had happened. I was in shock. Just like that, my life changed in an instant. That was scary. One moment I was planning my wedding in my head, the next I'm planning Richard's destruction. I knew he'd think long and hard about what I had said. He'll weigh his options and realize I have the upper hand in the situation. I just hope he doesn't try to call my bluff. Time was something I didn't have. In a little while he'd realize I wasn't pregnant and he'd win. And I *hate* to lose.

I felt nauseous after my fourth glass of Absolut, or was it champagne? I wasn't feeling well; I ran into the bathroom and threw up. I made up my mind to see a doctor first thing tomorrow morning. Since when couldn't I hold my alcohol? I tucked myself into bed and tried to fall asleep on a nauseous stomach and now a headache from stress and worrying. How the hell can you go to sleep like that?

46
JOSHUA TUNE

This morning it was exceptionally cold in the courtroom. I glanced over at Monique and her eyes were icy. Water would freeze on her ass in Hell. She was tight–lipped because I was about to get one up on her. Judge Madden and I go way back, and even though it's unethical, judges pick favorites all the time and tend to rule in their favor. I knew she adored me, and I played upon every ounce of her vulnerability. Every time Monique made an objection, you heard, "over ruled." I'd smile and look over at Monique and her co–counsel. Monique was meticulous though; she'd have her argument noted for the record. Her case was taking a beating from my slick maneuvering, and she didn't like it one bit. At this moment, she was expressing her displeasure to the judge about the testimony of the defendant's mistress.

Monique: "Your Honor, I have a request. This past Friday, October 10, I was served with a further response to discovery demand. Mr. Scialla and I were notified in court by counsel that the next person was also a witness. Your Honor, we have the name of an individual we have not been provided previously. We don't know whether this person is going to talk about being a friend or an actual eyewitness. Nevertheless, we request under the provision of CPLR 3101(a), that the prosecution be precluded from offering the testimony of this witness. We were not provided with the name, address, or identity of this person before, nor were we provided with any information as to what this individual would testify. We had previously been advised of other witnesses, but not of this individual."

The Court: "Counselor?"

Joshua: "Yes, thank you. Your Honor, Miss Hamilton is a liar!"

Monique: "Judge!"

The Court: "You're on very thin ice counselor. You'd better watch your step in my courtroom."

Joshua: "Well, to clarify this matter, it was on Thursday, October 9, rather than Friday, that we hand–delivered to the office of the defense notification of the name and address of this witness. Counsel knows she is not an eyewitness. Her testimony will be offered on the issue of a relevant conversation the defendant had with her regarding the murder of his wife. Moreover, when a case is put on the calendar, does that mean the investigation is supposed to stop? I still continue to seek out individuals who have something relevant to say, and the moment that we discovered that this person was cooperative and had information pertaining to the case, we immediately identified her to the defense. Your Honor, in the interest of justice, I would respectfully urge that the defense's application be denied, and that she be permitted to appear and testify."

Monique: "Just to make my point. Evidence that my client has committed a crime that's similar in nature, or one equally frowned upon, would promote a bias in the jury. They will be more likely to believe that he actually did kill his wife and render a guilty verdict. We would like to refer the Court to several Appellate Division decisions, which speak to this issue. The first is Williamston v. State; the second, Collins v. State. In both those instances, the late identification of a witness resulted in an erroneous decision by trial court to permit the testimony, only to be appealed finding a decision by the Appellate Division to order new trials because of that erroneously admitted testimony."

The Court: "You want to be heard?"

Joshua: "Your Honor, she's tap dancing around here. First of all the crime of fornication is not similar to murder. It's not heinous or violent. It is highly unlikely that the jury hearing that he had an affair would be sole cause to convict him or infer the defendant is a murderer. And the admission of improper testimony does not always warrant a new trial. The testimony can be so minor that it would be unlikely the defendant was prejudiced. Kaplan v. State makes that quite clear."

The Court: "Anything further, Miss Hamilton?"

Monique: "No, nothing further."

The Court: "As to the preclusion of the witness, well, in light of the fact that apparently this is a witness that was discovered only recently, and that you had been advised about them last week, I'm going to allow the testimony."

Monique: "Your Honor, I think—"

The Court: "You've been heard counselor!"

I smiled discretely at the judge, then over at Dominick, my co-counsel. We'd won this case. I already knew that and the feeling of victory was exhilarating. The defendant wasn't looking too pleased with his attorneys. I don't know if he knew what had gone on, but I'm sure he knew it wasn't good for him. His eyes said he was ready to go "postal" at any moment. He started to fidget around in his seat. The wood chair he was sitting in scratched the floor and made a screeching noise. Monique observed how agitated her client had become, so she leaned down and touched his arm to explain the situation. He yanked his arm from out of her grasp. This startled her. She pretended that nothing had happened and glanced nervously at me to see whether I had seen his aggressive ploy. I couldn't wait for the trial to end to be sure this animal was locked away where he belonged.

47
JOSHUA TUNE

"Whose pussy is this? Tell daddy . . . tell me!"

"It's yours . . . oh God . . . Josh . . . umm." I was making love to Monique on her dinning room table. I had her propped up with her legs spread eagle in a horizontal position. It had started to get really good when she said, "Whose dick is this? Tell me you cunt sucker."

My eyes flew open in horror, and not even two seconds later she slapped my face hard and said, "Whose dick is this?" I felt like a little sissy when I said, "Yours, baby . . . it's all yours." Then she started screaming, "Fuck me harder . . . harder . . . harder!"

That was music to my ears. I pumped in and out with gusto. I loved when she spoke nasty to me, it turned me on. Though I have to admit she could be a little controlling at times. She flipped over and let me enter her from the back. At first I thought she just wanted back shots, but when she told me to put it *in* the back, I thought I had died and gone to sex–heaven. I have always wanted to experiment with anal sex, but never found a woman uninhibited in that area. All of them were either too scared or too frigid. I entered her with ease and from then on she had me babbling like a baby. I came so hard, I screamed "Sweet Jesus!"

Exhausted, sex sweaty, with an exaggerated case of the munchies, we somehow managed to make it to the bedroom where we both collapsed face down on her king–sized waterbed. After she picked up the phone and ordered Chinese take–out, I finally got the wind back in my lungs. I was a satisfied man until she said, "I make love to you better than your wife, don't I?" I just smiled because I didn't think she seriously wanted an answer but she probed on. "Answer me."

"I thought it was more like a statement, you know you satisfy me."

"That wasn't my question, counselor," she retorted. Her voice was stern and demanding. The situation started to become uncomfortable.

When we first started this affair, she had barely mentioned Parker; I was the one always bringing Parker up, dumping my problems from home onto Monique's lap. Now the tables were turned. All she does now is bring up Parker and my marriage. "What's going on?" "Are you happy?" "How does she treat you?" And now this.

"It's different," I stated honestly, and then continued, "When I make love to you, it's hard, exhilarating sex. There's always an element of surprise. You don't look like you fuck. I know that surprises a lot of men. When I'm with my wife, it's soft and loving. Like she's a baby who needs nurturing. She makes love to me like she *needs* me. Also, inside, you two *feel* different. She's long and deep as if her pussy doesn't end, and when I enter her, her pussy grabs hold of me every thrust and never lets go. When I'm inside you, your pussy lets me explore."

I turned on my side so I could see her face to face. As I looked in her eyes I could swear they had turned dark. She didn't say anything for a long while, so I said, "What are you thinking about?"

"You're still having sex with your wife?"

"Well, I am married. That's what married people do."

"I thought I kept you satisfied."

"Monique . . . don't go getting insecure on me. I love making love to you. You two are just . . . different. There's no other way to say it. Besides, you asked the question."

"Baby, I could never be insecure. There's no other woman that can cook better than me, fuck better than me, or look better than me. There's no other woman smarter than me or can dress better than me. I was just trying to see where your head was. Making sure you didn't go getting all–sentimental because I'm fucking you so well. I wanted to make sure you were still getting it on with your wife, because I would hate to have to break your pompous heart."

She wrapped the sheet around her naked body. I admit she had game. I guess that's why she was a top trial attorney. But I'm better, so I said, "If I wanted to leave my wife today, you wouldn't have me?" I raised my right eyebrow to show her my curiosity. She looked me directly in my eyes and said with a voice I'll always remember, "If you left your wife for me, you'd leave me for the next pretty face. I wouldn't respect you."

Her words grounded me. I felt like a fool, thanks to Madison convincing me that Monique was after Parker's wedding ring. As I said from the beginning, all Monique was after was a good time. And I was the man giving it to her.

Monique got up to take a shower and I stayed in bed relishing the moment. When the water came on I decided to join her. Thinking about her smooth skin lathered up with soap, made me grow an erection. With my penis rock–hard, I opened the bathroom door without knocking and Monique was sitting on the toilet sniffing a line of cocaine. My hard penis quickly deflated as I watched in shock.

"Either come join me, or close the door behind you," she stated.

I wasn't sure if she was referring to the cocaine or the shower.

48

I prayed as I took every step to the trashcan in my bathroom. I held my breath, and then bent down on my hands and knees. I carefully took out the condom we had just used. I looked at the juices inside the latex and wondered if it was enough to get me pregnant. I had read that when women want to be artificially inseminated, the sperm is injected inside of them. They pay thousands of dollars for this procedure. I was going to do it myself for free. I put the sperm filled condom inside a small plastic cup. I stored it in the back of my freezer among the frozen steaks and ice cubes. Tomorrow, I would purchase a syringe, for an emergency situation, and insert the crème inside me when I was ovulating, but *only* if I had too. Until then, I will pray everyday that I won't be forced to do something so deliberate. Unfortunately, the only thing that can save my relationship right now is a baby. I have no choice. I *need* this pregnancy! I don't want to lose him.

49
PARKER BROWN-TUNE

"Peace."

"Yes."

"May I speak to Monique?"

"This is she . . . who am I speaking to?"

"This is Parker. Parker Tune." Silence from the other line. So I continued, "I'm Joshua's wife."

"Yes . . . Parker. He's told me so much about you. How can I help you?"

"Well . . . I um . . . I wanted to know . . . how exactly do you know my husband because he hasn't told me anything about you."

"What?"

"Please don't be upset that I called. I know this is forward of me, but sometimes you just never know."

"Know what?"

"Are you sleeping with my husband?" I said flatly. There was no more room for beating around the bush. She let out a coy laughter and I couldn't help but get jealous. She sounded so adorable on the phone. I hated her instantly. I was imagining how beautiful she must be. I couldn't tell from her voice if she was white or black though. Not that it really mattered. But they usually were black. Then she said, "Parker, I've known your husband since we were in high school. He's an old friend of mine. We've never dated before and we never will. I know he's married happily because you're all he talks about."

"I must sound like a neurotic wife. I really apologize for calling you under such extreme circumstances but ever since I found your number, he's been coming home late. I thought there was a correlation. I thought that he could be spending his spare time with you."

"Oh . . . we're opponents on a case. A high–profile case that I know we both want to win for the same reasons. I'm up late with my co–counsel all the time. But no one suspects me of having an affair with him because he's an old fart." She laughed and this time I laughed with her. She eased a lot of my tension, but intuition told me that Joshua was not up late working on a case. He was seeing someone; she was just the wrong someone.

"Monique, will you do me a favor?"

"Depends."

"Can we keep this conversation between us? Joshua will be very upset that I called you."

"Listen, girl, one thing that is fading is unity. We're sistahs. No one should be able to break our bond. If enough women stuck together, men wouldn't get away with half the shit they pull."

"You got that right."

"And don't be embarrassed that you called me either. I've done the same thing before myself. I was dating this guy and I had totally lost all my senses. I was doing stakeouts, drive–bys, g-i-r-r-l, this brother had me strung. I had turned myself into a stalker. I called the sistah that he was dating, and she said she didn't even know him. That I must have the wrong number. She didn't know I had been parked outside her home for two hours. Had watched him go in!"

"Yeah, some women don't mind being the other woman. I have to admit, I was never down with that program."

"Amen! But again, Joshua and I are only friends." Monique and I talked for well over an hour. She was so nice and she understood my situation. I told her everything Joshua and I had been going through. She was attentive, even asking questions. Intimate questions too. It felt good having a new ear to spill my problems into. Most of my friends were tired of me telling them the same old scenario. When we hung up, she told me I could call her anytime; she'd always be there to listen cause she knew how it was with these no–good men.

Now I have to go down to the spy shop and see what gadgets they have. My girlfriend Michelle told me about this place off 3rd avenue in Manhattan that had all the equipment I'd need to catch an unfaithful husband.

That was the easy part. The hard part is figuring out what I'm going to do if I find what I'm looking for.

50
PARKER BROWN-TUNE

Michelle met me at Bloomingdale's. We walked three blocks to 61st Street and 3rd Avenue to the spy shop. It was placed neatly between a bakery and a pet store. We stood outside looking at the gorgeous puppies in the window. I knew not to go in because they'd be too expensive, but one puppy kept calling me. It's little paws kept tapping the glass for my attention. When I turned to leave, the puppy stood on its two back legs and started to bark. It had straight black and brown hair. I asked Michelle to wait a moment while I ran inside.

When I went inside the storeowner told me that the dog was a girl. She was called a teacup Yorkshire Terrier. Her frail little barks were calling me "mommy." My maternal instinct kept saying, "purchase her."

"How much?" I asked the storeowner, who was ignoring me and catering to this uppity–looking black couple. As I stood there quietly waiting for her to acknowledge me, my patience grew thin. I cleared my throat but she still made no response. Finally, I aggressively tapped her on the shoulder. "One moment," she retorted. The two customers and the storeowner were standing admiring a baby Shitzo. No one was saying anything; they were just giggling, saying, "Ooh and ahh." Finally the couple asked how much. The storeowner replied, "$1000, but if you purchase him today, I can give him to you for $800, no tax. That's a great bargain."

After another ten minutes went by and the sale of the puppy was complete, the storeowner walked to the back of the store to fix some dog chains that were out of order. I wanted to explode but I kept my cool to see how far she would push it. I casually walked to the back and said, "I've been waiting here patiently for twenty minutes to be assisted."

"Really?" She said with a phony smile. I ignored her and continued, "I wanted to know how much the little Yorkie in the window is?"

"It's Yorkshire Terrier, dear. Are you looking for a companion?"

"Yes," I said ignoring her arrogance.

"They're very expensive, but you look like you can afford it."

"Well, I won't know until you tell me the price."

"She is $1200. But I can give her to you for $1100 plus tax."

"You gave the other couple a better deal."

"That's because you are purchasing a teacup. She won't get any bigger than three pounds."

"My husband will kill me if I make such an expensive purchase."

"What does your husband do?"

"He's assistant district attorney for King's County."

"Then I'm sure he can afford it. Besides, you look resourceful. I'm sure you'll think of something to explain why you made this purchase. You have such beautiful hair," she flattered and smiled circuitously as she led the way back to the puppy in the window.

Michelle came inside and rescued me. She had a 3 p.m. meeting so her time was limited.

"Either we go to the spy shop now or not at all!" Michelle stated.

"Spy shop? Well dear, that gives you even more reason to splurge at your husband's expense," the storeowner retorted.

The spy shop was small, but it had a lot of catalogs to look through. Whatever you didn't see in the store could be ordered and you'd have it the next day. Not bad. A young salesman came to help. He had to be in his late teens, early twenties. Probably a college student. It was difficult, but I discretely told him that I suspected my husband of cheating and asked if he had anything I could afford that could help me.

"How do you want to catch the adulterer?" he said. So much for assumptions. "By the way, my name is Robert," he continued.

"What do you mean 'how do I want to catch him'?"

"Is he screwing her in your bed, in your home?"

"I resent that remark. I'm not sure he is seeing anyone at all!" I was defensive.

"Sure you are, that's why you're here. Take a look around, ninety percent of our customers are women. Women who know. They just want proof so they'll get more than half, if you know what I mean."

I looked around the shop and saw he was right. The majority were women. Women in full–length mink coats and huge diamond rings. This was so sad. I didn't want to bust my husband to get a divorce. I wanted to bust him so he could see that what he was doing was not worth losing me for. Sometimes we all need a reality check.

"No. To answer your question, I don't think he's screwing in our bed."

"Then there's no need for you to get a surveillance video set installed, is there?"

"No, I think that would be useless."

"You never know. Many men screw other women right in the comfort of their own homes. Could I interest you in something small? We have the world's smallest video cameras, the size of a dime. Come look, I'll show you."

He led us to an array of video cameras. Some were installed in beepers, tie clips, flower pots. Everywhere. Technology was amazing.

"How about the new time–port X380 camera? It can take a photo up to two blocks away. He'll never know you were in the vicinity. It's on sale for $3,000."

"That's ten times too expensive. Anyway, I don't want a picture. I want something more concrete."

"Well, how much do you have to spend? We have a private investigator that could follow him around and give you a minute–by–minute replay of his day events."

"He'd kill me if he ever found out."

"Then kill him first." He said it in such a matter of fact way, it made my skin crawl.

"Have you ever used any of this equipment?"

"Yes. I used the telephone recorder and found out my fiancé was screwing my brother. I heard conversation after conversation. It's amazing how much a person will say when they don't have a clue someone's listening. It was one big joke." He looked bitter. But who wouldn't be after that revelation.

"Well, how much is the telephone recorder?"

"Two hundred dollars."

"I'll take it! Why didn't you tell us about this first?"

"I work on commission."

51
PARKER BROWN-TUNE

"What the fuck is this?" Joshua exploded as soon as he walked through the door? I jumped at his outburst. I was so jumpy lately, always trying to please him. Immediately, I felt as though I had done something wrong once again. I said, "It's a puppy. Her name is Sasha."

"I know it's a fucking puppy! What is it doing in my house and how much did *Sasha* fucking cost?" he exclaimed. I noticed he hadn't taken off his overcoat so I started to panic. I hoped he wouldn't storm out of the apartment. I feared he'd go to be with his mistress so I lied.

"She didn't cost anything. Lyric brought her for me because I confided in her that I wanted a baby and she figured this would cheer me up."

"Do I look like dial–a–joke? Lyric wouldn't buy her mother ice water in hell. She's frugal. Besides, she doesn't like you. Where's your pocketbook?"

"Why?"

"Parker, don't make me ask you twice." Joshua's blue eyes had turned so dark they looked brown. Sasha started to bark and that only made matters worse. I ran over to the sofa and retrieved my pocketbook. I handed it to him, not knowing what he was going to do. He went into the kitchen and poured my contents onto the table. Then he pulled out a couple of credit card receipts until he found the one. My hands began to tremble in anticipation of what would come next. Joshua lowered the receipt slowly, then calmly he said, "Do you think I have $1500 to waste on a puppy? Didn't I tell you we were broke?"

"Yes, Joshua."

"Didn't I say we needed to save money, and that you should cut back on spending?"

"Yes, Joshua."

"So, can you explain to me like I'm a six–year–old kid, how spending $1500 on a puppy and puppy accessories is cutting back?" His voice was so soft it scared me.

"I'm sorry Joshy, but I'm lonely. You're never home anymore."

"I work!" he bellowed.

"You're not working all the time."

"Stop it! Don't try to turn this situation around. The dog's going back!"

"I can't take Sasha back. You don't understand. The owner treated me like I couldn't afford Sasha and if I return her, she'll feel vindicated."

"Parker grow up. I'm warning you you'd better do it fast. You *can't* afford the damn puppy stupid, you don't work."

"Well, you do and you're my husband. New York law says that a spouse is entitled to half of everything accumulated by the couple during their marriage. So I'm worth half of you. I've been signing my name on the dotted tax line for the past two years, so I can certainly afford a puppy!"

I kneeled down and picked up my petrified puppy. She rewarded me with a thousand licks to my face and mouth. He had to be crazy telling me to return her. She was giving me the most affection than I've received in weeks. He breathed in and out for a moment trying to digest the situation. He slowly went to the kitchen drawer and pulled out a pair of scissors. He went to my wallet and cut up every credit card I had, including my ATM debit card. I had about twenty bucks in my wallet so I was furious. Then he gave me a long look and went right back out the front door.

"Joshua!" I called after him. He gave no response, so I called his name again then ran after him. He was descending the front step; his stride pompous and steady.

"Joshua, where are you going?" Still no response. We were outside now and he was heading for his car. I still had Sasha in my arms and she was shivering. I realized that it was around thirty degrees outside, and I didn't have a coat or shoes on. I started to turn around and go back inside the house but determination pushed me on.

"Joshua, can we talk about this? Please . . . don't leave!" I was begging him and still he kept ignoring me. I reached out to grab his arm and he yanked away from me. Tiny drops of rain began to fall on my face, but still I kept running behind him until we were at his car. He flipped the alarm switch and hopped in. Thinking quickly, I ran around to the other side of the door to open the passenger side but he was much faster than I was. He locked the door and put the car in reverse. I ran along the side of it tapping the window and calling his name. By this time, I was soaked and shivering. The rain was so heavy now it felt like tiny needles were penetrating my skin. But I was immune to the pain because the pain in my heart was much greater. I ran in front of his car so he couldn't move, hoping he'd sense my desperation. Our eyes locked through the glass and he said, "You'd better move or you'll be sorry." I stepped back aimlessly, and he sped off into the night.

Inside my apartment, I screamed out of anguish. I punched myself in my face, my chest and legs over and over again. I pulled at my hair and scratched at my face. I wanted to die. I felt lost, lonely and distant from my husband. I was in so much pain! I cried out of frustration and fear. I was losing my husband and there wasn't anything I could do. The pain was so intense and felt so heavy. Couldn't he see how what he was doing was affecting me? Couldn't he see how much I loved him? What could I do? God, please tell me what I can do? I know his new mistress can't love him like I do. Love him for him only, and not his car, money or status. She was probably some nickel and dime whore from the projects, no education and no goals. Someone who would do anything he said with the intention of taking him from me. Believe me, I know the games women play to get a man because I've played them as well, but never with someone's husband.

I lay in bed in the dark, listening to the storm dissipate. As the taps on my window became faint, I convinced myself that I still had hope, that this storm too would pass . . . slowly. I mean, why am I feeling so insecure? Josh hasn't asked for a divorce. He hasn't asked for a separation or even moved his clothes out the house. He loves me. He's just going through something right now.

52
MADISON MICHAELS

The circumstances surrounding my living arrangement with Maurice were not what I'd hoped they'd be. Ever since he got that new car, it seemed to replace me. It's all he talks about. The car needs service. The car needs a wheel alignment. The car needs. The car needs. What about what I need? I need my man to be at home with me sometimes.

Then there's the issue of always working late hours. They screwed him up at payroll during the transfer, so he's not getting paid at the moment and that's leaving everything unbalanced. I like stability in my life. Monotony. Furthermore, he's changed his shift at work, so he sleeps during the day and works nights, while I work during the day and wait up for him at night. All I do is sit around and wait for him to suggest something. I no longer do things alone such as going to the movies or museums. I don't go hang out with Lyric; in fact, I don't even call her. I don't go out with Joshua unless Maurice can join me. I've devoted my whole life to Maurice, and I love it and hate it at the same time.

I decided a hot bath would soothe me. After I bathed and put on a soft teddy, nothing too revealing, I pulled my hair back and put on some Victoria Secret Pear Body Splash. Maurice loved the scent. I took a long look in the mirror and saw a fat pig. Maurice was always complaining about my weight. I told him a little white lie that I was on a diet. Well, it's not all a lie. I am trying to watch what I eat. Honestly, I've always felt like a full–figured woman. The perfect size ten. And if I wasn't so shy, I would be flaunting my size 34–D cup breast in every man's face to get attention, but that's not me. My figure has always embarrassed me because I'd see the way men would look at my body and disregard my face, mind, and personality. But I NEVER felt like I had a weight problem until now. Maurice is right; my thighs are too big. My butt is too big and my size nine feet are too big according to him. He was quick to recognize that I don't have any ankles. Just leg and foot.

As I sat around the loft just pining away, I decided to light some candles and wait for Maurice to come home. Two hours would go by before the telephone rang. I rushed to it hoping it was Maurice because I was worried. I hoped he was all right because the line of work he did was so dangerous.

"Hello."

"Who's this?" the female caller asked.

"This is Madison. Who am I speaking to?" I really shouldn't have given my name to an anonymous caller, but it was already done.

"Madison, this is . . . um . . . Tina. I want you to do me a favor."

"A favor?"

"Yeah, I want you to go look underneath your right pillow. You do sleep on the right side of the bed, don't you?"

"Who are you and what do you want? What is this about?" I continued. I was very wary about this person, but nevertheless, I kept her on the line as I went to do what she'd said. Something inside me, maybe it was instinct or intuition, but something made me do what I was told. As I walked into the bedroom with the cordless phone, I could hear her whispering to someone, then giggling. As I held the phone with my left hand, I picked the pillow up with my right and there they were. A pair of red, lace, crotch-less panties. I threw the phone down and screamed in horror. Who? Why? I picked the phone back up and said, "Who are you?" My voice cracked in between each word.

"Ask Maurice bitch!" Click.

"This isn't happening" was all I kept telling myself in an effort to remain sane. I repeated the words over and over again while sitting in the corner of my living room. My body was trembling like I had just jumped into a tub of ice. I tried to control it, but at this point I couldn't control my speech. I was mumbling, crying, screaming and most of all I was scared. Did this mean that he didn't love me anymore? Did this mean that I would be left all alone again? I was sitting Indian–style but transformed myself into a kneeling position and started to pray. I asked God to please make this pain go away. I wanted to go and vomit the pain like bad food. I wish pain from the heart was that easy to get rid of. How could Maurice make love to someone in my bed? My conscience kept telling me that Maurice was sleeping with someone in my bed on my sheets. But my heart kept saying it was all a misunderstanding.

53
MADISON MICHAELS

Minutes felt like hours and my mind was running rampant with all sorts of obscene sexual positions of the two of them making love. She didn't have a specific face yet, but my mind equated her with beauty. I decided to go to my refrigerator and throw away all my fat snacks that just a moment ago I wouldn't let go of. I threw out all my ice creams, cookies, and cakes. I bet she's a perfect size six. She sounded like a perfect six on the phone.

I had the lid to my garbage can off, and it was damn near full with cookies, cakes and donuts. I was in a frenzy by now. Dumping ice cream down the sink and sodas, I was sweating profusely and crying all the same. My hot tears were mixed in with my salty sweat. I no longer smelled of Victoria Secret Pear Body Splash. I looked down at my plain nightgown and felt nauseous. I know I called it a teddy, but the reality of it was it was nothing but a nightgown. Then I rushed into the room to examine the panties. I picked them up to see the size. They had a "Pink Pussycat" label that read size medium. Medium? She could be anywhere from a five to an eight. I bet she was that perfect size six though. If I didn't have so much butt, I bet I could squeeze into these. Could she be a size ten? Well, I wouldn't know unless I tried them on.

I prudently took off my panties and began to try hers on. I needed to know if these would fit. I got them as far as my hips then gave up. When I took them off, I wondered what kind of woman could wear panties with the middle cut out? Lyric came to mind immediately. I asked myself if I could wear those and my answer was a firm "No." Then I rephrased the question and asked, "Could I wear those for Maurice?" and my heart said "yes" before I could finish the sentence.

When I heard his key hit the locks, I jumped up from out my sleep. I had fallen asleep on the kitchen table and my neck and back hurt. I had drooled down the side of my face, which had now crusted up, and my eyes were bloodshot from crying all night. It was a little after 5 a.m., and I could smell the liquor on his breath from outside the door. Maurice fumbled around with his key until I finally walked over and let him in. When I opened the door, he stood there for a moment looking at me. He belched, then pushed passed me and stumbled towards the bedroom. "Maurice," I called after him but he didn't answer. He kept moving in the dark ignoring my voice.

"S-h-i-i-i-t-t! Fuck!" he screamed. Then he did a one–leg hop to the edge of the bed. He'd hit his toe on the living room end table. "Ooooh, it hurts," he whined as he took off his shoe and began to rub his toes. I clicked on the light and immediately began to massage his foot. Without saying a word, I went and got a basin and filled it with warm water and Epson salt. I took off his other sock and placed both feet in the warm soothing water. He just closed his eyes and lay back in the bed. Ten minutes would go by before I had the courage to say,

"Maurice . . . who's Tina?"

"I'm asleep."

"No . . . you're tired, but you're not asleep. Please baby . . . tell me who's Tina . . . she called here tonight looking for you."

"I don't know any Tina!" His voice started to elevate and he kicked the basin that held the water, which splashed everywhere, then continued, "Don't start no shit tonight, girl. I'm not in the mood. You know I've been drinking. Now take your chunky ass in the kitchen and eat a pork chop or somethin' to occupy your time, but please, leave me alone."

"I don't think you need to be mean. I'm asking you an important question. Someone called *my* house, a female, who I don't know, asking to speak to you. I just want to know who she is," I said.

"Your house, huh?"

"Look, Maurice, right now we have some issues that need to be addressed. My house. Your house. Let's just put that aside for a moment. My feelings are hurt right now because I think you're being unfaithful to me."

We were standing face to face, and he was breathing that liquor straight up into my nostrils. All signs of being sloppy drunk were gone, and he seemed coherent. He took one step back, cocked his head to the right side, then said, "Say, Madison. If I was messing around, what would you do?" His voice was cocky and he appeared overconfident.

"I can't answer that question until you answer mine. No hypothesis." I was visibly shaking and I knew he could see me. What would I do?

"Are *you* cheating on me? They say that the one accusing is the one doing."

"You know I'm not that kind of girl."

"I don't know shit except my name!"

"Maurice, I was a virgin. How can you say these things to me?"

"*Maurice I was a virgin!*" he mimicked. Then he continued, "For all I know you could be fucking that white prick Joshua. Girls play that 'virgin' game all the time. All you had to do was contract your pussy muscle."

He was looking at me with contempt, as if he believed every word he'd just said. He had taken the evidence of my innocence, something that I thought was special, and made me question if I really had been a virgin. I was left standing there, clueless, trying to figure out how this conversation had gotten turned around.

Maurice stepped into the bathroom to take a shower. I waited patiently until he came back out looking refreshed with a monogrammed towel that I'd brought him wrapped around his torso. By this time, I'd refocused on what I needed to get out of the way. Before I could say anything, he rolled his eyes and said, "You still up?" He was visibly annoyed.

"I waited up to talk to you Maurice." I walked over to my side of the bed and picked up the red panties.

"Who do these belong too?" I had held them up in front of his face so he could see they were not mine. With a quick gesture, he slapped the panties from my hand. "Get that shit outta my face," he roared like a tiger. Frightened, I slowly backed away because alcohol can make some people violent. My hand was stinging from the blow, and my instinct said to back off. I turned around to get in bed when he accosted me.

"Didn't I tell you about turning your back on me?" I had no idea what he was talking about, but I played along anyway.

"Yes."

"Then, do I look like a glass of fucking water? Transparent? Do you think you can just fucking ignore me when you're ready?"

"Maurice . . . I wasn't . . . I–"

The first slap made an echoing sound in my ears. I never saw it coming. I felt dizzy and a sharp pain penetrated from my right ear to the back of my head. My eyes couldn't focus before more blows came and left me blinded with my eyes swollen shut. I tried to collapse on the floor and cover up my face but he had a tight grip on my hair. I felt tufts of my hair being pulled out. I felt blunt blows to my face, head and arms and I was screaming. "MAURICE . . . PLEASE STOP IT. YOU'RE HURTING ME!" He just continued to hit me more. Pound after pound, I tried to imagine when he'd ever stop hitting me. He seemed to enjoy it. Finally, when the pain became just pressure, and my whole body was numb and I couldn't move another inch or scream another word, he stopped.

The bitter taste of blood would linger in my mouth until I was finally over Maurice, and although I didn't know it back then, that was the first sign that things could only get worse. In the dawn of morning, Maurice helped me into a bath to wash away what he'd done to me. He'd cried and explained that he'd just lost control, and that this would never happen again. He asked me whether I could ever forgive him? And I answered "Yes," because I knew I could. I loved him.

54
LYRIC DEVANEY

"Congratulations, Miss Devaney. You're pregnant."

The doctor was wearing a white cotton hospital jacket with a stainless steel stethoscope around her neck. Her flaming red hair had been pulled back in a tight bun, and she had on thick, black–rimmed, 60's cat–shaped glasses. Her buckteeth were protruding through her thin lips. She had a very elegant voice, and it appeared she came from wealth. I could always notice such things.

"What did you say? I mean . . . I can't be." My hands immediately went to cover my stomach. I looked at the doctor, who was smiling. "What are you grinning about?" I snapped. I wanted to slap that smile so hard; it was killing me to keep my composure. She took a couple of steps back then buried her face in my file, then said, "You're twelve weeks pregnant. I thought you would be pleased. If you are not, there are other options. Naturally I'll have to refer you to another physician, I don't carry out abortions."

"Why do you automatically assume I would want an abortion? Because I'm young and black?"

"Young? There must be a mistake here; your chart says you are about thirty–five. Is that correct?" Oh, she was trying to come for me, but I did not have time to put her in her place. I had too much on my mind. I ignored her last remark, went to the calendar on her wall, and counted back twelve weeks. Just as I had expected I had no idea who the baby's father was.

Twelve weeks before, I had quite some weekend. I had had sex with three men in two days. First Richard, then Jay Kapone, and then that freakazoid rapist Erious.

"Doctor I'm keeping my baby. Therefore, if you have to, write out a prescription for vitamins, iron or whatever I am paying you to do. I suggest you start writing. My time is valuable. I am starring in a major motion picture. I'm going to be a star."

"Everyone is dear," she contested. "Didn't you know you're in Hollywood?"

Her words were reassuring and her voice was soothing but something about her was irking me. I took my focus off her and thought about keeping my baby.

Lyric with a baby? For some weird and wonderful reason I felt satisfied. Of course, she will be an only child so she can be spoiled just like her mother. She's going to private schools, ballet class, archery, horseback riding, ice skating, singing lessons, fencing; and she's going to have piano lessons whether she likes it or not. She will do everything I was not able to do.

Now, who could be this child's father? If I prayed to God, I would ask that he not let it be Jay Kapone. Nobody wants an ugly little child. If my daughter comes out ugly, what will I do? You cannot give it back. Everyone will laugh at me. Inside they will be overjoyed that Lyric Devaney brought an ugly mongrel into the world. Maybe I am being too hard on Jay Kapone. He has good qualities the child can pick up like being softhearted. Is that good or bad? Softhearted people always are fucked over. My mother told me that when I was knee high. By the time I was five, she was already giving me 'bitchology lessons' (that's what momma called it). Showing me the ropes about life. Teaching me reasoning and logic. Not the kind you learn in class, but the real McCoy. What you need to know about the streets and how to survive. You're either a survivor or a doormat. You choose. It's either one or the other . . . no in between.

I kept thinking about Jay Kapone being the father and got increasingly disgusted with his looks. Not to mention, Jay Kapone doesn't have the finances I need to support this child. Children are a liability, not a luxury! Naturally, I want Richard to be the father. Richard will bring culture into my child's life. Richard knows all about Leonardo DaVinci, Socrates, Aeschylus, Michelangelo, Monet, Winston Churchill, and just a slew of interesting people. My daughter will live a life of opulence.

I cannot wait to see Richard's face when my pregnancy starts showing. I will do something like show up at Gracie Mansion or at one of his fundraisers with my belly sticking out holding my back and doing that fake pregnant walk I see all the women doing for attention. He will start sweating, and his face will turn beet red and his small beady rat eyes will grow large with horror. His heart will probably give out on him at that moment. Oh, I cannot wait. I cannot help being so mean. I guess I don't know any other way. It satisfies me explicably.

Now, if the baby turns out to be Erious Jerome's baby, I will be set for life. Erious' money is as long as his dick. I wonder if I should marry him. He's worth over $400 million. If I married him, I would get half easily. However . . . he is a rapist, and I just cannot get with his morals. I have self–respect. Anyway, those child support–checks every month will be enormous. I'm not taking less than twenty thousand a month!

The more I think about my baby, the more excited I get. This baby is some sort of blessing . . . like Jesus. A gift or something from a higher power. God, Allah, Messiah . . . I don't know who, but somebody has blessed me for a reason. I can do this. Shit . . . I can do anything I want. I'm Lyric Devaney and nobody had better forget it!

55
LYRIC DEVANEY

Traffic going towards LAX airport was at a snail's pace. I pulled my black Cadillac Seville rental onto the emergency service road and rode the shoulder lane about five good exits before I was pulled over by a state trooper. "Fuck," I said underneath my breath as I saw the flashing lights through my rearview mirror. I contemplated making a run for it to avoid getting a moving violation on my license. I had already picked up two speeding tickets out here. I can't wait until this movie has finished shooting. I'm missing New York and my cozy duplex.

One more exit and I would have been off the highway and heading toward the Delta terminal. Madison and Portia were coming here to visit, and I didn't want to be late. I could see Madison panicking if I was not at the gate to meet her. She surprised me when she agreed to come and see me. I've been trying to get in touch with her for weeks but she's never around. If I asked when she was coming out, she'd give me an evasive answer. Finally, I got them both to agree to come at the same time. I paid for their plane tickets and neither complained about riding with the other one. I wanted to tell my two friends in person that I was going to have a baby before the press got wind of it. I'm showing a little bit, not much, and my morning sickness is gone. I'm four months along and I know that if this film doesn't wrap soon, it's going to cause problems. I'm doing a great job at hiding it from the crew, and I wouldn't dare let that bitch Terisa find out. Once my scene is done, I don't hang out on the set. I retreat to my trailer. And when the day is over, I head straight to my hotel room. I've been watching what I eat and taking my vitamins and fiber on the regular. I want a healthy baby, and I realize that I'm responsible for her health. She needs me. This baby makes me feel whole.

"License and registration," the trooper demanded.

"Why did you pull me over?" I replied to the officer who was looking like he was having a bad day. Why do we always ask the obvious when it comes to getting a ticket?

"I said license and registration, gal. You don't ask the questions! I ask the questions from here on out. You understand me?" He'd put his right hand on his gun holster to make a statement that he was in charge of the situation.

"What did I do? Some wild maniac ran me off the road!" I lied, still trying to avoid getting a ticket.

"Let me ask you for the last time. Do you have a license? Pull out the goddamn registration!" he shouted. I noticed he was riding alone so his car must be recording everything that was taking place right now. But since I'm black and from Harlem and we don't have respect for the police, I said, "You need to be out chasing down some real criminals, and leave the honest taxpayers alone!"

"And you need to respect this here badge!"

"Oh, fuck the badge. And while your fucking the badge, go fuck your mother!"

"Excuse me! Did I hear you right, gal?" His southern twang was stabbing at my eardrums. "Do I smell marijuana?" he continued. Ignoring his question, I reached in and pulled out my license and car registration.

"Get out of the car. I think I need to search the vehicle for narcotics. You look under the influence."

"I ain't under no damn influence of nothing, asshole!"

"Well, you have to be under something talking to me the way you just did. I could lock you up for disorderly conduct!" I jumped out the car and let his nosy self check through the entire vehicle until he was satisfied.

"You can get back in the car."

I sucked my teeth and rolled my eyes very ghetto style. Or is that considered childish?

"Do you know why I pulled you over Miss . . . Devaney?" I looked straight ahead and continued to ignore him.

"Oh, you're a smart aleck, aren't ya?" Still I had no response for him. He swaggered to his patrol car in his tight polyester pants and riding boots, to write up my ticket. He purposely took nearly twenty minutes probably to make sure every 'I' was dotted. When he came back, he started his idle conversation again. Sometimes I think those lonely fucks pull you over just because they are bored.

"Now Miss Lady," he said, voice as sweet as sugar, "if you weren't so cute, I would have had you in handcuffs by now. Anyway, I gave you one ticket for riding the shoulder. You can plead 'Not Guilty' by checking this box right here on the back and mailing it in to this address. But I don't suppose you'll do that because you're from out of town. New York City, is that right?"

Still I didn't respond. "Well anyway, you can plead "guilty" and mail the fine in to this address right here on the back of the ticket. And since you wanted to be a smart aleck, I also gave you a ticket for not having on your seatbelt. Now I know the law in New York City may not pay too much attention to those sort of things, but out here in California we obey vehicle traffic laws. Now where are you heading to?"

I still didn't respond. Why is it when these cops pull you over they're immediately rude and condescending? But once their deed is done, and all tickets are written out, they want to get to know you better, have a nice conversation with you, and fill you with bullshit chit–chat. Anyway, once he politely put BOTH tickets in my hand, I replied, "Officer, why are you still standing here. I said for you to go fuck your mother!"

I burst out into laughter, ripped the two tickets up, and threw them out my window. Joe Pesci would have been proud.

56
LYRIC DEVANEY

That behind me, I slowly made my way into the airport. I parked in short–term parking and still had a good ten minutes to spare before their flight arrived. Despite being totally annoyed at what had just happened, I still felt elated about my life. I was almost where I wanted to be. I was making big future plans, and I was just about to live out my dreams. The first thing I'm going to do when I get back to New York is purchase my mother a mansion. Something with nine bedrooms, outdoor and indoor Jacuzzi's, swimming pool, tennis courts, just whatever her little heart desires. Wait a minute. Maybe I'll just purchase her a modest home and purchase myself a mansion. I mean, what is my mother going to do with all that room? She doesn't entertain like me. And what would be the purpose of both of us having mansions? That's just a waste of my money, and when you're purchasing mansions, $15 million can run out pretty quickly. And besides, we don't need all our poor ass relatives coming out the woodwork shacking up in my mother's home. No, I think a modest home will satisfy her. As a matter of fact, I thought I should call her and see what she thinks. I haven't told her about my pregnancy yet.

My adrenaline started going again as I pushed her number on my cellular phone.

"Hello," my mother's raspy voice cracked. I could tell she had been drinking because her voice always got very hoarse.

"Mother, darling, how have you been?"

"Lyric, my baby, why don't you call me more often? You still out there in that L.A. with those gangs, those Bloods and Crips?"

"Yes, momma. I'm still working on the movie."

"Did they pay you yet?"

"Yes, momma. I've already been paid."

"Well good! You can send me some of that money because I'm not doing too well out here. The government done cut my food stamps in half and the hallway light has been out for two days. I called housing four times already. They said they was going to send someone out to fix it but ain't no one came yet."

"Momma, when did they cut your food stamps?"

"Last month. It was that awful Mayor Cardinale."

Ignoring her last remark, I said, "Why didn't you tell me sooner?"

"Lyric, you know I hate to bother you. You done moved out the projects and forgot about your own mother!"

"Momma, don't lay that guilt trip on me right now. I'm calling because I got good news."

"You know the projects ain't what it used to be. You know when I moved in Amsterdam Projects back in 1960, there wasn't ANY black folks livin' up in here. It was one other black family and me in this whole development. That's when it was only working white folks living here."

"Mother, darling, you've told me this story a million times. Didn't you here I said I have good news?"

"I don't know why I taught you to disrespect me so. Go ahead Lyric. My time is yours."

My mother sounded a little dejected. Her attitude would normally take us into a lengthy argument but not today. I said, "Momma, I'm pregnant." I smiled the words out. I heard a loud moan of disapproval, and it sounded as if she was choking on her dentures. She regrouped then said, "Lyric, how many children do I have?"

"One momma."

"And why did I tell you I kept that one child?"

"Because you were a fool."

"And what did I teach you not to be?"

"You taught me not to be a fool like you."

"So what do you call yourself right now?"

"Mother, darling, this is different than your situation." I so desperately wanted my mother to participate in my joy.

"Lord. Lord. Lord," was all I could hear her mumbling to herself.

"Mother, will you please stop and listen to me for a minute?"

"I done told all my friends my daughter is going to be a movie star. And you done thrown your career away before it even got started. See I had an excuse for my life turning out the way it is. I had you back in 1962. Back then abortions were illegal. You lay on one of those butcher tables and you may not see tomorrow. You ain't got any excuse. Abortion is as legal as liquor. All you gotta do is pay."

"Mommy, I'm not having an abortion!"

"Lyric Maria Devaney! Don't go getting soft on me. Girl, those just your hormones talking. Don't you know woman get all sentimental when they're having a baby? Soon, before you know it you'll be crying. Tell the truth, you been doing any crying?"

My mother went on and on until I said the magic words, "Momma it's different now because I have money." I stopped her mid–sentence.

"What you mean you got money? Compared to me you've ALWAYS had money. Just ain't want to share none."

"I can't go into details but I got enough for the both of us. As soon as I get home I'm getting you out the projects and buying you a little house of your own."

"You'd do that for me?"

"My momma didn't raise no fool!" I stayed on the phone with my mother for another five minutes before I saw Portia waving to me. She had on the latest Chanel shades and her long hair was pulled back with a mink pigtail holder. I could see she was sporting the matching black and white Chanel sneakers too. I was impressed. I also had those sneakers but mine were red and white. Portia was definitely screwing someone with a little paper.

"Lyric!" she bellowed out like I was the movie star I would soon be. We ran to each other and embraced like we hadn't seen each other for years. I admit that I genuinely missed her. We each took a step back to admire how the other one looked. I just had on a gray DKNY sweatsuit to hide my pregnancy. I practically had every color. Sweatsuits are all I've been wearing since I found out I was pregnant. I still looked sexy as hell even hiding my figure. A closer look at Portia and I could see that she had on a set of diamond earrings. The clarity was excellent. My anger began to build. So she purposely wore her hair pulled back to show off? She NEVER ties up her long, unstylish hair. I should have known she was up to something, graciously accepting my invitation to come out here with *Madison*. My eyes immediately turned from sincere to penetrating hard glares. Portia pretended not to notice my expression and flashed the latest nylon black Prada knapsack up under my nose. I also had this knapsack, which I purchased in Barney's New York for $800. My pressure was up, but then I examined her accessories closer. I mean she was trying, but no fashion award would be handed to her. Now maybe if she would have confided in me that she wanted to upgrade her wardrobe, I could have given her a few pointers. For instance, she had on the Chanel sunglasses and the matching sneakers. Plus. Then she put on a pair of Parasuco blue jeans (although, they did make her appear to have a heart–shaped ass) with a Polo tank top. Minus. And, yes, she had the Prada knapsack. Plus. She loses her points because she didn't have the matching carry–on luggage. Minus. In fact, she showed her true colors because she had the $29.99 luggage on wheels that every flight attendant in America sports. Then and there, I decided to allow her to try and dress like me. Why not? She could never pull it off completely anyway. And to show her that I'm not intimidated by anyone, I would even take her and Madison shopping this weekend at my expense and show them how it's really done. Show my girls some love. I looked around trying to find Madison so we could get this show on the road.

"Lyric," this unfamiliar woman was smiling a familiar smile. She looked sickly and undernourished. Her eyes were despondent and she held my stare, challenging me to say something.

"Yes? I'm Lyric Devaney . . . where do I know *you* from?" I said this with mucho attitude. I don't know why. Just because.

"Lyric, stop playing, it's me, Madi." I immediately looked at Portia and her eyes met mine with a hopeless expression. She shrugged her shoulders and I immediately became sick to my stomach. This person . . . Madi . . . was maybe fifty pounds soak and wet. She was as bony as the night is dark. She'd chopped off all her hair locks and strangely tried to go all–natural. Her nappy hair was begging for a perm and a weave. Her clothes were hanging off of her and her face looked gaunt. Her eyes were pulled deep in their sockets, and to be frank, she looked like a crackhead. Like she'd been hitting the pipe for the last two months. "What have you done to yourself?" I screamed, my pressure immediately rising.

"I've been dieting," she said with pride. She smiled and her teeth were yellow and stained. She repulsed me. She was either missing something or doing something. I hoped it wasn't the latter. I reached deep into my DKNY sports bag and pulled out my gold–framed Cartier shades and a DKNY baseball cap. I could not be seen with this creature.

I hurried up and ushered my friends into my car. I needed to get to my hotel room and find out what's been going on in New York while I was away. I promised one thing, and that's that Joshua's going to catch hell for not giving me the 4–1–1. I don't care if we're not speaking; Madison is my friend too.

57
LYRIC DEVANEY

"Madison you look sick!"

"I look slim. There's a difference," Madison walked over to her bedroom in the suite and put her bags by the bedroom door. Her jeans looked dingy and very worn while her shirt swallowed her whole upper body. Madi used to have large breasts but now they appeared as if they had dried up because I didn't even see an imprint. She's on a sick trip because her breasts were her greatest assets. She reached inside her cheap black leather bag and pulled out a pack of Newport cigarettes. I openly gasped.

"Yo, chill, how you know I ain't wanna sleep in that room?" Portia couldn't help being narcissistic. I don't know who made this chile think she was better than everyone else was. She ran over to each bedroom to inspect which one she thought was better. While she tediously wasted her time, because the rooms were identical, I had more important things to straighten out. But first, I had to get rid of Portia so I could talk to my friend.

"Don't tell me you started smoking," I scolded.

She inhaled for a good five seconds as if it were pot, then exhaled a couple of circles in the air. She'd probably saw this same move on a late 70's show. Madison had on that dark chocolate lipstick I see all the darker sisters wearing which I can't stand. It makes their already dark lips appear black.

"Portia . . . could you do me a favor and take my driver down to the set and pick my script up for tomorrow. It has the last two scenes I'll be shooting."

"Why can't you do it? I coulda stayed in the 'hood with my momma if I wanna get ran 'round like some maid," Portia challenged.

"Well," I started off, slowly biting my tongue from responding with a sharp remark, "I thought we'd go shopping today, then go club hopping, but first I have a meeting with one of the executives from Endless hair coloring and I thought we'd kill two birds with one stone. And I'd really hate to run into Winston Love." I threw Winston in for security. I knew her groupie ass wouldn't hesitate to go do this fictitious errand. She'll be gone at least an hour and that should be adequate enough to see what's the deal with my friend.

I thought Portia would never leave, but once she was gone, I tore directly into Madison.

"What the hell's gotten into you?"

"Lyric, don't start no shit, okay. I'm grown." Now it was my turn for my eyes to pop open with horror. I know this little heifer didn't just swear at me. "Excuse me?"

"You heard me twice the first fucking time!"

"Oh no you d–"

I couldn't even finish my sentence because she had gone into the room that I'm paying for and slammed the door. I started to run in there after her and jack her up, but I could see she obviously had some issues that needed to be worked out. I couldn't wait to call Joshua up and bomb him out. I didn't even wait for him to say "Hello." I yelled, "Why didn't you call me and tell me Madison needs to be committed!"

"Lyric, what are you talking about?" he seemed distracted, as if I caught him at a bad time.

"Madison came out to California looking like a poster child for a crack ad."

"Crack . . . California . . . slow down and tell me what's the deal. Is Madi alright?" I really hated the way he genuinely cared for Madison. I knew I had his full attention. I felt a sharp pain of jealousy, but I ignored it and concentrated on my friend's condition.

"Joshua, Madison weighs . . . maybe . . . ninety pounds. She looks sick and she's talking about being on a diet. There's no way you can lose nearly a hundred pounds in the time she's lost it and still be considered healthy."

"What are you talking about? She weighs ninety pounds? Are you sure?"

"I don't talk just to be talking. I was just looking at her! Don't act like you haven't seen her! She works for you."

"I haven't seen her. I've been going straight to court every morning and when I get to the office she's already off to school. Christ! My secretary told me she's been out sick these past few weeks, and I've been so consumed with my own goddamn life, I couldn't even make time to go see her. I kept saying I'll get around to it."

"This is all your fault. If you could keep your pecker in your pants, you would have more time to realize she was going through something."

"My fault? What about you, Miss self–centered. And what about Maurice?"

"Whose Maurice?"

"The boyfriend she's shacking up with."

"What!"

"Long story."

"Listen, she's tripping. This guy must have her on Quaaludes or Ecstasy because she's acting crazy!"

"No. He's a straight–up kind of guy. He's works for the F.B.I. Maybe they're arguing or something. You know how you women trip."

"Correction. Some women trip! Did you have this guy checked out?"

"Checked out? Why would I do that . . . he seems cool."

"You mean Mr. Overprotective Joshua didn't have Madi's first boyfriend checked out?"

"We have dinner . . . work out at the gym together . . . he seems okay."

"Well, Madison is definitely not okay but the picture seems a little more clear. He must have dumped her, and she's having a hard time getting over it. I feel much better now. I'll take her out on the town, take her shopping, and show her a good time. She'll eat at the best restaurants, Spago, Lenny's. When I'm done with her, she'll have forgotten all about this creep."

"You think that's the case?"

"Yeah."

"Ummm . . . if you find out differently let me know. I'll fly out and see what I can do."

"Your presence is not needed."

"You just had me thinking Madi was using drugs. If I can help, don't hesitate to call me."

"Oh, she's in bad shape. But I think the sun will do her good. Did I mention she chopped her hair off and is puffing on cigarettes?!"

"I'm on the next flight out!" Before I could try to persuade Joshua into not flying out, he hung up the phone. I didn't bother calling him back because I knew he'd come out anyway to check on his Madi. That's what I get for opening up my big, fat mouth about the cigarettes.

58
LYRIC DEVANEY

The shopping mall in Santa Cruz had the best department stores. I thought we'd start there and work our way to the boutiques on Rodeo Drive. Saks Fifth Avenue was holding a pair of Gucci sandals for me. The Gucci store had sold out my size, and after having them check all their stores, they concluded they were completely sold out. The salesman at Gucci said, "Why don't you try Saks?" So I did and Saks came through for me.

After picking up the shoes, it was time to do some major shopping. I wanted to go into Ralph Lauren because their fall collection had a pair of riding pants I needed to have in my closet, and this is where the drama began.

"I don't wanna go in no tired–ass Lauren. I want somethin' fly like Moschino or Versace!" Portia always had to be seen. "Portia, you can go into those sections. I have my cell phone, call me and we'll hook back up later. But right now I just explained I want those pants."

"No . . . I'll chill."

"Oh, if you're worried about the money, you can take one of my credit cards and sign for me. Don't worry about the cost . . . spend as much as you like."

"Lyric I gotz my own doe. I don't have to use plastic . . . I got paper!" Portia went into her Prada knapsack and pulled out a wad of cash and flung it in my face. It was probably more money than she's ever seen at one time in her whole life. I immediately got a headache. It just started pounding. Here I am trying to be all nice and courteous, and she was trying to break me down. So she's dealing with someone who has money. Big fucking deal. I've been dealing with hustlers since I was fourteen. I've since graduated to millionaires. But since Portia wanted to play . . . I'd show her just how far I could go. Instead of feeding into her bullshit, I decided to see whose money or *credit* was better.

Meanwhile, Madison was oblivious to everyone around her. She was in deep thought and I wished she would confide in me. I picked up my size six riding pants and was going to walk with them over to the sections Portia wanted to visit, when she picked up a pair herself and said, "Oh, these are phat! I'mma get a pair too." We both knew Portia didn't have anywhere she'd actually wear them, but she put the game in motion for me. So I said, "Madison, why don't you grab a pair too. What size are you now?"

"I don't like those."

"Well, what size are you anyway?"

"I don't know."

"Well, why are you dieting if you're still going to wear your old clothes size? Those jeans are falling off you."

"I have new clothes. I just didn't bring them with me. I want to save them for special occasions." Her last comment fell on deaf ears. She sounded pathetic and looked the same.

Portia and I carried our Lauren pants into the Versace section first. I used to love Versace until every hoodrat had to have it in their closet. Whether they stole it or fucked for it, they got it, and it just wasn't the same stepping out in Versace anymore for me. Plus, the colors became too flamboyant. A little too much gay flare was going on. But his couture collection is always fabulous and very expensive. So that's what I headed straight to. Meanwhile, Portia wanted to stay in the $200 jean section while I was in the $2,000 couture section. I grabbed two of everything I could hold and tracked Portia down in the dressing room. "Girl, I found us the hottest pieces. No one is going to have this shit. I even think I found us the perfect gowns to wear for my premiere." I thrust the clothes I wanted her to purchase in her hands, and I caught at how she tried to see the price tags without letting me suspect anything was wrong. Inwardly I smiled.

Madison came inside my dressing room cubicle and sat on the bench with a forlorn look. I wanted her to confide in me about what she was going through, but I thought it would be best for me to give her time to absorb it herself. I'm sure when she's ready to let it all out, I'll be the first person she'll speak to. I felt like our relationship had loosened a little bit, and I secretly wondered if we had drifted apart. Were we still as close as we used to be?

The DKNY sweatsuit came off with ease. I looked at the little pouch I was carrying and blew my baby a kiss. Madison was still looking down at the ground in deep concentration. I slid into this silk and chiffon, lime and dark green Versace gown and I knew this would be the dress I'd wear to my premiere. I still had about four other gowns to try on, but I knew this was the one. My now larger breasts seductively draped the front area, and my little belly was playfully sticking out. I looked adorable. Since Madison was in her own world, I decided to pull her out.

"Madison, what do you think of this dress."

"It's fine," she said not looking at all.

"Madison, you haven't even looked at me." I don't know why I was talking so sweetly. I felt like an angel. I think my mother was correct about the hormones making me sensitive. Slowly Madison looked up from the floor and her eyes focused on me. Her jaw dropped six inches while she sat there dumbfounded. "Well . . . what do you think?" I said.

"You're . . . you're . . . "

"I'm pregnant!" I cried. Unable to contain my excitement, I did a bunny hop around the dressing room. I sat next to her and looked my friend in what should have been happy eyes and when I saw the deep despair, I nearly lost it. Madison burst into tears, screaming and saying, "Oh, God . . . please help me." She was hysterical and hyperventilating. The sales associates heard the commotion and came banging on the dressing room door. I flung open the door for help. Madison was kicking and screaming and banging her head up against the wall. She looked like someone who just wanted to die to end all the pain she was going through. Everyone stood around in shock not really knowing what to do.

Then Madison stopped her frenzy and became unconscious. I felt anxious and looked around for Portia who was probably the only one who ignored the chaos.

"Portia!" I screamed. She bolted from her dressing room, naked, and ran straight towards me. She pushed through the crowd took one look at me, then at Madison, and immediately took control of the situation. I was trembling with fright. What if Madison was on some sort of drug and had just overdosed?

Portia told the sales rep to call the paramedics. The sales rep did as she was told. Then she cleared the area saying Madison needed air. She bent down to Madison and put some dresses underneath her neck to elevate her head. Madison was sweating profusely. Portia lifted Madison's eyelids then checked her pulse. It finally dawned on me that Portia's grandmother had been a registered nurse and must have shown her granddaughter how to keep someone stable. Portia reported that Madison's pulse was faint and that the ambulance had better "get the fuck here soon!"

59
LYRIC DEVANEY

When the ambulance arrived, two EMS workers came running back to where Madison was lying on the floor. The two men stopped only briefly to admire Portia, who was completely naked bending over Madison. They scooted Portia to the side and began to work on Madison. Portia stood there watching over her to make sure they knew what they were doing. Then the sales rep said to Portia, "Why don't you go and put some clothes on, dear. They know what they're doing. Your friend will be fine."

"I dunno who told you you could tell me what da fuck to do. I know I ain't got no clothes on! These men done seen 'nough pussy not to be affected by me. And besides, you're the only one clockin' me. So why don't you go take your lesbian ass back up front and handle your peoples. This here is a good friend of mine!" she bellowed. The old conservative woman smoothed down her suit and twisted up her face at being called a lesbian, deciding that it was too much profanity and nudity for her to take. She took Portia's advice and headed back out on the floor without uttering another word.

The EMS workers asked me a slew of questions.

"What happened?"

"I don't know."

"Is she taking prescription medication?"

"I don't know."

"Is she on any drugs?"

"I don't know." My brain was not functioning because of the panic. They told me what hospital they would take Madison to and asked if I knew where it was located. "Yes," was all I could eventually say. I still didn't know if Madison was going to live or die, and I'll admit, I was frightened.

Portia had to come and help me undress, so we could go meet Madison at the hospital. My hands were still trembling. "I know you ain't pregnant!" She said in astonishment. Suddenly, the news wasn't so joyful.

"Yeah."

"I know you ain't keepin' no baby!"

"Portia, not right now. Can't you see I'm traumatized? My best friend could be dead!" I snapped.

I didn't see the hurt in Portia's eyes, but I heard it in her voice when she said, "I thought I was your best friend. I've known you longer." Was she serious? I had to definitely pull myself together. I ignored her and slapped her hands away from around my waist. I didn't need this shit. I could undress myself. I put back on my sweatsuit and gathered my clothes that were thrown around the dressing room floor. Unfortunately, Portia and my war of the cash vs. credit cards would have to wait. I went to the register and did a charge/send because I didn't have any time to spare. When Portia saw I was still going to purchase my things, she ran back into her dressing room and gathered her outfits. To my amazement she had a couple of the items I had given her. When the sales person told her with a smile her total was $5,432.01, Portia didn't flinch.

"Do you want to open up a Saks charge card? You get 10% off your first purchase."

"No, thank you. I'd like to pay cash." Portia was talking very politely and proper. No ghetto twang was escaping her lips. She pulled out a roll of cash and counted out fifty–five crisp hundred–dollar bills. She patiently waited for her change while I impatiently waited for her to wrap this up. I noticed she still had maybe a grand left over. With Saks shopping bags in tow, we scurried out of the mall.

The hot Santa Cruz sun immediately warmed up my ice–cold body. I kept imagining walking into the hospital and the doctor saying, "Miss Devaney . . . we did all we could. She's gone." Portia had to drive the Lincoln because I was in deep thought. What could send a stable person like Madison over the edge? She appeared to be so solid and focused. Now, I, on the other hand, was always out of control. I felt something when I saw her flipping out. Like something inside of me wanted to join her. After all the turmoil I've been through, I'm amazed that I'm still here with my head held high. Every negative situation has seemed to only make me a stronger person. Some say God will only give you what you can handle. I'm an example of that. But what about Madison?

In New Patient Registration I gave Madison's name. "Are you family?" the clerk asked.

"Yes . . . I'm her . . . niece . . . Lyric Devaney. Perhaps you've heard of me?" Publicity for the movie was tremendous. Everyone was anticipating the opening date for "Silk." The clerk squinted her eyes then screamed, "Oh my goodness! Oh my goodness! It's Sassi! Tasha come here quick! Look . . . it's Sassi from Silk!" Her co–worker came running, joined with two other individuals.

They surrounded me and began to ask for my autograph. I was flabbergasted. They praised me and told me how beautiful I was, and I enjoyed every compliment. So this was a taste of stardom? It was welcomed. More people came to see what the commotion was all about. Some stayed and wanted my autograph too, while some just looked at me with no enthusiasm and kept walking. They were probably looking for a bigger star or not moved by celebrities at all.

Portia finally tugged at my shirt and reminded me that we were here for a reason. "I need to see my aunt." I reminded the clerk who had initially helped me. She walked Portia and me to the "Triage Unit" where Madison was lying on a bed sedated. She looked as if she was fighting demons in her sleep. Her eyes kept twitching, and her face looked frightfully odd. Before I could ask questions, the nurse on duty said she would go get the doctor, so he could speak with me.

The doctor came in and explained that Madison was anorexic. From the marks imprinted inside her mouth, she was sticking her fingers down her throat and purging. He said that she was undernourished and dangerously underweight. Her heart muscles had gotten damaged and were very weak. What he'd said next took Portia and me by surprise. "She's eight weeks pregnant, and the baby is in danger of having a birth defect. Her actions have been hard on the fetus."

"Is she going to lose the baby?" I said to the sympathetic doctor.

"We're doing everything possible to keep her and the baby stable. She's sedated now, but when she wakes up, she's going to have to work with us. Someone will be coming in to talk with her once she comes to. But for now, she needs her rest. She'll be fed intravenously until she gets her strength back."

"So what . . . like she's crazy? 'Cause Lyric said she was bugging out," Portia replied.

"She's not crazy. She's suffering from a psychological disorder. When people suffer from anorexia, they see themselves as fat. No matter how much weight they lose, they still see that same fat person. The therapist will explore the issues behind what made her go through this metamorphosis. And how she can control it. But she will need lots of love and support."

"Doctor, how long will she have to undergo therapy? She's not from here. She lives in New York." I thought how lucky I am that Joshua was on his way. I couldn't deal with Madison and her problems right now. It's like having a child before I have a child.

"She will have to remain in the hospital at least two weeks or at least until her weight is at an average level for her height. Then she can have out–patient treatment in New York if she chooses."

"She doesn't have a choice if it's going to make her better."

"You're wrong. Therapy is a choice. The patient has to want to get better. At any moment, she can sign herself out of the hospital."

"Well, I'm sure she'll want to get better for her baby," I chimed.

"I hope you're right about that. You ladies don't have to wait here. She won't wake up until tomorrow. Come back tomorrow during visiting hours and she'll be able to talk." The doctor talked a little more, then led the way out of the hospital and into a lot of questions and insecurities.

Joshua arrived around midnight California time. He looked so professional with his trench coat, briefcase and somber look. "I hope you brought a change of clothes in that briefcase because you're going to be here for a while."

60
PARKER BROWN-TUNE

Maybe . . . life isn't so bad. For the past two weeks, I've been having deep, meaningful conversations over the Internet with a wonderful man I met in the chat room. He's absolutely charming! We're both being very cautious, but we both want to meet each other. His name is Timothy and he's described himself as tall, dark–chocolate and handsome. But what I like most about him is he's editor–in–chief of Success Magazine. I've pitched my interior decorating idea to him and he thinks it wonderful. Further, he encouraged me to pursue my idea about having my own television show, educating people on how to interior decorate their homes to replicate celebrity homes but not at celebrity prices. Joshua is so negative regarding my career that I felt reluctant to share my aspirations with him or anyone.

Fortunately, Timothy made me feel so comfortable that eventually I opened up to him. He also said that if I'm as good as I say I am, maybe, the magazine can do a spread for me!

Yesterday during the chat, I think he actually wanted to have cyber–sex! I deterred the conversation but I'll admit he had me excited. I felt vibrant from the tips of my toes to my artistic fingertips. When Joshua finally did come in, he went off screaming about his "Goddamn telephone bill." I really wish he would lighten up or give up his mistress because she's not doing anything for his personality.

At first I was depressed thinking that there was something wrong with me. That was until I was home one day watching talk television. The host had a guest on her show that said men like Joshua are insecure and have low–self esteem, and they need women to help build up their confidence. They think that these women are catering to their needs, but in reality, *they* are the dependent ones. They are constantly looking for something because they are not happy within. That one television show gave me the push that I needed because, before that, I was mentally a mess.

Now I disregard Joshua's yelling and have stopped screaming along with him totally. But he keeps yelling for attention. Just screaming about whatever he feels is wrong at the time. I think he's noticed a change. I'm no longer begging for his attention or questioning where he is because, truthfully, I don't care. He's the one losing out on my good loving! I think there's a breaking point in relationships for everyone. I put up with his philandering long enough. I've cried enough tears, and I put in more than my fifty percent. So, why not leave him? I've thought about that on numerous lonely nights and the reason I stay is because I married him for better or worse. I'm hoping that this is the worse part of it and that eventually it'll get better. My husband is successful and has a future ahead of him. I want to be a part of that. I want to share his joy whenever that comes. Why should I let her have the glory after I put up with all the pain? Don't misinterpret what I mean. If Joshua ever humiliated me, I wouldn't hesitate to greet him in divorce court. I know he's disrespecting me by having affairs in the first place, but he respects me as well because he never parades his mistresses out in public, and once I find out, he usually gets rid of them quicker than you can blink. Notice, I said usually.

This latest fling has become time–consuming for him, and he seems reluctant to drop her. That bothered me for some time but since time heals all wounds, I've become a little numb to the pain. Perhaps I've convinced myself that she's a loser just like the rest of them. The last one was a stripper; this one probably works the grill at McDonalds. Isn't it funny that if the other woman has no accomplishments, it makes you stronger in dealing with the situation? But if she turns out to be a brain surgeon with a home in the Hamptons, you'll want to slit your wrist. That's the awesome power of the mind. Psychology has never been my thing.

61
PARKER BROWN-TUNE

Anyway, I've been so caught up in my Internet romance, I haven't had time to follow-up on Joshua's affair. I have about eight tapes that I secretly made of him using the phone, but I haven't listened to any of them. I would have bet my life wild horses couldn't keep me away. And they haven't . . . a cyber man has. How illogical is that? Anyway, I have to prepare mentally before I go listen to what I know will be devastating to me. Can I handle knowing? You always meet women who dig and dig for the truth regarding their mate's infidelities, and when they hear or see something that blows their minds, they totally lose it. They can't handle it and breakdown. My question to these women is "What did you really expect?" I already told myself that nothing is sacred and as long as the man thinks he can get away with it, he'll take that chance. I even think it makes the relationship more exciting for them living on the edge like that. You read that a man was murdered because he got caught in some man's bed screwing the wife. So you say, "Why would she sleep with someone in her own home where her husband lays his head? Did she want to get caught?" Truthfully, I feel it's the element of surprise. The prospect that you could get caught is a big turn on for some people.

Something I'll always remember is when I was twenty I found out my live-in boyfriend was sleeping with my roommate Susan. Once the truth came to light, I dropped the both of them. He came begging and crying to be back with me, and I told him "Go be with Susan." He looked at me and said something I'll never forget. In a raspy voice he moaned, "Once you found out about us, it took away the thrill. I realized what made her exciting and sexy to me is that we had to sneak around. Once you took that out of the equation, and I was free to be with her . . . I didn't want her anymore."

Secretly, I respected his honesty at a time when he'd been so dishonest. But this splurge of honesty did nothing for our relationship. I never got back together with him. I decided that he needed to be taught a lesson and that lesson would be losing me. Women don't realize how much power we have because we're always trading that very power in to be, excuse my French, assholes! Don't we realize that men are only as strong as we let them be? If I had taken my boyfriend back, it would have sent a message that this was acceptable behavior. Some may believe that everyone makes mistakes; I'm also a believer of this logic, but we need to realize that some mistakes are forgivable and some just are not! It hurt me to let him go because I thought at the time I was in love. But something in me just didn't want to trade my power in to be an asshole. I told myself if I'm hurting this bad about breaking up, he's hurting as well. He spent just as much time with me as I spent with him. Something in me wonders if I was stronger back then? If I've resorted to settling for a piece of a man. I haven't answered that question yet because the response may be painful. I'll admit I have compromised myself since I've been married. I also think that since I'm older now, looking at the prospect of growing old alone is frightening. Who wants to be divorced at thirty–four looking for a man? That partying scene is scary because you go to the clubs, and there are girls out there half my age grabbing the attention of the men in my age group. Look at Joshua dating someone barely eighteen years old. How can I compete with those opponents? I think I like having a security blanket.

TAPE I

"What are you wearing?"

"Can't you say 'hello'?"

"I wanted to skip preliminaries today. Tell, daddy, how much you miss me."

"Umm . . . daddy . . . I miss your big, white cock."

"What do you want me to do with my big cock?"

"I want you to jerk off then bust all over my chest . . . then . . . "

"Yes."

"I want you to slide it up and down my big, ripe breast . . . "

"Then what?"

"I want you to ram it into my wet, tight pussy!"

"Okay."

"Then I want you to fuck me hard and fast!"

"Like this?"

"Just like that daddy . . . umm . . . daddy do it harder. Harder!"

"Do you want me to cum?"

"Not yet daddy. I want you to flip me over and spank my ass hard!"

"Like that?" (smack, smack)

" . . . Umm . . . yes-s-s-s-s! Keep fucking me...your love's supreme."

"Who pussy is this?"

"It's yours daddy . . . all yours."

"Let me taste the pussy . . . open up for me."

"Ohhh . . . don't stop."

"Damn! You got some good pussy."

"You want to hear it?"

"Yeah . . . let me hear the pussy."

"Swish . . . swish . . . swish."

"Jesus, Mary, and Joseph! I love you . . . let me hear it again. Let me hear the pussy calling for me again."

"Swish . . . swish . . . swish. Like that?"

"Yeah baby . . . I'm getting ready to cum . . . ummmmmm God! Shit!"

"Me too . . . ohhhhhhh . . . aaahhhhhh. It feels so good!"

TAPE II

"Hey baby."

"Hey."

"You sound down. What's up?"

"I don't know if I can do this any longer. I mean...I thought I could handle you having a wife . . . but now my feelings are involved and everything is out of control. I think I want to see someone else."

"You know that would kill me. I can't bear to see you with another man. You mean too much to me."

"I'm starting to doubt our relationship."

"What do you mean by that?"

"If you love me . . . really love me...you'd let me leave you because I'm unhappy in this relationship. Emotionally, my needs aren't getting met. I'm in love with a man who's in love with someone else."

"No. You're in love with a man who's in love with you. Pumpkin . . . don't you know I'd run through hell with gasoline briefs on only if you were waiting for me on the other side."

"You're in love with me and in love with your wife? How can that be?"

"I love my wife . . . yes . . . but I'm in love with you! I can't explain what I exactly mean . . . but if I could walk away from my marriage without anyone getting hurt . . . I'd be with you in a second. Parker is not as independent as you...she needs me. She's a needy person."

"So stay there! I'm in love with you yes . . . but I am nobody's fool. Technically I am a free woman. So that means I can see who I want, when I want."

"I thought you told me that you didn't want me to leave my wife for you."

"I don't."

"Then what are you asking me to fucking do?"

"I'm telling you to re–examine your feelings. If you love me, then you should want to leave your wife for your own happiness not mine. Why should you stay with someone you're not in love with? Then once that's done, you should start to think about sharing happiness with me. I'll be here. But the truth will be, you left your wife because you wanted to, NOT because you met someone new!"

"Why do I feel like you're double–talking me?"

"Look . . . I know that this may be difficult for you, but you allowed yourself to be in this position. You pursued me . . . and now that you have me . . . it appears you can't maintain me. You're leaving me no choice but to take myself out of this equation. Not just for myself . . . but for your wife. Since she's so needy as you put it . . . I'll leave you alone and let her have you TOTALLY!" *(click)*

TAPE III

"Sweetheart . . . why have you been avoiding my calls?"

"I'm busy right now, Joshua."

"Did you get the roses I sent you?"

"Yes."

"Uhhhhh . . . what about the diamond tennis bracelet?"

"Yes . . . I received that too."

"Well?"

"Well, what?"

"I'm trying to apologize here."

"Your approach is much too weak and cliché for me to fall prey to this game. If you haven't noticed, I can purchase my own roses and diamond tennis bracelet. But I must say, you went well out of your way. I'll add that it would have been appreciated if I had received those gifts from someone who belonged to me, not some other woman's husband. Was there a two–for–one sale going on?"

"I didn't buy Parker anything!"

"Well, maybe you should have."

"She doesn't warrant those types of gifts. I look at you and see you deserve the best money can buy. You have class. Parker wouldn't know the difference between faux mink or the real thing."

"Please, Joshua . . . don't go off on another Parker tangent. I'm sick of fucking hearing about her! You think it's some sort of consolation if you speak about her negatively? Is that supposed to boost my ego?"

"No . . . not at all. I'm just trying to show you that I can separate you two and that I don't take you for granted."

"Joshua, I have to go. I have company and I'm being rude."

"Tell him to wait!"
"Did I say it was a 'him'?"
"How long have you known him?"
"Two weeks now."
"Have you slept with him yet?"
"No, I haven't slept with him."
"Well, why does he have to wait so long? I didn't.
You expect me to believe that bullshit?"
"You can believe what you want . . . but believe me
when I say it's over!" (click)

I sat there with embarrassing tears streaming down my face. Tape after tape I told myself that I could handle it. The humiliation was overwhelming, but I remained level–headed. I had this innate feeling that people actually marry for the moment. And commitment or for *"better or worse"* was just standard rhetoric. Actually, I would have been glad to stop listening after the first tape, but I needed to know who this mystery woman was. Her voice sounded so familiar I almost lost it and dialed my sister Tonya in Philly to accuse her of having an affair with my husband. But whoever she was . . . this predator was manipulating my unsuspecting husband.

You know, you come to terms with your mate having an affair or affairs and you know that sex is involved, but you think that's all they share with this other person. You tell yourself it's an unattached sexual relationship. Then reality hits and you find out they share so much with these women. They call them the same pet names they call you. They buy them presents on their birthdays and holidays. They share the most intimate secrets about themselves. Things they made you believe they only shared with you because you were special to them. One part that stands out a little . . . notice, I said a little, is the roses and bracelet. Joshua keeps screaming we're broke and I'm limited in what I can spend, but he runs out in a panic and buys this bitch diamonds! How dare he? He gave her something she can look at and think of him whenever she needs to. When he's gone, that bracelet will still be sparkling as a reminder of what they shared. The only diamond Joshua has given me was my engagement ring, and to tell the truth, that's nothing to run home to talk about. But as he so eloquently suggested, I'm not worth the good stuff.

I took a break from the tapes to look over our credit card statements to see what else he had given her and how much he'd paid for the bracelet. I went back a good six months and totaled up forty grand alone on gifts and flowers. This last purchase cost him five grand, which is more than he spent on my engagement ring when he shelled out a measly twenty–five hundred. I no longer felt sorry for myself. The tears were long gone. I swallowed venom and went back to resume my purpose trying to find out who this bitch was. Up until now he'd never said her name.

TAPE IV

"You've reached the right number . . . unfortunately at the wrong time. But please don't hang up. Leave your name and number and I'll get back to you as soon as I can. Ta, ta. (Beep)."

"Monique . . . pumpkin . . . I really miss you. I want to solidify this relationship and take it to the next level. Honestly I understand your ambivalence and I want to change things and be the man you want me to be. Since I won the case we were trying . . . a lot of opportunities have come my way and I want to share them with you. I want you to be the first to know I'm running for district attorney, and I want you to be by my side. Umm . . . I don't want to keep on talking to a machine . . . but if you're there . . . or if you're not . . . give me a call when you feel up to it. Love you. (Kiss)."

62
PARKER BROWN-TUNE

God and ten horsemen couldn't hold me back from going to kick her ass! Monique–of all people! I suspected her in the beginning, but then she threw me a curve ball and played me. I confided in her and told her all the intimate details of my marriage. We'd even gone out for cappuccinos. I actually thought she'd be my new friend. I *wanted* her to be my new friend. She was so refreshing and honest, I thought. First impressions are priceless because they determine how you'll respond to someone and your outlook on their character.

Fear pulled at my heart when I realized that the woman Joshua was seeing was no flunky. She was a top attorney who was smart and conniving and noticeably didn't have a conscience. Those are the worst kind. "A person without a soul" is what I call people like her. Walking the earth, destroying, and taking pleasure in their destruction.

I laced up my Nike Air Trainers and hit the concrete. In twenty minutes it would be Monique and me, and there'd be nothing between us but space and opportunity!

I arrived at Monique's plush highrise apartment building in her upscale neighborhood realizing all she is a high priced whore. I thought it would be best if I snuck past the doorman; I didn't want to be announced.

When I arrived at her apartment, she had her music up very loud. I rang the doorbell twice but no one answered. My stomach was all twisted up from anxiety, but I kept my faith that she'd be home. But determination told me that even if she wasn't . . . I'd wait around like a stalker until she arrived. Much to my advantage she was doing weekend house cleaning because she flung her door open with two hands filled with trash to dump into the compactor room.

"Parker, you startled me," she said. If she was nervous, her eyes never gave her away. She responded to me as if I come over every weekend. "What's up?" she continued.

"Monique . . . I'm so upset . . . it's Joshua again. I needed to talk to you. I hope you don't mind me intruding on you without notice?"

I pretended to be flustered and helpless. She motioned for me to come in, then ran back out to dump her trash. I took the liberty of turning down her music because I didn't want to miss one lie she would tell.

She came back in smiling and asked me flatly, "How did you find out where I lived?" Her eyes were accusatory and immediately put me on the spot as if I had done something wrong. She had me so shaken up I almost said I had gotten her address through my girlfriend who works for the telephone company. Thank goodness that before I became a rat, I got my composure back. I was going to play into this, but I realized she was a savvy attorney and knew exactly why I was there. The gig was up.

And since I really didn't want to ask questions, only to hear lies . . . I immediately lunged at her and so it began. We tussled and tugged at each other, biting and pulling each other's hair. I thought this fight would be an easy win, but she was much stronger than I thought she'd be. I imagined I would be throwing her all around the place but she had fooled me. We both yelled obscenities at each other like, "Bitch, Cunt, Slut, Whore!" Nothing was spared in our verbal assault. As we fell into furniture, knocking over vases and television sets, I realized that I couldn't let her win. If I can only have one thing, it should be victory in this fight. If she was going to get the golden boy, I needed to walk away with the golden gloves. I mustered up every bit of strength and remembered my high school days. I remembered kids teasing me with words like "freckle face," and "funky dred." Then I put it on. I remembered how to headlock, back flip, drop kick, uppercut, body slam and stomp out my adversary! I grabbed hold of her arm and twisted it back with one hand, while my free hand landed several punches in her face. With one swift maneuver I flipped her over my back, and she landed on the floor with a hard thud. My left sneaker stomped her head into her parquet floors until blood squirted out from her nose. I wanted her to feel some of the pain I was feeling. I didn't realize she was screaming so loudly until I heard her say the two mind–numbing words, "I'm pregnant!" She screamed until I let her go. She was bruised and beaten and barely able to catch her breath before I made her say it again. "What did you say?"

"I'm pregnant . . . and Joshua's the father of my baby!" All the color drained from my face and I felt faint. I remember hearing a hard knock on her door, and before I fell to my knees, I heard, "Police! Open up!"

63
LYRIC DEVANEY

Everyone was euphoric on the set. This morning would be our last day of shooting, and then tonight, the producers were throwing a party in my honor. I only had one scene to re–shoot, and it had me uneasy. Jacob wanted me to redo the scene where I'm in a casket after overdosing on heroin. At first I had opted to have a closed casket, have it written in the script that my mother wanted it that way. But then I realized that could hurt the film. People would want to see me lying there looking beautiful just like Nikki Guy did in the original movie with a white dress and a white carnation in my hair.

Reluctantly, I gathered my thoughts and prepared for the scene by practicing my breathing. Jacob said that I was too jumpy in the casket, and it was visible to everyone watching that I was not dead. I had told him that I had four consecutive dreams that I was really dead and everyone was at my funeral crying, dripping tears of hurt, hate, joy and confusion on my sleeve. He told me that when you dream of being dead, it's not you who dies; it's someone you know that will die. That freaked me out too, but I must admit I was relieved that if someone was going to the pearly white gates before their time, it wasn't me. I think that's why I freaked out over Madison. Could she be the one my dreams were about?

Madison and Joshua would be joining me on the set as soon as Madison was discharged. Joshua went to pick her up from the hospital, while Portia and I came straight to the set. I hardly got a chance to see Joshua since he got here last week because every waking hour he's been at the hospital at Madison's side, trying to get into her head as if he's some shrink. He's hoping she'll open up to him, but he said he hasn't had any luck so far.

Portia and I have been enjoying California. We hit every nightclub out here. I gave the paparazzi something to talk about on every occasion. It's been helping create a buzz about my movie "Silk." The anticipation is phenomenal. The press said, "Not since 'Grease' starring John Travolta has a musical been expected to be a summer blockbuster!" I was photographed dirty dancing with married leading celebrity men. I let them catch me giving superstar singer Adina a kiss on the lips. But what I'm most proud of is a quote I gave to Angel Magazine, for an article they did on me regarding Richard. The issue drops a week before the movie hits theatres. And the photo layout I did was flawless. I would only do the shoot with Andrea Guy. He's photographed Hollywood's sexiest celebrities, the likes of Sophia Loren, Dorothy Dandridge, and Marilyn Monroe.

The journalist asked me this question: "It was rumored that you and Mayor Richard Cardinale of New York City were having an affair. Is there any truth to that rumor?" He turned whiter than white when I replied, "Yes." That was all I would give him, but it was more than enough.

64
LYRIC DEVANEY

Marisol and Jay Kapone are so grateful that they hired me they gave me a $10,000 bonus and said that I was underpaid. I took their money, but I really didn't need a measly ten grand. But my number one rule is to never give anything back. So I kept it. The movie is expected to gross close to $200 million and I'm pissed that I didn't negotiate a percentage for myself as well. Now what black production has ever seen those figures? I've already been offered numerous roles, and I've been reading through wonderful scripts. Kenny, my agent, lets everyone know from the outset, I'm not taking less than $5 million for my next role.

Terisa is not expected to come to the party tonight. Word is she's taking a flight back to New York this afternoon after her last scene. A little bird told me that when she found out I was offered a two–record deal with Sony records she was outraged. They said she was screaming, "She has everything! I hate that bitch!" I laughed and laughed. Actresses can be so temperamental. She knew her career was over, but she didn't know how to handle it. She was doing so much coke I would swear she went through her fifty grand in a week. If it wasn't for my baby, I'll admit I came close to having a dependency for Valium and alcohol. But since I have something to live for, I left all that alone. I am now a drug–and alcohol–free mom–to–be.

Sony was the record company putting out the soundtrack for the movie. After hearing my vocal range in the studio, an A&R director referred me to one of the executives. After listening to me sing live, he wanted to make me the next R&B sensation. I declined on that and told him I wanted to be the next pop diva. Pop is where the money is, so that's where I want to be. He loved my business savviness and got the top writers and producers to start working on my album. A month after the movie drops, I'll be flown right back out to L.A. to record my album. I really don't mind coming back here as long as I'm working. I'll probably rent a beach house while I'm out here next time because I'll need to be comfortable. By then I'll be close to eight months pregnant, and I don't want to put any strain on my baby. I've already thought of a name for her. Oh, the doctor's already confirmed I am having a little girl. I knew I would. I'll call her "Brooklynn" after the only thing that instilled fear in me.

When I was younger, living uptown you'd hear horror stories about the Brooklyn girls. You'd hear all Brooklyn girls shoplifted, and all Brooklyn guys robbed. So being born and raised in Manhattan, I was taught not to go into that borough, and for years I didn't. When I started acting and modeling, there came a time when I really didn't have a choice. There may be an audition downtown in Brooklyn, then what would I do? Would I miss it? Well, soon enough I was faced with that dilemma. They were holding auditions at Macy's in downtown Brooklyn for models between the ages of fourteen through sixteen. I'd just made it at sixteen. I wanted the print ad because it was for Gap clothes, and I knew if I got the ad, it would make me even more popular in my high school among my peers. Anyway, I got on the downtown A–train and headed into Brooklyn. My smart mouth was closed tight, afraid I might get into an altercation with some bad–ass Brooklyn girl.

On the train I was flipping through my headshots, when a girl sitting next to me decided to strike up a conversation. When she asked my name, I blurted out "Brooklynn." Of course, the next question was did I live in Brooklyn. "Yup," I responded. She then asked to see my pictures and told me she lived in Brooklyn, too. The girl turned out to be Portia, and we've been friends ever since. She accompanied me to the audition and, subsequently, I got the ad. So that name helped me overcome a fear and gain a friend. This baby helped me overcome my addiction to Valium and alcohol and will also be my friend.

65
LYRIC DEVANEY

At the lunchbreak, Portia and I raided the fruits and vegetables to take back into my trailer to eat. Portia had been mingling all day on the set telling everyone she was my sister. Just as we were preparing to go into my trailer, Terisa blocked my path purposely. I guess she wanted one confrontation for the road.

"Congratulations," she chimed.

"Thank you," I returned.

"You don't even know why I'm congratulating you."

"I'm sure I did something wonderful."

"I'm congratulating you for stealing my job!"

"T-e-r-e-s-s-a, I really don't want to revisit this with you." My voice was a little edgy. Terisa had clearly been doing coke. The film was still evident like a fingerprint under her nose. She kept sniffing and her eyes were bulged out while she fidgeted as if she had had too much caffeine.

"Did you know your sister fucked her way into my role, and I'm going to tell everyone when I interview and her career will be ruined?" Portia stepped up quickly and said, "My sistah got the role 'cause she's a better actor than you. I've seen ya movies and you ain't shit. And if I heard right, you got what da fuck was comin' to ya."

"But I was supposed to be the star." Tears had swelled up in her eyes.

"Bitch please . . . you soundin' all stupid."

Portia's defending me like that made me feel as if I had family. I was raised as an only child, and sometimes I felt aloof. You're always detached because there's no one to be attached to.

When we got inside my trailer, I decided to bond with Portia. First we talked about what we'd wear to the party tonight, then I steered the conversation to something serious.

"Portia I have something to tell you, but you'd better not tell a soul." Portia's eyes grew large as she thought about what I might confide.

"I won't."

"You swear to God?"

"Yup." She did that cross–your–heart thing.

"You know men just gravitate towards me. They love me before they know me. I have that power over them."

"An' what?"

"Remember I paid for you and Madi to come out here, plus your hotel suite, plus I offered to take you shopping on me?"

"Yeah."

"Didn't you wonder where I got the money from? Wasn't that a little bit out of my character?" I said slowly. Portia exhaled and looked bored. I could tell she thought I had some juicy Hollywood gossip and all I was talking about was money.

"No. Shit, I didn't give a fuck. I thought you were splurging off your movie money. Anyway, I kin top that. Don't you wanna know where I git my paper from?" Before, I could respond and try to dominate the conversation again she continued, "I'm a dancer now at Club Heat up'n da Bronx. Sometimes I bring home a G a night." She smiled the proud smile of a businesswoman. Ultimately, I had to shut her up.

"You're a shaky booty girl? A stripper?"

"I'm a dancer," she retorted, jumping to her own defense.

"You dance in clubs while men stick dollar bills down your panties? While I'm thinking you got some fool tricking his money on you, you're swinging around poles like some jungle bunny!"

"What's the difference? You still selling yourself whether it's for one guy or ten ma'fuckers."

Observably, she must have thought I would condone this type of behavior, but I expected more from Portia. She's a beautiful girl, a little rough around the edges and ghetto, but that's part of her mystique. She could easily have what I had if only she didn't settle for less.

Society will say there's no difference between a prostitute and a call girl. I adamantly disagree. A prostitute will take $20 from a john, whereas a call girl doesn't take less than a grand. So, you say it's only money? This whole world revolves around capital. There's a difference between being an associate at a law firm or a senior partner. A doctor or a brain surgeon. And the difference is money. Everyone fucks for something--be it pleasure, a baby, money, happiness, companionship, revenge or rebound. But when you call the shots, it shows who is in control.

It took me a moment to respond to her question, but eventually I said, "The difference is there's no consistency in stripping. You may have a good night on Wednesday, but for the next month of Wednesdays you'll be struggling. Ask yourself the question you asked me, but this time add the word 'fuck' in the equation. I bet now I'm making a lot of sense."

"Chick, stop acting stuck–up! I like dancin'. It makes me feel sexy. Do you want me to show you how to make your booty clap?"

"Portia, there's absolutely nothing anyone can show me regarding sexual positions, relationships or fetishes. And if you want to dance so badly, find a man who would want to watch you. That's a real turn on for most men, and it's hard for them to find a woman willing to do it. So that can be your edge over the next female. But please...stay out of the clubs. Don't you know those streets will kill you?"

"Lyric, I don't attract the type of players you do. Those willing to throw their bank books in my lap. And I don't have talent like you do that will earn me $250 G's for one picture. So I gotta go for mines. I'm finally handlin' my bus'ness and you say chill. I say fuck dat."

"Portia, to tell you the truth you're lazy. You don't want to work hard for anything. If it's easy . . . you're down. I get what I get because I strategize. Anyone can do that. You can do it. Maybe not as good as me but it can be done. You know how many men would love to have you on their arms showing you off? But you don't give them a chance to want you before you give yourself to them. And you do have a talent. I looked at how you were with Madison and that was a talent. You could go back to school for nursing or better yet be a doctor. I'll pay for it if you want me to."

"Please, you know how hard dat shit is? I'm not smart enough for it."

"We'll, you won't know unless you try."

"Lyric, if I did let you pay, I promise I'd pay you back as soon as I git my license, wit interest. I ain't a slouch like da next broad. And I'll admit I always did wanna be a nurse just like my grandmommy."

"There will be no need for you to say you'll pay me back. I'm hardly going to get gray hairs arguing with you about returning my money. If there's one thing I learned in life about friends and borrowing money, it is that they don't pay you back. And I hardly want to get my blood pressure up calling you for my money and you making me feel like I owe *you* something while you avoid all my phone calls. Been there, done that. So I don't loan . . . I give. Besides, I'm straight like six o'clock."

"That baby must be messin' wit ya hormones. Since when ya cheap ass got so generous? And don't tell me da fame got you trippin'."

"I tried to tell you earlier that I came into some money."

"From where?"

"You swear not to tell anyone?"

"Didn't we square this away already?"

"Okay. Remember Erious Jerome?" I was whispering and looking directly into Portia's eyes. I could immediately detect uneasiness when I mentioned his name. She never did tell me what happened with the two of them. But if you let Erious tell it, he got him a piece and I'm sure that wasn't a lie.

"Yeah," she returned my voice tone.

"Well, Erious came to my apartment that Saturday after the restaurant . . . and . . . he . . . um . . . raped me and I . . . blackmailed him for fifteen million. I have it all on tape," I blurted out. I felt so relieved that I had finally told someone. The burden was weighing on my shoulders every day. Portia turned a deep pink; tears of frustration streamed down her cheeks. I immediately felt bad. The last thing I wanted to do was upset my friend. She was probably wondering why I hadn't confided in her sooner. Seconds felt like hours, so I got up and went to embrace my friend to let her know that I was okay. When I came within arm's reach, Portia exploded, "You lyin', triflin' bitch! Now I know where this lil' talk came from. You been fuckin' Erious Jerome all this time behind my back! *'Strategize. Do you know how many guys would want you on their arm?'* You violated me bitch!"

Of course her outburst startled me. And most of all, her perception of the situation had me wondering how I could have chosen such an anal friend. I didn't respond to Portia's accusations because there was no need. Besides, she was screaming so loudly I couldn't get a word in if I wanted to. All I was worrying about was who could possibly be listening. She continued, "You ain't nothin' but a sneak–fuck! You spoiled cunt. I hate you bitch. Riddle me this, why would he want you when he already had me! Me, Lyric. I'm fly too. I did everythin' to dat ma'fucker dat night. Why would he have to *rape* you like some stiff dick criminal who don't get no ass? He's a multimillionaire. A famous celebrity! But you want me to believe he was so *mesmerized* by your beauty dat he had to take it. Bitch please. Since when do rich niggas have to take da pussy when, since I've known you, you gave it away?"

"I think you have me mixed up!"

"Word?"

"Word!"

"Lyric, let me explain somethin' to you. You run 'round here with your nose way up in the air sniffin' your own ass like you betta than us 'cause you got paper. Dat paper is illegal. If you want to impress me, marry a billionaire. Betta yet hoe, 'come a self–made billionaire! But until you kin do dat, those dollars you got stashed away in some safety deposit box hardly prove to me that you somethin' special! You had to lie, steal and fuck for what you got, and you want to be a role model. Nah . . . I think I like Oprah."

"Portia, this is America. It doesn't matter where the money came from as long as I got it."

"It matters slut. It matters when just 'cause you can buy the latest Gucci bag and I can't, you feel as though you kin dis me whenever you want 'cause your money makes you feel like you hot shit. You not hot shit, Lyric. You old, lonely, and scared 'bout growin' old 'n bein' lonely. Everythin' you got is an illusion. Every relationship you have is built on lies. You lie just to lie and that's sick. These men don't know you. They know who you say you are and, sweetheart, that's too much work for me justta keep a man. I may be wild 'n ghetto, but I'm always myself and people can either accept me or reject me. I kin look myself in da mirror, and see me. When you look in your mirror who do you see? Cinderella? Or the ugly evil bitch you really are! God don't like ugly. While you're busy hoardin' your money for safe keepin', a higher power is probably makin' sure you ain't gonna be able to enjoy it."

"Poor Portia. And I mean that literally. You just can't accept the fact that everyone you've ever gone after went after me. You've held a deep resentment for me ever since we were young."

"Pearl always said you were jealous of me! My niggas never wanted you, you sick dumb bitch. They thought they could fuck you 'cause you were always flirtin'. Every time I thought you had my back, you'd stab me in it."

"You're a joke!"

"Then have a laugh."

"Portia, I'm not privy to these allegations. It sounds like a bunch of paranoia to me."

"Whatever!"

"Don't hate the player. Hate the game!"

"Yo . . . let me get up outta here 'fore I beat the shit outta you."

"Don't let the door hit your big head on your way out!"

"When you drop that baby, I'mma kick your fragile ass!"

"There's no time like the present!" Portia stared me down hard but I didn't back down. If I weren't pregnant, we would have gone at it. I am no longer the uptown girl with a fear of Brooklyn girls, and that ghetto lingo hardly made my heart beat any faster. I can get down just like the next girl. I will admit I am no match for Portia, she would have swept the floor with me, but I have heart. And that's enough. She stormed out of my trailer and I didn't stop her.

66
LYRIC DEVANEY

Around an hour after the commotion in my trailer, Madison and Joshua arrived. Madison still looked frail but her eyes looked a little livelier than they had previously been. She still was solemn and indicated to Joshua and me that she didn't want to stay on the set, so I had my driver take her back to the hotel. I slyly told them that Portia had an emergency back in New York that she had to attend to. Neither one of them pressed to know what the emergency was nor did I think either one of them realized she was even missing. I gave Madison my telephone number in the trailer for emergencies and told her NOT to give it to Richard if he called. Lately, he's been harassing me about considering an abortion. Someone must have gotten word back to him that I was really pregnant because I could hear the fear in his voice. His tone was no longer stern and disrespectful. He was almost pleading with me to have mercy for the sake of his political career. I told him I'd think about it, then I turned around and took nude pictures of myself with my belly exposed and made a collage and sent it to him at his office. He freaked, and I enjoyed every minute of it.

Joshua walked out with me to do my last scene. I hesitantly climbed into the mahogany casket lined in off–white cotton. At every take, I saw Joshua mingling with the staff. He was smiling and having a wonderful time. Occasionally, he would glance my way and give me thumbs up, or wink at me with a smile. He was genuinely having a good time, and I was glad to see him loosen up a bit. All the girls flocked to him in a matter of minutes. He had tanned to a golden brown. He looked scrumptious. Joshua had that magnetic attraction with women. I secretly wondered how his marriage was going? Since he'd come to California, I haven't had a chance to catch up on old times. It's been months since I've seen or spoken to Joshua, and I really missed his comments and company. I haven't even told him that I was pregnant! I was waiting for us to be alone because I know Joshua is going to want to quiz me on who the father is. I'm sure he'll want to be my child's godfather, uncle, or something.

After we wrapped up, I took a quick shower and asked Joshua if he wanted to grab something to eat. While I was dressing, with Joshua in the room, I surprised him when I turned around after fastening my bra and flashed my little belly. "Jesus, Mary, and Joseph, Lyric! You're pregnant!" Joshua exploded. Grinning, I said, "Isn't it wonderful!"

"Well . . . yeah . . . I guess. Is this what you really want?"

"If it wasn't, would I still be pregnant?"

"Why now? What I'm really trying to ask you is, what does a woman go through when she's determining whether or not to terminate a pregnancy?"

"Well, I never actually considered terminating my pregnancy. I just knew."

"What about the father? Did he have a say or did you make the decision on your own?"

"Well, I didn't have to consult with the father because I'm not sure who he is. I'm sure that doesn't surprise you." I smiled and went over to him and playfully messed up his blond hair. He smiled cordially, but there was a forlorn look in his eyes. I secretly wondered if he was judging me. So I asked, "Are you disappointed in me?"

"Lyric, I've only held love and admiration in my heart for you. I'm not judging you because in order to judge, you must first be free from sin. This I am not. I'm thinking now that my life is so complicated. Whatever happened to us?"

"Joshua, I know there must be something troubling you, for you to look so despondent, and to speak highly of a relationship that couldn't work. We're lucky our friendship survived. What would I have done without you in my life?"

"You'd be Lyric Devaney . . . superstar." We both laughed and he gave me a bear hug, and kissed me on my cheek. Then he congratulated me on motherhood. His blue eyes turned gray, and he sat there glum as I got dressed. As I looked at him through my mirror, he looked like a sad, confused, little boy.

"Joshua, I heard you won that big case you were working on."

"Yes."

"So, what's next?"

"I'm running for district attorney."

"Good for you. What does Parker think about that?" I really didn't care what Parker thought or how she felt. She rubbed me the wrong way all the time, but I could tell he was troubled, and if it wasn't work, then it must be play. Joshua shrugged his shoulders at my last remark then he said, "Lyric . . . I need someone I can confide in and since Madison isn't in her right mind and has her own issues to deal with, I thought I'd impose on you."

"Impose?"

"This conversation cannot leave this room."

"I understand."

Joshua took a deep breath, then exhaled. He looked directly at his fingers as he twirled them around, trying to stay focused. The clock was ticking on my patience, but I kept it together. Finally, he said, "I'm the not–so–proud father of a baby boy. Kaisha delivered an eight–pound baby boy two weeks ago and told me the bad news only hours after she had the baby. She fucking left a voice message on my voice mail at work to call her mother!"

You could clearly see Joshua was torn apart about this recent revelation. I was even shocked that such an intelligent man could be so stupid. I always say you never gamble with a person who has nothing to lose when you have everything to lose. Joshua had a wife and career, and Kaisha had a space reserved in her empty bank account for all his child support payments. I knew the last thing Joshua wanted to hear was me dumping on him. He wanted support and someone to tell him it wasn't as bad as he thought it was. "How do you even know the baby is yours?"

"I took a paternity test. Do I look stupid to you? The test came back ninety–nine point nine percent positive." I debated on whether I should answer his 'stupid' question, then decided against it. He was taking his frustration out on me and that was understandable.

"Did you ever try and talk her out of having the baby?"

"Lyric, can't you take a moment out of your busy schedule and program your air–head to listen. Didn't I tell you I just found out about it!"

"Don't try and belittle me to make yourself look like your stupid ass has got more in your brain beside noodles. I'm trying to help you out here!"

"I know . . . I know. Forgive me. I'm just tired. I haven't seen Kaisha for eight months. I broke it off at the request of Parker. Then I get a call from her mother that she had the baby and that I'd better get down to Long Island Jewish Hospital Center. I get there and her mother is screaming 'sexual assault on a minor', her sweet darling innocent daughter was seduced by me . . . that she's going to authorities unless I marry her . . . and I'm like freaking out."

"Does Parker know yet?"

"Jesus! No way! Parker is very emotional right now. She thinks I'm going to leave her for someone else. I can't imagine her knowing that another woman was the first to have my baby when she's been desperately trying to get pregnant."

"Parker wants to have a baby?"

"Yeah. But I told her that I wasn't ready. And God knows I'm not. Why am I being punished like this?"

"What about your wife? Don't you think this will be much harder on her than it is on you?"

"Parker doesn't know and will never know."

"So, you're not going to tell her about your baby?"

"No!"

"Are you at least going to claim this baby?"

"I'll support this baby, but that's as far as it goes. I don't want to see this baby or have any contact. His bitch mother is lucky I didn't ring her fucking stripper neck!"

"What's the baby's name?"

"Guess."

"Joshua?"

"Is that your final answer?" Joshua said sourly. He had me confused. I had thought much more highly of Joshua until now. I guess the old adage is correct, you never really know a person. I'm sure he's mad at Kaisha for keeping her pregnancy a secret, but that baby is the innocent victim here. I left the subject as it was and decided to deal with my own life. You get gray hair worrying about other people's problems. Joshua got himself into it; he should be able to get himself out of it.

67
LYRIC DEVANEY

The hot LA heat snatched my breath as soon as we walked off the set. I couldn't wait to get to my car. As I hopped in to escape the heat, the leather was so hot that it scorched my bare legs and I screamed in agony. Joshua took the keys and told me to go back inside until he warmed up the car and was able to put on the air conditioning. He didn't have to ask twice before I scurried off to wait in the shade for him to rescue me.

As I stood in the shade, I felt very lonely. The very thought of Joshua's consideration for my welfare touched me in a negative way. I started to feel that I would long for that manly feeling. I wanted a meaningful relationship with someone who would care enough to cool off the car when it was hot and warm it up when it was cold. Someone to open doors for my baby and me when we're entering restaurants. I wanted love! Not sex, pleasure, or adoration. I wanted to be loved by someone. People look at me and it appears I have everything. But they don't see my emptiness. Until now, I didn't see my emptiness. My baby makes me feel whole in one way, but I don't feel loved and that leaves me feeling empty. What if my baby resents me because she doesn't have a father? What if she doesn't truly love me either?

Joshua pulled the car around, and I shook off any negative feelings I had. I realized I was just feeling down because Joshua had set the tone with all his self–pity. I thought about all the good things going on in my life and the people surrounding me. Good people. And the part about not being loved was simply melodrama. Every man who has ever had Lyric Devaney was in love. Everyone except Richard. Richard was afraid to love me because I was different. Not only in skin color either. I was different because he couldn't control me. I was like a stallion when he was used to having ponies.

Madison was asleep when we got back to the hotel. I looked to see if she had ordered any food and realized she hadn't. I stormed directly into her room and shook her awake.

"Get up!" I screamed. She jumped out of her sleep and adjusted her eyes to focus on where she was. Finally she said, "What's the matter?" Her voice was whiney and baby–like.

"What have you eaten for today?" I continued, "It's nearly six o'clock in the evening and you haven't eaten yet?"

"Lyric, lay off of her. The doctor said it would take some time."

"Don't tell me what to do! You weren't with her when she freaked out."

"I'm not hungry Lyric, but I'll eat something. I promise. Order me something light."

"I'm going to order you some soup and crackers, some orange juice, Jell–O and a fruit salad. And you'd better eat it all!" I had her so petrified I think I could have gotten her to eat a hamburger at this point. Once Joshua saw I had the situation under control, he went into the shower to get ready for the party. He was most excited. I bet he wanted some West Coast pussy before he went back to New York. Just as I was about to order room service, the telephone rang. Portia was probably calling to apologize. I'll accept it for her own good. Besides, what would Portia do without me? I got her into all the exclusive parties. With me she got to meet celebrities and stay in the A–list crowd. She's nobody without Lyric Devaney. She'll miss the elite lifestyle and come crawling on her hands and knees, begging to sit in the front seat of my Mercedes. I'll make her play the back. . . for a while.

"Hello."

"Is Joshua there?"

"Who's this?"

"Lyric, I really don't have any time. I only have one phone call and I need to speak to Joshua."

"Why Parker . . . congratulations step–mommy!"

"Step mommy? What are you talking about?"

"You know . . . Joshua's brand new baby boy . . . Joshua Jr., Kaisha's son? Don't act like you didn't know that–"

Before I could finish my sentence Joshua had emerged from the bathroom totally naked with water dripping off his glistening body. I glanced over at Madison who had a pitiful look on her face. You could tell she'd heard this news for the first time. You could hear Parker screaming from the other line and when Joshua responded, he said, "Lyric's lying . . . she's a trouble maker . . . I don't have any kids . . . arrested . . . newspapers . . . Monique . . . I'm not . . . she's lying . . . pregnant . . . she's lying . . . don't sign any papers . . . don't talk to the press . . . I'm on my way!" Joshua flew through the suite like superman grabbing his things and trying to get dressed at the same time. Something had definitely happened in New York that he had to get back too.

"Leaving so soon?" I said coyly.

"Fuck you! Why did you have to go and tell Parker? I confided in you, Lyric, and as usual, you had to fuck me over!"

Innocently, I said, "I thought you said she knew."

"Liar! You're nothing but a liar. I told you she didn't know and you told her anyway. That wasn't your place."

"So she found out sooner than later. Better she heard it from a friend and not some stranger. I did you a favor . . . you should thank me."

"You know Lyric, there's nothing wrong with being a bitch. But have some consistency with it. That way people will know how to handle you. Why were you treating me kindly, if only to turn around and betray my trust? Stick to what you know, bitch."

"Good point. I do aim to please," I retorted.

"Lyric Devaney, if I never see you again it will be too soon. I hope you end up in hell with rats doing the jitterbug on your rotten soul!"

"Likewise."

And so that's how I ended the argument with Joshua. He had a lot of nerve talking to me like that, in my condition with my baby listening. I was only joking, trying to get a laugh in for the day. Parker wouldn't believe me anyway. She's such a fool for him. Parker will be half of a hundred and still wondering who the hell Joshua was sleeping with. I decided not to let Joshua's outburst upset me for the whole day. He's immature and selfish. When had I become a factor in his failed marriage?

68
LYRIC DEVANEY

Joshua was long gone before room service came with Madison's meal. She was a little uneasy about Joshua and me bickering. Lord knows she hated confrontational situations. I sat and watched her painfully swallow spoonful after spoonful. When it looked like she was ready to say she had had enough, I gave her a hard look and she picked the spoon back up and continued. Her temperament was calm today. She was no longer the irrational Madison cursing me out. She was back to normal . . . or so it seemed. I decided to pry into her business because I was a little bored, and I wanted to spend some quality time with her since she wouldn't be joining me for the party tonight. I'd be going alone. I started off subtly, "Madi . . . what made you cut off all your hair and try this new bald hairstyle?" Her hand immediately went up to her head. Then she relaxed and explained, "I cut my hair because it held so much negative energy, and I had to release myself or else I would never be happy."

"Happy with Maurice?" I questioned.

"Who told you about him?"

"Well, you didn't."

"No."

"Joshua did."

"Maurice is my boyfriend, and we love each other."

"If he loved you, would he let you starve yourself to death?"

"Lyric, you don't know anything about our love."

"I know you look like shit. What man wants to wake up every morning to Kermit the Frog? You look just as bald and green as Kermit is."

I laughed a little but cut it short when I saw the look on her face. Madison had toughened up a little bit since I last saw her in New York. I guess when she gave away her virginity, her innocence went as well. Still, I sought more information.

"You love this guy?"

"Yes. I told you we love each *other*."

"Then, why are you in this condition? When you're in love, you're glowing. It's written on your face. Your face looks like he dumped you. Is that it, Madison, and you're ashamed to tell anyone?"

"Lyric, we are still together. You're not the only one who can keep a man," she snapped.

"How are your grades in school? Are you still graduating this semester?"

"Look . . . I don't like being put on the spot. I didn't invite you into my personal life, so you can see your way out of it. If Maurice wasn't happy with me, would he have given me this?"

Madison got up and went to her suitcase and pulled out a small pouch. She loosened it and pulled out a necklace. I inspected the piece and responded, "This is a cute piece of costume jewelry. Did he make it himself?"

"Costume? What are you saying? This isn't real diamonds and rubies!" She snatched the piece out of my hands and was screaming at the top of her lungs. She had apparently thought this piece was the real McCoy. I hated to tell her otherwise, but it was painstakingly obvious.

"This necklace couldn't be worth more than ninety–nine cents at the dollar store. It's cute though." I smiled to let her know it had my approval. I don't know what came first, the hot soup flying across the room or Madison charging me and attacking me with every ounce of strength her pathetic body could muster. She was screaming that she hated me and that I was jealous of her relationship. We were both pregnant, so I didn't really want to strike her, so I just shielded myself as best as I could from her blows. Thank God, she was too weak and fragile to do any real damage. During the struggle, someone must have heard the commotion outside and called security.

Madison was throwing plates, knocking over lamps, kicking and screaming as they tried to remove her from my room. They asked whether I wanted to press charges, but I declined. I just wanted her out of my sight. She landed a couple of scratches on my face, and I was worried they wouldn't heal properly. Before she walked out the door, she stopped in front of me and said, "I may not have real diamonds, but I've got real love. People love me. Can you say the same?"

With that she spit directly in my face, then sauntered out escorted by two security guards. If I didn't say I was hurt, I'd be lying. I don't think I'd spit on a dog. The message screams that you're nothing. Madison spoke loud and clear that I'd crossed the line when I attacked her relationship. Some women are just like that. They value their partner of one day more than they value a friendship of years. In their eyes, the friend can be replaced. But could the man? Especially since we live in a world where it's so difficult for a black woman to get one. If I've learned anything in life, and I've learned many things, it's that life is not meant to be understood. This is something I understand perfectly.

I peeled off each layer of clothing trying to dissect the day's events. In a matter of hours, I had lost three friends and I was now alone. But if I looked on the bright side of the situation, I could relish the fact that I was going to a party tonight in my honor. I would be praised for the work I'd done on this film. That meant a lot to me. With this film I give something back to society. Years from now, people will still be able to see my hard work, and, I hope, respect it. How many people got a chance to achieve that?

I turned the shower massage on and let the hot water cascade over my body. It relaxed me and cleared my mind. I decided that as soon as I get back into New York, I'd fix what had been done. I would eventually get my friends back. If I didn't . . . who would accompany me to my premiere in New York at Ziegfeld's?

69
JOSHUA TUNE

I believe everyone has a soulmate. I just think mine died in some freak accident or had a sex change and is now living life as a man. I hate to be so cynical when it comes to love, but Jesus . . . it shouldn't be so difficult. I think I got four gray hairs in an hour's time. Parker is going to make me grow old before my time. My mother did it to my father, and now Parker is going to do it to me.

I had to sit in the airport four hours before I was booked on a non–stop flight going back to New York. I couldn't wait to get back east and straighten out this whole mess. I'll admit, when I heard Parker's voice and her accusations, I was visibly shaken. I almost forgot who was wearing the pants in this marriage. As time passed, I've gathered my thoughts and just want to get to the bottom of what happened. Parker said she and Monique were arrested for assault. No doubt, over me. I'm hoping the police department gave them both desk appearance tickets to appear in court at a later date to stand before a judge rather than sending them both through central bookings. That place is dirty and degrading, and no place for either one of my ladies. I'm sure Monique can handle herself regarding getting out of trouble; it's Parker I'm worried about. They can also charge her with trespass and burglary if Monique declares Parker was not invited into her home. I pray that Parker didn't tell anyone who her husband was. I can't have officials knowing that my wife has been arrested. That will affect my chances for getting into office for the upcoming appointment. The more I think about it, the angrier I get at Parker. By the time I reached home, I was steaming. To add fuel to the fire, the house was in disarray as usual. Her shoes were thrown everywhere, and there wasn't anything in the refrigerator to eat. That meant she hadn't gone food shopping. I guess she was waiting for me to come home to do it in between trying a heavy case and picking up the laundry.

I had to think about whom to call first. This was a discrete matter, and at this point, no one could be trusted. I started off safe and called the precinct as a concerned friend of the women. The police officer told me that Monique Hamilton had been released from the precinct after they had carefully reviewed the complaint and determined she was a victim. Parker Brown was held and taken to 100 Centre Street to be processed where she would spend the night in jail. The prick cop charged Parker with assault in the 2nd degree, burglary in the 3rd degree, trespassing in the 3rd degree, menacing in the 2nd degree and a slew of other misdemeanor charges. Assault two, if she's convicted, is a class D felony where she could spend up to six months in jail. I'm sure Monique had worked her magic with this case, calling her high-priced attorney friends who probably came to her rescue immediately. But Parker wasn't a complete fool either since she was married to me. There was no way she'd be the only one getting arrested. I'm sure the minute they slapped those bracelets around her wrist, she opted to have Monique arrested, too, by counter-pressing charges. I noticed she used her maiden name out of loyalty to me. If she had done otherwise, I would have been outraged. My face had previously been splattered on every newspaper printed in New York for getting the conviction for the succinylcholine chloride murderer. I was a local celebrity, and I loved every minute. Someone's even writing a book on the trial called "The Perfect Crime."

I debated on whether I should call an old colleague of mine and have Parker's case file pulled, so she could see the judge quickly. She'd already been in custody twelve hours, and I was sure she was frightened. Going against my better judgment, I decided not to make any contacts. I didn't want to have to owe anyone any favors when I got into office. Besides, this was a bullshit case. If I reached out for help, that would give people an invitation to pry into my personal life. Maybe I'll hire her private counsel to appear in court for her. I don't know what I'm going to do, but my gut says I have to do something! Parker must be frantic by now.

70
JOSHUA TUNE

What boggles my mind is--how in hell Parker found out about Monique. One of my friends must be leaking information to Parker because I've been very careful not to leave any clues. Could Madison have betrayed me and let Parker know about Monique? I quickly talked myself out of that notion; Madison's loyalty was towards me. I have an inkling that it could have been Dominick at the office. I've seen the way his lustful eyes concentrated on Parker's ass when she was in the room. And he's always making comments that if he had Parker at home, he would never stray. Yeah, that fat son-of-a-bitch is the culprit. I'm going to check him as soon as I get this mess straight. And what about Monique betraying me and saying she's pregnant? She knows that she was supposed to adamantly deny any involvement with me. Unless, Parker tricked her. No, Monique is too clever for that. I just can't picture Parker tricking a top-defense attorney into spilling her guts. I was stretching the situation real thin. I kept trying to envision the two of them rumbling like two wildcats from "West Side Story." I wonder who got the best of whom? They're both tough as nails but equally feminine. Parker's always hollering about kicking someone's ass, but that can be purely speculative. I've never seen her physically attack someone in all my time with her. And as for Monique . . . she's tough in a courtroom, but could she stand up to real physical combat? I would have paid top dollar to see this scene go down. I know I probably shouldn't be laughing or joking about this because it's serious, but I can't help but chuckle inside.

As I was unpacking my suitcase, the computer said, "You've got mail!" I hesitated for a moment, but my gut called me to it. Lately, Parker has been spending a lot of time on this damn thing. It's almost an obsession for her. I'm curious to know who was emailing my wife. I clicked on "One new message" and opened it up. It was

257

addressed from someone whose e–mail address was *'Thickdickulous@aol.com.'* Whatever that meant, I knew I didn't like it. I read quickly, but absorbed every line and my stomach suddenly felt nauseous. This prick was having cyber–sex with my wife! I debated on whether I should instant message him back as my wife or as myself. I didn't have time or patience to play any games, so I emailed him back and let him know that he had just reached *"blackkitten's"* husband! And that he should no longer use this email address. I was shutting it down. He never emailed back a response. I opened up all of her old mail and realized my wife was a cyber–slut! She'd been having an affair for the past three weeks. I was so disgusted and embarrassed at Parker's behavior. Didn't she realize she was a married woman?

My thoughts bounced back to Parker and Monique. I wonder why Parker had lied and said that Monique was pregnant? I needed answers! I took a quick, hot shower and decided to go to Monique's apartment to find out what had gone down. Monique will tell me what happened. The truth. Because I knew I couldn't trust my lying–ass wife. I ultimately decided to let Parker handle this one on her own. I hope she has a miserable night in jail.

71
JOSHUA TUNE

Monique opened the door with trepidation, and instantly I knew why. Her sweet innocent eyes were swollen and bloodshot. Her sexy lips were protruding and hanging limply as if gravity were pulling them to the ground. She had on an oversized robe that seemed to swallow her petite frame. I immediately embraced her and she moaned in agony. I gently let her go and kissed her forehead. Our eyes met and locked, then tears steamed down her chocolate cheeks. This was my entire fault. How could Parker behave so savagely? Suddenly, the situation wasn't funny. Monique led me into her once–opulent apartment. It looked like she'd begun cleaning up the mess. Broken glass still decorated her perfectly–buffed parquet floors. Pictures had fallen off the wall and come crashing down on the floor. Sofa, television set, vases, statues were all left broken or turned upside down and left in disarray. I was left speechless. Somebody was going to have to pay for the damages. And clearly because Parker was my jobless wife the responsibility would fall upon me unless I could get Monique to let bygones be bygones.

Monique and I had to talk in her bedroom because being in clear view out front was not in our best interest. She appeared to be weak and drained, and the strain of recent events had taken its toll on her. For a while we didn't speak. There was only movement. I laid her down in her bed and went to put on some tea. When I came back into the room with the tea, she was sleeping soundly. I decided to let her get her rest and went into the living room, rolled up my sleeves and began to clean up the mess. As I swept up every piece of glass, I wondered what my next move should be. My mind was just as broken as those pieces of glass.

After the apartment was cleaned and everything that was broken was removed, I sat back on the sofa and cleared my mind. I needed answers to make my next move. Hours passed before I heard Monique call out to me. I quietly walked into her bedroom and sat on the edge of the bed.

"I didn't think you'd still be here," she whispered.

"I couldn't leave you . . . not like this," I replied.

"I'm sorry Joshua . . . I never meant for this to happen."

"Well, what did happen?"

"You mean Parker hasn't told you?"

"No. I haven't spoken to Parker yet. I came to you first."

"I appreciate that. Oh, Josh . . . it was horrible. I opened my door and she just attacked me. She called me all types of names, accusing me of sleeping with her husband. I denied everything but she didn't want to hear it. Her and her friend–"

"Wait a minute. She brought someone else here, too?"

"Yes. They jumped me . . . she and another girl."

"That explains your condition. It was probably her bitch–friend Michelle. She's always in our business. How did she look? Was she short?"

"I can't really remember. All I remember is being beaten. All I could do was tell her that I was pregnant to get her off of me."

"Monique . . . how could you do that to me? Undermine our relationship. Why would you lie like that? Don't you think that only made matters worse for you?"

"I didn't say I was pregnant by you, silly. I told her that I was pregnant by my fiancé and for her not to hurt my baby. It worked! They stopped."

"Fiancé?" I spat. I immediately felt a twinge of jealousy.

"I'm not engaged. I just said that for them to stop. But I am pregnant . . . I didn't lie about that!"

"Monique . . . please don't destroy me like this. I thought you told me that you haven't slept with this new guy."

"I haven't . . . Joshua, I'm pregnant by you. You're the father of my baby."

Seconds felt like hours as we sat there in silence. At some point Monique reached out and grabbed hold of my hands. I think they were trembling. She brought my hands to her belly and said, "Our baby, Joshua. We're going to have a baby." The words, her words, had me hypnotized. I wanted to feel the joy I saw in her eyes, but it was all too complicated. I fell down to my knees and cried like I had never cried before. Hard sobs of anguish came rushing to the surface, and I was like a scared little boy. She consoled me and embraced me until I had calmed down. I crawled up in bed beside her and she snuggled in my arms. I kissed the side of her face, and there I lay until we eventually fell asleep.

When morning came I was more refreshed, and I focused on the decisions that would have to be made. I started off openly and said, "Monique, how far along are you?"

"Somewhere between eight and ten weeks."

"How long have you known?"

"I just found out before you left for California. I was going to tell you as soon as you got back . . . but then this happened first."

"Not to sound uneducated . . . but how did this happen? After the incident I told you that I had to make love to Parker right after you, we agreed to use condoms. That was months ago. You're only weeks pregnant!"

"I remember the night like it was yesterday. After court one night, we had a romantic evening in, you drank too much champagne and insisted on making love without the condom. You said you missed me. Do you remember?"

"No," I replied. But I guess anything is possible. I've been known to get drunk and forget what happened the night before.

"Well, I remember and I wouldn't lie to you about something this serious."

Fidgeting with words I said, "Umm . . . have you decided . . . umm to have–"

"I'm keeping our baby!"

"Monique, I'm married. What do you want me to do?" I was pleading with her to change her mind and get an abortion.

"I want you to do what's right. I want you to divorce Parker and marry me. I love you Joshua . . . and my baby needs you. With me by your side, we can go all the way. You can go all the way with your career. You don't owe Parker anything. You gave her the best you had. Now it's over. It's over because you love me. I know you love me Joshua . . . I can tell the way you make love to me. I feel you. I understand you." Monique came close to me, and all I felt was her breath upon my face. She was right. I did have feelings for her, but I didn't know if it was love.

"My wife and I took vows. I don't think I'm ready to turn my back on that just yet."

"She doesn't love you. Not like I do. She said it herself. She said she's only with you because you're a good provider!"

"You're a liar!"

"I'm not . . . just ask her. Parker has no upbringing. She's ghetto trash and that's transparent. You'll never climb the political ladder with her holding you back. Look how she could have compromised your career coming over here doing what she did. Tell me how that shows she loves you?"

"She came because she loves me. She loves me so much that she wanted to hurt you for loving me. If it were merely because of my status, she would have ignored you." I didn't dare tell Monique what I had discovered through Parker's e–mail.

"Joshua, if you tell me right now that you don't love me . . . I'll take my baby and go far away from here. You'll never have to see us again. But if you can't say those words . . . my door is open to you . . . but I won't wait forever."

72
JOSHUA TUNE

I left Monique's apartment with a sense of guilt looming overhead. One baby here, one baby on the way. What the fuck was I doing? Monique directly asking me to divorce my wife had shaken me up a bit. I felt like rubber being pulled in three different directions. I had three women in love with me, all vying for my attention and undivided commitment. It's like smoking a cigarette to the butt and having to make the decision to get one last drag, or throw it out because it's served its purpose.

I entered my apartment to find Parker flying around the house in a frenzy. Her eyes were red and puffy, and it appeared she'd been crying. She was noticeably packing some items into a suitcase. She ignored me as I came in and didn't say a word. She was upset which made me upset. After a couple minutes of watching her gather her things, and wipe a couple of tears away, I finally broke the silence.

"What are you doing?"

"What does it look like?" she hastily snapped.

"It looks like you're packing your things."

"Nope! I'm packing *your* things."

"What the fuck's the matter with you? Stop acting like a kid Parker . . . I'm not going anywhere!"

"You are getting the hell outta my sight or so help me God . . . I will make you very sorry!" she screamed. Parker was furious and I thought the approach I was using was inappropriate. I'd better calm down some and level with her.

"Parker, explain to me why you're packing my things for me to leave. I told you that Lyric is a lying bitch. You know that, pumpkin . . . come on. Don't let her come between us."

"Don't you dare call me *pumpkin*! And don't go dumping your actions on Lyric. As a matter of fact, I owe her for opening my eyes. I know about the baby, Joshua.

I spoke to Kaisha. And I also know about Monique's pregnancy. How do you expect me to feel?"

"I've never slept with Monique. I swear on my mother's grave! All this is a misunderstanding. She told me she tried to tell you the truth, but you didn't want to hear reason. And she definitely didn't say I was the father of her baby. But you and Michelle didn't even care. You just brutally jumped her anyway."

"How dare you stand in my home and quote what some other tramp told you! You're cherishing her words like they came straight from the Holy Bible. I'm your WIFE! Why do you keep forgetting that? And Michelle was never there. That's another one of her lies! She's manipulating you, Joshua."

"No one is manipulating anyone. And she doesn't have to lie to me? You're the one who has been lying to me."

"Me! Lying? What have I ever lied to you about?"

"Thickdickulous! Does that sound familiar? While I'm out working my ass off, you're gallivanting as a cyber–slut!"

"Don't you dare try and turn this around on me! You're the unfaithful one. Not me! And where have you been? Your ticket says you came home yesterday? How could you leave me alone in jail . . . and not even come to support me in court?" Parker collapsed on the couch as if all her strength had been zapped from her. She shook her head in disbelief.

"I stayed at the Marriott. I needed time alone to think," I said calmly.

"You were with her weren't you?" she asked.

"I answered that already. Now stop acting crazy and delusional."

"Crazy! Delusional?!? Why are you doing this to me? Me? Do you hear how you sound right now? You're cold . . . and distant. You just want me to roll over and accept you for who you are. Turn the other cheek and let you and your mistress carry on. You selfish bastard. I hate you!"

Parker lounged at me and was kicking, scratching and screaming. She was crying in agony as I tried to control her. I grabbed her by her hair and gripped her arms and flung her across the room up against the wall. That was the first time I had ever put my hands on her. Her eyes popped open in horror. Then she quietly said, "Get out." Her voice escalated and she sobbed, "Get out! Go to her. Go to that bitch! I hate you! I hate you, Joshua!"

I ignored her outburst and casually finished packing the suitcase she had already begun. I took out my cellular phone and dialed Monique right in front of Parker. I asked Monique if her door was still open and she sweetly replied, "Yes." With that, I grabbed my things and never looked back. I didn't have to make any decisions . . . they were made for me. Whether this was good, bad, ugly or an indifferent thing to do, none of it was made out of rationalization, I thought. I exhaled as I walked out of Parker's life and into Monique's.

73
MADISON MICHAELS

Maurice promised to pick me up at Laguardia airport in his Lexus. I was excited that I was going to be picked up in style. This would only be the second time I've been in it since he's gotten the car. This was going to be a treat. I didn't even get a chance to brag to the girls that my boyfriend drove a Lexus. They probably wouldn't have believed me anyway. It's so hard to believe that Lyric would be so jealous that she would lie about my necklace and say it was a fake when it's clear that it's the real thing. I should have done more to her than just spit in her face. She's a wench, and I have really started to hate her!

I'd called Maurice from the hospital, and he was genuinely concerned about my health. He told me to take it easy, and that we'd work it out when I got home. He asked if I wanted him to fly out West, but I told him I'd be fine and would come home soon. Although I hated to admit it, I didn't want him to meet Lyric in all her glamour. I'm sure he would have been impressed with the limousines, caviar and champagne L.A. had to offer. He wanted to know more about what the doctors said about my condition. He thought what I needed was rest and relaxation, not to be up in a depressing hospital. He was the one who told me to sign myself out. I did as I was told and called Joshua, and told him I was being discharged. I still have to tell Maurice that I'm pregnant. I don't know if I'm happy or not about it, and I am not sure how Maurice will feel either. Money is still tight, and I'm tremendously in debt. I wanted to get to know Maurice better before we decided to have a baby, but fate intervened and decided we would have to take it one day at a time while the baby was coming.

As I departed from my flight, Maurice was waiting in the standing area of the vestibule. I was so happy to see him, I ran and gave him a big hug. He embraced me and swung me around. He was smiling ear to ear and so was I. I guess I'd made a good decision taking a vacation away from him because things weren't working out. Whoever said "absence makes the heart grow fonder" was not lying. Maurice had on a light–blue Izod canvas shirt with beige khaki pants and a pair of penny loafers. He looked GQ, like one of the models in the magazine. He was clean–shaven and smelled great. I was proud to be his girl. I kissed his dark–chocolate cheek and we were off.

On the ride home from the airport, Maurice asked a lot of questions about the hospital and the tests they'd ran. I'm sure I had him worried when I told him they said I was anorexic. I explained to him that the diagnosis was incorrect, that I was not sick, and that I was just dieting to look good for him. He squeezed my hand tightly and told me that I looked great before and I look great now. My hand instantaneously went up to my short Afro. At first I thought cutting off my hair was a power move, to get rid of the negative energy and assert my self–esteem. I wanted to stand out from the women Maurice was seeing and make him notice me more. Now, my conscience was eating away at me and I felt like a fool. I keep getting funny looks from people who stared at my head when talking to me and not my face. Little kids pointed at me and giggled among themselves, then said things like, "She looks like a Bald Eagle." I asked Maurice whether my new haircut was too extreme and he said, "I love you for you. You don't have to go through a metamorphosis to please me. I've put too much strain on you Madi, and I'm sorry. Please forgive me. I'll behave from now on. I promise."

74
MADISON MICHAELS

When we got home, Maurice insisted on making me dinner. I took a shower and put on a pair of sweats, then propped myself in front of the television set in the living room so I could watch him work. I don't know why it felt so pleasurable watching him prepare dinner. He's been doing it for the past couple of months, and I love it. I'm sure he's never gotten any joy out of watching me. But women are different; the littlest thing can be pleasing to us. As I sat flicking through every channel, I thought briefly of how I'm almost flunking out of my last semester. My brain suddenly went on hiatus because of all the drama I was having with Maurice. I couldn't seem to think about anything or concentrate on anything except making Maurice happy. If we'd have an argument or if he was upset about something, that would ruin my day and thought process. I just wouldn't be able to function no matter how hard I'd try until he was speaking to me again. I told myself that I wouldn't worry about it today, not when I wasn't feeling so well. I'll worry about it tomorrow. Yeah, tomorrow I'll worry about school.

While Maurice was busy, I went down to check the mail. I'd been gone for some time, and Maurice didn't have a copy of the mailbox key. I was supposed to leave it with him but had forgotten. I was reluctant about going through everything. When the mail toppled out of the box, usually it was nothing but junk mail and bills. Nowadays I didn't even open up certain mail; I'd just toss it. Can't pay the light bill right now, toss! Try back in two weeks. Nevertheless, tonight I stopped on two bills that looked foreign. One was a Chase Platinum MasterCard bill and the other was a Capital–One Visa bill. They were both in my name. I opened the first one as I walked slowly up the steps back into my apartment. There before me was a bill for $25,000. Apparently, someone charged a man's gold Rolex watch from Tourneau on 34th

Street. I openly gasped. I ripped open the second one, and it totaled $6,000. There were a variety of things listed on the bill from department stores like Bloomingdale's, Macy's and various restaurants and electronic stores. I was furious. The only culprit could have been Maurice. I charged into the kitchen feeling light–headed and demanded to know where the bills had come from.

"Oh that," he casually replied.

"Yes, Maurice. Who authorized you to open up these accounts in my name? I can't pay for this, and neither can you." I felt defeated and frustrated. I buckled into the kitchen chair and began to cry my eyes out. This was all too much to take. He calmly sat down beside me and took the bills out of my clenched fist. Then, I noticed the watch. I knew it was from Rolex because Lyric has one too. But hers is platinum. How could I have missed it earlier? My perception is fading along with everything else.

"Neither one of us has to pay the bill. You and I both know that you didn't open up these accounts. All you have to do is call these credit card people, and tell them that you didn't make these charges and it'll all go away. I promise." I looked in his eyes and saw the devil! My mouth opened up in horror. Then I said, "Maurice, I can't do that. I would be committing fraud. You of all people should be aware of the consequences. The very people you work for will be knocking on my front door. Credit card fraud is a federal offense. I could lose everything I've worked so hard for in a second. No, what you have to do is take everything back, and I'll close these accounts. You shouldn't have done this anyway. You're way out of line here, and you have to fix it!"

In a balanced tone Maurice said, "I'm not taking back anything. Besides, I've used most everything already. They won't take it back used even if I tried. I don't know what you're going to do, but I told you how to handle it. If you want to play all goody–goody, then have fun paying back thirty grand!"

"Me! What about you?"

"I don't have that kind of money."

"Neither do I."

"Then do what I said. Madi, with your credit we could get a whole lot more things. This time we could get some things for you. I've only just got started."

The tears started to fall even harder because he was not hearing what I had to say. His greed was overriding his common sense, and in the long run, I would be the fall guy. My emotional state barely phased him. He continued, ". . . it's clearly not your signature. What can they do? Shit! Besides, they have insurance for this type of thing and we're not hurting anyone. You work your ass off five days a week, and what do you have to show for it? The white man has been slaving us for years. We need to take what's ours. You know those bastards won't even give us reparations for our past, present and future struggles. I don't know about you, Madi, but I want my forty acres and a mule!"

He looked satisfied with his speech. I was repulsed. I hate when black people do something wrong and blame white's for their actions. If the white man has so much control over their actions, why don't they praise the white man when they do something positive? It's purely conditioning, used as justification when they've gotten themselves into trouble and don't know whom to blame.

I dried my eyes because tears were useless in this situation. Nothing I'd say would convince Maurice to return that sparkly item upon his wrist. He was just as materialistic and ruthless as Lyric, and it made me sick to my already–nauseous stomach.

"Maurice, I can't deal with all of this right now. I'll think of something, someway, I'll have to pay for these items."

"Are you really noble or just an idiot in nobleman's clothing?" The remark stung, but at this point, could I feel anymore than what I was feeling?

I simply replied, "I'm not the one pretending to be someone I'm not."

"What do you mean by that? What do you know about me? Who have you been talking to?" he bellowed. I jumped to attention and tried to control my body from shaking. The way Maurice's mood would turn dark instantaneously had me wondering if he was using any drugs. I pushed back in my chair because I could feel a slap coming on, and I wanted to be able to block most of the impact.

"I really don't know much about you, Maurice, because you won't let me into that area of your life. You always tell me we'll talk later whenever I ask too many questions. I'm afraid that if I really knew who you really were, maybe I wouldn't love you so much. I'm talking about charging a Rolex watch and driving around in a Lexus you can't afford."

"Oh, I'm sorry I misunderstood. And why are you trying to play me? I can afford this shit, but I'm too smart for the average mind. Why should I spend all my money when I can get it for free?"

"But it's not for free. Ultimately, I'm going to be responsible for these items."

"So what? Didn't I buy your ass that expensive necklace? I tied up sixty grand on that. I could have brought my own Lexus and Rolex if I wasn't looking out for you!"

"Lyric said it was fake," I timidly replied. His face tightened up and his eyes merged together; he looked cock–eyed. I knew I had hit a nerve and I was praying that didn't mean I'd get beaten. I thought fast and tried to clean it up. "But I told her that she was a liar. I even spit in her face be–" The slap stopped my last remark. I felt the blood ooze out the side of my mouth. I didn't say another word. I hadn't even flinched. Our eyes locked. The second slap was more potent than the first. I guess because I didn't react the way he had wanted me to. My head hit the side of the wall and made a thumping sound. I felt a large lump immediately swell up on the left side of my head. Again our eyes locked. My breathing increased, and I heaved in and out. I didn't understand why he expressed himself so violently towards me. Whatever I said that got him upset were only words. Why couldn't he fight me back the same way? Verbally? I followed Maurice's eyes to the glass pitcher sitting on the counter–top and when he reached for it, I screamed, "MAURICE . . . DON'T . . . I'M PREGNANT!" But it was too late. He smashed the glass pitcher filled with cold fruit punch upside my head and knocked me off my chair. The pitcher broke into pieces and splattered everywhere. My forehead split open and blood gushed from the wound and dripped into my eyes. I don't know if it was the impact of the blow or the massive amount of blood, but seconds later, I passed out and woke up in a hospital recovery bed with Maurice by my side.

"I told the doctors you fell rollerblading," he whispered. Still groggy I managed to sit up in my bed. I felt awful. My hand went up and fingered stitches on my forehead. *Please God don't let me have a scar.* I was hesitant about speaking because I didn't know what to say. I was trying to piece together everything that had led up to me waking up in Kings County Hospital Center. Maurice wasn't saying anything, just looking at me with sad puppy–dog eyes, showing remorse. He gently leaned over and kissed my stitched up forehead that felt very tight. Then he cupped my hands inside of his.

"How does it look?" I cautiously asked.

"It's pretty ugly right now, but it'll heal up nice. . . I promise." He replied. I wanted to tell him how sick I was of his promises, but instead I said, "Let me see it."

Maurice went out to the nurse's station and came back with a mirror. I held it in front of my face, and I gasped at my reflection. My head was shaven where the stitches were sewn, and there had to be at least one hundred stitches that extended from the middle of my head all the way down to my right eyebrow. I had a feeling I was permanently disfigured. My mother may not even recognize me. The nurse came into the room as I was looking in the mirror. I could tell she felt sorry for me, and when she spoke, she couldn't look me in my eyes. But I did see her glaring at Maurice. She said I had to stay at least another hour until the medication they'd given me wore off. I said nothing. I just laid back and shut my eyes tight so no tears could escape.

75
MADISON MICHAELS

To say that my self–esteem was *almost* non–existent was an exaggeration. At this point in my life, I don' t think I knew what the word meant. I dieted even more now. Every chance I got, I ran in the bathroom to purge after eating each meal. Although it made my throat feel raw from sticking my fingers down into it, emotionally it made me feel better. I was also using laxatives and diet teas to cleanse my system. Maurice was walking around with a big chip on his shoulder. He couldn't shake his guilt for what he'd done to me. He occasionally tried to help out around the house by picking up his things. And he always cooked my dinner to try and help me get back my strength.

I didn't go out much now because I was ashamed and embarrassed at who I'd become. I was so disappointed in my life. I lay in bed day and night, most times alone feeling nostalgic. I felt like I had sacrificed so much for this relationship, and I was wondering if he was the one? Sometimes, Maurice convinces me that he's in love with me. Other times, I feel like I'm sleeping with the enemy and that scares me. I haven't been to work nor have I gone to school. I just lie in bed and let the bills pile up. I don't know what to do. My telephone rings off the hook with people calling to check in on me. The Dean of Admissions calling about my attendance, Joshua calling about his failed marriage, and Kenny calling about Lyric's premiere. I usually let the answering machine pick up. I just want to wallow in self–pity. Soon my telephone will be shut off as well, and honestly I don't care. I don't have to hear Maurice's other girlfriend using their code: call once then hang up, so he'll run into the other room to return her call. Then there's a zillion collection agents calling a trillion times a day telling me I owe some outstanding bill.

It was shortly after 3 p.m. when my telephone rang. I checked my caller identification and was surprised to see it was Portia calling. I hadn't heard from her since she left California. Portia has never called me, so I made a quick decision to answer the phone because I was curious to know what she wanted.

"Hello," I said.

"Whaddup, girl?!" Portia excitedly exclaimed. You heard her popping the gum in her mouth. click–clack, pop, pop, click–clack. She was a little too excited for my taste, but I responded with, "Nothing."

"Whaddup wit chu?" Not waiting for a response she said, "I have two tickets for the DMX concert at the Garden. All the niggas is gonna be there . . . the Lox . . . Lil' Kim . . . Jay–Z. Yo, that shit is gonna be hot yo."

"Sounds good. But um . . . Lyric's back . . . did you know?"

"Yeah, I knew!"

"Then why aren't you asking her first?"

"I don't fuck wit her no more . . . please. And I heard through the grapevine you don't either."

"You heard correctly. Me and her don't speak and frankly she gets on my nerves."

"True dat."

"She thinks she's all of that, and that everyone is jealous of her, and that she's better than everyone!"

"Word. I'm like . . . I don't have any ree–son to be jealous of you. Who you? You bleed like da rest of us. I was gonna beat the shit outta her scary ass, but I let her slide. She was like, 'don't hit me, don't hit me.'"

"For real?"

"For real yo."

"I cannot stand me some Lyric Devaney!"

"You know she ain't nothin' but a hoe right?"

"Yeah, I know! But she looks down on us and everything we do. Did you hear I spit in her face?"

"Git the fuck outta here! Word?"

"Yes, right before I left LA. I let her non–acting ass have it."

"Me, too. Yo this is wild. I screamed on her, then I jetted. I was about to do her yo."

"You know all her jewelry isn't real. A lot of her pieces are fake!" I don't know why I lied but they probably were. How would Portia or anyone else know the difference? We sure didn't have anything to compare it to. Then I continued, "And the pieces that are real, I heard she brought them herself and lied about them being gifts from her boyfriends. I believe it too. Look how she acts all stuck on herself, what man is spending his hard–earned money on her! Now I know how to make a man spend some cash."

"Well, you need to buy her nose 'cause she can smell rich dick!" Portia joked.

"Tell me about it."

"Anyone can git a nigga wit paper. Keepin' dat ma'fucker is another story!"

"And she's not as cute as she thinks she is."

"Who you tellin'? I look better than her!"

We laughed and laughed and talked about Lyric until our mouths were dry. I made up some story about going to dinner with Maurice, so I wouldn't have to go with Portia to the concert. Under different circumstances, I would have loved to go. And it was free! Portia said I didn't have to pay her for the ticket, but I couldn't let anyone see me like this. Portia would be mortified, but I'll admit, it was tempting.

After Portia and I hung up the telephone, I went to microwave the food Maurice had made for me. I stuffed my face with baked chicken, spicy mashed potatoes and mixed vegetables. I also had some butter pecan Haggan Daz Ice cream. After that, it was off to the bathroom. First I purged until I was throwing up water, then air. Next, I relaxed in a hot tub before retiring to bed. Suddenly, I didn't feel well. It was probably the baby and morning sickness. Maurice never mentioned my telling him that I was pregnant, and I'm glad because I won't be for much longer. I didn't tell anyone, but I didn't want this baby. I have this awful feeling that once the baby is here, Maurice will give all his attention to the baby, and I'll be left out in the cold. I know how men react to their first–born. I haven't had Maurice to myself long enough to want to share him with someone else. I'm told that you can have an abortion up until six months of pregnancy. Maybe, I'll call Portia and ask her to come with me to terminate my pregnancy. God knows, I don't want to go alone. I'll think of something to tell Maurice once it's done.

76
MADISON MICHAELS

I was lying on the bed with a cold rag on my face when Maurice came in with a bouquet of roses. I wanted to run up and embrace him, but I didn't have the strength. Maurice noticed my fatigue and came to my aid. "You like?" he smiled. I managed a weak grin and whispered "Yes." Maurice laid the roses on the bed beside us and got serious.

"Madi, I have to ask you an important question. Are you up to it?"

"Yes."

"It's come to my attention that you told someone you didn't love me."

"What?" I jumped up and sat up straight. Who was telling lies on me? I know it's that whore Lyric. I'll kill her!

"Does that mean the statement is not true?"

"Of course it's not true. You know I love you!"

"Prove it!" His face was stern, and I couldn't read him. I hoped he wasn't about ready to strike me again. I hadn't healed yet from the last beating. I had to express myself correctly. I didn't want to say the wrong thing to upset him.

"How?" Was all I could settle on and I hoped it was enough. It showed that he was running the show, I thought. He looked long and hard in my eyes then said, "Marry me, that's how." His pinky finger held a diamond engagement ring, which he taunted in my face. I squealed with delight and grabbed the ring to try it on for size. I couldn't help but hear Lyric's words . . . "It's a nice piece of costume jewelry." I wondered momentarily if it was fake. And if it wasn't . . . where had the money come from? Then I shook all questions and insecurities aside and relished in happiness. Of course, I'd marry Maurice. I'd said "I do" the first day we'd met.

"When?" I finally breathed.

"How about next week, Friday?"

"So soon?"

"Is there a problem?"

"Well, we barely know each other. There's so much about you that I don't know."

"Biggie and Faith Evans got married after just two weeks knowing each other," he reasoned.

"Well yeah that's true. I can't plan a wedding in a week. All of my friends . . . your friends . . . my family . . . your family . . . cake. Get the picture?"

"I don't need all of that. All I need is you. We'll go to City Hall."

"Never! I want to get married in a church with a minister. That's my dream . . . I deserve that."

"Weddings cost too much money. We'll go to City Hall next Friday. Unless you just don't want to do this."

"Of course I do! I love you so much, you know that. But um . . . next Friday is Lyric's premiere."

"Fuck that gold–digging slut! You're not going to her premiere. Besides, she's not your friend anyway."

Something about the way Maurice said Lyric was not my friend when he hardly knew her or our relationship made me shiver. "What do you mean she's not my friend?"

"She came here looking for you the other day while you were out talking about her premiere. I was in here alone and she started asking questions. I'm like . . . this girl is a Barbie doll. She's gorgeous . . . but fake. Then she starts coming on to me telling me how good I look, and how nice my body is. Before I know it, she is giving me head! I swear to God I didn't fuck her Madi . . . you got to believe me."

Maurice put his eyes down to the ground and didn't say another word. I was stalk white. Gorgeous . . . head? Those two words stuck in my throat like a clogged drain. How could my once best friend betray me like this? And over a man. My man. To say I despised Lyric was an understatement. If I weren't sick, I'd go straight over there and rip her tongue out of her mouth. This meant war! I didn't want her to see me like this, all banged up; she'd only laugh and make fun of me. Maybe, I'll pay some rough girls from the neighborhood to go and beat the shit out of her. Cut up her face or something. Leave her looking just as ugly on the outside as she was on the inside. Lyric's innate ability to push everyone's buttons as efficiently as she did was an uncanny gift. I hated her for making me feel as inadequate as I felt at this fragile time in my life. Damn her. Damn her to hell!

77
LYRIC DEVANEY

I adorned myself with a white mink and chinchilla fur from Fendi. I walked around my condo in full diva status. As my mink swept the ground and my stilettos from Gucci click–clacked against my parquet floors, I realized how happy I really was. Fame, money and power are all a girl really needs. When you have all those things, men are secondary desires. My face had been splashed across every credited magazine there was and they all wanted to know who Lyric Devaney was. I was at my best in every interview and the public loved me. The anticipation of my movie had shaken up America. My new publicist, Bryant Cody, was great! He called to tell me Celebrity Magazine was going to feature me as one of the fifty top sexy celebrities. I'll be in the June edition. He's not sure which number I'll be because it's up to America to cast their votes. I know I'll be in the top five. I'm not even worried about that. Whoever said the rich get richer must have been a philosophical scholar or something. Jasmine Cosmetics has signed me to a two–year contract as a model and spokeswoman for their product.

Since I've been back, I've gone on a major shopping spree to celebrate the completion of my movie and new found success. I had two tailored fur coats from Karl Lagerfeld being delivered to me in the next four weeks, and I can't wait. I bought a natural Russian barguzin sable–belted greatcoat. That baby cost me $150,000. And a Russian lynx for $195,000. I wanted at least one of them to be ready before my premiere, but coats like these were top quality shit! So I'll have to make do with the white mink, which is just as fabulous. I also stopped in Tiffany's and bought a buckle bracelet in 18k gold mesh with diamonds set in platinum with the matching mesh bib necklace. That set cost me twenty grand easy. Richard loved buying me gifts from Tiffany's. In fact, I will be wearing the two Etoile bangles with diamonds set in platinum he'd sent to me when I first got on the set for the movie as a good luck present. I also went into Barney's New York to buy a belly chain from jewelry designer Manon Von Gerkan. You could only get these from Barney's or Fred Segal.

My telephone, which I used to call my "private line," hasn't stopped ringing. Agents, groupies, movie producers are all calling, trying to jump on the Lyric Devaney bandwagon. Upscale restaurants are giving me invitations to have complimentary dinners to help lure in Hollywood's A–list.

I've only been back in New York a month, and I've already decided not to put my apartment on the market. I thought it would be better for me to let my mother move in here when I move out. Besides, what would my mother do with a big house? I'm sure she'll be more than grateful to have this place all to herself. Lord knows I'm doing more for her than she ever did for me.

Last week I was photographed home–hunting. Every newspaper and magazine reported that I was looking in the $5 million and up market for mansions in the Hamptons. Actually, I've already found one for $6.5 million. Ten bedrooms, sauna, three jacuzzis, six marble bathrooms, tennis court, recreation room, movie theatre and mosaic–tiled outdoor and indoor heated swimming pools. It used to belong to billionaire tycoon Geoffrey Lieberman and his wife Sandra before they put it on the market seven months ago. They originally had it listed for $13 million. When the sharks didn't bite, they lowered their price substantially. I hear that a lot of white people are trying to unload their property ever since that rap mogul moved into the neighborhood. So this was a deal I was going to steal. Once I'm settled in, I'm going to Habite' in San Francisco for all my antiques. They have eclectic furnishings.

Anything I do now is considered news. That's why I always come out looking great. I hide my pregnancy behind fabulous furs, and I usually throw on a pair of designer shades. Even at night. That's what most celebrities do. I learned that from being in Hollywood. It means I'm trying to disguise myself, but please, take my picture anyway for free publicity!

I wanted to pop the Cristal champagne, but due to my condition, I abstained. I wanted for every day of the rest of my life to feel like a party. What the hell . . . I've earned it. Yesterday morning, I invited Kenny over; and we got our shop on. I spent nearly a hundred grand on Gucci silverware and plates, Lenox China, Mikasa flutes, and handcrafted candlestick holders. I went to Hermes and purchased a $1,000 bathrobe and slippers. Saks 5th Avenue and purchased $5,000 Queen Helene sheets. Why? Because I could afford it!

The first thing I wanted to do when I moved in was host an opulent dinner party. Invite only the "in" crowd. I may have to exclude Madison and Portia. Joshua can come because he's acceptable and will be on the political list. When you have these parties, you have to mix up the categories. Musicians, politicians, actors, rappers . . . where would Madison and Portia fit in? Madison currently looked like a character from Sesame Street and Portia would fuck one–third of the men before the night ended. No. I think I'll have to nix those two. If only for that night. I'm sure they'll throw a fit and start screaming I've changed. I'll just quote some comedian, "Yes I've changed! I've changed my telephone number, my address, and the amount of money in my bank account. What? There's nothing else to it."

78
LYRIC DEVANEY

I know I had previously said that when I got back, I'd give my friends a call and mend all quarrels. Negative! Since I've been back, I've been making things happen. I've already written six songs for my debut album, landed a cosmetic and modeling contract, read numerous scripts and landed a $5 million role in a Malcolm Meade Cardozo film; all the while I've secured positive press. I could walk in public wearing a thong and rain boots and still be accepted. I swear, it feels I can do no wrong. So if they don't call me soon, they may not be able to reach me in the near future. Telephone numbers are unquestionably changing, and I can imagine how busy I'm going to be. It seems that I've outgrown them all in a matter of weeks.

I had Federal Expressed my movie premiere tickets to all of them, though. They had better not let me down by not showing up. I'd be furious. I still needed their support and praise. I need to be praised all night. I realized not one of them called me since I've been back. The nerve! Could they all still possibly be angry with me? If they still were, I'd say they were behaving childishly. We've argued plenty of times and were still able to mend our quarrels. But now since I'm rich and famous, they can't seem to be able to swallow their pride and call me first. The green eye sure is busy these days. Well, I refuse to make the first calls. They better take those priceless tickets as a peace treaty and act like they know what I know.

At 2 p.m., Kenny came by to be nosy to find out what I was wearing to my premiere. He was so nervous, fidgeting around making me nervous. I was lying across my sofa relaxing because I had less than an hour before my hair stylist was due to come. Also, a masseuse and manicurist were also hired to come by to relieve my tension and give me the perfect French manicure. As I lay there in my own zone, I noticed Kenny's mouth was open and nothing tangible was coming out. I realized that he irked my nerves. It was then that I decided I'd get rid of him as soon as possible. He wasn't even the one to get me this deal, but he got paid a portion of my earnings when he didn't earn me shit! The nerve of him being all proud of me like he was my mentor or something. Like he paved my way when I had to claw my way through Jay Kapone and Terisa. And who had my back? I had my back! As he was gesturing and flaring his gay arms all around the place, I secretly wondered if he gave it or took it?

Kenny started fussing over the gown I was going to wear to the premiere tonight. He insisted that I wear a white carnation in my hair like the trademark in the movie. I really agreed to wear the white carnation because I was wearing my new–white mink and chinchilla fur tonight. I decided that I'd do just that and get a kick out of the press. I know management had invited Nikki Guy to make an appearance. I told Kenny to call her back and ask if she could come dressed like Sassi as well with a red sexy dress and red rose in her hair. She accepted. I want her to sit next to me, and let the public see the 60's meet the 90's.

"Kenny"

"Diva!"

"Hel–lo," I said and gave him two snaps up. Then he totally took it out of context and started snapping *his* fingers and twirling around on his tip–toes calling me "Mrs. Divine Diva." I was mortified for a moment. I started thinking. When did Kenny start respecting my "old ass" as he had so homosexually put it.

"Miss Thang . . . you spent a lot of cash yesterday. Do you think it's wise? Wait until you secure a couple more movie roles, and then we can go paint the town red. But for now . . . as your agent . . . you need to slow it down."

I guess money brings the gay out of people because he was full–fledged at this point. "Kenny, I wanted this to wait until after the premiere tonight . . . but since you brought it up . . . let's get right to the point. You are officially fired!"

"What?" he spat.

"You heard me correctly. You're lazy, cynical and you don't work hard enough for me. I can see it now...a script landing on your desk and you're thinking . . . she's too *old* for the role. So to avoid all of that, I have to let you go. I need someone who believes in me."

"Miss Diva . . . Miss Diva." He said while shaking his head in a sympathetic manner. "Well, you are everything I ever thought you'd be. This has nothing to do with my constant teasing about your age. You think you've reached the top of the pinnacle and you don't need anyone else? Didn't you ever hear it's lonely at the top? Look around you. Who do you see? Don't think I didn't hear what went down with you and your friends in California. You may be on top today . . . but you can just as easily slide down that same ladder that you climbed up. And don't forget whose shoulder's you used. And no matter how you distort the truth in your mind, you would not be in "Silk" if it wasn't for me. No agent nor friend would have told you about the casting call because everyone sees through you. You're hated by many and loved by none."

"Kenny, stop acting like a sissy and take being fired like a man. My friends have nothing to do with this equation. You are not viable to me. It's that simple. So I simply decided to take you off payroll. Don't worry, you can still keep your ticket for the premiere tonight."

"You know they say left–handed people owe the devil a day's work. I guess left–hearted people like you will owe him a lifetime. I hope you don't slip up and trip up because if you do, no one will be there to catch you!" Kenny exclaimed. Then he went into his pocket and pulled out his pass for the premiere and threw it in my face. The rough plastic edge popped against my head. I immediately jumped to my feet and lifted my hand to bitch–slap him, but he caught my wrist and we stared fiercely into each other's eyes. With force, I snatched my arm away and on my way up to my bedroom I told him to "get the fuck out!"

"Love . . . I'll skip out of here and into court. I will have my attorneys get so far up your ass, the gay jokes will be on you!" I never replied to that remark, but he did oblige me and left promptly.

79
LYRIC DEVANEY

As I lay upstairs in my bed, I drifted off into a light sleep and woke up in a sweat ten minutes later. It felt like I had been asleep for hours. I had this same re–occurring dream that I was falling from the Empire State Building but that I never hit the ground. I have that anxious feeling in my stomach that you have when you're on a rollercoaster. And in my dream I'm screaming. These dreams are eerie and are starting to get to me. First it was the casket, now this recent dream of my falling into nothing but darkness. Something just doesn't seem right. These weird empty dreams have me feeling a little edgy.

For some reason, I didn't want to be alone, but I had no one to call. Even though I didn't want to face reality, I admitted to myself that I really missed Richard. It seems that just yesterday we were making love. Now were doing our best to make each other miserable. I think I had threatened Richard a million times since I found out about the baby. Then I humiliated him in Angel Magazine and never once did I think about his political future. I could be taking away his livelihood, and I don't even know if he's the father of my baby! How could I say that I love this man and at the same time do everything in my power to try and destroy him? And what about his love for me? Actually, he never said he loved me. He just implied it. Could I actually be a victim of double–talk? Is it possible that Richard never, ever loved me? The proverbial reality of it made me feel nauseous, and it wasn't from morning sickness.

Thinking about love and my happiness, I thought about my baby, Brooklynn. She's taking too long to arrive. I wish I could snap my fingers, and she'd appear to share tonight with me. I'd buy her a miniature white mink and chinchilla coat exactly like mine, with a little shoulder bag to wear like she was grown. All little girls want to carry a purse like their mommies. Speaking of mommies, I haven't spoken to mine since I got back. I picked up the phone and speed dialed her. She picked up on the first ring.

"This is momma," she crooned. My mother had everyone call her "momma."

"Hi, mother."

"Lyric . . . my baby . . . where have you been?"

"Mother I've been shooting a movie. I told you that already."

"Well, why haven't you called? I'm still your momma, and you know I don't have no long distance. So you back now?"

"Yes, I'm back. And that premiere to my movie is tonight. You should be able to catch a glimpse of me on the news this evening."

"Catch a glimpse of you. No, I'm going to see my baby in person. I'ze told all my friends that my baby is a star and when she has that big movie premiere, I'm going to be right there with her on television. I done saved up and went and bought me a nice dress and shoes from "Bargain Land" on 125th Street." Her voice smiled.

"Mother you can't go." I said irritated that she'd want to.

"What you mean I can't go?"

"Mother, tonight is no place for you."

"Oh . . . you 'shamed of me, huh?"

"No, mother. It's not like that. What celebrities have you ever seen take their mothers to premiere night or to the Oscars for that matter? But I will acknowledge you in my acceptance speech when I win a Oscar for my role in 'Silk'." As I spoke the words, I envisioned myself up on the podium accepting my Oscar.

"Lyric Devaney . . . I'm fifty–one years old, and I'm not getting any younger. I think I deserve a little excitement in my life before I leave this here good earth. I want all the perks of being a celebrity mom . . . and maybe I can meet me a rich husband to live out my last days with. You know the doctor said I ain't got much longer . . . chile why you want to take away my last chance to kick up my heels?"

"Mother . . . I didn't want to tell you because I was embarrassed, but they only gave me one ticket and I have to use that for myself," I lied.

"Well, you'd think the star would get treated better than that. Now what am I supposed to tell all my friends in building three?"

"Tell them your back was acting up again. They'll understand."

"Oh . . . alright. Well, now that you're all famous . . . when am I getting my house you promised me? Lord knows i'ze sure is tired of smelling these pissy staircases 'round here. And the gunshots at night nearly make me jump out of my skin."

"Mother, I've decided to let you move into my condo, and I'll move into the house. This is much better for you because you can't keep up with a big home all alone."

"No, I'ze don't wants no apartment condo! That's for you young folks. I want a house like you promised me. I want to live out the rest of my days in luxury...like the white folks. I want to plant vegetables in my garden like I did down south before you were born." My mother's voice was slow and paced, and she was getting on my nerves.

"Mother, you make me so mad I want to strangle you!"

"If you ever lift a finger at me, you won't bring it back down!"

"Look," I said, ignoring her threat, then continued after I breathed, "you're not getting a house because I don't want to buy one for you. You will do just fine in this here apartment. Stop being ungrateful!" I screamed.

"No, you's the one being ungrateful!"

"Me? Ungrateful! What have you ever done for me?" I smugly replied.

"I gave you life . . . and don't you ever forget that. I should have flushed you when I had the chance . . . but I didn't! You also had the privilege of living life as an only child!"

I nearly gasped at my mother's blatant honesty. I'm supposed to be grateful that she brought me into a world of poverty, where I had to struggle to get ahead ever since I was twelve years old.

"Let me slap you with reality! You fucked for pleasure and had me, so deal with the pain. I don't owe you shit! You didn't have an abortion because you couldn't afford one. And you were so enthralled with my father, you'd do anything to keep him including getting pregnant. When he didn't turn out to be the man you thought he was, you rearranged your life and I went along with it. So don't act like you've been a slave to my life, and now you're waiting to reap your rewards! This is sex education 101 . . . use condoms if you don't want children!" I slammed the phone down so hard I thought I split it in two.

I swear to God, I now know why I had had an occasional drink in the past!

80
MADISON MICHAELS

Maurice and I were married a couple of days after he proposed. Neither my family nor my friends were invited. And Maurice had no relatives; so basically, we had no one but each other. It killed me not to invite my mother or Joshua, but this wasn't the type of wedding I had wanted. And Maurice promised that as soon as we got our money right, we'd have a large wedding with a huge wedding cake, and I would be able to invite all my friends and family. So, for now, we grabbed a nice guy from off the street to stand in as our witness and went to City Hall.

The wedding was nothing like I had imagined, but Maurice was persistent about marrying me. I think it gave him a thrill to get his way all the time. Despite being married to the man I loved, I still didn't feel the bond I had expected to feel with my husband. Nothing changed. In fact, we didn't even consummate our marriage on our wedding night. Maurice dropped me off that afternoon and went right back out. He said he had "business" to take care of. When I asked him "what business?" he replied that he had to go and hustle up some money to buy an outfit for Lyric's premiere tomorrow. He said she personally had Fed–Ex ship a ticket for him, and him alone, to attend the event. There wasn't anything in there for me. When I protested against his going without me, he said, "Baby, wild horses couldn't keep me away! Everybody who's anybody is going to be there, and this is my chance to make my presence felt with sexy ass Lyric!"

81
MADISON MICHAELS

I woke up bright and early Friday morning to get my plan in motion. Maurice had arrived home 5 a.m. and he was inebriated, so I knew I didn't have to tiptoe around the house; he'd never hear me anyway. I went to his pockets and pulled out all the money he had. To my amazement it was close to $200. If he asked where the money had gone, I'd say I never saw it. He'll think he lost it coming home in a stupor. I know I really should have asked Maurice for the money, but I knew he'd only say he didn't have any. Besides, he had set the tone for taking things without permission. I'm only following his lead. And I technically was his wife, so maybe it's time he started paying some bills.

I took a quick shower and put on a black T–shirt and Levis, my black Reeboks and then I was off. Today, I was going down to "Pink Houses" projects in East New York, Brooklyn to find two of the toughest girls that I knew walking on earth. My biggest challenge would be hiding from Portia. The two girl's names were Redbone and Sweepy. I had met them when Joshua and I were in court prosecuting them for attempting to rob their very own friend, Tisha. Apparently, they wanted to rob Tisha of the new gold jewelry she had acquired from her current boyfriend Merciful, a local hoodlum around their way. The girls rode her up in the elevator, and when it stopped on the second floor, two guys opened the door with guns drawn and told Tisha to give them her jewelry. Tisha, smelling a set–up, refused to let go of the jewels and lashed out and began fighting Redbone and Sweepy in the elevator. Outnumbered, she was clearly no match for her friends.

Tisha testified that Sweepy had snatched the gun from one of the masked gunmen and started letting off shots. Miraculously, no one was hit. Redbone and Sweepy were each facing seven to fifteen years upstate doing hard time if they blew trial. Everyday, they would come into court with their court–appointed attorneys and strike up a conversation with me asking me to "hook them up" with a plea bargain. They proclaimed their innocence on each and every occasion. Although I knew I should not be involved with the other side, something in my heart went out for these bad girls. They looked so innocent and were very attractive girls who didn't seem as if they could handle hard time upstate. But their police files told another story.

After weeks of trying to convince Joshua that he had enough on his plate to handle, that he should push this case through and concentrate on his more important cases, I finally penetrated his concrete exterior. I got him to let them cop–out to three years, so they'd only do one and a half if they had good behavior. They jumped on the deal and off to jail they went. That was two years ago. Sweepy did the one and a half, but Redbone got hit with six extra months for fighting. She apparently got sliced in the face with a jail–made shank by a lesbian who suspected her of fooling around with her girlfriend. These two girls, before they went up north, said they owed me a favor . . . today I wanted to cash in on it.

After walking around in circles for four hours, asking everyone in sight if they knew Sweepy or Redbone, my feet were swollen from exhaustion. I realized no one was willing to give up that information to a perfect stranger. They probably thought that I was an undercover cop trying to bust the two unsuspecting girls. As I was sitting on the project bench resting and devising a plan, I noticed a lady somewhere in her early thirties, looking down at the ground, kicking leaves away like she'd lost something. I went over there to ask if I could help her with her search. Her face was twisted up and her body was twitching. As I spoke to her, she rocked back and forth. Her clothes were too small and worn. She smelled like last week's trash. "Did you lose something?" I asked. She opened her mouth wide and smiled a toothless grin.

"Oh, I ain't never seen you cop from 'round here be foe. What cha got? A twennie?"

"A twenty dollar bill?" I nervously responded.

"Twennie dollars of crack rock. Don't chu hit the pipe? I needs a hit and fast . . . stop playin," she exclaimed.

"I . . . don't do drugs."

"Well you should 'cause you sure looks like you been beamin' up to scotti. I know a crackhead when I'ze sees one."

I was speechless. My hand immediately went up to my scar. She continued, "Girl, I ain't talkin' 'bout no scar. Your face and weight gave you away. You a walkin' zombie just like I is! Now let's beam up together. We friends. You treat me this time and I'll turn a quick trick later and that one will be on me." Every time she opened her mouth, I smelled hot do–do.

"No . . . no . . . you're mistaken. I don't smoke crack. I thought you lost something and I wanted to help you. I'm just looking for my friends." I was so embarrassed that I stuttered through my sentence. Her left eyebrow went up suspiciously, and she stared at me intently to see if she could see a sign of weakness. "Are you Poe Poe?"

"Poe Poe? Excuse me, I'm not sure who she is," I said.

The crackhead literally fell down to the ground rolling around laughing hysterically. Then she stopped and hopped up with one quick gesture. I guess the show was over. Walking away she mumbled, "You must be the police then." Thinking quickly I ran after her and slid ten dollars from out my pocket. "I'm not the police. I swear! I'm just out here looking for my friends. If you help me find them, I'll pay you." Hearing the word 'pay' made her quick little steps come to an abrupt end. "You don't look like you got any cash on you. How much you gonna pay me if I tell you where your friends are?"

"I'll give you ten dollars?"

"Who ya' lookin' foe?"

"I'm looking fcr Sweepy and Redbone. Do you know them?"

"You tryin' to git me killed for a itty bitty amount of money? If you are Poe Poe, do you know what they'll do to me?"

"For the last time I am not the police. I need to hire them for a job. And if you don't tell me where they are, when I find them I'll let them know you almost made them miss out on making some money. They won't be pleased!" I had put a little base in my voice to let her know the situation was serious. Then I flashed that ten bucks like it was ten grand. She fell for it—hook, line, and sinker. She snatched the ten from my hands and pointed me towards Building 32 on Stanley Avenue and Building 45 on Caveman side.

82
MADISON MICHAELS

I started out toward the closest building. This is where Redbone lived. I rode up in the piss-smelling elevator to the 6th floor. She told me to go to apartment "6Z." As the elevator made its way up, I heard rap music blaring from the hallway. My intuition told me it was coming from the sixth floor. Just as I thought. I got off the elevator and my eardrums nearly burst. Two girls were walking down the long and narrow hallway with a boom box stereo. I immediately recognized them both as Redbone and Sweepy. A smile of gratefulness splashed across my face. As we got closer, I could see them both staring me down with a penetrating glare.

"Yo, who dat?" Sweepy spat. Redbone reached into her back pants pocket and pulled out a razor. They were just a couple of steps away from me now, and my heart was fluttering from fear. Redbone looked a little masculine since I had last seen her and that four-inch scar on her cheek didn't help much. She had on a pair of white Puma sneakers with a black stripe, a black bandana with two ponytails tied tightly underneath and a pair of blue Guess overalls. Sweepy was wearing a bright red, tight, t-strap cotton dress that contrasted with her dark-brown complexion. They clashed in sophistication and complimented each other ghetto fabulously. Sweepy's hair had gel in it and was slicked back into a ponytail with a weave piece dangling. She had on a pair of Doc Marten's combat boots and an inexpensive Liz Claiborne pocketbook draped over her shoulders. Jail had certainly used them up. Any innocence they had once possessed was gone and replaced with a callous, distant look in their eyes. They looked too old and worn out for their young years. I knew I'd better speak up, and soon, before I wouldn't be able to make it out of there in one piece.

"Sweepy, Redbone, It's me, Madison Michaels."

"Yo, how she know our names?" Sweepy kept asking Redbone the questions as if she had all the answers.

"Who da fuck is Madison Madison, what da fuck!" Redbone laughed.

"It's me . . . Madison . . . two years ago . . . criminal court. I did you two a favor." I smiled hoping they'd soon recognize me before this got ugly.

"Oh dip. It's da bitch from the court house!" Sweepy exclaimed.

"Wow, you look fucked up. What happened to you?" Redbone countered.

"I ran into some trouble. That's why I'm here. I'm hoping you two can help me out. Pay me back that favor you owe me."

"Wait a minute. We don't OWE nobody shit!" Redbone's smile quickly evaporated, and she tensed up and became hostile.

"Yeah fuck dat! We still did hard time up north. So what da fuck you talkin' 'bout OWE? I should cut your ass right here and now!"

As they moved in closer towards me I yelled, "Wait a minute! I didn't mean owe. I wanted to pay you two to do a job for me. Let's just let the past lie there. Who knows? I may be able to do you guys more favors. I have high connections. I'm an attorney now with the D.A.'s office. You may need me in the future," I lied.

I could tell they both were thinking about what I had to offer. Redbone broke the silence, "I just caught a case for snatchin' this broad's chain on da A–train. Do you think you could hook me up? This time I don't want to do *no* jail time. Tell your office I said to kiss my ass!"

"Sure, I could probably get that bullshit case dismissed." I was talking their lingo and saying what they wanted to hear.

"What 'bout me? I just got caught in Macy's for boostin' some shit. You'd think they would give me a shopliftin' class then let me go! But those crackers are tryin' to give me two years upstate. Yo, I can't go back up north," she whined.

As I stood there listening to them bitch about their delinquent problems, I was eager to get my situation handled. Time was running out. I made every promise I could, then finally asked the question–"I wanted to pay you girls to bust somebody up. Today! And I need my name to remain anonymous. I'll pay for the job to get done, but you must be discreet. My career and all," I cautioned. Both their eyes lit up when I said pay.

"Yo dat shit gonna cost some paper yo."

"How much?"

"Fifty dollars a bullet!" Redbone spat.

"Bullet? I don't want you to shoot nobody." I was impressed with their gangster mentality. And the thought was tempting.

"You said 'bust somebody up.' What da fuck does that mean?"

"I want you to beat someone up. Really bad. And you must, must slash her face into tiny pieces where plastic surgery won't be able to fix her."

"Is she da bitch dat slashed ya face?"

"No . . . no . . . that was different. Anyway, how much for that?"

"Same price!" Sweepy said before Redbone could open up her mouth with a lower bid. I dug deep into my jean pocket and pulled out my one hundred and seventy dollars to peel off the fifty dollars when Redbone snatched my whole stash.

"Thankz partner," she sneered. I thought about getting angry, but I knew better, so I just let it slide.

83
MADISON MICHAELS

On the A–train to Lyric's condominium, we devised a plan. I would knock on Lyric's door and when she came to open it up for me, they'd push us both back into the apartment and act like it was a robbery. After they duck tape the both of us, they were going to ask Lyric for her prized jewelry. And the minute Lyric refused to give up the goods, which I knew her materialistic ass would do, they'd cut her up like mincemeat! When the smoke clears, Lyric will be stitched up and so will I. She'll see I have stitches on my forehead, and I'm sure she'll be so concerned with her cuts, she won't realize that mine are old. Also, I'll have her eating out the palm of my hands. She'll have to pay for my re–constructive surgery as well as her own.

The situation got out of hand when I told them what jewelry to ask for. They decided they wanted to kill Lyric for her jewels! I had to tell them that she really didn't own the jewelry they were going to ask for. That's why it was such a great plan, because the object was for her to refuse. I told them she was going to refuse because she didn't have it to give. It took some convincing before they actually believed me, but fortunately they did. And not a moment too soon, because the next stop on the train was Lyric's.

84
MADISON MICHAELS

By the time we arrived at Lyric's apartment, I was afraid we had missed her. The premiere would begin in less than two hours, and I was wondering if she had to make a couple of stops first. My stomach was tied up in knots and my mouth was dry and pasty. I looked over at Redbone and Sweepy; they were as cool as ice cubes in lemonade.

We crept up to the second landing, undetected by neighbors. The building was usually quiet, and you hardly ever saw anyone. Everyone kept different hours. Redbone and Sweepy were off to my right, waiting in the cut for Lyric to open up the door for her good old friend Madison. At first I knocked timidly because my hands were shaking. I kept wondering if these two strangers would lose it and cut me up as well as Lyric just for the hell of it. Then I rationalized that they needed me. I was the attorney who'd get their cases dismissed. With newly found courage, I knocked even louder on her door. Still no answer. A quick vision that she could be in there giving Maurice a blow job made my blood boil.

I reached for the doorknob and turned it. To my surprise, it opened. I walked in and motioned for Redbone and Sweepy to come in, too. I put my finger to my lips letting them know to be quiet. All three of us tiptoed up her plush carpeted stairs, heading for her bedroom. She must be totally engrossed in the mirror admiring herself getting dressed for the premiere, I thought, tuning out the whole world. Anticipation had my adrenaline pumping when I thought about how she was finally going to get hers. I wished that afterwards I could spit in her face again. Or maybe take the razor and get a couple of slashes in myself, but I knew I could never do that without getting some serious jail time. No, I'll let my thugs–for–hire take care of the small things. Because after I teach Lyric a lesson, I'm going to be into bigger and better things as Maurice's wife.

Lyric's bedroom door was open, and I could clearly see she wasn't in there. When I looked to see the bathroom door ajar, I turned around to clue Redbone and Sweepy in that this was it. They were too busy casing the joint, pointing out what they wanted to take. I heard Redbone telling Sweepy they could beep B–Boy to come back and get the big screen television. These fools were going to get us busted! If they thought that these nosy neighbors weren't going to call the cops watching Lyric's household being looted by some dusty project bums, they were wrong. How could they take those items out inconspicuously? Again, I worried about the possibility that I could be dealing with amateurs. Why hadn't I realized that if they were so professional, why were their rap sheets longer than my telephone bill? They're sloppy and stupid. I gave them a look that said "Let's get the party started," and got their attention. Once they were behind me, I pushed into the bathroom yelling, "Lyric . . . who are these people? What's happening to . . . "

I was stopped dead in my tracks by the morbid scene. Lyric was completely naked, hanging over the side of her bathtub, filled with water, with her right wrist slit. Blood was everywhere. The peach carpet in the bathroom was soaked with blood and had turned a deep burgundy. There was an empty bottle of Moet champagne lying on the floor and an empty bottle of Valium prescription pills. From the frightened look plastered on her face, it was clear she was dead! No one said anything for minutes. I leaned over to check her pulse on her neck and felt nothing. She finally went over the edge and committed suicide I thought. Her left hand was wrapped tightly around her protruding abdomen. I looked at her in disgust!

We all backed out of the bathroom at the same time, and I closed the door back the way it was. Luckily, we all had gloves on, so we didn't leave any prints. I looked at Redbone, and she was trembling and tears were streaking down her face. "Ohmigod! Ohmigod!" She kept mumbling.

"Will you keep her quiet," I said to Sweepy who I could see was casing the joint like I now was.

"We need to call an ambalance," Redbone continued.

"We ain't callin' no motherfuckin' ambalance for dat bi'och! I know who she is and I ain't catchin' no murder charge. The fuckin' mayor is gonna make someone fry in the electric chair for killin' his hoe and it ain't gonna be me!" Sweepy blurted out.

Who knew she kept up with politics? She was right about not calling an ambulance. We'd have to hang around and explain how we found her. Had we seen anything, blah blah blah? I didn't want any part of this scene. I hope the bitch died slow. I'm just angry she was in la la land, all intoxicated and drugged up. She always was a coward.

85
MADISON MICHAELS

I left Redbone and Sweepy in the hallway, trying to get it together. As soon as I entered Lyric's bedroom, I spotted a beautiful white mink coat. A huge smile came upon my face when I thought about what Maurice would think when I came home wearing this baby! I ran to it and immediately tried it on. Then I ran to her dresser to find her jewels but none were there. As I was rummaging through her room, I grabbed anything of value quickly because I knew we had to get out of her apartment. Redbone, who by now had it together with Sweepy right behind her, came in to see what I was doing. Both sets of eyes landed on the coat at the same time. "Yo up that!" was all Redbone said to me. I knew she meant the coat. That made me mad. They already had my money, which I knew I wasn't getting back and they hadn't even done anything. Now they wanted the coat. I convinced myself that if they didn't have weapons, I could take on the both of them. Redbone's outburst had me thinking I had more balls than these two imaginary gangsters. But they did have weapons and outnumbered me by one, so I reluctantly took off the coat and handed it to them. Sweepy ran downstairs and got a couple of garbage bags and started throwing Lyric's clothes inside them. I just sat on the bed watching them load up all the good stuff. I knew not to go and pick up anything because whatever I'd grab, they'd just take from me. I listened to their idle conversation and became more and more infuriated.

"Yo we hit the lotto."

"We gonna be rich. You know how much we could git for dat coat?"

"At least some big bucks . . . maybe two hondred!"

"Damn . . . she got all the flyest gear up in here. Yo, I got first dibs on dat Donna Karen jumper!"

"Let's take everythang. Nobody know she in here dead. We could go git a truck and make it happen."

"We can't do that, stupid. She famous. Someone is gonna come lookin' for her ass sooner or later. We got ta git up outta here foe we go down for this."

"We ain't goin' down foe shit. We already gotz a hookup in the DA office sittin' right here."

"Her ass going down too, stupid. Let's take what we kin carry and bounce."

While they went back and forth with the nonsense, I had cleverly spotted Lyric's Gucci pocketbook tossed in the corner near her bed. And if I knew Lyric, she'd have at least a grand up in there AND her credit cards. When they had their backs turned, I reached down and with one swift movement, I picked it up and stuffed it down my pants.

Once outside, Redbone and Sweepy were an awful sight to see. They both were struggling down the block dragging oversized plastic bags with silly grins on their faces. I let them walk ahead of me because I thought it would be best to distance myself from them. If anything went down, I'd deny ever knowing them. I'll say they were trying to set me up because I had them sent up north. They had basically forgotten about me, anyway, once they were out in the fresh air away from any possibility of getting caught.

Once we got to the train station, we went our separate ways. They never even stopped to thank me for the money or the clothes they had gotten from Lyric's house. None of that would have been possible if I hadn't put them down.

86
MADISON MICHAELS

When I got home, Maurice wasn't there, but he left an angry note on the refrigerator telling me that if I didn't put his fucking money back, he'd break my fucking fingers when he got back in tonight. I swallowed hard and finally reached inside my pants and pulled out Lyric's stylish Gucci bag. I threw it over my shoulder and ran into my bedroom mirror to admire how it looked on me. I smiled with delight once I realized that it was all mine. Then it suddenly hit me that I needed to check it for money. I ripped it open, pulled out the wallet, and tossed the bag on the floor. When I opened the wallet, it contained an enormous number of crisp $100 dollar bills. I counted out $3,000! My heart skipped a Sweet Dixie beat. I then counted out her credit cards. I thought I had died and gone to glamour girl heaven. I wiped the perspiration off my forehead and took out two $100 dollar bills and laid them on the kitchen table for him. Then I took the Gucci bag and put the wallet back inside and hid it in the hamper in my bathroom away from Maurice. Tomorrow I was going to shop until I dropped. God knows I needed it! After all of this, I was exhausted. I took another shower, put on my nightgown, and went peacefully to sleep.

The telephone ringing startled me. I jumped up and looked at the clock. It was 11:15 p.m., and Maurice wasn't in yet. I put my hand to my heart, thinking this would help slow it back down. Breathing in and out, I realized this must be Maurice. I finally picked up on the fourth ring, "Yes . . . who is it?" I asked sweetly. All I heard was someone sobbing uncontrollably into the phone. I couldn't make out what they were trying to tell me. I thought that this could be some sort of joke from one of Maurice's mistresses.

"Who is this?" I demanded. The sobs came further apart and you could tell that the person on the line was trying to get him or herself under control.

Finally I heard, "Madison, it's me . . . Joshua. Something horrible has happened. Have you heard? It's Lyric. She's . . . she's been hurt really bad. She's been rushed to Bellevue Hospital in critical condition . . . " he sobbed.

"You mean she's not dead!" I bellowed.

"No. She's barely hanging on . . . how did you know? Did you see it on the news?" he questioned.

I rolled my eyes then said, "Umm . . . no . . . I meant I hope she's okay. What happened?"

"It appears she tried to commit suicide. Her limousine driver found her wrist slit. That's all I know. I'm on my way over to the hospital. I want you to meet me there. I know this must be hard for you, but we need you strong right now. I need you to call Portia, and I'll call her mother."

Joshua broke out into tears again and became all choked up. Then he said, "This is all my fault. I should have been there for her. Who knew what she was going through? She must–" I had to cut Joshua's whining ass off mid–sentence.

"Joshua, I'm so upset right now. Let me call Portia and meet you at the hospital. We'll talk then," I said dismissing him.

I hung up the phone and ran to the television and turned on "New York One News." The first thing I saw was Lyric's condominium being filmed on the news. All her neighbors were standing around, some sobbing, and some shaking their heads in remorse. The story was just coming on. The reporter said, *"This is Gilt McGronner, from WLTV, Channel Ten news. I'm here on Sixty-Eighth Street and Park Avenue at the home of superstar celebrity Lyric Devaney, star of the movie "Silk." When Ms. Devaney was late coming down for her movie premiere tonight, her limousine driver became suspicious and went up to investigate. There he found an unconscious Ms. Devaney, who was then rushed to the hospital in critical condition for an apparent suicide attempt. Ms. Devaney was also pregnant, a fact that was concealed from everyone. People are speculating about whether the mayor is the father of her love child and whether this is the reason she tried to take her own life. The Mayor was reached but had no comment on the situation. But he did say it was a great tragedy. We'll keep you posted as the police fill us in on the details. Apparently, the police are also investigating a possible burglary. It appears that some things are missing from the superstar's home. Our prayers definitely go out to Lyric Devaney. This is Gilt McGronner, WLTV, Channel Ten news."*

I clicked off the television and paced my bedroom floor. It was virtually impossible for someone to survive when they had lost so much blood, especially when they wanted to die. And she had taken liquor and Valium. Anyone knows that mix is lethal. If she wants to die, then why don't she just fucking die? What is she holding on for?

I ran my finger over my scar then I realized I was trembling. What had I gotten myself into? What if someone had seen me around Lyric's condo today leaving with two thugs and bags of Lyric's belongings? I'll spend the rest of my life in jail for this shit! No! I needed to calm down. And how the hell did the police know shit was missing? Probably the large gaps in her closet. They have trained eyes for things like this. I should have known better. But what could I do? Redbone and Sweepy would have taken her things even if I had protested. Just then I ran into the bathroom and pulled out Lyric's wallet. I cut up all her credit cards, license and her wallet into pieces and threw it in the garbage. I stuffed the twenty–eight hundred in my bra and exhaled. I knew I should really get rid of her Gucci bag, but I couldn't bring myself to let go of it. I had never had anything that expensive before.

I convinced myself that no one could prove that the bag was Lyric's. I reached for my Nine West, four–year–old pocketbook, took out my wallet, put it in my new Gucci bag and tossed my old bag in the garbage and dumped all evidence into my incinerator. Since I didn't really want to speak to Portia on the phone, I left a voice message on her pager telling her briefly what had happened and for her to meet us at the hospital. Last, I wrote a note to Maurice and stuck it on the refrigerator telling him where I was going to be for a couple of hours.

I opened the cupboard and grabbed Maurice's Hennessey bottle. Even though I didn't drink much, I knew I needed something to do the acting for me. I swallowed down two glasses, brushed my teeth, popped a Cert's candy in my mouth, and I was off to be live on stage. Just like I had learned from Lyric.

87
PARKER BROWN-TUNE

The livery cab service I called could not get me to Bellevue Hospital fast enough. I sat there fidgeting while arguing with the cab driver to speed it up for what seemed like an eternity. Ten minutes ago I had heard on Channel Seven News that Lyric had tried to commit suicide tonight. I dropped everything and flew out of the house in my nightgown with a trench coat covering me up. While sitting in the cab, I realized that Joshua must not have known what happened to Lyric because he hadn't called me. I pulled out my cellular phone and called his when a woman answered on the first ring.

"Yes," she said.

"Um . . . do I have the right number? May I speak to Joshua?"

"Who is this?"

"His wife!" I responded. I was annoyed that Monique would be answering his phone so soon. There was absolutely no need for that. He never let me answer that goddamn phone, I thought to myself. And although my feelings were hurt for that moment, I pushed them aside and concentrated on why I was calling him. Lyric's situation was far more important than my marital problems at this point. It took a while before Joshua finally got to the phone. I heard a lot of whispering and someone covering and uncovering the phone. When he finally did say hello, I was so hot; I think my ears were on fire.

"Parker?"

I just ignored his phoniness.

"Joshua, I have some really bad news for you. I just heard that—"

"I know. We are at the hospital already." We? I thought to myself. So it's official. He did go running right into the arms of Monique after all. You'd think a husband needed time to breathe and figure out what he really wanted to do before he transitioned himself into another relationship. Men are just different. They need companionship, and there is no such thing as rebound in their books. Slightly annoyed that he could have found out such tragic information and not have tried to contact me sealed our fate. "Very well," I retorted and ended my call. I sat back in the cab and said a silent prayer for Lyric. As I closed my eyes, a couple of teardrops slid down. I wondered if I was crying for Lyric or for the realization that I had lost my husband. My marriage was over.

When I arrived at the hospital, reporters were everywhere. Some were live and on the air, while others were trying to get an inside scoop regarding Lyric's personal life from everyone who went to the reception desk to ask for her room number. The hospital made it very clear that only family was allowed up on the floor. When it was my turn, the reception nurse asked me my name. When I told her, she said, "Sorry, you're not on the list." I was furious. "Well, who made the list?"

"Joshua Tune. He's an assistant district attorney and a very close friend of Ms. Devaney." She smiled when she spoke of Joshua, and it was clear she was smitten. He must have used his charm on her.

"Well, I'm his wife!" I declared. She gave me a strange look and had to call upstairs to verify that I was who I said I was.

A reporter lurking nearby thought I was a perfect snitch to dish the dirt on Lyric and sprang out at that exact moment. While the nurse was writing out my pass, he slid over to me and said, "What station you working for?"

"I'm not working for no goddamn station!"

"So, what's your game, slim? I've seen Mr. Tune tonight and he has a hot cutie draped over his arm. So, if you're his wife, the other woman must be his daughter." I knew that if I answered to that derogatory remark, I'd let him know he had gotten to me. I decided that ignoring his remark would be in my best interest but he continued, "So, do you really know Lyric Devaney." He looked me up and down and made a smirk on his face as a gesture to let me know he hadn't believed that I knew

Lyric. When I swung around and looked him directly in his eyes, we were both caught off guard.

"Reggie?"

"Parker Brown!"

"What the hell are you up to harassing people coming to see Lyric?" I scolded.

Reggie and I had gone to high school together. Our mothers used to call each other cousins. They were best friends until they moved away. No one kept in touch like we said we would. Reggie was still handsome as ever, and even though he had never made a pass at me, I knew that he was attracted to me. But out of respect, he never acted on it. He stood 6 feet 2 inches and had an athletic body frame. His high cheekbones and full lips gave him sex appeal. His face had matured and his dark–chocolate complexion glowed.

"I'm a journalist for Celebrity Magazine. My job is to dish out the dirt. It pays the bills. Say, do you really know Lyric Devaney?"

"She's a friend of mine," I somberly said.

"Then I'll let you go to be by her side. I hear she's really messed up bad," Reggie said sounding more humane and sympathetic. Then he continued, "Are you really married to Joshua Tune?"

"Yes . . . I am."

"I always knew you liked milk in your coffee." He smiled. As I walked towards the elevator, he asked, "Could I call you sometime?"

"I'm listed."

88
PARKER BROWN-TUNE

When the doors to the elevator opened, my heart dropped. The reality hit me that we *could* actually lose Lyric. I know she and I bickered a lot, but she was still someone I admired. No one should leave this earth like that with such a promising future ahead of them. As I walked down the long white corridor, I could start to distinguish faces. Everyone was looking down the corridor at me as I approached, making me feel unwanted. Monique and I made eye contact and she squirmed around for a moment, then held onto Joshua's arm in a territorial grip. Joshua had his hands firmly tucked into his pants pocket trying to give off the appearance that he was handling the situation. I knew him better than that. I knew inside he was torn. I could read it in his eyes and the way his forehead had crinkled lines that creased and looked permanently apart of his face. He looked at me and nodded. I just rolled my eyes and kept moving. Lyric's mom was pacing up and down the corridor with her Bible in her hand quoting Scripture.

Her mom was extremely attractive for her age. She didn't look a day older than forty. Her clothes were worn and outdated, but you could tell that once upon a time, they were very stylish. Her sandy brown hair was pulled back tight in a ponytail that reached about one inch above her butt. She strikingly looked like an impoverished Lena Horne.

Madison was sitting down in a chair looking unusually calm. I thought Madison would have to be sedated at this point considering she was usually so fragile. In fact, she looked a little bored and distracted, as if she was ready to go home or there was a more important place she'd rather be. I must have been reading her wrong. Everyone takes tragedies in their own unique way. I remember when my father had a heart attack at work and the phone call came to the house, my mother burst out laughing. She didn't find it funny. She was scared and that was all she could do to keep it together.

I decided that Madison was my best ally. I went and sat by her and gave her a big hug. We embraced, and it felt like I would shatter her to pieces. She was nothing but skin and bones. I knew her situation from a nosy intern at Joshua's office. One day I called for Joshua, and he wasn't in the office. I then asked to speak to Madison, and she wasn't there either. But he didn't hesitate to tell me the 4–1–1 on how horrible Madison looked. And he was very accurate, I might add. As we sat there, I tried very hard not to concentrate on her appearance. That large slash adorning her forehead and face was unsightly. I decided to stare straight ahead and not to ask her any personal questions regarding her circumstances. I sat there wondering how two beautiful black women could destroy themselves the way Lyric and Madison had. What was missing from their lives that drove them to act irresponsibly?

"Peace Madison. How's Lyric doing?" I tentatively asked.

"Fine."

"The doctor said she's stable?" my voice asked with hope.

"No."

"So how do you know she's fine."

"Because she ain't dead!" Madison replied. I was startled by her tone but didn't push any further because I was aware of the stress she must be under. I swallowed hard and walked over to the one person I knew I could get details from. Joshua and Monique were engrossed in a deep conversation. They both felt me walking towards them, turned around, and stopped talking mid–sentence. I did my best not to make eye contact again with Monique. I kept my eyes focused on Joshua.

"Joshua, have you heard anything?" I said. Joshua cleared his throat before he spoke. This was an awkward situation, being so formal with your husband.

"They still have her in surgery. Right now, they're

trying to save the baby. They are performing a Cesarean." His voice was weak and he was stark white.

"What are Lyric's chances?"

"The surgeon said it could go either way." With that grim information, I walked away. I didn't go back to sit down next to Madison, nor did I go and disturb Lyric's mother. Everyone had their own space and just patiently waited for what we hoped was going to be good news. Lyric was a fighter; she'd pull through. Whatever she was going through when she took those pills, I hope she realizes it is not important now. She must *want* to live for the sake of her baby.

Perhaps twenty minutes had passed before I heard an awful moan, then a shriek. It was Portia. She came flying down the hallway in high–heeled shoes as if she had on Nike Air Trainers. Her outburst startled everyone. She ran directly to Lyric's mom and embraced her. She was crying so hard, she couldn't talk. Everyone gathered around her to calm her down. Her light complexion was bright pink and her face was tear–stained. Mrs. Devaney calmly walked her over to a chair and sat her down while I ran to get her some water.

"Let it out chile . . . just let it out," Mrs. Devaney said. Portia buried her head in her chest and just let go. My heart went out to her because she was clearly the only one who couldn't handle the situation. When she finally calmed down, I gave her the water.

"How is she? Please don't tell me she's dead!" she cried.

"No, she's holding on. My Lyric's a fighter. She doesn't know any other way."

"I can't lose her . . . I can't lose my best friend. God can't do that to me . . . we not speakin' . . . I need to tell her that I'm sorry . . . I'm so s-o-r-r-r-y."

She sobbed uncontrollably again. Just then Joshua couldn't take it anymore either and broke down also. He turned and walked away quickly with his hands dug deep inside his pockets, like a little boy hoping no one would see him cry. Just when I was about to go after him, Monique took off first. I remembered that was no longer my job. I stayed back and tried to comfort Portia.

Portia was going on and on about her argument with Lyric. She was telling Mrs. Devaney that she didn't want to lose her friend while they were mad at each other over a man.

"She's gotz to make it," she kept saying over and over again. Just then she looked up and her eyes focused on Madison who was just sitting there and hadn't said much since I got there.

"Where the fuck you git dat bag?"

"I um . . . ah . . . I bought it," she fumbled. Portia sat up straight and wiped her face and nose.

"From where?" she asked suspiciously.

"A store!" Madison snapped.

"That's Lyric's bag, you bitch!" Portia screamed.

"It is not! It's mine!" Madison yelled back. These two were clearly showing the signs of being under the pressure of losing a close friend. Hospital security ran over to them and threatened to throw them out if they didn't quiet down. Madison retorted, "I'll be leaving shortly anyway," underneath her breath. Then Portia, equally as quiet, mumbled, "Since when your broke ass kin afford a bag from Gucci?" Madison never responded. It was clear that there was a standoff going down. So much for friends coming together during tragedy.

89
PARKER BROWN-TUNE

The minutes seemed like hours as we all impatiently waited. Finally, the head surgeon came out with a grim look on his face. As he walked towards us, Joshua and Monique ran behind him trying to catch up. He went directly to Lyric's mom as we all huddled around to hear the news.

The doctor exhaled, then began, "Your daughter is not expected to make it through the rest of the night. She's lost a lot of blood and the tranquilizer mixed with alcohol has her in an irreversible coma. We did everything we could for the baby, who is six months premature weighs only one pound one ounce. She's not expected to make it through the night either. The baby suffered cardiac arrest during the Cesarean and had to be resuscitated. Another pediatric surgeon had to open up her chest and massage her heart. During this procedure a malfunction occurred and oxygen was lost between sixty seconds to a minute and a half. She lost a lot of oxygen to the brain and even if she did make it, she'd require strict medical attention around the clock. Are you Catholic, Mrs. Devaney?"

All Lyric's mother could do was nod her head 'Yes.' She was clearly destroyed by this information. "Then I suggest you go down to the chapel and have the priest come and pray for your daughter and granddaughter. I'm sorry."

The doctor walked away quickly, and I could see the grief on his face. I'm sure that's the hardest part about being a surgeon. The fatalities. Then telling the family.

My heart was heavy but I refused to give up hope. As it stood, Lyric was still with us. Mrs. Devaney came back with the priest, and we all headed to the Intensive Care Unit to say our last goodbyes to Lyric. Mrs. Devaney and the priest went in first. I watched from the window as the priest said a prayer, then took out some oil and anointed Lyric's head. Then he did a cross three times in the air and left.

When he departed, we all went inside. Lyric had tubes up her nose, hanging out of her mouth, and in her arms. She looked as if she was ten years old. So helpless as she lay there. The mere sight of her threw everyone into a frenzy. Mrs. Devaney finally lost it and collapsed into Joshua's arms. "My baby . . . my chile . . . God please don't take my chile. Take me! Take me!"

Everyone hugged and comforted each other in this time of need. Monique had stayed back outside the room, and I could feel her eyes burning a hole in the back of my neck. She was making sure I didn't make a move to comfort Joshua.

I walked over to the side of the bed and grabbed hold of Lyric's hand. "Lyric . . . you're strong. Don't give up on us. If you can hear me, squeeze my hand Lyric. Lyric fight! You have a little girl who needs you," I said and waited patiently to see if she would show some sign of life, but I felt nothing. Mrs. Devaney then led us in prayer. We recited Psalm 23. Portia was on Lyric's opposite side, holding her other hand. She kept bending over, kissing Lyric's face and whispering, "Please don't leave me here all by myself. You all I got. I'm sorry. I'm so sorry."

For some reason Portia thought that Lyric had done this to herself because they were at odds. "Portia, this is not your fault," I said trying to comfort her. She never even looked up. She just kept concentrating on Lyric.

As the hours went by, everyone had eventually propped themselves up in the hard hospital chairs they made available to us. Every now and then, we would all gather in prayer. Around 5 a.m., Madison announced to everyone's amazement that she had to go home and see what her "husband" was doing because she hadn't heard from him all night. Until now no one noticed the ring on her finger or the large hole in her head. She walked over to Lyric and leaned over the side of the bed. Then, clutching that Gucci bag tightly underneath her arm, she whispered something in Lyric's ear. I didn't hear it but Portia jumped up and said, "What did you say?!"

Not these two again. Startled, Madison jumped back away from Lyric's bed and said, "I said 'Please don't die'."

"It sounded like you said, 'I HOPE you die'!"

"Portia, what's the matter with you. Why would Madison say I hope you die?" Joshua had had enough of their bickering throughout the night.

"I know what I heard!" Portia was adamant.

"You're wrong!" Madison said gathering her things and flying out of the hospital room. I started to go after her because I knew that Portia was just making it clear that Lyric was her best friend. But I figured that she just needed to be alone and probably didn't like seeing her friend in this condition. Besides, those two were always vying for Lyric's friendship. Madison said her good–byes and disappeared into the early morning hours.

90
PARKER BROWN-TUNE

At approximately 5:20 a.m. we all heard, "Beep, beep, beep, beep . . . Code Blue. Code Blue . . . " Lyric's respirator was beeping uncontrollably. Then about four nurses and a slew of doctors came charging down the hallway and into her room. They screamed for everyone to get out, and we all quickly realized what was happening wasn't good. Everyone had panic–stricken faces. I was visibly trembling from fearing the worst.

We all watched in horror as they tried to jumpstart her heart. Every five seconds you'd hear, "Clear," then they'd zap Lyric with another electrical bolt, and her body would, literally, jump off the bed and collapse back down. For ten straight minutes this went on. Even long after the monitor signal that followed her heart lay flat, indicating that she was gone, the crew wouldn't give up. Ultimately, someone had to come out and tell us that we'd lost her. Lyric was gone. I felt her spirit leave the room, and I knew she'd be at peace in heaven.

The doctor walked over to Mrs. Devaney and reminded her that she still had a grandchild holding onto life in the nursery who needed her love and support. Since Lyric had died and the father hadn't been named, the next of kin was Mrs. Devaney who would ultimately have full custody unless the father of Lyric's child stepped up. We all agreed that Lyric hadn't told anyone who the father was.

"What chu saying?" Mrs. Devaney spoke to the doctor with newfound strength.

"I'm just simply saying that a social worker will want to know that the baby is going to be in capable hands."

"Baby? My baby just died, sir. That's where my responsibility ends. I spent most of my life raising Lyric and not enjoying myself because I always put her needs before mine. Now I'm determined to live out the rest of my life traveling and living in luxury. Not watching no retarded chile."

Everyone stood around and the moment became very tense. The doctor simply walked away in disgust. Up until now, no one had even bothered to go see the baby because we were all so consumed with Lyric. Mrs. Devaney spun around and directed all her attention towards Joshua. It didn't even phase her that she'd upset the doctor. As Lyric lay dead in bed with a white sheet covering her head a couple of feet away from her, Mrs. Devaney said, "Joshua, you're a lawyer right?" I could tell Joshua didn't want to disrespect Lyric's mother, but he was upset at her words. "Yes, I'm an assistant district attorney. Why?"

"Because you can tell me how I can git my money."

"What money?"

"Lyric's money, you silly fool. Did you think I just won the lottery?"

"No . . . but I bet you think you just did." With that, Joshua turned to leave. Monique and Portia followed behind him. Mrs. Devaney lingered for a moment then left as well, never turning around once to look at her daughter.

Something led me down one floor to the nursery. I expected to see some of the gang giving the little one support, to try and hang in there but no one came. I looked at the itsy–bitsy baby with the word, "Devaney" splashed across the incubator. She was no bigger than my hand. It was amazing that a baby could actually be that small. The respirator was helping her breathe in and out. "That's right . . . take deep breaths, baby girl," I cheered. "You're going to make it! Make it for your mommy. She's in heaven now . . . with the angels."

91
PORTIA JONES

Damn yo, how could I lose my homegirl? Shit is just fucked up now. No more chillin' in the Benz, frontin' like it's my shit. No more V.I.P. at the clubs, drinkin' bubbly with the celebs. I just can't understand how she gonna go out like dat? We peoples. She should have come to me, I was always down for whatever. I always had her back.

"Hootie hoo . . . " someone called. I was upstairs in my bedroom. I ran to my window and looked out. It was my other homegirl Peaches.

"Whaddup girl."

"You comin' down?"

"What ch'all doing?" I asked.

"We 'bout to smoke this spliff. We waitin' on you. It's Peanut, Crossman, and Boog. You down?"

"Yeah, I'm down." I closed my window and was headin' out when my moms stopped me.

"Where you runnin' to this fuckin' late? Ain't nothin' out in dem streets but death. You see what happen'd to dat other chile. She ain't killed herself, she was murdered. I know, dem cards done told me," she said.

"Pearl not tonight. I'm sick'a hearin' 'bout those Tarot cards. All my damn life you been practicin' dat Voodoo shit. If you kin see so much shit, see us out da damn projects!" I snapped on my moms.

"You better watch your tone 'fore I break dat broom over your head." I looked at my moms and rolled my eyes. Then she continued, "She in here now. Dat dead girl is here! She needs my help." I grabbed my jacket and slammed the front door on her constant babbling. "Chile, you better git in here and wash these dishes in that sink . . . " Pearl called after me.

When I got down below everyone was outside on the bench. Chillin'. Everyone did head nods. There was three blunts bein' passed 'round. Peaches hit me off wit the quickness. "Wassup," Peaches smiled.

"Hey girl," I said as I took a long drag of the blunt, and then passed it to Boog.

"We heard 'bout your girl goin' out like dat." Peanut said.

"Yo, that shit is ill," Crossman exclaimed.

"Yeah, I'm fucked up right now. I don't even want to think 'bout it, yo."

"Portia you lookin' right in dem jeans, ma. When you gonna let me hit it again?" Crossman questioned.

"Nigga please. Scabeatit! You ain't gettin' no more of this. Ya broke ass! Please, I don't wanna hav'ta whip a bitch ass over you. What!"

"Nah, my girl nice wit hers yo. She can handle."

"She can handle who? I'll fuck her up all the way from here to Ft. Green, Bed Stuy, Tompkins . . . " I laughed.

Crossman and I used ta fuck back in the dayz 'fore he hooked up wit his new chick, Tandie. In the projects people like to keep shit goin', so every now and then someone will tell her dat Crossman was out chillin' on the bench wit me and my peoples. She is 'posed to be steppin' to me.

The weed had everyone feelin' nice. B.I.G had just dropped his double CD and Peanut had the boom box on blast. *". . . my Detroit players, Tim's for my hooligans in Brooklyn . . . dead right if the head right biggie there ever' night . . . "* we all sang in unison. I jumped up and started doing the crip dance, the bankhead bounce, then da butt. We were all trippin'.

"Go Portia, it's ya birthday. Go Portia, get busy!" the crowd cheered as I worked up a sweat. We soon all fell back on the bench wit a mean case of the munchies. In between snackin' and snappin' on each other, Redbone and Sweepy came through wit a bag full of shit they had just boosted from the department stores. They had mad shit.

"What'z up couzin'," Redbone addressed the crowd.

"Whaddup," everyone responded.

"Wassup," Sweepy said. Sweepy wasn't from our side so no one said shit to her. Redbone decided to do all the talkin'.

"I got some fly shit to sell. Who got paper?"

"What chu got?" Peaches inquired. Redbone went into the plastic bag and pulled out a white mink coat. We all gagged. "How much yo?" Everyone quizzed.

"$200 dollars."

"Damn, my girl would look fly in dat shit Red, but I ain't makin' no sells tonight. Let me take it and you come see me tomorrow and I'll hit you off." Crossman said.

"Nah, nigga. You sell fuckin' crack ever' day. You ain't got two bills?" Redbone retorted. Crossman pulled out a pocket fulla crack viles to prove he didn't make a sale. But Redbone didn't care. She wasn't givin' up her shit to Crossman witout gettin' paid. We were all lookin' through the big bag pullin' out all type of shit. Sweepy was clockin' us to make sure no one stashed anything.

"What 'bout you Portia. You ain't got two bills?"

"Nah, I'm broke yo."

"All those damn foster kids your moms got and you can't get two bills?" Peaches asked.

"I know you ain't tryin' to snap on my moms bitch. 'cause I will take all my frustration out on you and beat you down yo."

"Damn, why you wildin'." Peaches mumbled.

While we were all tryin' to come up with some money to buy some of the fly shit, Crossman made a sale, but it wasn't enough for the coat.

"Yo, I could beep Justice–Born, he's really feelin' me right now." I was tryin' hard to get the coat.

"That bird ass nigga! He's grimy yo." Crossman said.

"Let me find out you jelly." Peanut responded.

"Jelly, nigga look at the ice on my wrist and neck. This platinum kid!"

"Nigga that's white gold! Stop frontin'."

Redbone pulled me to the side while the guys kept goin' at it. "Portia, you keep it real. Mad niggas out here feelin' you. You stay fly. Here's my beeper number, if you git the paper, hit me yo. I'll hold the coat for you."

"I know these bitches out here can't fuck wit me. But my girl just died, so I'm chillin wit the niggas right now and the dancin'."

"Who?"

"Lyric Devaney, the star of da movie "Silk" was my homegirl. That's why we out here trippin'," I explained. Redbone, lookin' a little shaky, grabbed Sweepy then bounced to git breakfast at the Galaxy. I walked back over to the bence to hear the rest of Crossman and Peanut snappin'. We were all laughin' until our stomachs hurt. Boog was calm because he was drinkin' a forty and it balanced his high. He was cheap as shit drinkin' out the bottle so no one could get none.

Just then 5.0 jumped from out two vans with guns drawn and rushed us. Boog dropped the forty, which came crashing to the ground and everyone tossed their blunts. They grabbed Crossman and swung him up against the fence and started to handcuff him. He had sold to an undercover officer. One of the cops was tryin' to make Crossman spit out the crack viles he tried to swallow by hittin' him in the face.

"Spit it out motherfucker," the cop kept yellin.

"Damn, ya'll some 21 jumpstreet ass niggas!" I yelled.

"T–N–T, A–Team ma'fuckers!" Peaches screamed.

There were five white cops and one black cop. The black cop had Crossman pinned up against the fence fuckin' him up. He was the undercover Crossman sold the crack to.

"Shut the fuck up bitch, before I push your wig back," the black cop said to Peaches, using our lingo.

"I wouldn't even let it go down like dat, partner! Take off that badge, and I'll show you who the real bitch is!" Boog challenged.

"Go the fuck upstairs before I arrest all of you's for obstruction of justice!" The big burly white cop said.

"P-e-a-r-l . . . P-e-a-r-l . . . these cops are harassin' us. Call the news. Call seven on your side!" I called up to my mother. The cops finally got the hint when everyone in the projects looked out their windows and started throwin' bottles, cans 'n garbage at them, and yellin' all types of obscenities. They finally left draggin' Crossman with them. "Keep ya head up Crossman!" We called behind him. He just smiled.

92
PORTIA JONES

It ain't surprise me dat the day we gonna bury my home girl, my fingernail would break! "Ain't this a bitch!" I thought. Now how I'mma run down and git this shit fixed 'fore the funeral?

Her moms planned the funeral wit the help of Parker. I ain't no help. I was buggin'. I may have lost ten pounds of my booty fat from stressin'. When I look'd in da mirror, I knew I hadda snap outta that shit. Havin' a flat ass just ain't cute.

So any way, they decided that it gonna be a joyous day 'cause Lyric went home to our Holy Father. They ordered five, all–white, stretch limos instead of that black bullshit. At her grave, two cages of white doves were gonna be released at the end of the service. She'll be sportin' a fly white dress, gloves and a white carnation in her hair. They got a white casket with white satin linin'. Her moms said she gonna break on any peoples comin' dressed in black. They gonna be assed out.

Everyone hadda have a special laminated pass to get in, that V.I.P. shit. She gave out a coupla passes to the press who had said good things 'bout the movie "Silk." The first three days it grossed $60 mil. Lyric would have been geesed.

I took one last look in the mirror at my form–fitting, red dress. I looked fly, yo. Matta fact, I'm the flyest bitch in Brooklyn. These bitches can't see me. My jet–black long hair was wild 'n wavy 'cause I had washed it in the shower and let it air dry. I got that good shit da bitches crave for. Ever' black person wanna be mixed with Indian. Ever' hoe wanna pretend she's a virgin. And ever' nobody wanna know somebody famous. Those are the rules of the universe. Lyric taught me that! I stood back in my high–heeled red, patent–leather shoes, grabbed my crème shawl, and bounced.

As I stepped outta da limo in front the church, I glanced 'round and saw Lyric's mom bein' interviewed by the news. She was chillin'. She had on a white, gold and navy–blue Chanel business suit that Lyric had bought 'bout two years back. It was still fresh. Lyric had so many clothes with tags still left on them. She could get busy shoppin'. Her mom's also had the Chanel bag firmly under her arm and a perfect French manicure. My stomach got all squeamish just lookin' at her. Ain't that fucked up? I thought she would hooka bitch up and give me Lyric's gear. How she gonna be like that. You see how people are?

93
JOSHUA TUNE

The crowd that surrounded the barricades all held up signs that read, "You will be missed," "Rest in peace," "Oh Sassi . . . make peace in heaven." The camaraderie was extremely rare. Thousands came out to say good–bye to Lyrics' memory. I hadn't realized that I was standing frozen in the same place until Portia came up behind me and gave me a warm embrace. I turned around, startled only to see a pathetic frame of a woman. Monique was one step behind me, not allowing me out of her eyesight. I knew I looked just as unsightly. I was unshaven and my clothes were unruly. The stubble from my chin scraped up against her cheek as I returned her hug. Lyric's death had affected us all. My eyes were sunken in and the brims were lined in red. You could tell I'd been crying for days. "How are you holding up, kid?" I softly asked. At any second you could tell I would fall apart.

"I'm doing okay," she replied. We looked deep into each other's eyes and knew that we should end the conversation at that point. I took a deep breath and allowed Portia to lead me into the church. The organ music was playing a melancholy tune. They play that tune at every funeral you go to. I thought they planned this to be a joyous occasion.

The casket appeared to be ten miles down the road. It was surrounded by tons of beautiful flower arrangements. Each arrangement, trying to outdo the next, was fighting for floor space and attention. There was Parker, dressed conservatively, holding a single white rose. She had on a peach dress and matching sandals, and it appeared she was talking to Lyric. All three of us approached with caution. My legs were trembling with each step. Parker turned around and smiled when she saw us. It even seemed like she smiled at Monique too which was kind of odd.

"Hi guys . . . doesn't she look beautiful?" she exclaimed.

We all looked down at Lyric. And she was right. Lyric even looked beautiful lying in a casket. Her skin looked smooth not pasty as I had imagined. Her makeup was flawless, and Lyric would not have accepted anything less. She looked like she was sleeping, waiting to get up and go out on a date with some young rich guy she'd just met. Oh . . . my heart was numb with grief! Portia and I broke down at the same time. Parker pulled us to the casket and had us kneel down on the step and pray. Then she told us to talk to her. Tell her how we felt. "Let it out," she suggested. She then left us there sobbing uncontrollably until we eventually stopped.

94
PORTIA JONES

At some point all the peoples came 'n from outside and the service started. I looked 'round for Madison, but I ain't seen her anywhere. I did see Nikki Guy and she looked fly. Mad celebs were there, too, givin' condolences and showin' luv. I clocked as Jay Kapone and Marisol came walkin' in wit sad faces. I leaned over and asked, "Joshua, where the fuck is Madison?"

"She wasn't feeling well this morning and had to be rushed to the hospital. She's vomiting again. She's broken up about Lyric. After the burial, I have to go and see her. I have to start keeping a better eye on her. She worries me."

Wit that his words trailed off. I couldn't help but think da sick–bitch threw her fingers down her frail throat to avoid bein' here wit me. I'm on to dat bitch. I've been havin' a fucked up feelin' in my stomach 'bout Madison and Lyrics' death. Shit just don't feel right. I know there's no connect. . . but somethin' is there. What, dat somethin' is, I don't know yet.

The Reverend Clifford Dale performed the sermon for Lyric. He sure was preachin'. He preached so good I'mma go to church every once in a while. It sure wouldn't hurt gettin' a lil' God in my life.

Standin' off to the side was good ol' Mayor Cardinale. He was sharp in a blue–tailored suit wit a light gray silk tie 'n gold cufflin's. He took the handkerchief outta his pocket and dabbed his forehead for sweat that wasn't there like a lil' faggot. Two secret service men had his back. His face was stern as he held his composure. He sure did take a chance comin' to Lyric's funeral. The press is gonna eat for dayz off him bein' here. I watched him off and on until my eyes wandered over to the six–foot nine, brown–skinn'd brother I was all too familiar wit.

Erious Jerome came through and hovered in the backa da church, tryin' to remain invisible. At six–nine there ain't no hidin'. Nigga pa–leeze. When the choir got up to sing, "His Eye is on the Sparrow," I excused myself and headed to da back. From the stupid look on his face when I came up, he wasn't pleased that I had came to say whaddup. Wit eye contact we both nodded at each other. When I spoke, he had the nerve to pretend he didn't 'member me. Then he faked, "Oh yeah, we did meet, didn't we?"

It took me all but two seconds to shut him down. "Look nigga don't play wit me I'm grown. Knock it off! It's officially a wrap for you. I got da rape–tape. If you wanna keep catchin' wreck on the b–ball court, a ma'fucker betta have my doe. I want twenty–mil."

I stood there and watched the color drain from his face. His fat, juicy lips started to twitch uncontrollably and he reached out and grabbed my arm wit such force I thought it would be yanked from its socket. In a low, growlin' voice he said, "I don't get fucked twice without lubrication, you bitch!"

"Don't make me snuff you up in here! Keep grillin' me like dat ma'fucker." I retorted and yanked my arm back, then continued.

"Live at five . . . you got the digits." As I walked away, I could feel his eyes burnin' a hole in the back of my neck. When I turned back around, he had jetted. Now all I gotta do is git my hands on that damn videotape.

Lyric's moms got up after the eulogy and asked if Lyric's closest friends had anything to say about her. Joshua and I looked at each other, and I nodded for him to go first. Parker was now sittin' next to me, comfortin' me as best she could. She looked exceptionally cute and satisfied. Somethin' in her life had changed, but I didn't care enough about Parker to be nosy. Joshua stood at the podium and cleared his throat several times before he began. Tremblin', his hands gripped the microphone and he said, "From the first day I laid eyes on her, I knew she was someone special . . . someone way out of my league. Her sun–kissed face dipped ever so slightly in warm caramel could lighten the dull interior of any hopeless heart. She thrilled me. She chilled me. And also instilled in me that you only live once. So do, be, say, whatever the hell you want! Her death tells me that you don't always have tomorrow to say 'I'm sorry for hurting you.' Or 'I will never love anyone like I love you.'" He was lookin' directly into Parker's eyes as he said those words. Tears were streamin' down his face, and he was snifflin'. He had captivated everyone in the audience with his vulnerability. He was bein' a lil' too soft for me 'cause I like a thug, but, it is what it is.

Then he got his composure back and continued, "I will never be able to tell Lyric how much I love her. But maybe I can make two wrongs right by telling someone else here today that I love . . . " But, Joshua never continued. Everyone sat baffled and eager to hear the rest of his sentence. Joshua turned stark white 'fore our eyes as he stared straight ahead. Soon everyone caught on and turned around to see what he was lookin' at. There she stood. Lyric Maria Devaney had come back to life. The last thing I saw before I fell out was her chestnut brown eyes.

95
L. DEVANEY

When I arrived at the church, my heart was beating with trepidation. I wasn't worried because I always had an anxiety attack right before something big was about to go down. But I had just the remedy inside my Steve Madden pocketbook. I inhaled deep on what would be my last pull off my Newport cigarette and vowed once again to quit. The nicotine made me feel lightheaded. I turned around to make sure no one was watching me then discretely pulled out a small can of "Old English" malt liquor and took a quick swig. The warm liquid traveled through my body releasing fluids that kept me in the right frame of mind.

"Today was my day," I muttered to myself and I planned to see it through. Thirty–five years I've waited for this day and, without warning, it's here. But, just like a true Devaney, I was already prepared. Step by step I climbed the cathedral stairs. I heard the organ silently playing while someone was speaking with such remorse and conviction my heart almost went out to him. Midway down the aisle, I froze in place. Goosebumps went down my spine because the whole church jumped on their feet and stared at me so incredulously that I instantly had this self–satisfied look upon my face. Just then pandemonium broke out! *Were these crazy people going to attack me?* I wrapped myself with my own arms to stop from quaking, but I stood firmly in place. People were tripping over each other in an effort to exit the church and escape the eerie feeling that filled the air. Everyone was screaming and yelling and pushing past me, damn near knocking me over, making me lose balance for a split second. The press was running past me, too, stopping briefly to catch a quick flick to sell in their magazines and newspapers. Their huge expensive cameras clicking one hundred times a minute while their flashbulbs blinded me. Little children were separated from their parents, helplessly crying out for their mothers or someone to help them. Young women were being trampled on by strong young men, who never stopped to lend a hand to help, concerned only with their welfare. Before I could say or do anything to calm the situation down, it was too late. I had originally planned a big speech, but as everyone knows, nothing ever happens the way you envision it. I looked at this pathetic crowd as the reverend and his gospel choir stampeded off the stage and knocked over the casket that stood in their way. Nothing was sacred. As the casket came crashing down with a thud, I felt her eyes on me. I looked over and my mother was standing there with that same dismal look of disapproval that I knew too well. I winked and blew a kiss in her direction and thought, "Show time!"

96
L. DEVANEY

"What are you doing here?" her words were snappish, and I didn't like her tone one bit. I guess she didn't realize I was no longer a little girl. We were in the lobby of the church, now nearly vacant. It was my mother and four other people I didn't know. One girl had to be revived because she had fainted and needed air. Everyone was staring at me in astonishment, until I realized no one knew.

"Who are you?" said the glassy-eyed, white man with skepticism. His red inflamed nostrils showed that a line of coke was not a *rare* event in his life.

"My name is Lacey. Lacey Devaney . . . I'm Lyric's identical twin sister." The same girl fainted again and was caught before she hit the ground by the white male.

"Why you come here 'fore. Spreading family business? This is your sister's day and you chose to try and take it from her as you usually did when you were children."

"That's nonsense. I never *tried* to take anything. I just did! Besides, this is my sister's funeral, and I should have been permitted or even invited to come."

"You knew exactly what you were doing, you heathen! Coming here dressed up like Lyric in that white dress with white carnation in your hair. How you know what she'd be wearing?"

"Maybe because we're twins. I just felt it."

"YOU LIE JUST LIKE YOUR NO-GOOD FATHER!"

"Leave my father out of this, bitch! He took care of me when you threw me away. He's three times better than you are, and I ended up better than your spoiled brat did! Your love left Lyric swallowing a handful of pills and chasing it down with a bottle of liquor!"

"Shut your mouth! Don't you dare blame what happened to Lyric on me! I loved her! I was the only one who truly loved my baby!"

"You smothered her when we were children. Your paranoia and selfishness divided a family. If you hadn't spoiled Lyric so much, I would have lived a normal life. Lyric was always jealous of me! Jealous of the attention I'd get whenever I came into a room she was in. You saw that, and kicked my father and me out of your lives, made me call you 'auntie' and say over and over again that Lyric and I were cousins who looked alike. You're a crazy mother! And Lyric was a nut case, too!"

"Don't you dare come in here pointing fingers and disrespecting your sister's name. That's blasphemy!"

"Oh shut up! You crazy bat! You sent my father to an early grave. All he ever did was love you. I had to hear all my young life how much he loved you. That you were never satisfied because he didn't make the kind of money you demanded. He took you from an overcrowded shack and put shoes on your bare feet and that was the thanks he got in return. How dare you demand more money from him when you weren't even used to going to the bathroom indoors? You were a country bumpkin who thought her good looks could give her a free ride!"

"I deserved a free ride and your lying ass father promised me a bed of roses, but instead I got pregnant!"

"Yeah, you got pregnant and blamed him for that. Right up until you gave birth, all you ever did was nag and complain. When you went into the operating room to give birth, you wouldn't let him come inside with you to show support. You shut him out of that beautiful experience. Then when I came out, seconds after you had delivered Lyric, you blamed him for that, too! The only thing you said he ever did right was to give you Lyric. But you made it clear, even in the delivery room with doctors and nurses all around, that you didn't want two kids. Those two kids would drain your youth away, and you needed to maintain it because you'd be famous soon. Well look at you now, thirty–five years later. You're nothing now, and you were nothing back then but trailer trash minus the trailer. Daddy told me that you practically grew up living in a cardboard box, and he rescued you from that life. And guess what? Your rich–ass daughter left you broke and still living in the ghetto."

"Yeah well, that all may be true, but as the smart folks on television say, 'That's my past. I'm rich now!'"

"So you think!"

"So I know!"

"All you have ever known was your love for Lyric. I remember you coming in the room telling me that I no longer would be living with you anymore. I'd be moving with just my father. Do you know how messed up you left a five–year–old child? When you wouldn't accept my father's phone calls or even come to visit me, I cried. I cried every night for ten years. I listened to my father cry until his heart gave out! He'd cry all through the night and in his sleep he would call out your name. My father cried because he loved you, but he loved his daughter more. He cried because he knew you would have let him stay, but it was me you didn't want around! I upset your spoiled brat. I could always outdo Lyric in anything she wanted to do. If she scored '100'. . . I'd score '101.' If she did a back flip, I did a triple backward flip with ease. If she came in first place, I got grand prize."

"But look at *you* now. What you got? Nothing! And my Lyric is a big time star!"

"Your Lyric is dead!" I spat.

My mother hauled off and slapped my face. I looked over at Lyric's dead stiff body in the casket that had been picked back up from off the floor, and I smiled openly. Then I let out a psychotic mechanical laughter that would have made a snail's skin crawl. I had accomplished what I came there for. I smoothed down my white dress, rearranged my white carnation in my hair, and stepped outside to address what was left of the press that impatiently awaited me. Today was my day. Finally! And it had just begun. My mother had no idea what I had planned for her! I wasn't going to let anyone ruin it for me. It took thirty–five years to actually win, and it felt good. Even if it was by default!

97
JOSHUA TUNE

I sat in my office with my feet up on my solid oak wood desk contemplating the morning events. Lacey . . . the name surreptitiously crept through my mind repetitiously. If Lyric was pretty, Lacey was beautiful. Although they were identical twins, Lacey had that extra "oomph" that left you in complete awe. She was stunning with an innocence that escaped Lyric. Monique had insisted that I accompany her "home," but I declined.

That "home" didn't nowhere near compare to the real home I had left behind. Monique was so territorial about everything. She made it very clear that she had paid *"mucho bucks"* for her furniture, and I'd better not even lay a glass down without a coaster underneath it. Her rules and regulations were turning me off, and inside I wanted to run back to Parker with my tail in between my legs, begging for forgiveness. But my stubborn pride wouldn't let me. How do you go back and admit that you thought the grass was greener on the other side, but in reality it was really all an illusion? Overnight Monique had changed! Or was she always like this and I'd missed the warning signs? And to put the cherry on top, if I thought that Parker was insecure and obsessive about me seeing other women, Monique took the cake, grand prize, and the trip to Hollywood! I've even caught her smelling my underwear for cum stains. If she couldn't account for an hour of my time, she'd start screaming, "I know you were with that bitch Parker!" Then I'd retort, "If Parker's a bitch, then you're a home wrecker!" That always shuts her up quick.

I don't understand women. She went after me, Parker's husband, with every ounce of persistence one could muster, and for some reason, she was angry with Parker and considered Parker a bitch? The logic was too confusing to try and decipher, so I just let it go as a woman thing. So it wasn't hard for me to make up the excuse that I had lots of work to do back at the office.

Actually, that was really true. The reason I call it an "excuse" is because I knew I had no intentions of getting any work done. I was so far behind with my caseload ever since Lyric's death, I had to ultimately dispense cases to the new attorneys who were eager to make a name. Besides, my head paralegal and law student, Madison, never came into the office anymore. I wondered if she still collected a paycheck.

I made a mental note to go and see Madison in the hospital this afternoon as I took out my razor blade and began chopping up the five–hundred dollar's worth of pure cocaine I had copped this morning before the funeral from a real thug in the 'hood. Thanks to Monique I now had an expensive cocaine habit that I couldn't shake. However, I was nowhere near being a junkie. Monique's dark chocolate ass had better start laying off the coke with that baby growing inside her. They, well hell, I, as district attorney, will prosecute to the fullest mothers who abuse drugs while carrying a fetus. What the hell was I thinking? Jesus, I had no clue. Three rows of coke later and I still couldn't answer that question.

98
JOSHUA TUNE

The stale hospital odor permeated each floor, making me sick to my stomach. After Lyric's untimely demise, I vowed never to step foot into another hospital under somber circumstances; but of course, Madison was worth making an exception for. I didn't want her to end up feeling hopeless like Lyric and doing the unthinkable. Still, it didn't quite sink in that Lyric had taken her own life. It was so unlike her, and it saddens me to know that you could know a person but never really quite know them.

I had stopped by the deli and bought six red roses for five bucks to brighten the atmosphere. Inwardly I wondered if her no-good boyfriend would be there. The guy was a prick who was driving Madison crazy! When I called this morning, her mother was by her side almost frantic. The doctors had no idea what was wrong with her. She was now throwing up involuntarily without any medical reasoning. She swears up and down she's done with purging her guts out but just when she quit, her body said, "Not so fast slick!" The doctors have pinched and poked every inch of her body and ran almost every test and, still, nothing conclusive.

When I walked inside, I saw the body of a twelve-year-old. Madison looked so fragile underneath the thin white bed sheet that was outlining her skeletal frame. Her throat was parched, and her lips were dry and crusty. Her hair had begun to grow back and was in a nappy Afro style. The disfiguring scar on her forehead was still screaming for attention. She mentioned something about falling in the shower. I was skeptical, but she never had any reason to lie to me. She was all alone. When she saw me, her eyes lit up but her body was unable to react. It was clear that she was in so much pain she could barely move. It appeared that practically overnight something had come and sucked every bit of life out of her. I sniffed a couple of times then cleared my throat before leaning down and planting a kiss on her left cheek. I squeezed her hand and said, "How are you holding up, kid?"

She squirmed uncomfortably, then whispered, "I'm in pain. Joshua . . . please help me . . . I'm dying . . . I just know it . . . Lyric's come back to kill me."

"That's nonsense Madison. You're delusional right now. What the fuck they got dripping in your arms?" I retorted inspecting the intravenous tube that was inserted in her arm. The last thing I needed was for her to take me on a trip. I was already bouncing off the walls coming down from this sweet high.

"I'm serious Joshua . . . she came here this morning and said I'd be next!"

Five more minutes with Madison and I'd be hallucinating. To distract her, I buzzed the nurse. As soon as she walked in, I exploded, "What the fuck type medication you got her on? Fucking Ritalin?"

"I beg your pardon."

"You heard me you fat bitch! She looks like shit and she's going crazy as well!" I snapped.

She didn't answer me but directly ran to get Madison's doctor and the security guard. They came back in the room like the Three Musketeers. The doctor recognized me from my picture being in the papers and news press conferences I held during the succinylcholine chloride murderer's trial. He told the security guard he could handle me and told the nurse to go back up front to her station. She grunted underneath her breath, but did as she was told. The doctor came further into the room and said, "This is not Ritalin she's taking for psychosis. It's Demerol for the pain. She's in a great deal of pain."

"What's wrong, doc?"

"Actually, I don't know. But I assure you, we'll find out. We're still running tests but right now, I don't have a clue. All we can do is give her something for the pain."

"So why is she seeing ghost?"

"We've noticed that she's been babbling since she came in. She's lost a lot of fluid and is not properly nourished, so it's common to have side effects. The body is not working according to its full potential right now."

The doctor rattled on and on about not knowing what was ailing Madison. I took a deep look at this overpaid yuppie and wanted to punch him out. I don't know but lately I've been filled with so much rage; it's almost uncontrollable. I decided that it would be best if I left. I was in no condition to help Madison out right now. I told Madison and the doctor to excuse me while I used the restroom and made a quick exit from the hospital.

99
JOSHUA TUNE

Once the fresh air hit me, I felt much better. I glanced down at my watch and realized that I could go back "home" because Monique wouldn't be there. It was Friday evening and she always went to visit her mother for dinner. Same time every week I would have several hours of peace. This sure put pep in my step. When I got off the elevator, there was a tall, well–groomed black guy aimlessly waiting by my door. For a second I thought I would be robbed and beaten but realized cheap two–bit hoodlums don't rob people while wearing a ten thousand dollar Patek Phillipe watch and Salvatore Ferragamo shoes. Still I approached with caution.

"Are you lost?" I asked in my tough guy voice. "I'm looking for Joshua Tune," he said.

Thinking quickly I observed a briefcase and realized this could be it. Parker had finally done it. She was suing me for divorce, and this punk was going to serve me the papers. I thought about lying and saying I wasn't him then realized I could run, but couldn't hide from the inevitable. "That's me," I said, then sniffed a few times before clearing my throat. That had become a habit.

"Can we go somewhere and talk discretely?" he asked.

"First off . . . who the fuck are you?" I countered, annoyed because I now wanted to get inside to take another hit to alleviate the stress of the day. I welcomed the opportunity not to share my shit with Monique's greedy ass.

"Pardon your profanity," his crisp accent corrected my blatant disrespect.

Lately, all my etiquette had gone out the window. When I'm high, I have no energy to waste thinking of proper words or phrases. I say exactly what's on my mind. Something in his eyes said that I'd better get my shit together and fast. As quick as a blink, I straightened up, got my composure, and rephrased my question. "I need to know who you are before we start relocating to someplace discrete, don't you think?"

"You're correct. Please accept my apology, but the situation has me a little on edge. Allow me to start from the beginning."

"Please do!"

"My name is Herbert Ballentine, and I'm a private detective. A few months back, I was hired by a Miss Lyric Devaney who came into my San Diego office to inquire about my getting information about someone."

He looked around to make sure no one was lurking in the hallway before he continued, "I have the information she requested, but I can't help but think that Miss Devaney couldn't possibly have killed herself but was murdered by the same person she had hired me to investigate!"

I felt myself go weak in the knees. This was all too much for me to take. My heart palpitated three times faster than normal, and I had started to perspire uncontrollably. My throat became dry, and all I wanted to do was take an ice-cold shower. I unloosened my tie to give my throat room to squeeze a couple of words into the atmosphere.

"Jesus, Mary, and Joseph! What's this have to do with me?" I managed to get out. He noticed something was wrong and asked if I was all right. I assured him that I would be okay and pressed him to answer my question.

"Of course, sir. Miss Devaney told me that if I found anything substantial that I should forward the information to you. That you would know what to do with it because she'd be busy with her career."

"Get to the point!" I exclaimed. Couldn't he see I was in agony? He curled his eyebrow in a peculiar manner and had the balls to say, "You should really lay off the cocaine. It'll mess you up bad."

"I now beg your pardon!" I bellowed with every ounce of embarrassment.

"I know the symptoms. I used to indulge but cut it out way back in the 80's. Kick the habit, it's costly." He reasoned as if we were old college dorm buddies. Too high to be embarrassed for too long, I let his comments ride in the universe while I dug for my key to let him in.

100
JOSHUA TUNE

I wondered if the nosy neighbors had heard anything. This being a predominately white building, these uppity white people couldn't stand that I was shacking up with a black woman. They spied on us all the time, thinking we were strange. Once inside I excused myself and went in the bedroom and snorted four more lines. I was in there a good thirty minutes before Herbert got impatient. He knew exactly what I was in there doing. When I came out, I gave him a stern look that said, "Mind your business, I'm grown!" He was sitting in the dining room with pictures and paperwork spread all over the table. He didn't wait for me to start asking questions, he just jumped straight into the story:

"Maurice Mungin, A.K.A., Victor Jones, A.K.A., Corey Blackman and the list goes on. His birth name given to him by his grandmother who raised him because his mother was addicted to heroine is James Smith. He was born thirty years ago in a women's prison in upstate New York. James learned at a very early age he had a gift with the ladies and later turned that gift into something lucrative. He started off swindling them for money to just get by. Make them buy his sneakers, pay for name-brand jeans . . . small-time stuff like that. When he turned twenty-two, he decided he wanted more. His first victim's name was Mary. Mary would later be found dead in her bathroom from a bizarre accident. She had allegedly slipped in the shower after coming home in a drunken stupor, bumped her head, and choked on her own tongue. Her parents told the police that their daughter's death was no accident. No one listened at first. When they found out that a $20,000 policy was in his name as beneficiary, it gave the police a motive.

They brought him in for questioning but he had an airtight alibi. They followed every lead, dug as deep as they could in his past, and was on the brink of getting a civil suit filed against them for violating his civil liberties before they had to close the case and rule her death was an accident. They stalled as long as they could because they knew with the case being open, he couldn't collect on his policy. And they also knew that once the case was closed, he'd be gone just as mysteriously as he had come. His second victim was Stacey."

He passed me a photograph of a sweet looking light–brown girl who didn't look more than nineteen years old. Then continued, "Her mother didn't know she was dead until two years had passed. She was a loner and had run away from home several times. James found her and immediately married this needy person. One day her mother had gone to the cemetery to see her late husband. The clerk gave her the plot name and number of her daughter. ("There must be some mistake . . . I'm coming to see my husband . . . he just passed away,") said the mother. They told her that her husband was there as well as her daughter. Further investigation would show that Stacey had apparently taken a shotgun and blown her brains out. Her mother had no idea her daughter was in the same town, let alone seeing a psychiatrist and battling depression. The doctor said he couldn't help her. The mother knew that there was no way her daughter could take a shotgun and kill herself. She was too afraid of guns.

'If everything I'm saying seems circumstantial, then explain how someone four–feet–eight inches with arms long enough to hold a shotgun and pull a trigger?' her mother pleaded.

All this happened inside the sheriff's office. Her mother had brought in a shotgun to demonstrate what she was talking about. Feeling like the Keystone Cops, they rushed and reopened the investigation. By that time, all evidence had been destroyed and they had nothing to work with. But the detective on the case did come up with an insurance policy that was paid out to a Clarence Boyd, A.K.A., James Smith, who was now long gone. When his luck had finally run low, he was on his third victim. Her name was Nancy. She was in the hospital for unknown stomach pain. They checked, and a policy for $100,000 was riding on this woman's head. The sheriff's department brought him in for questioning but didn't have anything to hold on him. When he was released, he did the gingerbread man. Later, they tested Nancy in the hospital and found she was being poisoned by arsenic. She refused to press charges and adamantly stuck by her story that she had poisoned herself. That was one year ago. Our guy is now shacking up with a Miss Madison Michaels. And I'm sure he's not done yet."

101
JOSHUA TUNE

He finally stopped speaking for a moment and just watched the expression on my face. In front of me were copies of police reports, insurance policies, pictures of dead girls and interviews with family members.

"Why hasn't he been stopped yet? All this evidence . . . "

"I'm the only one who knows that James Smith is all these aliases. He is wanted in several states on suspicion of murder, but no one has put it together that he's a serial killer!" he said. I had a document in my hand and hadn't realized I was visibly trembling.

"You think he's trying to kill Madison?"

"I think he's killed Lyric!"

"Oh my God! What do we do?"

"No . . . what do *you* do? I've done my job and I'm leaving this nice file in your capable hands. Aren't you some sort of hotshot district attorney?"

"I used to be," I muttered.

"Listen buddy . . . you've got work to do. And like I said earlier, leave the drugs alone. You're going to need a clear head. If he thinks you're on to him, you may be next on his list!"

Herbert concluded our meeting and left me pacing the floor. It all was making sense. I knew Lyric couldn't have killed herself! If he touched one hair on her sexy head, I'd fucking slay his ass in court! What should I do?

First thing I needed was a shower. After the shower, I took another hit of the blow, then called the hospital and told the doctor I needed to meet with him in his office. Then I called Detective Scotti Holmes, a cool dude who I wanted to investigate Lyric's possible murder that I could trust to keep quiet. I needed to do everything by the book. Up until now, Lyric's death was inexplicable. I was back. I could tell. This case is going to do it for me! I could smell victory!

At the hospital, I got right to the point. I had no time to waste.

"Doc, I need you to test Madison for arsenic."

"Do you know something?"

"I will once the test comes back positive," I stated.

The doctor stared intently into my eyes then replied, "Now that you mention it, you may be on the right path. I do not know why I did not see it myself. Arsenic is carried by the blood into all parts of the body, and is found in the brain, the bones, and in the marrow. It can even be found in the fingernail. Do you think someone is trying to murder your friend?"

"Yes, I do!" I said and looked gravely into his eyes.

"Well, I'm sure her bout with anorexia didn't help their goal much."

"What does that have to do with it?"

"Arsenic is eliminated through the kidneys and the liver and passes through the bowels, urine, and may be pushed out by vomiting. It manifests itself first usually in vomiting, a natural expellant against this irritant, as in bowel movements. Whoever is trying to kill her was probably adding it to her food a little at a time so she wouldn't taste it. When she started purging, whatever she took in came right back out, thereby taking longer for their plan to work."

"Why would someone use this method if it's traceable?"

"In some cases of death from arsenic, no arsenic is found in the system. I'm thinking that they must have increased dosage to speed up the process hoping the poison would accumulate in the system more rapidly than she could push out by vomiting. What's happening now to Madison is that her body is naturally irritated by this and the tissue, her kidneys, heart, and her nervous system are being destroyed. Eventually, she will be unable to recuperate and death will come within a few weeks."

"She's not going to die is she?" I pleaded with my eyes.

"Not if what you just said is the culprit. I have to go now; I'll keep you posted. In addition, have a doctor look at you. You do not look so good. Have a physical."

"Sure thing, doc. Thanks."

Inside the comfort of my BMW I let the music of the late Tupac Shakur blast out of my speakers. *"I'm not a killer but don't push me, revenge is like the sweetest joy next to gettin' pussy!"* I let my head nod back and forth to the beat to gather my thoughts. Next, I called the office and had Dominick look into an insurance policy on Madison. I told myself I wasn't going to speak to him for not showing up at Lyric's funeral but I needed him, for now. In addition, I had Judge Madden sign a search warrant for Lyric's apartment so any evidence collected wouldn't be thrown out for illegal search and seizure. I was going to do it right down to the last detail. I called Detective Holmes to meet me over at Lyric's place in about an hour. I had to stop at "home" first and get Monique mother's telephone number so I could tell her I'd be out late working on a case. I didn't want her scolding me when I came home late.

102
JOSHUA TUNE

The apartment was quiet and still . . . just the way I liked it. I went into her drawer, got her telephone book, and called her mother's house for her. I know she'll be so surprised and glad to hear from me because I never call there. Nor have I ever met her parents. She said that I showed no interest in her anymore. "Hi, this is Joshua. May I please speak to Monique."

"She's not here!" Her mother snapped, confirming she'd heard nothing but bad things about me.

"Did she just leave?"

"She wasn't never here to leave," she chuckled. *Was she laughing at me?*

"Oh, I must be mistaken. I thought she said she was going to her mother's this Friday. That must have been last week."

"She wasn't here last week either!" she admonished. She was definitely trying to send a subtle message.

"Very well!" I said and slammed the telephone down. Where the hell was she going every Friday? In addition, why would she have to lie? I immediately put my mission on hold and cleared my thoughts. Could she be . . . ? I couldn't even complete the thought because it was silly. However, silly or not, I had an inclination to do something I vowed I'd never do. I decided to snoop around in her things. After tearing the apartment up, I stumbled upon a little red diary. Each passage was timed and dated, so it made it very easy to find just where I'd be. I didn't care about what she did before me, but I was certainly going to find out what she was doing now!

103
JOSHUA TUNE

Finally, after flipping through each page about how she was plotting to take me away from Parker, I dug deep and pulled out gold. It read:

I prayed as I took every step to the trashcan in my bathroom. I held my breath and then bent down on my hands and knees. I carefully took out the condom we had just used. I looked at the juices inside the latex and wondered if it was enough to get me pregnant. I had read that when women want to be artificially inseminated, the sperm is injected inside of them. They pay thousands of dollars for this procedure, but I was going to do it myself for free. I put the sperm–filled condom inside a small plastic cup. I stored it in the back of my freezer among the frozen steaks and ice cubes. Tomorrow, I will purchase a syringe for an emergency situation, and insert the crème inside me when I'm ovulating, but only if I have to. Until then, I will pray everyday that I won't be forced to do something so deliberate. Unfortunately, the only thing that can save my relationship right now is a baby. I have no choice. I need this pregnancy! I don't want to lose him.

My stomach turned over and my complexion drained, but I still had the strength to read further. How could she purposely impregnate herself with my seed to trap me?

This baby growing inside me was the answer to all my prayers. I have been seeing John for ten years and still he's unable to leave his wife for me. He's just that devoted to his children. That's what I admire in him and love so much. When I told him I was pregnant with his child, he said impossible! He's always used a condom since our first encounter. Ten years later, he's still wrapped up tight. I pleaded every time we made love to let me feel his juices exploding inside of me, but he wouldn't have any of that. Finally, I came up with a plan to impregnate myself. When it worked, and I told John that the condom had broken, he shut down all communication for four straight weeks. He wouldn't have anything to do with me until I told him he wasn't the father. I lied to have him back in my arms. Our Friday rendezvous rekindled my passion, so I am carrying my lovechild. In the mix, I had to tell Joshua that he was the father of my child. My baby is going to need a father and Joshua is okay. He's a fool, but he's tolerable. I think he's ambitious and will go far. With me behind him, he'll become a millionaire and his face will be known in the political arena internationally. Joshua would have stayed stuck on stupid had he remained with his uneducated wife, Parker. Taking him was as easy as taking candy from a baby. That's what I despise most about him. He was never a challenge, unlike John.

The words went on and on. She kept referring to me as a "fool," not a real man like "*her* John." Oh, how I despised that bitch! She had ruined my marriage and all I was was backup? That tramp–slut will never work a day in this town again when I get through with her. I grabbed that same duffel bag I had moved my things in and packed to move my things out. I hope she's having a good fuck because Joshua Tune will show her how it's done. Ten minutes later, I was on my way to Lyric's condominium. I had some real shit to deal with first.

104
LACEY DEVANEY

It was 8 a.m., and I was on my way into Manhattan for the reading of Lyric's Last Will and Testament. I had to be there at ten, and I didn't want to be late. First, I had to sneak out of the Days Inn Motel in Queens where I had been staying for the past three days. I usually didn't resort to such tawdry tactics, but my whole life savings were spent on this trip up to New York from South Carolina. I had lived there practically my whole life since father and I were kicked out of my mother's domain.

South Carolina was a beautiful state but it was slow! I couldn't wait to sink my teeth into New York's nightlife. I've heard so much about the China Club and Club Imperial that I'm going to make a point of getting into one of them tonight to celebrate. All my girlfriends back home would die to get just one night out in the Big Apple. I remember we would all sit around IHOP eating breakfast, dreaming about what we'd do if we could squeeze an extra couple of bucks from our paychecks and take a trip to New York. Everyone fantasized they'd meet a rich man to sweep them off their feet and take them away from their boring life. My dream was to live across the street from Central Park and go on romantic horse–and–carriage rides at night with my beau.

The gang was skeptical when I told them that I had family up North in New York. They couldn't understand why I'd never go to visit and let them tag along. Then when adolescent Lyric starred in her first commercial, I became a local celebrity. Everyone wanted to get close to me. I had no idea what was going on when my telephone started ringing off the hook. Friends, enemies, acquaintances--all called to ask me the details about *my* latest commercial. Totally in the dark, but like a true Devaney, I caught on fast. I let that ride for many years until people started to suspect that the girl that was in the print ads, commercials and small film parts couldn't be the same girl working at Checkers fast food restaurant for minimum wage. When I turned eighteen, I confided in my best friend Kim that the local celebrity wasn't local at all, but my identical twin sister named Lyric who lived up in New York City. She was the only person I let in on the awkward family secret. She grew to have a deep hatred for both Lyric and my mom and supported me in every way. She became the sister I'd always yearned for. From that point, we grew even closer. She always told me that I'd have my time to shine one day.

We both followed Lyric's career through a microscope. There really wasn't anything to get green over. Then she scored with "Silk!" The publicity alone would make me puke. I had to see her face glowing in all interviews, "Who are you," "Entertainment Access," and the covers of all the top magazines. She'd made it and I knew it. I thought all she'd ever amount to was a whore for the sleazy mayor of New York. Of course, I knew that the gossip that surrounded their relationship was completely true. Lyric was nothing more than a spoiled Jezebel, and I hated her dead corroded guts! I hoped maggots were eating out her perfect lips and pretty eyes at this very moment. The thought was rather pleasant and made me smile.

Kim was the brilliant one who had concocted this whole scam. My coming to New York and claiming Lyric's assets and fortune was her idea. I couldn't believe my luck when I was watching the evening news and saw EMS wheeling out a body wrapped in a white sheet with the journalist broadcasting that Lyric Devaney had tried to commit suicide. *"Die bitch!"* I thought. *"Suffer!"* I had been following her career all my life, and this was the first good news I'd ever had. Then she died. One day later my telephone rang, and it was Kim and her words to me were, "G-i-r-r-l, get dressed . . . you're on the next flight to New York!" So here I am broke, eager and on my way to inheriting millions. Kim had developed the plan. She remembered that I'd said I could forge signatures. I used to do this for play on our parents' old checks. I'd just practice signing their names. Therefore, when Kim said I'd have to forge Lyric's last will and testament, I had faith that I'd be able to do it perfectly. The only obstacle I could think of was that there would already be a Last Will and Testament in someone's possession. Kim answered that question before I could verbalize the word "fear." She dug up one of Lyric's latest articles where she mentions her attorney Gary Scheck. Kim said all I had to do was show up in his office, feel him out, and if he seemed bribable, explain to him how we could *all* share Lyric's fortune.

105
LACEY DEVANEY

When I arrived at Gary Scheck's office, I surprised myself. I felt an immediate attraction for him. He was quite handsome. He had dark olive skin, jet–black cropped hair, and full–pink, sexy lips that displayed a manicured mustache. He was well groomed, wore an expensive suit, Bruno Magli shoes, 14–carat gold cufflinks, and a solid, silk tie. We both stared into each other's eyes for a long time. The look couldn't be considered just casual. I'm sure he was quite taken by my beauty as well. I wondered if Lyric had slept with him. As if reading my mind, he said, "You are just as, if not more, beautiful than your sister. She used to date my partner. Amazing woman . . . your sister." Well that answered everything. But still, as much as my body was telling me to flirt, my mind kept me grounded. I didn't date white men. I'm far from a racist; I was just a realist. At the end of the day, all you have in common is great sex. And I've had my share of meaningless relationships. In any case, this was strictly a business trip, and I was taking it seriously.

I looked him directly in the eye and made my proposition. At first, he refused to entertain the idea. Then his horns started protruding and greed overtook any fear or loyalty that had originally existed within his being. When he told me that Lyric had a Swiss bank account that contained over $15 million, several safe–deposit boxes, a condominium she owned, a Mercedes–Benz, furs, jewelry, and had put down a deposit on a $6 million mansion, I nearly peed in my pants. Soon his ingenious legal mind was helping seal this plan airtight. He came up with loose ends neither I nor Kim had thought of.

He drafted up another Will just as he had done for Lyric; this time I was the sole beneficiary, and excluded my mother and my sister's unborn child. Lyric had left my mother twenty percent of her estate and the condominium. The other eighty percent would have been held in trust for her unborn daughter. She left Madison all her jewelry, which appraised at an estimated $1 million. To Portia, she'd left her all her clothes, furs, video equipment and shoe collection. Last on that list was Joshua, to whom she'd left her Mercedes–Benz and custody of her daughter, which he'd share with his wife Parker.

Gary told me that Lyric had come to his office the afternoon of her suicide, and he'd drawn up a Last Will and Testament for her. He said she seemed distracted and kept talking about this eerie feeling surrounding her.

"I told her it was fame, the baby and preparing for her premiere that had her feeling anxious. How wrong was I? All along she was just preparing for the other side."

He said this solemnly but never feeling sad enough to stop what he was doing. When he got down to an insurance policy for $5,000 with my mother as the beneficiary, I told him he could leave that. "Let her have it. She'll drink it up in two days!" I said matter–of–factly. He thought that we should leave everyone else's inheritance intact so as to not alert anyone. He wanted just to concentrate on the $15 million.

"Negative!" I said. The only thing I'm giving away is custody of Lyric's retarded child. I thought a moment on that and realized that a potential lawsuit was sure to ensue. Someone had to be held liable for what had gone wrong in that operating room. I considered the impending millions and almost awarded myself custody.

However, considering the matter further, I realized having Lyric's daughter in my home would be just as bad as having Lyric there. Then I thought about punishing my mother with custody of Lyric's retarded child. My vain mother would lock that child up in a closet and *throw* away the key. Meanwhile, she'll have access to her millions! No! I'll respect my sister's wishes and give the child to that couple. Well, that couple isn't really a couple anymore from what I could observe. In addition, that woman hanging on his arms was hardly going to use my niece's money to buy sable furs to drape over her whorish body. She was a home wrecker just like my no–good sister! No, I think that homely–looking person, Parker, will do just fine with the kid and the impending money. Nevertheless, *MY* money and assets were not being divided amongst these losers. I did not travel thousands of miles to half fulfill my plan. There was no way her scrubby friends were getting their hands on anything. I reminded Gary that he demanded fifty percent of the pot so charity was not an option. What they don't know won't hurt them. They had no idea these assets were really theirs anyway. "You can't miss what you've never had!" My daddy taught me that. Then it dawned on me, right in Gary Scheck's office that I also had to share my now–reduced cut with Kim. In addition, just as that thought came in, it went right back out. Lyric was *my* sister. What makes Kim think she should get any of this? Shoot! I felt like a leprechaun who just followed a rainbow and found gold! Life is so good.

When it came time for me to sign, I looked over Lyric's signature for a moment. Her L's were curvy and elongated while her D's were oblong and boxed. She definitely had a flare with her signature. Lyric had the signature of a true movie star. I could just imagine her practicing her signature for long hours until it was perfected and she was satisfied. Even as a child, she was obsessed with perfection. A five–year–old bratty perfectionist bitch! That is how she will always be remembered.

I took a plain white sheet of paper and went to work. It would take me seven minutes to perfect her John Hancock. Before I signed on the dotted line, I took one more look to make sure not even a handwriting expert could distinguish between genuine and forgery. When I was sure it was perfect, I signed the legal document to solidify the deal. Gary and I shook hands and that was the last time I saw him. Today we would meet again under lovely circumstances.

106
LACEY DEVANEY

When I arrived at the posh office building on 49th Street and Lexington, I saw wealth. Young white women wearing oversized Louis Vuitton pocketbooks with huge bumblebee, Jackie Onassis shades. Their hair was pulled back tight to bring attention to the huge marquis–cut diamond earrings that decorated their ears. Everyone had large wedding rings set in platinum. These women didn't look more than twenty–two years old, and it appeared they had everything. The house, car, husband, career, child and nanny at home. I exhaled because in less than an hour I would be eating caviar and drinking champagne. With Lyric's money, I did not need the husband, career, child or nanny at home. With money, loneliness is not an option. You can buy life, love, companionship, friends, material things, and even a child if you want to. With money, I can buy happiness.

When I walked in the reception waiting area, the secretary told me to have a seat. I sat down on the firm, dark–brown leather sofa until I was guided into a huge conference room where Gary Scheck was sitting at the head of a large, oval, mahogany table. I noticed that no one had showed up for the reading of Lyric's will except my mother who strolled in ten seconds after me.

"What she doing here?" she exclaimed.

"She was notified to come, just as you were," he said.

"You're only supposed to call the people in my daughter's will who's gettin' somethin'. Just 'cause she think she famly, don't mean she need to be here!" she spat. Inwardly, I gleamed. Gary Scheck ignored my mother's ignorance and announced we'd give the others a fifteen minute courtesy. As the minutes ticked away in silence, I prayed no one would make the reading.

"Make this as smooth as silk God. Please . . . You owe me!" I'll admit I was a little nervous about Joshua showing up because he was an assistant district attorney. He might suspect something was up. The reason he would even be coming was that I lost the battle with Gary about not having Lyric leave her friends anything. Therefore, he decided that $5,000 per friend would satisfy everyone.

Finally, he started reading. There was a lot of legal jargon in the first couple of lines. Then he got down to the nitty–gritty and began:

> *"I, Lyric Maria Devaney, residing at 9000 68th Street and Park Avenue, New York County, which I declare to be my domicile, do make and declare this to be my Last Will and Testament.*
>
> *FIRST: I revoke all Wills and Codicils heretofore made by me.*
>
> *SECOND: I direct that my Executor, hereinafter named, pay all of my debts, and expenses for the administration of my estate soon after my death.*
>
> *THIRD: I give and bequeath the sum of five thousand dollars ($5,000) each to be given to Madison Michaels, Joshua Tune, Portia Jones, and Linda Devaney. In the event that any person shall not survive me but shall have died leaving issue who shall survive me, such issue shall take equal shares per stirpes the share that his parent would have taken if he or she had survived me. If no issue is survived, the remaining shares shall be divided equally among the survivors who survive me.*
>
> *FOURTH: I bequeath my life insurance policy which has a five thousand dollar ($5000) cash value to Linda Devaney."*

I watched my mother's expression from the corner of my eyes. It didn't quite register yet that all she was getting was ten grand. She smiled at first, then when Gary tried to move on to the next person, she couldn't help herself.

"Why you movin on? You can do all of my inheritance at one time. Don't be rationalizing my portion out. I'm a big girl. I can take it!"

"Mrs. Devaney, that is your inheritance. That is all your daughter willed to you. Now I must move on. I have a meeting after this," Gary retorted. He was shrewd and blunt. I liked his style. I wondered if I turned him into a crook or if I had just enhanced his bank account. My dad said, *"Crooks can't be converted. They're bred at birth and can only be enhanced."* No matter how snippety Gary's tone was, it was no match for a poor woman living in the projects. She was not going to make this easy.

"What you mean 'that's all your daughter left you?' Are you out of your cotton–pickin mind? My daughter had two hundred and fifty thousand dollars! And it's rightfully mine. And that condominium is mines too. She promised it to me right before she left this earth. So you better look over that will one more time 'fore I have my attorney do it for you!" she barked. Her pale skin was blood red and her veins were protruding from her neck. She was mad as hell.

For a brief moment I thought that we should have slid this ghetto–trash misfit the measly two hundred, but hate got the best of me, and I shook that thought right out. Besides, it was too late. She didn't even know what Lyric was working with. Gary gave my mother a long hard stare and said in a tight, controlled voice, "Mrs. Devaney, you can either sit still and stay for the conclusion of the reading of this will, or I will have security escort you out of here right now. And you can have any attorney you want try to contest this Will. In addition, I guarantee once you mention the name Gary Scheck, you will not get very far. Pursue this, and that $10,000 you just inherited will be gone on billable attorney time!" He said pompously. Then he shuffled his paperwork to ensure that he had her complete attention. The room was pin–drop quiet. After painstakingly listening to him bequeath her only $10,000 she patiently listened for him to finally get to me:

" . . . and to my sister Lacey, whom I owe my deepest apology for what my mother has done, I bequeath my entire remaining estate. That includes my condominium, mansion, furs, jewelry, clothing, Mercedes, stocks, bonds . . ."

SIXTH: "Lastly, I bequeath custody of my beloved daughter to Parker Brown-Tune, who I'm sure will provide a stable home, with values I'm sure she wouldn't learn had she lived a privileged life with me."

WITNESS: I sign, and declare this my Last Will and Testament, in the presence of persons witnessing it at my request, in the County and State of New York.

And that's how I walked out of Gary Scheck's office a millionaire.

107
JOSHUA TUNE

The search warrant for Lyric's condominium did not turn up any leads. I kept thinking *"What if Maurice didn't have a chance to kill Lyric? What if he intended to do it but she took herself out first?"* Then I shook that right off. There was NO way Lyric committed suicide. It just wasn't in her character to do something so distasteful. In addition, to slice her own wrist! No way, my gut kept telling me. I should have seen it sooner, but I was flying too high on blow to catch the little clues. Now her murderer could get away with it! If so, I will never forgive myself. All evidence had probably been destroyed with all that traffic in and out of her place. Had the investigation been treated as a possible murder from the beginning, maybe we would have been able to find something beyond question.

Detective Holmes went over every area with a fine-tooth comb. Every inch of her bedroom and bathroom was dusted for fingerprints. Once we got a print that was conclusive, it was lifted, preserved and forwarded to our forensic laboratory. We also collected her kitchen and bathroom garbage, and her bed sheets were all redirected to the lab as well. That was the best we could do under the circumstances. I pulled all her telephone records to see her last calls, and Detective Holmes interviewed all her neighbors. No one saw anything out of the ordinary on that day. One neighbor said she had seen two strange-looking girls dragging garbage bags from the direction of their building, but she couldn't conclusively say whether they had come from her building or were just passing by. In addition, she added, there was a third girl walking steps behind the twosome. But what did that really mean? Detective Holmes took the information, but we both knew it was not leading anywhere. We needed to know if any strange men were lurking around the area. I had a picture of Maurice that I had gotten from the private detective

Herbert Ballentine. No one recognized him. I made them look long and hard. I tried to coerce a little, but no one took the bait.

Once I finished there, I told Detective Holmes to call me as soon as the lab had something irrefutable. I suggested that maybe he should put a tail on this Maurice, what's-his-name, character. He was too dangerous for us not to know what his next moves were going to be. Also, I was awaiting the call from the doctor regarding Madison testing positive for arsenic. Even if it killed me, I would put this case together. Even if it were on circumstantial evidence alone, I would win this case for my girls. This prick *murdered* my friend and was attempting to murder the other one. I could not let him get away with that!

With that business taken care of itself, I headed straight to Parker unannounced. I had to salvage my marriage. The whole ride there I wanted to kick myself for being such an asshole. I thought I really had something special with Monique. What an illusion! I started to remember all the reasons I married Parker in the first place, and it brought a smile to my face. Any man would be proud to have her on his arm, but I wasn't going to let that happen.

I pondered about what strategy I should use. Possibly make her believe it was all her fault I strayed from the marriage? Maybe, just beg for her forgiveness? Should I strong-arm her . . . maybe act aggressive and force myself back in? Perhaps appeal to her sensitive side and cry real tears? I wasn't sure which card I'd pull, but I was prepared to do anything to get my foot back in the door. I knew if she'd let me make love to her one time, I'd be back in her good graces. Women were weak like that. All it took was one rump around the sack, and you were back! At least until you fucked up again; and they'd remember all the past, present, and what's to come bullshit you will put them through.

108
JOSHUA TUNE

When I arrived, I took a deep breath and got the show on the road. I rang the doorbell and she answered immediately. When she opened the door, she looked adorable. I wondered briefly if she was expecting company. You could tell she was visibly surprised to see me. I smiled my boyish grin and her face soured. She tensed up and became standoffish, "What are you doing here?" she questioned. She had Erykah Badu playing softly in the background.

"I'm sorry to come without calling first, but I thought you wouldn't let me come to see you."

"You were right to think that."

"Could I come in?" My voice was low and soothing. The way I'd talk to her when we were making love. She took a minute to contemplate my question, then she moved aside and let me in. The apartment was spotless. No shoes lying all around, no dishes piled up in the sink. She had fresh flowers decorating the place and the fragrance smelled sweet. Oh, how I missed home! My eyes led me to her computer that was turned into a work area. She had stacks of paperwork and books piled up high on each other. Curiosity couldn't keep me from walking over and taking a look. Each book was about opening your own business. "You planning something big here?" I asked.

"I'm opening up my own interior decorating business. I needed to do some research first. It's time I got out and lived *my* life. Do what makes me happy, not wait around for someone to give me happiness," she retorted. I knew that last sting was about me. Acting as if her words were casual, I ignored her sarcasm and said, "You know you'll need to name yourself CEO, plus you'll need a CFO to handle your finances. I could help you with that if you want me to. And in exchange for sex, I'll work free of charge" I joked. She didn't laugh at all. Not even a slight smile. I knew this was going to be rough.

And I knew that she would want to discuss everything. We never did get a chance to talk about what happened; I had just left her hurt and confused. Sometimes I don't know why men do the things we do--always in search of satisfaction, mowing down innocent bystanders in the way. I was such a creep.

I watched her leave the room and come back with an envelope that she handed to me. I thought maybe it was a letter expressing her feelings about our relationship. Before we'd gotten married, whenever we would argue, she'd always send me these terrific, sexy letters in the mail telling me how much she loved me and wanted our relationship to work. The letters would give all the reasons we should stay together and make our relationship work. It had become so that whenever we'd argue, I would look forward to the letters. It was great because I never had to swallow *my* pride. She always let me keep my manhood. She said our relationship was bigger than pride. She sure did treasure what we had.

"What's this?" I asked when she handed me the envelope.

"I want a divorce, Joshua. Consider yourself properly served!" she retorted.

I dropped the envelope as if it was on fire. My hands began to tremble, and I started to sweat profusely. I ran my hands through my hair a couple of times, swallowed hard, then I started slowly.

"Parker . . . baby . . . listen . . . I can make it right again. I don't want to lose you. You want to hear me say I fucked up. Okay, I fucked up! But we can get through this. Please, just don't leave me . . . not now . . . not like this. Just give me one more chance, and I swear I'll be the man you married. In fact, I'll be better than the man you married. I'll be the man you want me to be." I was looking directly into her eyes as I said these words. She looked directly into mine and said, "I can't even sue you for wasting my time!"

"I want to get back together," I adamantly said, ignoring her last remark.

"The sad thing about this whole situation is that you started to think your golden dick was actually gold," she said sarcastically. I quickly thought about the

California tan I had acquired and felt guilty. Then she continued, "I mean that shit in a good way."

"Why are you doing this to me. Didn't you hear anything I just said?" I pleaded.

"I heard everything you said. But I lived through everything you did!"

"Come on, Parker. Don't punish me like this. I wanted Monique for a couple of days . . . you knew I wanted you for a lifetime. I was building with you. Can we *please* make it like it was? You have no reason to be jealous of Monique. I never, ever loved anyone like I love you!"

"I wasn't ever *jealous* of Monique. These women are trivial. Different time, place and face. It's the act that scorched my heart. When I realized you were cheating, it hurt me, but I told myself you'd let it go, she didn't mean anything to you. When your need for Monique overruled your *respect* for me, it tore me up inside. It felt like someone had ripped my soul from my body, if you can ever imagine that. When I thought I'd lose you, I had two options. The first one was I could leave you. Alternatively, the second . . . make her leave you one way or another! Luckily, I never got a chance to make the choice. You made it for me. There's no telling what I could have done and frankly, you're not worth it!"

"Were you in love or just in love with the concept? How can you just let it go so easily?" I rationalized trying to appeal to her womanly sensitive side. I went to stroke her face, but she pulled back and rolled her eyes at me. She had a lot of anger built up inside, and I feared that this was the end. I was crushed. But I continued, "Parker, I love you. Do you hear me . . . I love you!"

"You love me, huh? Did you love me while you were fucking Monique? Were you loving me while you were making fucking babies all around town! Did you love me while I cried in bed alone night after night? Where was your love then? Answer me! You better fucking answer me, Joshua!" she screamed, then burst out into tears. I was wise enough not to try to comfort her. I hated to see her cry though.

"Parker, I want you to know that if we don't get back together, you're irreplaceable. And I'll always regret hurting you the way I did," I said earnestly.

"You didn't deserve to be the one to say goodbye. After everything I have been through loving you, you had the nerve to walk out *my* door. You wanted Monique so bad . . . well you got her. You got just what you asked for!"

"No one . . . I repeat, no one is going to love you like I did!"

"Well I sure hope not!" she spat.

I drove around for hours since I had nowhere to go. It was just past 11 p.m. when my pager started to go off with Monique's number. Of course, I didn't answer it. First thing in the morning, she'll realize I was the wrong white boy to fuck with. I checked myself into the downtown Brooklyn Marriott for the week. I knew I had nowhere else to go. I had to find an apartment and get myself settled. I knew Parker was going forward with the divorce. Hell, if I were her, I'd get a divorce, too. She didn't deserve to be treated the way I had treated her. No woman did. But by the same token, I thanked God I was a man. Men did not put up with such nonsense; we're not built for bullshit.

109
JOSHUA TUNE

At exactly midnight, I was settled nicely into my room. Simultaneously, I was paged twice. The first page was from Madison's doctor and the second was from Dominick. I called the doctor back first. "What's up doc?" I said as if my heart hadn't just been torn apart.

"Go find yourself an attempted murderer. The test came back positive for arsenic." We hung up, and I realized I wouldn't get any sleep tonight. I called Dominick, who said that he had been trying to get a hold of me all day. A policy existed for a half a million dollars and Maurice Mungin was the sole beneficiary. I called Judge Madden's private line because I needed a search warrant for Madison's apartment tonight. I didn't want this prick to spend another day free. Then I called Detective Holmes and told him it was on! Before I set out, I did a few more lines to get my adrenaline pumping. My first stop was the hospital to break the news to Madison. How she'd handle it was a mystery to me.

110
MADISON MICHAELS

Pain overwhelmed me to the point that I wanted to end my life . . . only I was afraid of the consequences. Being Christian made me aware of the repercussions of taking my life without God's permission, and I didn't want to end up where I'm sure Lyric had! Lately, with great regret, I realize I've been rather foolish in decision–making, and I wanted to smarten up before it was eventually too late.

My illness and all the medication the doctor had administered left me emaciated and parched; my lips were dry and cracked. Briefly, I wondered if I had contracted AIDS from unprotected sex with Maurice. But the grace of God saved me from that. That was one of the first tests the doctor ran and, fortunately, it came back negative.

I called the house for Maurice every chance I got, but he never picked up or called me back. Things weren't going well for us, and I was concerned that he wasn't interested in me anymore. I *needed* him. I thought that after I had the abortion, everything would go back to normal. That I wouldn't be feeling ill, and I would be able to help mend our relationship, and ultimately he'd treat me the way he had when we first met.

By now I knew Maurice didn't work for any FBI. I don't know if he had ever worked for them, but I can conclusively say I know he doesn't work there now. In fact, he doesn't have a job at all, so he needs my help and needs me to be strong. It's so difficult for a black man out here in white America. He was probably too ashamed to tell me, thinking I'd be biased.

I lifted myself up in bed, which took my last bit of strength, and reached for the phone. I dialed my home number one more time and held my breath until someone picked up.

"Beth?" I said, remembering my landlord and old friend.

"Um . . . yes, how are you doing Madison?" She yawned.

"I'm okay. What are you doing there?"

"Well, I do own the place!" she retorted angrily. Then continued, "Have you forgotten because I haven't received any rent from you in months?"

"I'm sorry. I've been um . . . it's been rough. But I promise as soon as I get back on my feet, I will pay you back every dime I owe you," I said, deeply embarrassed it had to come to this. She was such a good friend, and my irresponsibility had obviously affected her. Lying used to be abhorrent to me, but now it seemed to be my second calling. It's just that I didn't think she *needed* the money. Her parents were so well–to–do.

"Not necessary," she replied.

"Beth, is Maurice in there with you? I mean, is he there?" I was scared Maurice had heard the whole conversation about me renting the loft and Beth owning it. When Beth had called, I explained my situation about Maurice and asked that whenever she came up to New York, could she please not mention her owning the place. I told her it was childish of me, but my new boyfriend was under the impression that it was really mine. She said she understood, but now she's blabbing her big fat mouth about our personal business arrangement.

I thought I heard her whisper something, then she came back to the phone and said, "Madison . . . I really hate to do this while you're in the hospital sick and all, but I think you're going to have to find new living arrangements when you're discharged. I've already packed up your things. They're waiting by the door for you. This isn't working out."

"Beth, if it's the money . . . I–"

"Madison, I'm so sorry I have to do this."

"Where will I go? I have nowhere to go or any money. You know my situation. Beth, please . . . I'm begging you to reconsider. I know I've said some inane remarks and I'm mortified for having been so stupid. But please, don't take the roof from over my head for being a jackass!"

"Look, this is hard on me, too. My parents are way too upset with you. They said you're using my kindness for weakness. You've made me look like a complete idiot in their eyes."

"Well, can I at least have another month to relocate?" I begged.

"Why can't you go back home to live with your mother?"

"What?"

"Madison, I'm sorry . . . but you have to go!"

"Beth . . . please!" I cried.

"Madison, please don't beg. It embarrasses me as well as you. Where's your dignity?" she scolded. She exhorted me to leave there quietly because making a fuss would only humiliate me.

"Beth, may I please speak to Maurice, so I could tell him that we have to move?"

"You don't get it, do you? Can't you grasp the bigger picture? *You* have to move. Maurice is staying right here with me!" she snapped.

"Say this is a joke. A cruel, sick joke," I whispered. She softened her voice a little then said, "Listen Madison, I've already told Maurice that he should explain the details to you in person. I'm making him come to the hospital today to see you. You are my friend and I don't want you hurting more than you should. It's just something that happened. No one's to blame here."

"No one's to blame here! How long has this been going on?" I screamed.

"It just started but we're sure we're in love."

"Love? He loves me! I'm his wife!"

"For the moment. He loves me Madison and we're planning on getting married after he gets your marriage annulled," she spat.

"You don't even know him."

"Didn't that rapper marry Faith Evans in two weeks?" she rationalized.

Those had been Maurice's words. Beth knew nothing of rappers or R&B artists. The betrayal I felt seeped down into my bones and emerged from them as a deep, agonizing groan. I slammed the phone down and screamed, "WHITE BITCH" over again, and again, until the nurses ran into my room and gave me a sedative to calm me. I was visibly trembling until my body began to feel heavier and heavier, and I drifted off into a restless sleep, envying those who have never experienced the pangs of abandonment from someone they loved.

111
MADISON MICHAELS

I had been asleep for three solid hours before I felt someone tapping my shoulder in a rough manner. Sleepily, I opened my eyes and there stood Maurice with Beth attached to his arm. Tears just started flowing uncontrollably because to hear it was one thing, to see it was another.

"Come on Madison . . . don't do the crying thing. Do you want us to feel pity for you? Okay . . . we do. Now can you please knock it off? What do you want us to say? That we're insensitive and selfish? Okay, we are. But you can't ignore love in the name of friendship," Beth stated.

I never even glanced at her. My eyes were totally fixed on Maurice. I wanted to hear him say it. I knew that there was no way he could look me in the eyes and say he loved Beth. As he stood there stone–faced, I noticed he looked exceptionally good. He had on a cream–colored suede jacket, dark blue jeans, and brown Prada shoes with a thick brown suede belt. But what caught my eyes was the expensive diamond–flooded watch that nearly blinded me. He saw where my eyes were fixed, "Oh that! My baby woke me up to it this morning. It's a birthday gift," he announced proudly.

"I thought your birthday was five months away," I managed to get out. He shot me a dirty look then retorted, "That shows how much you know about me. I'm glad we're over, we should have never gotten together in the first place, but you tried to trap me."

"What do you mean *trap you*?" I said. Ignoring my question, he continued, "Look, I'm only here to tell you face to face that I'm in love with Beth and that we're through. Beth wanted me to do this in person, so there won't be any misunderstanding amongst us." He squeezed Beth's chubby hand, then leaned over and gave her a big wet kiss on her fat cheek. She melted and smiled a wide grin. Her green eyes sparkling with admiration.

As they gazed into each other's eyes, no one considered the agony I was going through. They could have cared less that I had tubes hanging out of my arms, had absolutely no color, and could barely speak without sharp pains bolting throughout my body. Beth went on and on about how she insisted he come down and tell me in person that it was over and that it was in my best interest that I hear the bad news from him. That way I wouldn't be delusional about the relationship and how she didn't want to hurt me. I wanted to say that hurting me was exactly what she wanted to do. If she cared so much about my feelings, why didn't she let him come alone instead of clinging to his arm in a territorial manner exhibiting her own insecurity. I know because I've held onto that same arm just as tightly when we were together.

I was too weak for fighting. I was literally drained. I let them both give me 'good–bye' kisses on my forehead because I was too weak to protest. Each kiss burned through my skin like holy water on a demon. And I felt like I was in hell. God was punishing me for what I'd done to Lyric. Some philosophical people say its karma. Others say, "What goes around, comes around. But not always in the same fashion." And the sad thing about all of this is that if Lyric were alive, she'd tell me what I could do. Lyric had an answer for everything!

112
MADISON MICHAELS

It was shortly after 5 p.m. when the doctor arrived with Joshua by his side. I did my best to smile through my pain and greet them. But I just couldn't. I didn't want Joshua to know what Maurice had done. He'd be so disappointed and feel sorry for me and I didn't want to be pitied.

The pain in my body couldn't come close to the pain in my heart. All I kept thinking was how I was going to get my revenge on Beth as soon as I was well enough. How dare she betray me? Do I have "sucker" stamped across my forehead? I know Maurice just fell into her arms because of my sickness. He was just being a man and feeling lonely. As soon as I'm out of here, I'll get him back. I just know it.

"How are you doing, sport?" Joshua said. He looked a little apprehensive as he spoke. I looked into his bloodshot eyes and nodded my head. I really didn't want to see him. I didn't want to be bothered, and he kept popping up, aggravating me. All I wanted was to be left alone. But considering that he was my one and only true friend, I reached my hand out for him to take hold of. I knew he was just being so sweet and that he truly cared about me. He came and embraced my hand, then looked away. The doctor then stepped forward.

"Are you in pain, Madison?" I didn't answer him. Since it was too painful for me to say what I really wanted to say, I decided to ignore him. Why would a doctor ask his patient such a dumb question. He continued in monotone.

"Madison, I'm afraid I have some bad news for you . . . We've found out what's been making you ill." He paused.

I sat upright as best as I could. I've been waiting to hear this forever, and he was dragging it out. "It appears to be arsenic," he continued. "You will be treated but will have to convalesce for months before returning to a normal lifestyle," he concluded.

Did he just say "arsenic?" I thought to myself. Now how in the world would I have arsenic in my system unless someone intentionally had given it to me? And people only do that when they're trying to kill you. I decided that when my mom came to see me, I'd have her discharge me from this hospital. If I stayed a day longer, I'd end up in a coffin. It was obvious that the test didn't show anything, and that this "*so–called*" doctor was taking stabs at what my illness could be. The treatments were not effective; therefore, my condition was not improving. Whatever he has dripping in my arms through my veins may even be deleterious to my health. From my disgruntled expression, he could tell I was not satisfied with this explanation.

The doctor looked to Joshua to continue where he'd left off. Joshua, still holding my hand squeezed it tighter. Then he said something like " . . . Maurice is trying to kill you . . . murders . . . other women . . . fraud . . . not his real name . . . Lyric hired a private detective . . . he's going to be arrested."

"He's going to be arrested for what!"

"Jesus, Mary, and Joseph! What have I been explaining this past ten minutes? Christ Madison . . . he's going to be arrested for your attempted murder."

"You can't be serious," I fought back, all signs of pain and struggling disappearing.

"And you can't be this naïve! Look at you, you're dying right before my eyes!"

"I'm anorexic remember? I did this to myself. I must be relapsing." My mind searched to find a reason I was in this hospital in my condition. What Joshua said was unimaginable. I lay there experiencing one of the most troubling times of my life and I had no one to help me through this.

"Listen, kid. I know this is a trip for you. But the facts are the facts. This scum bag is going to fucking pay for what he tried to pull," he bellowed. I sat in horror at what could be true but then the love crept in and I knew Joshua was just like the rest of them. The enemy!

"You lying son of a bitch!" I screamed.

"No . . . he's a liar . . . a murderer . . . and a con artist!" he countered. Then he grabbed hold of my shoulders and shook me really hard as if he was shaking sense into me. I winced in pain, and then burst into tears.

"Why?" I cried. "There's no motive. I have nothing!"

"You now have a $500,000 insurance policy bounty over your head and Maurice is the beneficiary."

"No!" I screamed in denial. But something in my gut said Joshua couldn't make such a thing up. Something kept forcing me to listen. Something kept telling me it was all true.

"Repeat after me, 'Maurice poisoned me.'"

"No!"

"Say it goddamnit! You'd better say it or, so help me God, I'll slap some sense into you!" he roared. My eyes opened wide from shock, and then realization sank in.

"Maurice poisoned me," I said almost in a trance.

"Say it again . . . 'Maurice poisoned me.'"

"Maurice poisoned me," I whispered, then let out a loud wail. Joshua tried to grab hold of me, but I fought his embrace. I knew he was trying to soothe me. I just sat there rocking back and forth for a while trying to grasp what I had just been told.

"Good girl. Don't you worry, Madi. I'll make him pay for what he put you through." Joshua grabbed me in a big bear hug and this time I didn't resist. Once in his arms I released a loud, blood-curdling moan that epitomized exactly how I felt at that precise moment.

BOOK TWO
2001

113
PARKER BROWN-BATTLE

" . . . Cheers for Jennifer Lopez on her new movie . . ." I was perusing the newspaper that had an article on the hot, new Latin superstar. The article mentioned how her career had climaxed, and I was so proud of the Bronx native kicking the door opens for minorities in Hollywood. I'd read somewhere she demanded $9 million a movie. She's now the highest–paid Latino actress in history. But she's not resting on her laurels; she's starting a clothing line in the footsteps of her former boyfriend Sean Combs. Reading all the publicity on Jennifer always made me stop to think about Lyric. She would have been just as big, if not bigger. Lyric had the 'it' in make it. Her movie "Silk" grossed $200 million making it the highest–grossing black film of all times.

It was shortly after 7 a.m. when the door to my room was pushed open. "Ma, Ma." Mia said. I ran to my little bundle of joy and picked her up in a bear hug. Then with the other hand, I tickled her until she kicked and screamed with laughter. Mia brimmed with zest, and I was particularly joyful this morning. Mia was Lyric's daughter, miraculously I was left custody in her Last Will and Testament. Soon after that there was a long court battle with Lyric's mother. The court felt she had grounds because she was the child's biological grandmother and immediate family. I tried to work it out with Mrs. Devaney for visitation rights, but she wanted it all or nothing. It was painstakingly obvious that she had no desire to love and nurture her granddaughter. She was in it for the $8 million settlement Mia received from the New York City Health and Hospital Corporation. Mia had cerebral palsy and would never live a normal life. She could barely talk or ambulate on her own and would need help from a neurologist, ophthalmologist, rehabilitation therapist, and physical therapist for the rest of her life. She would never be employed or be able to maintain her own household. Sometimes I wonder if she'll ever realize she's different from others. I often think about what she's missing. Then I compare it to all the love she's given by me, and I know she'll make it. As long as I live, she will always be my baby.

I couldn't wait for the legal details of Mia's case to be over. It would be a travesty of justice if she were ripped from my home. I'm the only mother she knows. We even have our own way of communicating. She's learning a little sign language in her program class and I am working with her everyday.

I put her down while staring at her lovingly. With cinnamon skin just like her mother and long wavy ponytails, She's so pretty. But she was too tall to be just shy of four years old. She had long fingers and toes and could pass easily for a six–year–old. No one had any idea who her father was, and no one has stepped forward to claim responsibility as her biological father. Everyone knew Lyric was seeing the mayor, but it was clear her father was not white. I guess the father wanted to remain anonymous or simply didn't know about his child. It wasn't as if Lyric was a one–man woman.

Mia and I went in the kitchen to have us a bowl of cereal. She loved Captain Crunch and that soon became my favorite too. Sasha came running in and Mia started playfully screaming and chasing her around the kitchen. Shortly after our breakfast my sleepy husband came into the kitchen and greeted me with a big kiss and hug. I looked at him adoringly and embraced him around his waist. Mia immediately became jealous and fell down on the floor, kicking and screaming in a fit. I had to let him go and run to my baby.

"You're spoiling her by letting her get away with that nonsense."

"What am I supposed to do? Just let her bang her head on the floor?"

"Certainly not sweetheart. But we need to get her trained."

"Trained? Is she a dog?"

"Parker, why are you so defensive with me? You know exactly what I am saying. I want a little love and affection from my wife without interruption as well."

"Steven, why are you jealous of a child?" I had Mia in my hands rocking her quietly. She was holding on to me tightly and loving the attention. Mia loved Steven too in her own way. She just hadn't learned how to share yet because everything she wanted I gave to her. I know it's my fault but she's just a baby. My baby!

Steven was the doctor who'd tried to save Lyric's life. We'd met when I kept coming down to ICU to see baby Mia fighting for her life. He'd also come down to check on her. A friendship blossomed but that was all. I was going through my divorce from Joshua and felt very fragile at the time. Steven was never married, and he was extremely patient. Two weeks after my divorce was finalized we were married in a small ceremony, and I've been happy every since.

Steven is a strong, loving, black man who has only encouraged me along the way. His chiseled good looks, strong exterior and warm heart nurtured me back with love and allowed me to let go of my pain and move on. I can remember a time when I'd play my phone conversation with Kaisha over and over again in my head until I wanted to explode. Lyric had told me Kaisha had had Joshua's child, so I called her. She confirmed it and practically laughed in my face.

"Yes . . . I have Joshua's firstborn!" she gloated.

"Well, good for you. That's all I needed to know." I casually replied, even though I was torn up inside. I wanted to hang up but she pursued, "Eat your heart out bitch!"

"For what? Am I supposed to be envious of you and your baby? You have two decades of hard work ahead of you, so lace up your Nike's because it's a long run . . . hun!"

With that I slammed the phone down and cried my eyes out, but I know I left her with something to think about. She was too young to have a child, and truthfully I didn't envy her for that. I don't relive those moments anymore. I've since opened my own interior decorating business, and I'm doing very well. Steven and Mia make my life complete. We're also planning to start a family of our own. I'm hoping to give my husband a son and Mia a brother.

Thinking about the past, I realize that if I had not gone through so much pain with Joshua, I wouldn't appreciate Steven as much as I do. I cherish what we have and couldn't be happier with the way my life turned out.

114
PARKER BROWN-BATTLE

The water running in the kitchen sink had drowned out the ringing of the doorbell. Mia, who was sitting up in her highchair watching me, was pointing her finger towards the door. I shut the water off, then ran to the door calling out "Just a minute." I was in the middle of making dinner and that's what held my concentration. I could remember a time when I only went into the kitchen to open up Chinese delivery. Joshua did all the cooking. With Steven spending so many hours at the hospital, I learned to cook to keep myself busy. And also, it gave me great pleasure to see the appreciation for my efforts in his eyes. He always made me feel like I made everything perfect. In his eyes no one could cook better than his wife.

I opened the door to my ex–husband who'd dropped by unannounced. It really pissed me off when he did such things. Part of him still wanted to have the control over me while the other part wanted to see how things were going in my life. I was hip to him. I only bit my tongue about him coming by because he always used the excuse that he was coming to see Mia.

"Umm . . . something smells delicious," he said.

"Thanks. I hope my *husband* likes it. I'm making him barbecued shrimp and Caesar salad. His favorite."

"When did you become such a chef? When we were married, your specialty was take–out," he sarcastically replied.

Ignoring his remark, I cut to the chase. "What are you doing here?"

"Gee whiz. I'm stopping by to see the baby. I missed little Mia."

"You drive all the way to Smithtown, Long Island unannounced to see Mia. What if we weren't home?"

"Then I'd drive right back to New Jersey. No big deal." He shrugged. Joshua had lost his edge. He didn't have his little boy charm or good looks anymore. He looked worn and tired. I knew it had nothing to do with our divorce. During the divorce, it was rumored that he and Monique had broken up and the baby she claimed to be his really wasn't. I never asked him anything about his personal life or about Monique. Nor did he ever open up about what had happened to him. When the scandal broke and hit the newspapers, I ignored the tabloids. It wasn't my business or concern. My chapter with Joshua was over. All my friends would call and say he'd gotten what he deserved, but I would never let them go into details.

I watched him play with Mia for a while until dinner was ready. I didn't eat because I always ate with my husband, but I fed Mia and put her to sleep. Joshua declined dinner and said he'd already eaten. I told him he could stand to gain a pound or two. He was extremely lean. But no matter how his personal life was doing, it didn't stand in the way of his professional life. He had gotten his act back together in that area. Case after case, he made headlines. It was no secret his next stop was district attorney, then attorney general.

When everything had settled down, he finally got to the purpose of his visit. He took a deep breath and his eyes got very dark.

"Lyric was murdered!" he finally said.

"Didn't this issue come up years ago, but you couldn't prove it?"

"I can now."

"What are you going to do? Round up the usual suspects?" I joked. He didn't laugh. Instead he went into details.

"Parker, you're never going to believe what I'm about to tell you."

"Well . . . shit . . . if it's gonna get me killed too, then you can keep that little piece of information."

"I'll ignore that comment. Listen, I'm over at Lacey's mansion."

"Lacey?"

"Anyway . . . I'm over there and we're drinking, having a good time. Then she pulls out Lyric's video collection and asks, 'Are you on any of the tapes?' I'm like, 'no way!' But in my mind I'm freaking out because I couldn't conclusively say no. For all I knew, I was . . . you know?" he said. My face grimaced because for years he and Lyric denied ever being involved. He saw my reaction and kept the story moving. "Anyway," he continued, "we were sitting there totally tripping. We set everything up and realized there was still a tape inside the video camera."

"Let me guess . . . the tape had Lyric's murderer on it."

"Is that your final answer?"

"Didn't the police investigate the crime scene? You were there, too."

"Nothing ever came to fruition. We must have overlooked that there was a tape left inside the recorder. I didn't let them confiscate Lyric's video collection because I thought it was irrelevant. I knew there were only sexcapades on them, and I didn't want them getting into the wrong hands. A dirty cop could have sold them to the tabloids for big money. So, in trying to protect Lyric, I let her murderer remain free for four long years," he said. He was obviously in pain.

"I guess you feel like the scarecrow looking for a brain."

"No, I'm more like the lion looking for courage. You're never going to believe who murdered Lyric Devaney."

115
SENATOR RICHARD CARDINALE

The New York Times, to my disgust, had former President Bill Clinton on the front page. The article said that he was in Quebec with a Harlem T–shirt on. His big, stupid grin infuriated me. This guy was such an asshole. "Nigger lover" I spat. I always loathed Clinton. Partly because I was Republican and mainly because I denounced his views on foreign policy and castigated him for his attitude towards minorities. You would think that after all the humiliation he put this country through, he would be exiled or outcast. But the public loved him. He was a martyr in the black community, a legend to white women who deemed him adorable, and a role model to dumb white men who wished they could get away with half of what he had gotten away with.

Now here was a man who had the world in the palm of his hands, and he behaved like a childish brat. Over and over again, he got caught with his hands in the cookie jar. Sometimes people were so smart that they were dumb.

After reading an article about a plane crashing in Japan with tourists from the United States and Canada, and other countries in the Occident, I tossed the paper in the trash and put on my Barry Manilow CD. I was in my office awaiting Estelle. She'd arrive in thirty minutes. Just enough time for me to smoke a joint. I reached into my 18K gold cigarette case and pulled out a pre–rolled joint and lit up. As I inhaled, I felt all the tension in my body release. It had been a hectic week as usual. Being in office less than a year was a 24–hour thing. It was my 25th wedding anniversary, and I was taking Estelle out to dinner. She'd wanted to go away on a romantic trip, but I would hear of no such thing. I loved Estelle, but not in a sexual way. In fact, I had to remind myself to actually touch her physically every six months or so. She just didn't turn me on like the young girls did. Vivacious little whores ready to do any and everything for the good senator. It was nice being white with money *and* power.

After I'd smoked my joint, my secretary whom I thought had gone home for the evening buzzed to say Joshua Tune was here to see me. Joshua. The mere mention of his name made me think of Lyric. Sexy Lyric. I hadn't thought twice about her since her funeral. What the hell did Joshua want? And who did he think he was, showing up unannounced. He's been making quite a name for himself lately. I guess he thinks he's hot shit.

"Tell him to make an appointment. I'm busy!" I replied. I heard a low commotion, a little noise, and then he barged directly in with my secretary trailing behind him. I waved her out, infuriated that I hadn't had a chance to deodorize my office first.

Annoyed, but calm, I remained laid back. I didn't say a word. I just stared at him, making him feel awkward. Of course, that was my motive. After making a spectacle of himself, he finally sat down and began speaking.

"I got something you need to take a look at," he said, flashing a videotape.

"You came all the way to my office to show me a video? Do you even care to explain what this is about . . . or is this show and tell?"

"Just watch it!" he snapped, rather cockily.

I don't know if it was the marijuana or the determination in his eyes, but I did as I was told. As he popped the tape in, I took a look at my manicured fingers and decided I'd have Sun Li Chen come in tomorrow to cut my cuticles. She did a wonderful job on my nails and gave great head.

Ten minutes into the tape, I was livid. This blew my high. But Joshua would never know. I remained calm and got right to the point. "How much?"

"You think I'm here to blackmail you?"

"Everyone has a price."

"Not me. Lyric was my fuckin' friend!" He bellowed. I didn't mind the screaming. No one was in the building. I'd sent my secretary home. We were alone. I studied him real hard before saying, "You know,

Benjamin Franklin said, "Three people can keep a secret if two of them die."

"Are you threatening me?" Joshua cautioned.

"I'm merely quoting a scholar," I retorted.

"Is that so? Please, allow me to return the favor, 'To know what is right and not to do it is the worst cowardice.' Confucius."

"I see. I see. And your plans for your future? I hear first district attorney, then attorney general?"

"Maybe. Maybe not. That used to be the plan, but I hear your position just may be opening soon."

"'You've got to be very careful if you don't know where you are going, 'cause you might not get there.' That was Yogi Berra."

"'When written in Chinese, the word 'crisis' is composed of two characters. One represents danger, and the other represents opportunity.' John F. Kennedy," Joshua retorted.

I laughed and then said, "'There can't be a crisis next week, my schedule is already full.' Henry Kissinger." I sat back and enjoyed this wordplay.

Joshua looked at me intently, then said, "A man without integrity is like a body without a soul."

"Who said that?"

"I just did!" Joshua acknowledged.

116
SENATOR RICHARD CARDINALE

Shortly into our altercation, my wife stormed in. She had on a pastel–green Escada two–piece pantsuit with a clutch Fendi handbag held tightly under her arm. Her blonde hair was newly bobbed, and she looked wonderful in a masculine way. Immediately her smile faded when she saw Joshua.

"Estelle, I'd like you to meet Joshua Tune. He's an assistant district attorney in Brooklyn."

"I know who he is," she replied crisply.

"Mrs. Cardinale, would you have a seat please," Joshua said.

"What is this all about? Richard, we have a seven o'clock dinner reservation at Windows on the World," she snapped.

"Estelle, our good friend Joshua has something for us to watch," I said, my tone hardly reflecting the anxiety that was building within me. Joshua had already pressed rewind and play on the VCR as Estelle came around and had a seat next to me. She flopped down and openly sulked like a child who does not get her way.

The video tape came on and Lyric was hanging up her telephone. Someone had said they were coming over. Minutes later she walked out of the room to get her front door. Her face was fully made up and she had clothes thrown all over her bed. Moments later she was back in her bedroom followed by Estelle holding a .357 magnum with a silencer. Lyric purposely maneuvered herself directly in front of the camera lens.

I glanced over to look at Estelle. Her face was stark white. She obviously had no idea that Lyric had had such equipment in her house and was clever enough to click it on before her arrival.

"Estelle . . . don't you think you're taking this too far?"

"Shut up, you slut! Don't you understand my husband means everything to me? How dare you try to take away my foundation? Did you really think Richard would divorce me for *you*? Did you actually think I would consign my life over to you?"

Estelle was in total control with her handgun never wavering. She was in a rage and her face was distorted with disgust. Estelle continued, ". . . and to try and blackmail Richard about a nigger baby! How dare you threaten to go to the tabloids and tell all sorts of perverted sex stories and ruin his career? What do you think that would have done to me? Did you ever stop to think about me? He's *my* husband . . . not yours!" Lyric tried to get up off the bed and ease around to where I knew she kept her nickel–plated .25, but Estelle backed her back down.

"No you don't, whore! I know all about the gun underneath the mattress. My husband told me everything!"

Now it appeared that once Lyric knew she was not in control of the situation, she started to panic. Her hands were visibly trembling, and she was searching to find the right words.

"I never intended to go to the tabloids, Estelle. That notion is ridiculous. And I never told Richard that this was his baby. You'll see when the baby is born she will be darker than tar. And I'm so over Richard. I used him as a ticket to get into Hollywood. Nothing more, nothing less. I've made it to the big time. I'm in. See, I'm going to my premiere tonight," Lyric pointed toward a white mink coat hanging in her closet.

"You are?" Estelle raised her eyebrow in a peculiar way, then let out an eerie, psychotic laugh that could have chilled your skin. She was acting like a complete maniac and I was embarrassed.

Lyric clutched her stomach and said, "Well yes, I am going to my premiere tonight . . . right?"

Estelle just stared at her like she'd lost her mind.

Tiny tears streamed down Lyric's cheek, and then she said, "What are you going to do in here?"

"No . . . what are *you* going to do in here?" Estelle reached into her pocket and tossed Lyric a bottle of pills. Then she continued, "You can either take the pills and leave here like a lady, well maybe not a lady . . . a dignified whore is more like it," Estelle sarcastically chimed, then said, "Or you can feel thirteen bullets enter your face and leave this earth unidentified!"

"What is w-r-o-o-o-n-g with you? Are you *crazy*? He's only a man!" Lyric screamed. She was furious, and you could hear the helplessness in her voice. She stood up slowly so as to not make Estelle nervous and cause the gun to go off. She was wearing a silk slip and robe. She slowly let her robe fall off around her legs and pulled her slip tight to outline her small belly. "I am carrying my baby in here. A baby that I love so much. A baby that I want to see come into this world. How can you ask a mother to kill her child?" Lyric pleaded on deaf ears. More banter went back and forth, but my mind had drifted off, just looking at Lyric's full ripe breast. I thought about the wild sex we would have and immediately grew an erection with my wife inches away from me in deep shit.

The tape rolled on with Lyric begging and pleading for her life. It was quite sad seeing her grovel. My heart went out to the kid. Finally, giving in and opting to take the pills, Lyric said a remorseful prayer to God to take her baby to heaven and to forgive her for what she was about to do.

The Lyric Devaney I knew was a fighter. I wondered what made her give in without one? Was Estelle really that intimidating? Or did she think realistically and say she wouldn't get far trying to lunge for the gun? I thought about what I would have done in the same circumstance, and conclusively affirmed I would have to call someone's bluff. Maybe Lyric felt that she would be shot several times. That my wife was acting like a lunatic; so therefore, she knew she was too vainglorious not to have an open casket. I wondered briefly if my wife would have really shot her in the face had she not swallowed those pills? Observably, I realized that Estelle would rather drink cyanide poison than give up her political throne. She was having the time of her life being my wife. I concluded that not only would she have pulled that silent trigger thirteen times, but she may have also stopped to reload.

As Lyric was swallowing each pill, she warned Estelle she'd be caught within 24 hours. Estelle laughed in her face. I turned around to see that Estelle was not laughing now. Forty minutes into the tape Lyric passed out. Estelle went over and felt her pulse. Then she did something extremely bizarre. She undressed Lyric and hoisted her up over her strong shoulders and left the room. You could hear water running in the bathroom. Later Estelle returned to the room and took a long look around before leaving.

117
SENATOR RICHARD CARDINALE

Joshua hopped up and clicked the tape off. Estelle remained cool as a cucumber. She looked over for me to say something. I realized now was my time to do the negotiating for my dim-witted wife.

"Okay, Joshua. My wife coerced Lyric into killing herself. Like I said before, where do we go from here?"

"You can go wherever you want. But your wife will turn herself in tomorrow morning, nine o'clock sharp! The only reason I'm giving her the common courtesy of turning herself in is because there are five innocent children to think about. And I wouldn't want them to see their mother getting hauled off to jail."

"Do you have any idea what this is going to do to my career? Or bigger than that, what I'll do to *your* career?"

"Respectfully, you can shove your threats up your narrow ass!" he shot back. Then I realized I couldn't try and bully this guy. I needed to appeal to his sensitive side because careerwise he doesn't feel he needs me.

"Listen, Joshua, look at my wife. She can't go to prison . . . it'll kill her. Prison is no place for a lady."

"Your wife looks more man than you or I. I'm sure she'll fit right in! Besides, she should have thought about that before she committed murder."

"Enough!" Estelle interjected. "How dare you come in here and throw accusatory statements around about me while painting your slut friend as a victim. She wanted to take my whole life away from me! My whole life! When I found out she was sleeping with my husband, I had two options. One, I could leave Richard. Or two, make her leave Richard . . . for good! I opted for the second choice. There was no way I was throwing in my towel. I came first!"

"Tomorrow . . . 83rd precinct . . . nine o'clock!" Joshua said with disgust.

"Listen to me you meager–waged hypocrite. Had I thought Lyric made a Freudian slip by trying to blackmail my husband, I would have shown her forbearance. But she purposely and maliciously set out to blackmail Richard, and I was not able to repress my anger. She got what she deserved!"

"I'll make a note of that," Joshua retorted and stormed out.

"This is all your fault!" Estelle raged and had the effrontery to accuse me of ultimately killing Lyric.

"My fault? How could you be so dumb? I have people who take care of such things on payroll. Ex–secret service . . . CIA . . . one phone call is all it would have taken, and she would have disappeared for good. How dare you jeopardize my future on a meaningless black girl? Her threats were harmless. If I felt like I would stand to lose my position, don't you think I would have taken care of the situation?"

"Then why did you come to me and spill your guts about her blackmailing you?"

"I thought you were my friend first, Estelle. Business partner, second. Wife, last. We've always had that understanding. Now you demoralize my trust. I've had several affairs. You didn't go around killing them. What was it about this girl that made you snap?" I pursued. Her face was flushed, showing signs of vulnerable weakness. She didn't answer, and I realized for the first time in my numerous liaisons, Estelle was jealous of someone and unfortunately for Lyric, she was it.

I made Estelle go back home and wait for me. I had several telephone calls to make before tomorrow morning. Joshua made a big mistake giving a man with my power time to formulate a plan. Didn't he realize that this not only affected Estelle, but it could prevent my presidency?

118
JOSHUA TUNE

The morning didn't start off like I thought it would. I expected to be on a natural high, knowing that in a couple of hours Lyric's murderer would be brought to justice. Instead, I had this sickening feeling in my stomach that I couldn't shake. Lacey was still asleep and that was no surprise. She went from a bubbling, optimistic woman to a nocturnal, grumpy millionaire. If she wasn't high, she was being a bitch, and I was seeing more of Lyric in her than she'd ever care to admit.

Realistically, she was obsessed with Lyric. That's where I came into the picture. She wanted me because Lyric had me. She had spent her whole life trying to prove she was different from Lyric and that she was her own individual to the point when she wanted to possess everything Lyric ever owned, touched, or wanted to conquer. Lately, I've been noticing that she's been bitching about money. It's no wonder, the way she's been pissing it away these past few years. She had wads of cash in a safe built in the wall in the bedroom behind a huge portrait of her. And that mountain of money was getting lower and lower every day.

Glancing over some open mail I noticed she hadn't paid her property tax on this property and the state was threatening to put a lien on the house and land. I tried to give her legal advice and tell her she'd better take care of her business before she lost everything Lyric had worked so hard for. She flipped out on me. She hated when I spoke about Lyric in a positive way. Then she'd always have to remind me that academically she was always smarter than Lyric. Then I'd tell her to get an identity. My arguing with her always caused me to do a couple lines of coke, even if I was already high.

This morning I didn't plan on doing any coke. I wanted to kick the habit. I opted to be straight, but Lacey woke up before I had a chance to leave and she started in on her nagging. She was mad that I was having Estelle arrested for Lyric's murder. She had even tried to destroy the videotape. She told me to "Let it go." When I ignored her, she had the nerve to suggest she'd kick me out of her house. Since this was where I had been for the past four years, I knew I had to do something and fast. When she started screaming and throwing my clothes around, I knew she needed a hit and fast. We'd run out of coke late last night, so my only option was to go and cop some. I went to the safe and grabbed what I needed. When she saw what I was doing, she quickly calmed down. She walked over and gave me a wet kiss on my lips, then grabbed my balls through my pants into her grasp. I winced from the pain, and pulled back slowly.

Glancing at my watch I called Detective Holmes to tell him I'd be a little late making it down to the station. "Why ya runnin' late, buddy? This is what we've been waitin' on for years," he said.

"I gotta make a quick stop."

"Oh no . . . you're not goin' where I think you are! Tell me it can wait until after the arrest."

"Can't. I'll explain later," I said then hung up the phone. I decided I'd go and cop this last blow for Lacey, but after it's gone, she's going to have to give it up. I had already made up my mind in the shower to kick the habit starting today. And if she doesn't comply, then I decided I'm gone for good! Her beauty was mesmerizing, but I wasn't in love.

119
JOSHUA TUNE

With videotape in hand I set out. On my drive into the seedy part of East New York, Brooklyn, I had a chance to think about what Estelle had said. When she said she had two options, and the second one was to kill, I immediately thought of the conversation Parker and I had had four years ago right before our divorce. She'd had said the same thing about Monique. Jesus, Mary, and Joseph! Do men actually make women feel so desperate that they think murdering their husband's mistress is an option? I realized the shoe could have easily been on the other foot, and Parker could have thrown her life away on a loser like me.

Before I had taken the tape down to the Cardinales, I had to do a quick edit job. No one will ever know that the tape kept playing well after Estelle had left. Then Madison arrived with her street thugs and they looted the place. Madison could have easily called an ambulance for her friend, but she didn't. She let her bleed to death while stuffing a pocketbook down the crotch of her pants. The kid deserved to be in jail! But I realized that she was already there . . . mentally. Now everything made sense. And the other two girls identified as Redbone and Sweepy were dead. Redbone was killed when she and her boyfriend tried to rob a neighborhood drug–dealer. They went in, duct–taped him up, and demanded his drug money. After torturing him for hours, his brother came in unexpectedly from out–of–town and started shooting first, no questions asked. They were killed instantly. Subsequently, the brother got acquitted of murder charges because they had entered unlawfully into his home. But he did one to three for the illegal firearm.

Sweepy was killed mysteriously by a hit and run on Linden Boulevard on her way to McDonalds. It's rumored that she and her crew had jumped a girl just days before and beat her critically. The girl's boyfriend vowed revenge for their messing with his lady. Police questioned him on his whereabouts, but he had an airtight alibi. No arrests were ever made.

I try to look on the bright side of all this death and tell myself that Lyric's soul was finally at rest. I don't think of her often because it is too painful. She'd always be the love of my life whether she knew it or not. This morning I cried a little for her soul, then my heart lightened up. It felt like she was sitting in the car alongside me. I glanced over but no one was there. Or was she?

120
JOSHUA TUNE

I had Jaheim blasting from my CD player when I arrived at Pink Houses projects on Stanley Avenue in Brooklyn. *"I'm a hustler baby . . . I left keys to the drop and the cash in the lockbox girl . . . "* I sang along. The song was so hot. I beeped my horn twice. I had already called Bee–For–Real on his cell phone and placed my order. I had the lingo down pat. I said I needed a half brick on 15th Street. He came be–bopping down the lane with a toothpick in the corner of his mouth. He wore a black knitted hat, black sweatshirt, black jeans, a two–way pager, cellular phone and my package. He smiled cordially and leaned in the car through the open window.

"Wassup man." I said and slapped him five.

"Whaddup. You got dat?"

"Yeah . . . I got dat," I said poking fun at the lingo. Then I reached in my jacket pocket and pulled out $15,000 held together tightly with rubber bands.

"How much is this?" he asked as I handed him the cash. I looked at him incredulously but answered anyway. He was probably high off that weed. That high tends to make you slow and illiterate.

"15 G's like we said."

"What cha buyin' man?" He quizzed. Just then my cellular phone rang and I answered it with agitation.

"Who the fuck is this?"

"Joshua, I don't have time for your mood swings man, I'm in L.A., in jail. I was just arrested for rape! I need you man."

"Who is this?"

"Erious. I'm in deep shit. This young bitch said I raped her!"

"Look . . . dude . . . I can't handle this shit right now. Let me call you later."

"Motherfucker, there ain't no later for–" I just hung up the phone. His shit is too heavy right now. I'm in the middle of a drug deal. Bee–For–Real resumed his position. "What chu want man?" He inquired.

"What the fuck's the matter with you? I'm not buyin' Christmas cookies. I'm here for the coke! Jesus, Mary, and Joseph! Do you have it or not? Stop wastin' my fuckin' time I have somewhere I need to be!" I yelled.

"Oh dip . . . I thought you wanted to buy some chronic. My bad!"

"Why would I give you fifteen thousand for some fuckin' weed? You know I don't touch that shit."

"I'm just fuckin' wit you man. Here it is. Uncut just like you like it." He smiled and finally pulled out the coke wrapped tightly in Reynolds wrap plastic. Briefly, I thought about taking a hit right then and there, but decided against it. This case was going to do it for me, and I wanted to remember every bit of my success. Bee–For–Real looked around and then stepped back from my car; I never saw them coming. As I went to start my ignition, four detectives came with their guns drawn telling me to "get out the fucking car, asshole!" As my heart sank to the ground, my life flashed before my eyes and stopped at the meeting yesterday with the senator. Why had I underestimated him?

As the handcuffs were being slapped on my wrists and I was being read my rights Detective Holmes stepped out and patted Bee–For–Real on the back and told him he had done well. They had gotten everything on tape. No doubt he was paid by the senator to set me up. Amazingly, instead of feeling any contempt for Detective Holmes, I had to actually commend him for seizing an opportunity. This was a dog–eat–dog world, and everyone had to look out for themselves. Once I was safely in the back of an unmarked car, one of the detectives grabbed the videotape that was on the front seat of my car. He yelled, "I got it!" Detective Holmes did a head nod, and the situation was wrapped up.

He personally escorted me back to the 83rd Precinct to book me on possession charges. Logically, I made no statements to him. When we got out of the car in front of the precinct, he skillfully had the press waiting for my arrival. Lights flashed everywhere and I was nearly blinded. Reporters all scrambled to ask me questions as Holmes tried to scurry me past them like he had no idea they'd be there. One reporter asked, "Mr. Tune . . . how do you feel right now being on the other side of the law?"

"Like I just ate a moron sandwich!"

121
MONIQUE HAMILTON

It was a sweltering day. I was listening to AM radio when I heard, "Assistant District Attorney of Brooklyn, Joshua Tune, was busted today for buying and attempting to distribute narcotics with a street value of $80,000. His career is over..."

Joshua had made the front page of every newspaper and tabloid in America. He was "Live at five;" on the eleven o' clock news, a CSNN exclusive, and it was all so very fucking good for him. I wonder how he liked it with the shoe being on the other foot. Four years ago he ruined my career. My life will never be the same. He exposed the fact that I was having an affair with a very affluent, influential and so–very married judge. Pages of my diary were *given* to every tabloid, and I was exposed for trying to trap the judge with my lovechild. The whole nation hated me for impregnating myself with his semen. The headlines read "Desperate Damsel in Distress Tries to Trap Married Judge." The article used words like "deceitful," "crazy," "unstable," "conniving" and worse of all, a "home wrecker."

I was let go from my position with my firm. They said if I went quietly they'd give me six months severance pay. I was glad; I didn't want to be there anyway. Every morning I was greeted with a nasty reporter asking disrespectful questions! "Why would an intelligent woman like yourself do something so heartless and moronic?" "Didn't you care that he was married?" "Do you believe in God?"

Day after day I'd get bombarded with accusatory statements and offensive questions. I just couldn't handle it. After being ousted from every social event, I then decided to live my life in seclusion. Shortly after that, I had my baby.

John packed up his family and never spoke to me again. Eventually, it cost him his marriage. His wife just couldn't take any more of the publicity, and it put a strain on their already failing marriage.

I had to ultimately fight him for three long years in court before an Appellate Division Court overturned the lower trial court ruling and decreed he had to pay child support. It was a landmark case. Even though the child wasn't conceived with mutual love, the DNA proved he was the father; therefore, he had a duty to support his child. So, he gave a check every month but refused to have anything to do with him. He's never seen our child. I eventually lost my will to practice law and started teaching English in a public school in lower Manhattan.

I'll admit the only thing that makes me happy is my son. I named him John after his father. What I did may have been wrong for most, but looking at my son, it was right for me. I still love John and haven't been with anyone else since he's left. Somewhere in my heart, I believe he'll be back. But my mind tells me it's never going to happen.

I may find love one day; I may have missed my opportunity. But whatever fate has in store for me, nothing can be worse than the loneliness I've been subjected to.

122
PARKER BROWN-BATTLE

"Oh . . . my . . . God! Oh . . . my . . . God!" I screamed when I saw Joshua on "Live at Five." I knew it had something to do with what he had told me about the senator's wife murdering Lyric. There was no way Joshua would touch drugs, let alone *buy* them to distribute. He had his whole career at his fingertips. I sat up all night waiting for the news to hit about Estelle Cardinale. When it didn't, it confirmed that this had been a set up.

Around 11:00 p.m., I reached up on the top of my closet and got the videotape Joshua had left with me for safe keeping. My hands were trembling because I didn't want to be next on anybody's payback list. I wanted so badly to confide in my husband, but I knew he'd worry and tell me not to get involved.

As I paced the floors, I decided that Joshua was no longer a concern for me. I had a new life. I put the tape back and went to check on Mia. She was sleeping peacefully. I bent over and gave her a kiss on her forehead, then stepped back to admire her. For a second, I thought I saw Lyric's face flash before me. I felt a cold wind and the hairs on the back of my neck stood up. Something pulled me back to my closet, and I got the videotape back out. I had no idea what to do with it or who to give it to. When Joshua was led into the station, his friend, Detective Holmes, was the arresting officer. He must have been paid off.

Hours later, I finally came to a resolution. I went to my basement and made several copies of the videotape and waited for the morning. First thing in the morning, I went to my local post office and mailed a copy to every news anchor on every local channel in New York City. First come, first serve. I didn't care who broke the story, but I was sure they all would bust a gut just watching the tape. Joshua would be overshadowed by the publicity of Lyric's murder. In a matter of days, he'll be yesterday's news. Then he can focus on getting himself out of deep shit.

After I came back from the post office, I went inside my huge, modern house and thanked God for everything he had given me. I also thanked Lyric for her gift as well. I'm happy in my life, satisfied in love, and I am never, ever lonely!

123
PORTIA JONES

"Ouch. Damn it . . . kid . . . stop beating on your momma like that." My baby was kicking my butt. I was six months pregnant and ready here and now to drop this load. It was early afternoon on a Saturday, and I was on my way to see Madison. My boyfriend Troy was preparing lunch for us, and he stopped to touch my belly up as he usually did when I told him the baby was kicking. Troy and I weren't married, but we had been dating for three and a half years now. He was a train conductor, and my first solid relationship. I loved Troy enough to be faithful and that was a big step for me. He helped me turn my life around, and I loved him so much for that.

I had given him a lap dance at the club I was stripping in, and we had been seeing each other ever since. He convinced me to go back to school and get a degree. I completed a four-year degree in three years. I'm now an RN at Long Island College Hospital. I absolutely love what I do. Of course, I have Lyric to thank for steering me in that direction.

I never did get to blackmail Erious for raping Lyric. Lacey never let me get Lyric's video collection from out of the house. She just took everything and relocated. In a way I'm glad. I had to learn independence. If I had gotten the money I would never have learned how to be a responsible adult. I was living my life too carelessly, and now I appreciate every aspect of it.

Troy and I will eventually get married. But right now our financial situation is precarious with the baby coming and all. Anyway, I don't need a ring to solidify my relationship; my man does that for me everyday.

I took the B12 bus to Kings County Hospital Center. I could have gotten there with my eyes closed. I was going to the G building where Madison was. Her doctor called and said she was not progressing, and they would have to transfer her to Creedmor Psychiatric

Center in Queens. It would be harder for me to go and see her without a car.

Poor Madison. She had just flipped out one day shortly after Maurice had committed suicide. Maurice never did make it to trial for poisoning her with arsenic. I think that poison burned out some of her brain cells because she had been so smart and determined. I guess if someone went through what she did, they could snap, too.

Before she flipped out she was mad as hell. She was so bitter. She was determined to see Maurice spend the rest of his life in jail for what he'd done. She'd gone back to school and gotten her law degree. She regained all her weight back and recovered nicely. Then she got the bad news that she wouldn't have her day in court. On the eve of his trial, Maurice punked out and hung himself in his cell.

We were together having lunch when she received the news. She's never been the same since. That was a year ago.

As usual, she was sitting by the window muttering to herself some strange poem she'd written. She held this poem tightly in her clutched fist as if she were choking someone's neck. Preferably Maurice's.

As she rocked back and forth, I came around and hugged her. She never hugged me back. I sat down in front of her, but she never looked at me. She just continued to rock and mumble. I began telling her about my day, the baby, work, Troy, but she never responded. Today, I decided I wanted to get in touch with her since I wouldn't see her for a while. I moved in real close, to hear the word of what she was saying, but the sound was barely audible. I took her hands softly and opened her clutched fist and took the paper she held and it read:

My Dearest Maurice . . .

> *I always thought we'd have tomorrow*
> *I always thought you'd explain everything*
> *About you and me with concise clarity*
> *I wanted to be the one to make you eat*
> *your heart out.*

The one to make you say 'damn' I messed
up
I wanted to be the epitome and
personification of revenge.

I wanted to see regret in your eyes
Make you regret your lies
At night in jail muffle your cries
As you realized you messed up by
deceiving me.

I wanted living without me to be sheer
torture
Make you want to throw away all the
sentimental things your new girlfriend
bought you
Come crawling on your hands and knees
saying you used to see clear when I was
near
Now you can't see . . . without me.

Then I would smile and walk quietly into
the sunset
But the sun set on all my dreams
And I can now only see you in my dreams
And it seems life has cheated me
And once again you cheated on me . . .
with death.

You two met and she won you for all
eternity
And the pain I feel inside will last all
eternity
Cause internally I am DEAD
Did I mention I missed your funeral?
And I never did cry.

O! the joy I felt when I first heard the news
Who knew?
What reaction your death would do to me
Now in the aftermath I'm disappointed, see

*Cause I didn't get a chance to see you
suffer!*

*Perchance,
Is it possible?
You left me a woman scorned
So what I felt inside for you didn't allow
me to mourn
Only to vent
On the unpleasant time we spent
Trying to get it together,
However, that time would come never
But your time came now
God is the only one judging you now!
I hoped you said your prayers in jail at
night
While waiting for the sun to go down!*

That poem nearly ripped me apart, and I finally understood what she was going through. I stayed a little longer and promised to come and see her real soon. She didn't hear me. She only heard her words . . . over and over again in her head.

124
LYRIC DEVANEY

My work is done here in this life. I can now go on and be at peace. There's a long journey ahead of me, so I better get started now. There are a lot of people there I want to meet. Marilyn, Dorothy, Malcolm, Martin, Tupac and a slew of others. Aaliyah just arrived. Such a pretty young girl. Younger than me. Good thing there's no jealousy or envy in this beautiful place. We've decided to walk towards the light together. I want to tell her all about my daughter Brooklynn and what a big star I was and could have been. I'm sure she wants to talk about all her accomplishments, too.

The one thing I learned in *life* is that it's too short and unpredictable. So don't put off being happy for tomorrow because it's not promised. And if you *love* yourself first, all others will follow. Most importantly, loneliness can be overcome by believing in God. Not some man who thinks he is one. I thought briefly about staying around to see what evil Lacey was up to but that wasn't my job. I'll leave that in the hands of God. She has to find herself, and then maybe she'll finally be able to let go of that bitterness.

In life we have so many questions that ironically get answered in death. Everything is so ambiguous, it makes living seem like a jigsaw puzzle. The answer is right there; we only have to seek it out. Had I known I had everything I needed right there in front of me, I would have been at a different *peace* when I was mortal. I've decided that once I earn my wings, I'll spend most of my time watching over Brooklynn. She needs me. Now *that* little girl is beautiful! Almost prettier than her mother when I was her age. I did say almost, didn't I?

ACKNOWLEDGMENTS

I love you **Poochie**, Henrietta, Mother. You always wanted the best and set out to get it. I follow your example. I see so much of you in myself. I let your choices be my blueprint; therefore, I will move a little more wisely. However, I have my own mind, so I have made my own mistakes. **Monique.** My mother's firstborn. Your spirit, caring nature, and enormous support have pulled me through my darker years. If it were not for your encouragement, this book would have taken longer to complete. I owe you so much. I hope I can give it back monetarily, but if not...there is always love! **Tisha.** My middle baby sister! You have the patent on making me laugh. I miss your sense of humor and eclectic style. Your leaving New York has made me a stronger woman. I can no longer look to you to fight my battles with me. No one could ever take your place in my heart. Loving and missing you more each day. **Katrice.** "You ought to be in pictures." My beautiful, talented niece. I admire how you admire me. However, I pale in comparison of your talent, wit, and wisdom. I wish I were half the young lady you are when I was your age. **Aunt Renee.** You are so adorable. You are and will always be my favorite aunt. I have such fond memories of you dishing out love to my sisters and me. Your humor and presence were never taken for granted. **Cecily.** My favorite cousin. Somewhere our paths crossed and we grew closer. You have always been there for me no matter how bizarre, dangerous, or plain silly my circumstances were. I love you, and hope that, if you need me you know I am just a phone call away. What? There ain't no more to it! **Natasha.** I will never forget when I needed a shoulder to lean on, friends were nowhere around. When everyone decided to flee because of my situation, you came and embraced me. Your steadfastness was the Crazy Glue that sealed our friendship. I love you and hope to see you up on the big screen soon. If not, it will be a travesty of fate. **Michele.**

It took me a minute to understand you, but now that I do, I see you have so much to give. You offered me help without my having to ask on several occasions. You trusted me with so much before we had a chance to establish a rapport. You have inspired me in your own unique way and I just want to say you are a good person, thanks. **Tasha.** Toast. . . 'to a book that never closes. . . ' (smile) You are in all my fond memories. **Bruce.** You have made a dull environment tolerable. Your calm mannerisms always seem to relax me. You are genuinely a nice, caring and giving person. Thank you for all your help...and the ballets and opera and... **Erica.** Friend, colleague, college buddy, and former partner. It is always interesting having a conversation with you. Your realistic views always challenge me and then you throw in a twist of humor. Your original characteristics are captivating. Stay wise, cool, and real. Good having you as a friend. **Oldham.** You believed in me. You protected me. You have been there for me repeatedly. You made me feel safe in an unsafe environment. I owe you my sanity. Stay cool you handsome, sexy, devil you! **Nelson.** You are always a phone call away. Always making time for me whenever I need you, no matter how overwhelmed your law practice may have you. You always say kind words and make me laugh uncontrollably. I take solace in knowing we will grow old together as friends. Moreover, if someone were crazy enough to take my hand, I would be honored if you were by my side to give me away. P.S., I am staying out of trouble! To **Flowmentalz** and **Kirk Nugent.** The hottest, most helpful spoken word artists I have ever known. I have a tremendous amount of respect for your work as artists. You opened your doors to me when I needed someone to lead me on the right path and I have not looked back. Thank you for helping me reach my dream without the propaganda so many wanted to give out. **Vlad**, my savior. If I can't do it. . . Vlad will do it for me. You are so helpful, informative, and giving. Not many people genuinely have the quality...you are blessed. Thanks for all your support. **Kaesun**, my sweetie! You are kind, sweet, humble, giving, sharing, and my friend. I liked you from the start. You have always supported me in my writing endeavors and I just wanted to say thank you. Last, but not least I want to thank **Jimmy** and **Colbi**, for getting me through my days. You two are too much for one girl to take. **Dione Alexander,** my hair stylist like no other. Good luck on all your endeavors. Don't let anyone say you can't do it. **Maribel's,** I've been dedicated for a decade (whoa). I wish I had stock in your place (smile).

If I've left anyone out, I really didn't mean to. Forgive . . . forgive . . .

I wanted to thank all my friends who came into my life at different stages, for lending an ear when I needed you to listen and offering a joke when I needed to laugh. Stay cool, much love to all of you.

Most importantly, I want to thank my family who stayed with me through the storms of life, the pain of love, and as a result, I was never lonely.

Oh . . . I could not end this without acknowledging Pink Houses in East New York, Brooklyn.

ORDER FORM

MELODRAMA PUBLISHING
P. O. BOX 522
BELLPORT, NY 11713
(646) 879-6315
www.melodramapublishing.com
melodramapub@aol.com

Please send me the book Life, Love & Loneliness by Crystal Lacey Winslow

_____ @ 15.00 (U.S.) = _____
quantity

Shipping/Handling*   = _____

NO SALES TAX

Total Enclosed   = _____

*Please enclose $4.00 to cover shipping/handling ($6.00 if total more than $20.00)

☐ If you wish to pay by check or money order, please make it payable to Melodrama Publishing.

☐ To charge your order to a major credit card, please fill in the information below.

Charge to   ☐ American Express   ☐ Visa   ☐ MasterCard

Account No. _____ _____

Expiration Date. _____

Signature. _____

Print Name. _____

Address. _____

City. _____ State. _____

Zip Code. _____

Send your payment with the order form to the above address, or order on the web. Prices subject to change without notice. Please allow 4-6 weeks for delivery.